CHANGING PATTERNS

Also by Judith Barrow

Pattern of Shadows

CHANGING PATTERNS

by

Judith Barrow

HONNO MODERN FICTION

Published by Honno
'Ailsa Craig', Heol y Cawl, Dinas Powys, South Glamorgan,
Wales, CF64 4AH

1 2 3 4 5 6 7 8 9 10

Published with the financial support of the Welsh Books Council.

ISBN 978-1-906784-39-3
Cover photograph: Bert Hardy/Stringer, Picture Post, Getty Images
Cover design: Jenks Design
Text design: Elaine Sharples
Printed by [to come]

For David

Acknowledgements

I would like to express my gratitude to those who helped in the publishing of *Changing Patterns*...

To all the staff at Honno for their individual expertise, advice and help. To Janet Thomas for her thoughtful and empathetic editing.

A special thanks to my dear friend and fellow author, Sharon Tregenza, for her constructive criticism and encouragement throughout.

Lastly, as ever, for David; always by my side, always believing in me.

Chapter 1

16th June 1950
Llanroth, Wales

Sometimes Mary couldn't believe he was there. She would reach out and touch Peter just to reassure herself that after five years apart they were together again. He'd given up a lot to be with her.

'You are happy?' He slung his arm around her shoulder and pulled her closer.

The breeze ruffled their hair. The tide was on the turn and Mary watched the waves collide and dissolve. High above, gulls hung motionless, their cries lost in the air currents.

'Mmm.' Mary rested against him. The smell of the mown lawn on his skin mingled with the salty tang of spray blown off the sea and the faint smell of pipe tobacco. 'You?'

'Of course.'

She turned her head to look at him, brushed a few blades of grass from his cheek. In the four months since he'd found her he'd lost the gaunt pallor, the weariness, and gained a quiet contentment.

'It is good, the two of us sitting here, alone,' he said.

'Tom won't be long though, he'll be back from Gwyneth's soon. He said he was only just digging her vegetable plot over for planting tomorrow.'

'I do not mean Tom. He is family.'

Mary allowed a beat to pass. 'I know you didn't, love. And I know what you really mean. But it's not our problem. If people don't like our being together that's their lookout.' She kissed him. His mouth was warm; the tip of his tongue traced the inside of her lips. Through the thin cotton of her dress she felt his hand cup her breast.

Smiling she drew back. 'Tom?' she murmured, her voice rueful.

They sat peacefully on the doorstep of the cottage, each savouring the other's closeness.

1

Gradually the sun disappeared behind the cliffs. The trees became shifting silhouettes and the wind slapped the surface of the sea into rolling metallic arcs and carried the spray towards the cottage. Mary licked her lips, tasted the salt.

'It's getting chilly.' She shivered.

Peter stood, reached down and lifted her to her feet, holding her to him. *'Ich liebe dich,* my Mary.'

'And I love you.'

A few moments passed before she forced herself to stand back and, giving him a quick kiss, take in a long breath. 'Now,' she said, 'I'm late sorting tea out. If you put those things away, I'll go and give that batter a whisk. I'm making Spam fritters to go with that mash from last night.'

She stood on the top step watching him walk down the gravel path to where he'd left the lawnmower and then glanced towards the cottage next door. Although it was only just dusk the window in Gwyneth Griffith's parlour suddenly lit up and the oblong pattern spilled across the garden. Tom emerged out of the shadows swinging a spade in his hand and turned onto the lane. Mary waved to him and he waggled the spade in acknowledgement. 'Tom's coming now,' she called out to Peter. 'I'll stick the kettle on. He'll want a brew before he eats.'

The van came from nowhere, a flash of white. Mary saw it veer to the right towards Tom. Hurtling close to the side of the lane, it drove along the grass verge, smashing against the overhanging branches of the blackthorn. Caught in the headlights, her brother had no time and nowhere to go. Frozen, Mary watched as he was flung into the air. She heard the squeal of the engine and the heavy thud of his body on the bonnet of the van. The spade clattered along the tarmac. Peter threw open the gate and was running before she could move.

'Tom,' she heard him yell. Somewhere, someone was screaming. She was screaming.

The van had gone.

2

Stumbling towards the inert body of her brother, she passed one of his wellington boots. Looking up she saw the other incongruously dangling from a branch. There was a crunch under her shoe and she bent down to pick up Tom's spectacles. One lens was shattered and it fell from the frame as she held it to her breast. She didn't feel the glass cut into her fingers. The van's engine faded into nothing. The only noise was the awful sound of Tom's guttural breathing. Peter gently turned him over, cradling his head.

Trembling Mary dropped to her knees. Tom's eyes were closed, his face a blank mask.

'Help him, Peter.' Mary forced the words past the hard lump in her throat, all her nursing training deserting her. 'Help him. Please…'

Tom took a long shuddering breath.

In the fading light Mary watched the dark pool of blood spread.

Chapter 2

Ashford, North of England

'You think all you need to do is flutter your eyelashes and Ted will let you do anything. Well, let me tell you, my lady, one day, you'll come unstuck.' Hannah Booth narrowed her eyes as she glared at her daughter-in-law and took a long noisy slurp of tea.

Ellen chopped the onions with quick impatient cuts, willing herself not to react to the constant carping.

'Leaving me to look after William and…' Hannah wiped her mouth with the back of her hand. 'And the other one.'

'She's called Linda. God above, can't you even say her name? My – our daughter is called Linda. L-i-n-d-a.' Ellen glared at Hannah.

There was a moment of apprehension on the older woman's face before she spoke again, this time with triumph.

'Don't think I won't tell him how long you were out this morning, doing the so-called shopping…'

'What else do you think I was doing, Hannah?' Ellen clenched her jaw. 'I was in that queue outside the butcher's over an hour.' Her feet still tingled with pins and needles from standing so long.

'And what did you bring home?' Hannah pushed a fat forefinger at the small brown paper parcel on the kitchen table, the blood already seeping through. 'Two ounces of lamb's liver. Hardly enough for one.'

'That one being you, of course.'

'Well, why not? I need the iron, the doctor said.' Hannah banged her mug of tea down on the table and crossed her arms across her large bosom.

'Because it's Ted's money that bought it and it's Ted that'll be coming home from work hungry.' It was an automatic response. But to be honest, the way Ellen was feeling about him these days, he could whistle for his tea. She was sick to death of him going on about how good his new shop assistant was. Anybody would think he fancied her.

A small chill settled in her stomach. She pushed it away, aware that Hannah was still watching her.

'And you'll cook it before you go off gallivanting, will you?'

'It's work. My singing … is my work.' Ellen ground out the words as she threw the onions into the frying pan and gave then a stir.

Hannah snorted. 'Work? Prancing about in front of some blokes with nothing better to do? In a frock that leaves nothing to the imagination?'

'I sing in a respectable club.'

'Huh!'

Ellen turned the gas off on the cooker. She couldn't bear to be in the same room as the woman any longer. She washed her hands, getting as much lather as she could from the hard green bar of soap; she wasn't leaving the house stinking of onions. 'I'm going to get ready.' Sod the liver. They could fight over who would have it when he came home. And his mother could cook it. It would make her get up off her fat backside. 'I'm not having this argument again, Hannah.'

'You're not leaving before Ted gets home?' It was as much a challenge as a question.

Ellen stopped on the first tread of the stairs, holding back the heavy green curtain. She didn't turn around. 'The kids are in bed if that's what you're worrying about.'

'I'm not. I don't mind looking out for William.'

'There are two children up there.' Ellen's fingernails dug into her palm. 'Are you saying you won't look out for Linda? Should I tell Ted you said that?' She spun around to face Hannah.

Hannah scowled. 'I just said…'

'Yes?'

'Nothing.'

'Good.'

When Ellen came back downstairs she wore the new black satin strapless dress her friend Edna had made for her in exchange for two summer frocks that were too big for her. She sat down carefully at the table; the dress was a little tight but looked all the better for that. There was a stony silence in the room. She defied her mother-in-law, setting out her make-up. Pulling the top off the small tube of red lipstick, she held up the thin Yardley compact and peered into the mirror.

'I don't know why you think you need all that slap.' Hannah watched Ellen. 'I never bothered much with tutty myself. Eddie didn't like it. Very old-fashioned my hubby. And neither does my Ted. He says he likes a girl to be natural.'

Ellen pressed her lips together, moving them from side to side to even out the lipstick. 'Does he? He's never said anything like that to me. He always says I look beautiful.' Her glance at Hannah was defiant.

'Oh yes.' Hannah pursed her mouth. Without her false teeth in, her top lip covered her nostrils when she sniffed. She didn't take her eyes off the younger woman. 'Natural's best, I always think. Then there's no nasty shock for the man in the marriage.'

No wonder Mr Booth had a heart attack when Ted was a kid then, Ellen thought, slowly pressing face powder on her forehead and studying her reflection in the mirror before closing it with a snap. She waited a moment before saying, 'I've been asked to do a stint at the Astoria in Manchester next Friday as well.'

Hannah frowned. 'What about Ted? Does he know?'

'He won't mind.' He never minded what she did as long as she was happy. At least that's what he said. Had he said it more often lately? Was that because he was working late more regularly? With her from next door. Ellen stopped that train of thought.

'You going on the bus looking like that?'

'No, I'm getting a lift from one of the band. Harry. He lives locally. He'll bring me home as well.' Put that in your pipe and smoke it, as Mam used to say, she thought. 'Tell Ted, will you? Tell him I'll see him about one o'clock.' They'd have an hour then before he got up to go to the bakery. Time enough to show him what he'd been missing these last couple of weeks. She smiled to herself.

'Right, I'm off.' She pushed her feet into her silver peep-toed shoes and shrugged on her coat, adjusting the fake pearl earring that caught in the collar. She lifted one leg and then the other, looking over her shoulder, checking her seams were straight.

Just for mischief she said, 'Wish me luck.' She wouldn't admit it but she was nervous. This was only the second time she'd sung at the Embassy Club in Bradlow and the last time it felt as though she was battling against the noise of the chatter around the bar; as though she was invisible.

As she walked down the hall she heard Hannah mutter, 'Dressed up like a tart…'

Ellen slammed the front door and looked towards Shaw Road. A man walked by and wolf-whistled under his breath. She pulled her coat tighter and glared at him.

A black Ford Prefect pulled up at the end of the street. Harry. Ellen waved as the driver sounded his horn.

Avoiding the cracks in the pavement she teetered towards the car on her high heels. 'I'm entitled to a life,' she muttered, 'miserable old cow.'

Chapter 3

'What the fuck?' Patrick lurched onto his back and lifted his head off the pillow. Downstairs the telephone shrilled out again. 'What time is it?'

Jean pulled on the cord of the Lazy Betty and squinted at the alarm clock in the brightness of the light thrown out over the bed. 'Twenty past twelve.'

Patrick sat up, buttoning his pyjama jacket and reaching for his dressing gown.

'Who will it be?' Jean said. It felt as though the pulse in her neck was choking her. Her first thought was of her mother. That was quickly rejected; her mother didn't have a telephone.

'How do I know?' He sat on the edge of the bed, half turned away, half facing her. 'I'm not a fucking clairvoyant.'

Jean lay back. Outside the night was still. The room held the quietness within its walls. She couldn't even hear the normal hushed movements of her daughter deep in sleep in the next room. She got up and tiptoed across the landing. Jacqueline, undisturbed by the telephone, hadn't moved. Jean stroked back the lock of hair that fell across her daughter's face and gently tugged the covers higher.

The telephone rang again. She stopped at the top of the stairs, her hand clasping her throat, but couldn't make out Patrick's words. She went back to bed.

Eventually he slipped under the sheets, barely disturbing the eiderdown, and turned his back to her.

'Who was it?' Jean waited.

He didn't answer.

She touched his shoulder, her skin prickling. 'Patrick?'

When the sobs came, they were jagged; an explosion of grief. All she could do was to hold him, her cheek resting on his shoulder. Finally, when he turned, his face was white, his features rigid.

'What is it? What's happened?'

Patrick threw an arm across his face, covering his eyes against the light. His lips moved stiffly. 'Tom's dead.' Slow tears trailed down the sides of his face.

Jean gasped. 'What? How?'

'Not now,' he said.

'How?'

'No.'

She could hear the pain in his voice. 'Patrick?'

'No!'

He flung the covers back. She watched him leave the room, slamming the door behind him.

Almost immediately it re-opened. 'Mum?' Jacqueline was wide-eyed.

'It's okay, love.' Jean lifted the corner of the bedclothes. 'Get in.' When Jacqueline snuggled alongside her, stretching her arm across the soft width of her stomach, Jean felt the rapid beat of her daughter's heart. 'It's okay,' she repeated, 'nothing to be scared of.'

'Dad was shouting.'

'Well, nothing new there then, huh?' Jean gave her a squeeze, trying to add humour into her voice. 'You know what he's like. Up and down like a yo-yo when something doesn't suit. He's just being silly.'

'Why is he cross?'

Jean heard the fear in Jacqueline's voice. 'It's nothing for you to worry about, honest, love. He'll be fine again in the morning. Everything will be all right.'

But would it?

For the rest of the night Jean stared sightlessly up at the ceiling, not knowing what would face her in the morning. Patrick's lifelong jealousy of his older brother and the hatred he'd shown Tom for his stand as a conscientious objector hadn't grown any less over the last five years. She'd stopped asking him to go with her to see Tom and Mary in Wales. It only set him off on one of his tirades. And Mary seemed happy enough that he stayed away.

But what about Jacqueline? How would she tell her? She adored her uncle. He'd always made a fuss of her whenever they'd visited Wales. Would she even understand? The last one of the family to die was Patrick's mother and Jacqueline hadn't really known Winifred.

She made herself wait until seven o'clock before she went downstairs. Patrick was sitting in the kitchen staring at the empty grate and drinking whisky.

'What happened to Tom?'

He shrugged. 'Hit and run.'

'Who rang?'

'That bloody Kraut.'

'Do they know who … ?'

'Oh yeah,' his tone was sarcastic, 'that's why it's called a hit and run.' He emptied the glass and slammed it down on the arm of the chair. 'Course they don't bloody know.'

'There's no need to be like that.' Glancing at the almost empty bottle of whisky, Jean bit back a remark about his drinking. Instead, she said, 'I don't know how to tell Jacqueline.'

He whipped round to look at her. 'Jacqueline? Why should you tell her?'

'He was her uncle.'

'Huh!' Patrick shrugged. 'She doesn't need to know – not yet anyway.' He shifted in his chair. 'Get us a brew?'

9

'She will need to know, Patrick.'

'Why?'

'Because we should go.'

'Go where?' This time he didn't turn his head.

'You know where. To see your Mary.'

'Why?'

'Why? Because your brother's dead. Because she's your sister. Because she's my best friend. Because she needs us.'

'She's got that Kraut.'

'And that's what it's all about, isn't it? It doesn't matter about Tom or Mary, or even your daughter…' Jean kept her voice even. 'I'm going. And I'm taking Jacqueline. You can please yourself.'

Chapter 4

Ellen sat on the chair by the side of the piano while the musicians packed their instruments and shuffled off the stage, untying their black dickie bows and undoing the top button of their shirts. Harry, the drummer, winked and grinned at her as he passed, his round face red and glistening with sweat.

'See you in a bit. Going out for a bit of fresh air.'

Oh yeah, Ellen thought. She glanced down at the dance floor. The chubby girl who'd been eyeing him all night from the edge of the stage had disappeared. 'Don't forget I'll need a lift home,' she whispered, 'and don't have me hanging around outside on my own.'

High up on the ceiling the large crystal ball slowly turned round scattering small snowflake impressions over the crowd. The clock on the wall was wreathed in swirling blue cigarette smoke; the air reeked with the stench of nicotine and sweat. Ellen practised her breathing exercise, relaxing her throat ready to sing, and wished she hadn't. She checked the time: eleven thirty. Another fifteen minutes and the club would close and the crowd ushered out.

Her palms were damp and she surreptitiously ran her hands down the side of her dress, leaving smudged marks. It was ruined anyway. The stupid saxophonist had spilt some beer on it coming back on stage after the interval. Besides, it was so tight it rubbed under her arms and around her waist whenever she moved. All she could think about was getting home and out of the bloody thing.

She stood and adjusted the microphone out of habit; it was set perfectly for her. She cleared her throat and switched it on, smiling at the depleted crowd of dancers. The chairs at the back of the Palais were full of boys and girls smooching but there were still some left on the dance floor.

'I'd love to get you on a slow boat to China…'

The crowd began to move, a disjointed mass of huddled couples and girls swinging one another around.

Over by the bar a man jumped up on top of the counter.

Ellen faltered.

'Some idiot wants a fight,' the pianist called over his shoulder, 'keep going.'

'All by myself, alone.'

'Come on,' the man yelled, tearing off his shirt. 'You want a fight? Well here I am. I'm ready.'

Ellen watched as he started jumping around on top of the bar and jabbing at the air like a boxer. There was raucous laughter and then someone grabbed his legs and he somersaulted out of sight onto the floor, amid cheers.

She raised her voice. *'Get you and keep you in my arms evermore…'*

At the back of the room another scuffle broke out. Ellen could see Eddie, the bouncer usually at the door to the foyer, coming towards the stage, struggling to keep hold of a smaller man who was determinedly fighting him off.

'Leave all your lovelies weeping on the…' Her voice trailed away. She dropped her arms to her side, fear tightening her throat. 'Ted?'

He was still in his white overalls.

The pianist swivelled round to see what was happening. 'Ellen?' She took no notice of him. 'Ted? What is it? The children?'

'No.' He held out his hand. Ellen looked around. The dancers were still, watching her in shared curiosity.

Bewildered, she let Ted lift her from the stage. 'Tell me what's wrong. Why are you here?' She felt the sting of frightened tears.

'Get her things,' Ted said to the pianist. The man moved swiftly without questioning. 'I'll tell you outside, love.' He covered her shoulders with her coat and kept his arm around her. 'I've got the van. Come on, Ellen,' he said when she hesitated. 'Not here.'

'What's going on?' The manager of the Palais came from his office and stood in their path as they crossed the dance floor. 'You can't leave yet, you haven't finished your stint.'

'Shift out of the way.' Ted shouldered him aside.

Ellen registered the unusual aggression in her husband. She looked back at the manager.

'Don't bother coming back – you're fired.'

Right at that moment she didn't care. Something dreadful had happened and the sooner they were out of the place the sooner she'd find out.

'Was it an accident? I don't understand.'

'I told you, love. Peter just said the driver didn't stop. It sounds as if whoever it was panicked.'

'I don't understand,' Ellen repeated.

'Come and sit down.'

'No, I can't.'

Ted had almost carried Ellen into the house and now he held her close. She pushed back to look at him, bewildered. 'What if it wasn't an accident?'

'It was,' Ted insisted. 'Why would it be anything else?' He stroked her hair. 'You know that's a bad corner outside Mary's house.'

12

'Of course it's possible it wasn't an accident,' Ted's mother said. 'You never know.' Although it was almost one o'clock in the morning, way past the time she normally went to bed, Hannah was still up, sitting in her armchair. She pulled the cord of her maroon dressing gown tighter in a vain attempt to cover her nightdress and laced her fingers over her stomach. 'Perhaps somebody didn't like what … who … he was.'

'Shut up.' Ellen clenched her fists against Ted's chest. One day she'd swing for this woman.

Ted spoke at the same time. 'Yes, shut up, Mother. And go to bed, there's no need for you to be here.'

'Well!' Hannah heaved herself out of the chair. 'There was a time you'd never have spoken to me like that, Ted Booth.'

He didn't answer her. He put his face close to Ellen's. 'Hush now, love. Try to calm down. We'll speak to Mary tomorrow. Find out what happened. Peter didn't say much when he rang the shop. He was upset and I think he had enough on his plate trying to look after Mary.'

'She'll be in such a state she won't know what to do with herself. She adores Tom,' Ellen sobbed. 'We have to go to her. Now.' She pulled at the lapels of his overalls to stress her words. 'Now, Ted, right away. She'll need us.'

Hannah stopped in her tracks at the bottom of the stairs. 'You'll take – the kids with you?'

'Of course we bloody will.' Ellen didn't look at his mother. 'I wouldn't leave them with you. I wouldn't leave a dog with you.'

'Well, you've changed your tune. You've foisted her – them – on me often enough in the past.'

'Mother!' Ted roared. 'Go, get out – go to bed.'

'Well!' Crimson with annoyance she jerked the curtain aside and hauled herself onto the first step.

They waited, listening to the creak of the stairs under her heavy tread before either spoke again.

'We have to go to Mary, Ted.' Ellen could hardly get the words out. She felt as though her chest was bursting.

13

'We can't.'

'Tomorrow, in the morning then, as soon as it's light.'

'Now just a minute, love.' Ted took her face between his hands. 'Look at me.'

She stared at him.

'There's nothing we can do. It's happened. And Mary's got Peter to look after her. I think she'll want to be left alone. At least for now.'

'What are you talking about?' Her eyes widened. 'Of course we have to go. She's my sister. He was my brother. I want to be with her.' She couldn't believe what he was saying. 'I need to be with her.'

'Not yet.'

'Yes.'

'No, love. When it's the funeral.'

How could he be so cold, so practical? Ellen pushed him away, took a few steps backward until she walked into the table. She gripped the edges. 'I can't stay here. I can't carry on as though nothing's happened. We have to go.'

'I can't leave the shop just like that.'

'Why not? You've got Archie. You've said he bakes as good as you.' Her voice was shrill.

'I can't.' Ted came towards her, holding out his hand.

She knocked it away from her. 'Why?' she demanded again. She moved, putting the table between them. She didn't trust herself not to hit him.

'There's still the shop. I can't ask him to do both. He can't bake and serve – wouldn't be fair to ask him. And Doreen doesn't know all the ropes yet.'

'She's been working for you for months. If she doesn't know how to serve by now you should sack her.'

'No. I'm sorry, Ellen, I can't leave the shop just like that.'

'Then shut the bloody place.' Why he was arguing about something so important to her? So awful?

And then she knew. It wasn't the shop he didn't want to leave. She put the flat of her hands on the table, held her breath, swallowed. For a long moment they watched one another.

'Then I'll go on my own.'

Chapter 5

'Where've you been for the last two days?' Nelly Shuttleworth hoisted the two heavy baskets of shopping onto the kitchen table and rubbed at the marks that the handles had left on her arms. Breathing deeply from her walk from the bus stop, she glanced through the back door where her son was slouched in a chair in the yard.

'Why?' George didn't turn round. A swirl of cigarette smoke rose above his head.

'Because I'm asking, that's why.' Nelly took out a long pin from the crumpled black felt hat, pulled it off with a sigh of relief and scratched her head. 'You go off without a word for two days and don't expect me to ask where you've been?'

'Because it's none of your business.'

'My house, my business. So, where've you been?' She unloaded brown paper bags of sugar and tea onto the table. Twisting the ends of the tissue paper wrapped around a large loaf, she put it into the white enamel bread bin in the pantry. Resting her hands on the stone slab she tried to catch her breath. The old corset she was wearing was now too small for her; she'd have to chuck it. 'George?'

'For Christ's sake, I said – business!'

'And I asked what sort.' Nelly spoke sharply. 'If you're going to bring trouble to my door I need to know.'

'Stop fucking nagging.' George felt around on the flags by his feet, picked up a small stone and aimed it at a ginger tom that appeared on top of the yard wall. He missed but, frightened by the clatter against the bricks, the cat sprang onto the roof of next door's lavatory. George grunted in satisfaction.

'Watch your mouth.' Nelly tipped potatoes, carrots and peas from the other basket into a big ceramic bowl. 'And there's no need to be cruel either.'

George stood and came to lean against the doorframe. 'If anybody asks, I was here all the time.'

'Who'll ask?'

He lifted his shoulders. 'Dunno. Anybody.'

'And the truth?'

'If you must know I was in Manchester with Harry Bradshaw.'

'Up to no good, then.' Nelly set her mouth in a grim line.

'Just some old business I had to deal with.'

'What old business?' Why did she suddenly feel uneasy? She studied him. There was something in his eyes; a glittering excitement, a look of malicious triumph. Nelly wondered which poor sod had got on the wrong side of her son this time.

'Nothing for you to bother your head about.' George walked over to her, put his arm around her shoulder. 'Nothing to bother about at all.'

Chapter 6

'I wanted to be here. I couldn't bear the thought of you on your own.' Ellen spoke in shuddering breaths and clutched a sodden handkerchief. As soon as the children had gone to bed she'd burst into uncontrollable tears.

'I'm not on my own, love, I've got Peter.' Mary gave Ellen a wan smile. 'Still you're here now and I'm glad.' Even as she spoke Mary wondered why she'd said it. It wasn't true. She wanted only to be left alone to grieve.

Having Ellen and the children here meant she had to be strong. She'd realised that as soon as Ellen fell tearfully into her arms, leaving Peter to lift the children from the train. Her sister still assumed it was her right to be indulged and protected, Mary reflected with some bitterness, and that *she* would provide that comfort when all she wanted to do was to sleep to block out the awful images of Tom dying in the road.

Despite this, it hurt that Ted hadn't come to Wales. He had been Tom's best friend once. The least he could have done was brought Ellen and the children in his van, even if he had to go back to the shop. Stranger still, her sister hadn't once mentioned her husband.

'Where is Peter?' Ellen wiped her eyes and hiccupped.

'Next door. He went round to see if Gwyneth's okay. She's been in a right state since … since it happened. She was very fond of Tom, you know that.' And getting Ellen's hysterical telephone call in the middle of Saturday night hadn't helped.

'Did she see what happened?'

'No.'

Ellen sighed. 'I suppose that's something, anyway. An old lady like that.' She gulped.

'Yes,' Mary said softly, 'it was horrible.'

'Did you see the driver?'

'No, just that the van was white with an orange oblong line along the side. It came from nowhere.'

They sat in silence. A car passed on the road outside. Listening to it Mary closed her eyes.

Ellen leant forward on the settee, crossing her arms over her waist and swaying back and forth. 'I did love our Tom, Mary, you know that.' It had to be the tenth time she'd said those words since she arrived. It was obvious Ellen expected some sort of reassurance. 'I didn't always understand him, you know, all that pacifist stuff during the war. I mean, I know he didn't want to fight, he was so – gentle. But deliberately doing things so he kept going back into prison? Why did he do that?'

'I've told you before. He believed war was wrong,' Mary said calmly. 'They kept trying to get him to go back to work in the Civil Service. He wouldn't work for a Government which had taken the country to war.'

'But it didn't get him anywhere, did it?' I mean, what did he achieve?'

'Enough now, Ellen.' Mary went over the sideboard, took two clean handkerchiefs from a drawer and gave one to Ellen. 'Try not to cry any more, love, you'll make yourself ill. How about going upstairs to see what the children are doing?'

'I can't.' Ellen blew her nose. 'I don't want them to see me like this. Will you go instead?'

When Mary came back, Ellen was moving restlessly around the room fiddling with the curtains, straightening the horse brasses on the wall, running her hand over the long white crocheted mat on the sideboard where all the photographs were.

'They're asleep,' Mary said. 'Must be yesterday's journey on the train.'

'It took ages and it was hard work trying to manage both of them on my own.' Ellen picked up a portrait of Tom and their mother standing arm in arm in the garden, both in wellingtons and overcoats. 'When was this taken?' She waved the frame in the air. 'I've forgotten.'

'Just after we got here. March, '46.' Mary watched the careless gesture and half lifted her hand, afraid Ellen would drop the photograph. It was the only one she had of the two of them together. 'Why didn't Ted bring you?'

'He said he would have if I'd waited until he could sort something out with the shop. I can't see why he couldn't just shut it for a couple of days.'

'So you've fallen out.' It wasn't the first time they'd quarrelled and Ellen had turned up on the doorstep.

Ellen shrugged, her apparent unconcern contradicted by the tears that trailed down her cheeks.

'Do you want to talk about it?'

'No.'

'Okay. I'll make a brew in a minute.' Mary took the photograph from her, wiped the glass with the sleeve of her cardigan, and carefully put it back in its place. 'It was freezing cold the day this was taken,' she remembered. 'But they insisted on getting the vegetable plot ready for planting. Mam went mad at first when I got the Kodak out and took this of them.' She touched their faces. 'We have to remember the good times, Ellen. Tom was a good brother. You don't have to try to understand what he did, how he thought.' She smiled. 'I'll always be grateful to him. If he hadn't written that letter and left it with you, Peter would never have found me.'

'It's not every day an ex-POW knocks on your front door.' Ellen gave her a tremulous smile.

'And I'll always be grateful you didn't turn him away.'

'Our Patrick was there, that day. Sometimes it seems he's always at our house.' Ellen spoke absently. She leant against the back of the settee and wiped her hands over her face. 'I was scared to death. It could have caused right ructions. You know what a moody bugger he is at the best of times. Think how he'd have been if he'd seen him; just one mention of the war, Bevin Boys or the Germans sets him off again.'

'Perhaps it will never be over for him.' Mary bit her lip. They'd all grown up on the receiving end of their younger brother's temper. 'He put the telephone down when Peter first rang him to say what had happened. He had to try again.'

'Typical!' Ellen nodded. 'Apparently, the other day a chap who lives on Church Road, an ex-POW from the Granville, asked him for a job on one of his market stalls. Ted said he thought Patrick was going to hit him.'

Mary flinched at the mention of the prisoner-of-war camp where she'd been a nurse and Peter a German detainee. An image of Frank Shuttleworth flashed through her mind. She forced it away. His face haunted her sleep. To hear the name of the camp spoken so casually made her stomach turn. Even though it was where she and Peter had first fallen in love, they didn't talk about the Granville. As though each of them instinctively knew the distress it would cause. 'Did he hit him?'

'No, just gave him a pretty nasty mouthful from all accounts.'

'If Patrick's still hanging on to old resentments it's his own doing. I don't really care.' She did, but she wouldn't acknowledge the hurt. 'I've spoken to Jean. She says he won't be at the funeral but she will.'

'That's big of her. She'll probably come swanning in trying to organise everything as usual.'

'Stop it, Ellen.'

'Well, she didn't like Tom, not really.'

'She's my best friend. And she's our sister-in-law as well. She should be here.'

'So should Patrick.'

'It's his choice.' Mary shrugged.

She studied Ellen for the first time since she'd arrived in Llamroth. The black sweater and A-line skirt revealed how thin she was, and her blonde hair, scraped back into a French pleat, emphasised the gauntness of her face and the dark shadows under her eyes. 'You look awful.'

'Thanks.'

A thought struck Mary. 'Has Linda broken up from school for the summer holidays? Is it the end of term?'

'No, it doesn't matter if she misses a couple of weeks.'

A couple of weeks? It could be longer than that before the funeral. The police had told her there would have to be a coroner's inquest first. Surely Ellen wouldn't want to be away from home, from Ted, all that time? 'You'll have the truancy man coming to your door.'

'Well, I'm not there, so there's not much he can do, is there?'

There was something else the matter with Ellen. Mary could feel it in her bones. She gave a quivering sigh. 'What's wrong?'

20

Ellen glanced at her, incredulous. 'Our brother's just been killed, that's what's wrong.' She looked quickly away.

'You don't need to tell me that,' Mary flared. She'd lived with the images of Tom's last moments for five days now: cradling his head in her lap in the middle of the road, knowing he was dead; Peter gently holding her back when the ambulance took him away, the screams she couldn't stop; Tom's blood saturating her skirt, dripping from the hem onto her legs.

'You don't need to tell me that,' she repeated, more softly this time, seeing Ellen's stricken face.

Chapter 7

Mary took the last peg from her apron pocket and fastened Linda's skirt on the washing line.

Glancing up at the back bedroom window she saw the curtains were drawn. It was almost midday and Ellen was still sleeping. Peter had taken the children to the beach and silence hung over the house for the first time in two days; during the last hour she'd fluctuated between silent tears and unexpected anger.

'Has the policeman gone?' Gwyneth appeared at her back door. Her voice was husky and, unusually for her, her grey hair was uncombed and she was still in a flowery dressing gown. She looked as though she'd aged years in the last few days, her face pallid, her eyelids red and swollen.

'About an hour and a half ago,' Mary said. 'Are you all right, love?' She felt the burn of empathetic tears.

'No.' It was almost a whisper. Then Gwyneth straightened her shoulders and drew herself up to her full five foot. 'What did he say … *y plismon*?'

'He said, with no one else to see it…' Watching her friend struggle to compose herself, Mary stumbled over the words. 'As no one else saw what happened, we can't prove Tom was killed on purpose.'

'Peter didn't see?'

Mary shook her head. 'No, he only heard.'

'But it was still a hit and run, Mary? They're going to find who did it?' Gwyneth's question ended on a wobbly high note.

'He said they will try.' Mary let the angry tears spill out. 'Oh Gwyneth, what am I going to do without Tom? What am I going to do?'

They stood looking at one another, helpless in their shared grief. Then the older woman made a small decisive nod of her head. 'Have you time to come round, Mary?' she said. 'I've something to show you.'

Mary stared at the familiar writing, her lips moving as she read the letter again.

> *My dear Gwyneth,*
> *I've wanted to write this for some weeks but have felt unable to. I want, no I need to tell you how much I loved your son.*

'Oh Tom,' Mary murmured. She looked up at Gwyneth.

'I know.' The old woman put a trembling hand on Mary's shoulder.

> *From the moment we met, Iori and I knew we would be friends, knew we would want to share our lives after this awful time was over.*

'It would have been so difficult for them, Gwyneth,' Mary whispered. 'They'd have been thrown in prison, hounded.'

A flash of dread shot through her. It would be like that for her and Peter. She was under no illusion about the bitter prejudice of some people. To them he would always be the enemy.

Sometimes we would talk into the early hours in our cell, about what we would do for work, where we would live. Iori wanted to go back to Llamroth. I didn't mind as long as we were together. We both knew it wouldn't be easy, that there could be problems but we didn't care.

'They would have done it too,' Gwyneth said, reading the letter over Mary's shoulder with her. 'Iori was always determined as a boy.'

'And Tom.' Mary's misery lessened for a moment. She felt the hint of a smile move her lips until she read Tom's next words.

But I let him down Gwyneth. I didn't save him. I couldn't save him and I'm ashamed of that. And I will live with that all my life.

'He must have written this sometime in March or April of '45,' Mary said slowly. 'Before he was released from prison. He must have had it smuggled out. He took a big chance it wouldn't be found.'

She reached up and covered Gwyneth's hand with her own, remembering Tom's homecoming.

As a nurse she'd seen many cases of shock but Tom was the worst she'd encountered. Perfunctorily released from Wormwood Scrubs, he'd arrived dirty, unkempt and withdrawn. For days he'd shambled around the house as though she and Mam weren't even there. The only emotion he revealed was his loathing for Arthur Brown, the man their widowed mother had decided to marry.

Until the morning Gwyneth's letter arrived offering them the cottage here to rent. He'd sat in silence after reading it, struggling to retain some control until, with great gasping sobs, his grief poured out. The life in Llamroth that he and Iori had planned would come true. But without Iori. And it was too much for Tom.

He'd clung to Mary, his anguish uncontrollable as he struggled to describe what had happened to Iori; the way seven of the prisoners had beaten his friend to the ground with fists and makeshift clubs, others blocking the doorway so he couldn't get into the cell where Iori was trapped. Sobbing, he'd told Mary how he fought, punching, kicking and screaming, trying to climb over those who watched, cheering and laughing, urging the attackers to more violence.

Mary shuddered remembering his words.

'I couldn't get to him … I tried … I really tried … his face was unrecognisable … all smashed in.'

She'd never told Gwyneth. She never would. Reliving that moment was almost too much for Mary to bear.

But then she read the next few lines and her throat tightened. She swallowed against the loud pounding in her ears, struggling to breathe.

I should have protected him. I have sworn to myself that no one I love will ever, ever be hurt like that again. I will make sure of that. I hope you can forgive me for not saving your son.
Tom Howarth

A cold sick feeling rippled through her body. There was a line in a letter she and Mam received from Tom at the time of Iori's murder that had stayed with her over the years. *I wanted to kill them when I saw what they were doing to Iori*, he'd written. It had stuck in her mind because it was completely at odds with all her brother had believed in. A dreadful thought forced itself to the front of her mind. She squeezed her eyes tightly to get rid of it.

Carefully folding the letter again she stood up and enfolded Gwyneth in her arms. They rocked, gently crying. At last Mary kissed the older woman's forehead. 'Thank you,' she whispered, 'for reminding me of the time Tom was happiest.'

'Even though he wrote it when he was in such pain?' Gwyneth looked up at Mary. '*Nid oedd unrhyw beth i'w faddau* – there was nothing to forgive. Tom made my Iori content with himself for

24

the first time ever. I will never forget how glad I was when they met. And when I realised they loved one another.'

'I know.'

'I can say it to you, Mary, can't I?'

'Yes.' She patted Gwyneth's hand. 'Yes, you can, love.'

'I do miss Tom. He was like another son to me. I wish him and Iori had had more time.'

'I know,' Mary sighed. 'Thank you.' They smiled at one another even as the tears still hovered.

There was the bang of a door and lots of chatter from next door.

'That'll get their mother up.' Mary gave a small laugh.

'Don't let Ellen take advantage of you, *cariad*, you're always too soft with her.' Gwyneth stroked Mary's cheek. 'Take care of yourself – especially now.'

'I've got Peter,' Mary said.

'Yes, he's a good man. He'll look after you. But, remember what I said, *bach,* she'll let you run round after her, if she can.'

Mary gave Gwyneth another peck on the forehead. 'I'll remember.'

But it wasn't Ellen on her mind when she stood outside the front door of the cottage. It was Tom – and the realisation that he'd been lying to her all these years.

…no one I love will ever, ever be hurt like that again. I will make sure of that.

Chapter 8

The sea was sluggish in the heat; ripples of quicksilver on the slight roll of water reflected the bright light of the sky. Linda, oblivious to the temperature, ran along the foamy edge joining sand and sea, yelping when she stood on one of the many pebbles scattered about and seared by the sun.

The sisters sat on the beach in identical poses, chins resting on knees, skirts and arms wrapped around legs.

Mary sighed. She needed to talk to Peter; to tell him everything. But how? Perhaps it would change his opinion of Tom. And she hated the thought of that.

'You okay?' Ellen took her eyes off her daughter to give a quick look at Mary.

'Just tired.'

'Me too.'

'She's enjoying herself,' Mary said, watching Linda. It would do the little girl good to get some sea air. She looked too pale, too thin. 'She's all arms and legs, that one.' She glanced down at the sleeping little boy on the blanket between them, his bottom in the air, his chubby fist tucked under his chin. 'And he's tired out as well.' She forced a smile and shielded her eyes to look around. 'I love it here. It's gloriously peaceful, even with all the holiday-makers.' She watched a family walk by, the mother carrying a picnic basket, the father laden with blankets and windbreaks, the three children swinging brightly coloured metal buckets and spades. A lump rose in her throat. 'I thought we were settled for life here.' She stopped.

'Will you go back to Ashford?'

'No. Oh no, take no notice of me.' Too many bad memories. Mary picked up a shell and began to make a pattern in the sand. 'It's better for Peter here. I don't think we'll get as much trouble here as we would in Ashford. We haven't so far, anyway.' It suddenly occurred to her that things might be different – Tom not being with them anymore. She blinked hard. 'Tom will be buried here. I couldn't leave. I wouldn't want to.'

And any trouble from anyone, she was more than a match for them. She'd grown up battling with the gossips tittle-tattling about her family. She set her mouth.

They sat for a while watching Linda eyeing up the children who had just arrived; sidling towards them as they began to build sandcastles.

'Do you ever think back to when *we* were kids?' Ellen turned her head so her cheek was against her knees.

'Of course I do.' Mary grimaced. 'Constant rows, Mam trying to keep the peace, Dad roaring drunk every weekend, coming home ready to clout any of us who looked sideways at him, Patrick goading Tom all the time.' She stopped talking but her thoughts continued: Tom taking me to the park out of the way, rowing to the middle of the lake there in one of the boats, resting the oars and letting us drift while I cried; making me laugh when the tears finally dried up.

He wasn't here now to comfort her. He would never be here again.

I have sworn to myself that no one I love will ever, ever be hurt like that again. I will make sure of that.

Had Tom lied to stop her fears that the police might one day come after him? Or had he been frightened she would judge him? Surely not.

Her thoughts were disrupted by Ellen's sudden peevish voice. 'You and Tom were always close. I remember you gabbing away to him all the time.'

Even now, Ellen couldn't help being jealous. Mary's instant anger was quickly replaced by guilt. She and Tom were always close. Perhaps, without realising it, they had shut out Ellen when they were younger. Maybe that was why Patrick always resented Tom. She sighed. It was too late to think about that now.

Ellen bit at the skin at the side of her thumbnail. 'I've always been left out – I've never had anybody in the family on my side.' She frowned, a deep furrow between her eyebrows.

'Never had anybody on your side?' Mary closed her eyes. 'Do you want me to list all the times you've shouted and I've come running? Even since we moved here? Every time you needed help?'

It was as though she hadn't spoken.

'Mam was too busy keeping the peace between everybody and Dad didn't care.'

'Look, Ellen, I'm struggling to get through what's happening now, let alone what happened years ago. Why drag all that stuff up? You were Dad's favourite, for God's sake.'

'Only on his terms. Only as long as I did what he told me to. Have you forgotten that time I had the chance to be in a show in London but he stopped it?'

'I remember the screaming matches, the rows,' Mary said wryly. 'I don't know how you managed to get away with half the things you said without being clouted.'

'He stopped my one chance to make it big.'

'Not this again.' Mary rubbed the tips of her fingers over her forehead. 'Your voice is still lovely, Ellen, you're still young. There's time for you to achieve anything you want to.'

'Huh!'

'Nobody stops you singing now.' She was almost on the verge of asking Ellen to go home until the funeral. It was too hard. She didn't want to sort out her sister's problems anymore. 'You know,' she said, 'it would be good if, for once, just the once, you stopped thinking about yourself and saw what was going on around you.'

Ellen inspected her thumb; it was bleeding slightly down the side of her nail where she'd chewed on it. She wiped it with her handkerchief. 'I'm here, aren't I? I came to be with you.' She smoothed strands of her blonde hair off her face and refastened them. Next to them the baby squirmed onto his side, making small sucking noises.

All I want is a bit of peace and quiet, Mary thought. Fat chance of that. She shielded her eyes again and watched Linda, trying to ignore the heavy sighs from Ellen. But it was impossible. 'All right,' she said crossly, 'what is it?'

Ellen sighed again. 'If you must know, I'm going mad in that house. Ted's mother drives me mad. You have no idea what a nasty cow she is and I don't know how much more I can take.'

'But you always got on.' Mary knew Ellen had moaned through the years about her mother-in-law but she'd no idea things were

28

that bad. 'You were quick enough to move in with her five years ago.' And leave me struggling with things at home, she thought.

'That's mean, our Mary.' Ellen twisted around to look her. 'You know it was because we thought Ted was dead, that he'd been killed in action. She begged me. She couldn't bear being on her own.'

'But when you got the telegram saying he was a POW, you could have come home then. I still needed help with Tom, with Mam, with trying to work and keep the house clean. I'd have welcomed you with open arms.' Mary relaxed for a second. 'Tom was overjoyed. They'd been such friends before the war. I've always thought hearing about Ted was the turning point for Tom getting better. I needed you at Henshaw Street. I was desperate for help.'

Ellen straightened her legs, wriggled her toes in the sand. 'By the time Ted was due home, you were full of all your plans to come down here with Mam and Tom.' Mary heard the antagonism. 'You left the week he arrived.'

'Only so you and he could move into number twenty-seven. I thought that's what you wanted.' Mary studied the pearly pink and silver on the curved inside of the shell. 'I remember worrying about all the gossip you'd face, how you didn't seem to care that everybody would say you were "living over the brush".'

'Says she who'd been having a secret affair with a POW in the Granville.'

Mary's face flushed but she couldn't help smiling. 'Yes, well…' She put a hand to her cheek. 'You could have told me you'd got a special licence and were married.'

'And spoil all the fun of the nosy parkers?' Ellen lay back on the sand, arms folded under her head, gazing up at the sky. 'Anyway my moving in then has nothing to do with what's happening now. I'm at the end of my tether with the old cow.'

'You're more than a match for Hannah Booth, however crabby she is.'

'I can't do right for doing wrong.'

'Since when?'

'Since you and me brought Linda home from that foster place.' There was a catch in her voice. 'She's never taken to her.'

'Bringing Linda home was the right thing to do.' In a sudden shift of mood, Mary felt a surge of anger at Ted's mother. 'Why haven't you told me this before? It's not like you not to shout it from the rooftops if something's wrong.'

'I thought I could stick it out.' Ellen pulled a face.

'And now you can't?'

Ellen didn't answer. 'Remember going to the foster woman?' she said instead. 'The day we went to fetch Linda?'

'You did the right thing getting her back.' Mary gave Ellen a quick hug. 'Always remember that, whatever Hannah Booth says.' She would never forget the sight of Ellen carrying Linda out of that house in only a terry towelling nappy and a grubby red cardigan, so dirty it was almost impossible to tell what colour it actually was. But it was the child's grey eyes that distressed Mary; the fear in them, the tears quivering on her long lashes, as though she was too frightened to let them fall. And she'd clung so tightly to Ellen they'd had difficulty tucking the blanket around her.

Mary had vowed then it didn't matter who her father had been. She'd always be there for the little girl – and for Ellen.

Now she fought down a rising sense of dread. 'Hannah doesn't know who Linda's father was, does she? You haven't told her?' If that got out, it could cause problems for them all.

'No, of course I bloody haven't,' Ellen said. 'I haven't even told Ted. It's enough for the old bag that Linda's not Ted's.'

'What exactly does she say? Or do?'

'Everything … nothing … not when Ted's there anyway.' Ellen paused, blinked hard a few times. 'I can't take any more.'

'You need to explain properly to him.'

'I can't.'

'Why?'

'Just can't.'

Mary waited.

'*You* don't resent Linda?' Ellen searched Mary's face, obviously looking for a reaction. 'I know I hurt you but you've forgiven me? For what I did with Frank?'

'Ellen, I love Linda. She was the best thing to come out of the whole mess.'

There had been so many times over the last five years when she'd thought Linda was the nearest she'd ever have to a daughter. She loved both of her nieces but Linda had a special place in her heart. In the few months since Peter had come back to her, she'd allowed herself to hope that one day the two of them would have a family of their own; to acknowledge her yearning to hold her own child in her arms.

'Frank was your boyfriend and I was stupid enough to think he fancied me. Not just using me to get back at you.'

'It's all in the past. I've told you that often enough.' Mary turned her face away. She tucked her hands under her armpits. 'Frank was a bully, worse than a bully, you know that.' She hated the sound of his name in her head but she couldn't get rid of it. Frank Shuttleworth, the man she once thought she loved. The man who'd raped her, one cold wet morning on the canal path. Who'd died, drowned in the canal. Murdered, she was sure now, by Tom, her brother.

The self-loathing and the memory of scrubbing her body until her skin was sore for months afterwards all at once returned in a rush of bile in Mary's mouth. She swallowed, screwing up her face against the sourness.

She waited until the taste and the memories subsided, the silence heavy between them.

When she turned towards Ellen, the afternoon sun was full on her face and, for the first time, Mary noticed the habitual downward pull of lines around her sister's mouth. She's not been really happy for a long time, she thought, pushing away the images that haunted her almost every day. 'So,' she said, changing the subject, 'what are you going to do about Hannah?'

'I just wish I'd been strong enough to say no to Ted when he asked if she could come to live with us.'

'I still don't know why you didn't.'

'It's complicated. And Ted loves Linda so much. He idolises her. I thought I owed it to him to try to get on with his mother.' Ellen scrunched herself into a tight ball, pulling her knees to her chest. 'But she's such bloody hard work. I knew, once she got her feet under the table, I knew she was there to stay. And she's made sure of that.'

Ellen stood up, brushing the sand from her blouse. She looked down at Mary, her dark blue eyes brimming with tears.

'How, Ellen? Whatever she says or does, you need to tell Ted.'

'I can't. I don't think he wants to know.'

'Rubbish. Ted wouldn't want you to be so unhappy. He's a good kind man.'

'He's too soft, especially with that old battleaxe.' Ellen frowned. 'Anyway, he's different now.' She rubbed the back of her neck in a quick impatient gesture. 'I can't explain. I just can't get through to him at all. It's like me and the kids aren't enough anymore.'

'I'm sure that's not true,' Mary said.

'I think it is.' Ellen scooped up the still-sleeping little boy and held him close to her. She gestured to Linda to let her know they were leaving the beach. Her daughter ran towards them, protesting.

'He loves you.' Mary folded the blanket they'd been sitting on.

'Does he?'

'You know he does. And he's a good provider for you – the shop—'

'Is the reason his mother's still with us,' Ellen blurted out. 'He got it courtesy of his mother's money.' Her mouth twisted into a bitter line. 'That was the way she got to stay. She sold her house and lent him the money. And she never lets us forget it.'

Chapter 9

They stood in silence inside the porch of the large red-brick Council building. Leaden clouds pressed down, forcing light from the day, and the slanting rain bounced on the concrete path. Mary heard the wet swish of the passing traffic on the other side of the wall surrounding the grounds. The soil on the flowerbeds was trammelled with running water. Raindrops dripped steadily from the leaves of the laurel bushes spread out on either side of the doorway.

'I've got to get away from here.' Ellen knotted her headscarf under her chin.

Mary caught hold of her arm. 'Wait until it bates.'

'No, I can't.' Ellen pulled up the collar of her coat. 'I'll see you back at the house.' She hurried away.

Mary stared after her.

'Your sister is upset.'

'And I'm not?' Mary turned to Peter. The inquest had passed in a confusion of words she hadn't been able to follow. 'If she's that upset why hasn't she asked Ted to be with her, whatever she thinks he's done? That shouldn't matter. Or at least it shouldn't for now. He's a good husband. And, before the war, he was Tom's best friend.' She fumbled with her raincoat.

'Perhaps you should have spoken to him?' Peter moved to help her.

'She wouldn't let me. Told me to keep my nose out.' She shrugged away from him. 'I'm okay.' Her voice was sharp. 'Sorry.' She let him ease her arms into the sleeves. 'I'll be glad when Jean gets here. Perhaps she knows what's been going on.'

'Patrick?'

'No.' There'd been no mention of Patrick. Did she want him to come with Jean, being honest with herself? No. He'd done too much to hurt Tom when he was alive. And there was no chance he'd be civil to Peter.

She looked back into the porch at the door. 'What was said in there … the verdict, that phrase "unlawful killing by person or persons unknown" was the same as at Frank's inquest.' Her voice rose. 'That was what that other Coroner said then.' She was distraught, angry that in death there was an unbreakable connection between her brother and the man who had almost destroyed her life, even if it was only the cold and bureaucratic words.

'But nothing else is the same, Mary. Tom, he was a kind, decent man. Shuttleworth was *ein Sadist.*' Peter gathered her in his arms. 'He and his cronies at the camp enjoyed the power he had over us. The war did that to many men.'

She buried her face against him. 'It's just not fair.'

'Things are not fair, *Liebling,* but, perhaps, as the Coroner said, we must wait—'

'For what?' she interrupted, lifting her head, her face flushed with pent up anger. 'For the police to find out who did it? For someone to own up? We both know that won't happen.' She waited. He didn't say anything. 'In there it just brought everything back again. All those months when he followed me around, the things he did to frighten me into going back to him.' She lowered her voice. 'The way he got away with shooting you, trying to kill you.'

Peter put his finger under her chin. 'Look at me *Liebling.* We cannot let that man ruin our lives. *Er ist weg* … he's gone, he's dead.'

His voice was firm, dismissive, but there was something about his expression. She searched his face. His gaze shifted away from hers but not before she saw the evasion in them.

She frowned, confused, letting him gently fasten the buttons on her raincoat, the silence stretching between them. Since his return she'd believed that one day they would reminisce about the Granville because, as well as the fear of being caught, there were special memories there that bonded them forever. But it hadn't happened. This was the first time Frank's name had been raised and she'd been the one to start talking about him. Peter spoke only of the man's cruelty in the camp. Not that Frank had raped her.

An icy cold ran through her. Could he only deal with what Frank did to her by pretending it hadn't happened?

Don't be stupid, she told herself. Peter had come looking for her. He loved her. If the thought of Frank raping her disgusted him so much he wouldn't be here now. Surely?

'Peter?' She stopped. This wasn't the place. She'd pick her time, just as she would to tell him what she'd discovered about Tom. 'Let's get home,' she said instead.

'*Ja.*' He looked towards the gate. Water pockmarked the puddles on the path. 'We must run, I think.'

At the kerb they jumped back as a bus passed throwing up a wave of oil-skimmed water and then, heads bowed, they ran without looking until they were under the awning of the newsagents on the other side of the road.

'Sorry.' Mary collided with a young woman sheltering there.

'S'all right,' the woman laughed, 'you wouldn't think it was July, would you? S'pose we should just be glad it's not freezing cold.' Her voice changed to one of recognition. 'Matron?'

Mary peered from under her headscarf.

'Nurse Allott … Vivienne, I didn't know you lived around here?'

'I don't.' The young woman shuffled back to let them take cover. 'I came with some friends who live up the coast – Cardigan way. They're in the shop.' She made a vague gesture whilst looking with curiosity at Peter. 'Hi,' she said.

He dipped his head. 'Hello.' His accent sounded thicker than usual.

With a sudden stab of anger, Mary saw the sideways shift of the young woman's eyes and the hardening of her features. 'This is Nurse Allott, Peter, she works on one of my wards at the hospital,' she said, adding deliberately, 'my…' Boyfriend sounded ridiculous. She was twenty-eight. 'My fiancé, Peter.' She linked arms with him. 'He was a doctor in the hospital at the camp where I worked before.'

By the time she was next in work it would be all over the small hospital. She didn't care except that sooner or later it would get back to the Board of Governors. She wasn't sure how they'd take it. She laughed, a bright artificial sound. 'I do have a life beyond the hospital. As do you, I see.' She could hear the stilted tone in her voice but couldn't help it.

For a moment all was still.

'Oh. Yes, I see.' Vivienne Allott turned and flicked a hand towards the shop as the bell above the door jingled and a couple jostled their way out. 'Actually, we're here to see if we can register the death of my friend's husband. He's been posted "missing" since '41.'

The silence stretched between them.

'Anyway, must go.' The young woman shifted from foot to foot. She lifted an impatient hand at her friends as they nudged her. 'Er – I read about your brother in the paper, Matron. It must have been awful. Did they…?' She stopped. 'Have they arrested anybody yet?'

'No.' Mary's lips felt stiff forming the word.

'Oh, I'm sorry, I shouldn't have asked.' Vivienne Allott moved away. She didn't acknowledge Peter.

'That's all right.' But it wasn't. Mary fumed. Talking about Tom to someone like this, someone who purposely snubbed Peter.

They watched her move away through the crowds, her head close to one of the women. Mary saw them look back at her and Peter. She gave them a false smile, furious that she was the subject of their gossip.

Peter had a strange expression on his face. A nerve pulsed at the corner of his eye that Mary hadn't seen before.

'I'm sorry about that stupid girl,' she said.

'I think we are both sorry we met her,' he said, tracing her face with his fingers. 'Now…' Ruefully he looked up towards the edge of the awning where a line of water ran along the pole and streamed in shining elongated drips onto the passers-by. 'I am afraid we will have to get wet. We must leave here and go home.'

Home without Tom. It was something she had to get used to. 'Yes,' she said, turning, avoiding a newsstand by the shop window. 'Oh Peter.' She read the headline with dismay.

'North Korean Troops Storm across the 38th Parallel into South Korea.'

This conflict was one she'd tried not to think about. It was a reminder of a fear that caused her sleepless nights. What happens to us, Peter, if another war brings out all the old resentments? What if I have to lose you as well as Tom? 'It's impossible to believe that another war has started so soon,' she said softly.

Peter pressed her hand to his side with his arm. 'It is not the war of the British. Truman has sent in troops. It is America's war.'

'Until they involve us,' Mary said. 'What happens then?'

Peter lifted one shoulder. 'We can only wait to see.'

Chapter 10

'Thanks Ted, it was good of you to ring.' Mary scowled at Ellen who was glaring back at her from the sofa. 'I'm sorry she's not here at the moment. I think she must be next door at Gwyneth's picking up the children. We had Tom's inquest this morning.' It chilled her just saying the words.

She listened with a hand over her other ear against the hum of voices from the wireless, making small assenting noises. 'Yes, I'm – we're all fine – children too, yes.' She sighed. 'I know, I'm sorry, I have tried.' Finally, 'I will ask her again to call you. Yes, I promise.'

Putting the receiver back onto the cradle of the telephone she said, 'You'll have to talk to him sometime, you know. I can't keep putting him off and why should I?'

Ellen shrugged. But when she looked at Mary her make-up was washed away by tears.

'After this morning I'd have thought you'd have understood life's too short to play these games.'

'Don't, Mary.'

In the lull that followed Mary could hear the children laughing next door; a bus trundled by on the lane; the drone of a bee or wasp circled the parlour before escaping into the kitchen and out through the back door. The rain had finally stopped and weak spikes of sunlight fell across the room like slivers of glass, lighting up the horse brasses on the wall. A random thought flitted through her mind: perhaps the hot days of June were coming back.

'We need to talk,' she said again, taking in long slow breaths to stay calm. 'It's not just Ted's mother, is it? What's wrong between you and Ted?' Mary waited, watching Ellen playing with one gold hoop earring, her hand shaking.

On the way home from the inquest Peter had said that she needed to take care of herself; that her sister must sort out her marriage on her own. Yet, even though those awful last moments of Tom's life haunted her all the time, she still felt compelled to sort out Ellen's problems. You're a fool, she told herself.

Ellen picked up her packet of Craven 'A'. 'Damn!' It was empty. She flung it into the hearth.

'Tom kept some cigarettes in here.' Mary walked over to the roll-top desk in the corner of the room and opened a drawer. Her brother's broken spectacles were at the front in their case. Mary opened the lid and touched the wire frames with the tips of her fingers as though they would burn her.

'I didn't know he smoked.'

'He didn't, not often anyway.' Mary picked up the packet of Capstan and closed the drawer with a snap. 'Not your brand but they'll have to do if you're desperate.' She tossed them over to Ellen. 'Well?' She hoped she didn't sound as tired of all this as she felt.

Ellen sucked hard on the cigarette before answering. 'Okay,' she said, with a deep sigh and gulping a few times. 'However much I hate her, I have to say it's not just his bloody mother.' Her eyes filled. 'Ted's having an affair. He's messing about with the girl he took on in the shop.'

'From next door? The couple who moved in after Mrs Jagger died?'

'The same.' Ellen was crying again. 'And I'm not going back home and I don't want him here, not until I've decided what to do about it.'

Chapter 11

'Do you believe this of Ted?' Peter made quick regular jabs at the damp soil with the hoe, clipping out small weeds. 'Has she spoken of it again since yesterday?'

'No.' Perched on the low stone wall that surrounded the back garden Mary heaved a long sigh. 'It seems far-fetched from what I know of him.'

'You said he knows he was not Ellen's first or even second choice?' Peter spoke thoughtfully, careful not to say Frank Shuttleworth's name in case it upset Mary. In case it brought too many things out into the open. 'Do you think he is, how do you say it, playing Ellen at her own game?'

'It's so long ago, Peter. Why would Ted wait until now to have an affair? And anyway he worships her.' Could Patrick have been mischief making? He had made trouble between Ted and Ellen before. But why would he?

'And Ellen thinks it is the neighbour?'

'Mmm, a girl called Doreen Whittaker. She moved next door

39

after the old lady who lived there died. Her husband's in the Territorial Army or something. So, if there is anything going on, it's a fairly recent thing.'

'Has Ellen the evidence? There is something she has seen?'

'No … I don't know. She won't talk about it now.'

Peter leaned forward, resting his chin on his hand on top of the handle of the hoe and studied Mary. He thrust the hoe into the ground and went to sit beside her. Taking her hand in his, they sat without speaking, watching the skylarks swoop and dive above the fields beyond the garden.

The leaves of the apple trees fluttered, shooting flashes of late afternoon sunlight across their faces. The first new stems of beetroot and the long straight leaves of onions were sturdy in the ground. In the greenhouse healthy tomato plants were creeping up the staked canes. To Mary it seemed wrong that the garden still flourished without Tom, but she couldn't say anything to Peter. She knew he thought it was what she wanted. And perhaps it was.

She could hear the gramophone through Gwyneth's open windows: '… for parting is not goodbye/ We'll be together again.' Mary listened until the song ended.

'Gwyneth's in one of her melancholy moods again,' she said.

Peter glanced at her, puzzled.

'Frank Sinatra,' she explained, gesturing towards next door. 'When she feels sad she always plays his records.'

'Ah.' Peter bowed his head. 'And you, meine Geliebte, how do you feel? You look pale.'

'Tired,' Mary admitted, 'upset by the inquest, dreading the funeral, worried about Ellen.' And aware, yet again, how he'd avoided mentioning Frank Shuttleworth.

'Ah, yes, Ellen.' Peter chafed his palms together, rubbing dried grains of soil from his fingers.

Mary heard the pensiveness in his voice. She guessed that Peter wanted her sister to go home and leave them to grieve on their own. But would he be that selfish?

'I'm sorry, *Liebling*.'

Had her thoughts about him shown on her face? 'No.' Mary turned her face to his. 'Hush.' He was only thinking of her, she reminded herself. Just as not talking about Frank was his way of not upsetting her, she was sure of that.

He brushed his lips over her forehead, across her cheek until his mouth met hers. '*Ich liebe dich*,' he whispered.

She locked her fingers together at the back of his neck. 'I love you too, Peter. I always will.' Was this the right time to tell him about Tom and what he'd done? But his next words took her by surprise.

'So? We will marry. *Ja?*'

It was what she'd been wanting, waiting for. She didn't hesitate. 'Yes,' she said, 'oh yes, we will marry.'

It wouldn't be easy. There would be opposition, even hatred from some. But being together was what she'd dreamed of during the war. She refused to acknowledge the apprehension that trickled down her spine.

She would wait for the right time to tell Peter that she'd realised it was Tom who'd killed Frank.

Chapter 12

THOUGHTS STOP PRAYERS WITH YOU STOP ARRIVING THURSDAY ONE O'CLOCK TRAIN STOP LOVE JEAN

Mary was tense waiting at the station, walking first one way towards the bridge that arched over the single line of tracks, and then the other, until she reached the end of the platform where old wagons were shunted together, their steel wheels rusted to the sidings. There she turned her face to the sun; the mix of warmth and the slight breeze felt good on her skin and for a few moments she relaxed.

Then the signal juddered and clanged upwards and she heard a faint high-pitched shrilling. Shielding her eyes she turned, seeing only a trail of smoke at first. And then, all at once, with a great rush of noise the black barrelled engine steamed alongside the platform, followed by three carriages and the post wagon.

She was sure Patrick wouldn't be with Jean. Even so, Mary couldn't help looking beyond her when she saw the familiar plump figure bustle off the first carriage and drop her suitcase onto the platform. To Mary's relief there was no sign of her brother. She watched Jean help Jacqueline to jump from the step of the carriage and when the little girl ran towards her holding out her arms Mary lifted her and hugged her. Jean walked towards her in her usual manner, the slight waddle, worse in recent years, with feet planted outwards in what Winifred used to call her ten-to-two-feet march.

The two women hesitated as if unsure of each other, then hugged.

'Look at you, skin and bone,' Jean said, pursing her lips, her head to one side. 'Doesn't suit you.'

Mary noticed the short sleeves of her friend's yellow dress cutting into her upper arms and the roll of flesh around her waist above the belt but said nothing. In spite of everything she was glad Jean was here. She missed her and, regardless of their split loyalties between Peter and Patrick, she realised she needed her friend now. 'Thank you for coming.' She had to shout above the sudden loud hiss of steam from the locomotive. She kissed the top of Jacqueline's head. 'Lovely to see you too, love.' Grabbing hold of the little girl's hand she pulled her away from the hot spray that shot out from between the coupling rods. 'Come on, let's find that bus.'

It took Jean until they had settled on the single-decker before she said, 'Patrick says sorry he can't get away. He's too busy. One of the women who works the stall for him in Bradford is sick so he's having to run between there and Rochfield all week.'

'It doesn't matter,' Mary said, doubting he'd ever think of apologising for anything. Her younger brother – her only brother now she realized with shock – was such a bigot. Jean didn't need to make excuses for him. Mary's resentment, that even Tom's death wouldn't bring him to see her, was exacerbated by knowing Patrick wouldn't come because of Peter. And Jean knew that as well.

'Ellen?'

'She's struggling.'

'Hmmm. I went to see Ted. He was really upset about Tom. He couldn't come – his mother had a turn and he couldn't leave her.'

I'll bet she did, Mary thought. 'It's a shame he couldn't find someone to stay with her,' she said. Holding onto the back of Jacqueline's seat as the bus driver changed gears with a grind and stutter of the engine, she had to raise her voice above the rattle. 'Ellen could do with him here.' She stopped, not wanting to talk about Ellen's problems.

Jean wagged her head. 'Ted's going mad without her in the shop. He told Patrick his bread orders have gone right down – right down.'

'I thought the girl who's moved into Mrs Jagger's house was helping him?'

'Doreen Whittaker? Hmm, yes, well, she's neither use nor ornament as far as I can see. And a right flighty piece if you ask me.'

'Flighty? How do you mean?' Mary tried to sound unconcerned.

'What I said. She's not been in the town much above six months and from what I hear she's worked her way around quite a few of the local men.'

'Ellen says she's married.'

'Doesn't seem to stop her. He's in the Territorial Army and in Nottingham a lot, so they say.'

43

The bus picked up speed and the noise made it impossible to talk for the next few minutes. They swayed in their seats as the vehicle swung around the bends and twists of the narrow, hedged-in road.

When the bus stopped accelerating and quietened slightly, Jean spoke again. 'How Ted puts up with that mother of his I'll never know. Twice last week he didn't open the shop because she said she was having a funny do and couldn't be left. He says only Ellen can deal with her when she's like that.'

Perhaps it was as Ellen said. Perhaps Ted didn't want to know what problems his wife had with his mother. Mary kept quiet.

'I offered to look in on her but she was having none of it. It had to be Ted or nobody with her,' Jean said. 'She'd do better if she didn't eat as much. She's enormous now – just sits all day in that corner like a great fat spider, watching everything that goes on.' She leant forward as the bus stopped and a line of people scrambled up the steps. 'Jacqueline, come and stand by your Auntie Mary.'

The little girl squeezed onto Mary's knees instead and Mary gave her a cuddle as the bus lurched forward. 'All right, love?' She savoured the way the little girl snuggled trustingly against her but was troubled by the sadness in her eyes. 'You okay?'

'No Uncle Tom, Auntie Mary?' Jacqueline's chin quivered. 'I wish he was back from Heaven.'

'Me too, sweetheart, me too.' She kissed her. 'Linda's really looking forward to seeing you. She's so bored with her little brother. She said we had to hurry up so she could have someone proper to play with.'

Jacqueline giggled. 'I've brought my John Bull printing set with me, Auntie Mary.'

'Oh, she'll love that. Did Mummy buy you that for your birthday?'

Jacqueline nodded, her thumb tucked into the corner of her mouth.

Jean pulled at her daughter's hand. 'No thumb sucking,' she said. 'I can't stop her doing that.'

'It doesn't matter.' Mary smiled at Jacqueline.

'Linda missed Jacqueline's birthday party because Ellen brought the kids down here,' Jean said.

'Then we'll have to have another party, won't we?' Mary hugged her niece. 'Two birthday parties, all thanks to Auntie Ellen. Not bad eh?'

Jacqueline cuddled closer. 'Smashing!'

Mary watched the conductor making his way towards them, stopping at each passenger and leaning against the metal poles as he turned the handle of his ticket machine and dropped the fares into his leather satchel. She searched in her handbag for her purse. 'Ellen sent a telegram to Ted to say she was staying here for a while to help me.' Holding up a shilling she said, 'Two and a half, please,' and waited until the man gave her two pink tickets and a blue one and moved past them before she said, 'but, to be honest I'm not sure she should stay. Peter and I don't think it's doing her any good being here. She cried all the way through the inquest and now she says she can't go to the funeral, even though Gwyneth's offered to have the kids.'

'Some support.' Jean's mouth twisted. She didn't acknowledge the mention of Peter. 'How is Gwyneth by the way?'

'She's struggling as well. It's brought everything that happened to Iori back. She lived for him. All she's said is that Tom and Iori are together now. She has her faith.'

'Hmm.'

Mary could tell Jean was embarrassed. Stubbornly she continued, 'We all knew Tom loved him, Jean. We're just not allowed to say.'

'Well,' Jean faltered. 'Well, that's as maybe.' She sniffed, her mouth turned downwards. 'That's as maybe.' They travelled a while in silence. When Jean next spoke she sounded defensive. 'I did try to make Patrick come, Mary. He's not an easy man, you know. He's a past master of bad moods.'

'You're telling me. But you can hold your own on that score, I know. I've been on the receiving end of your moods many a time.' She leant towards Jean, touching her forehead with her own, noticing at the same time a small bruise on her friend's cheek. 'What did you walk into this time?' She smiled. Jean was very short-sighted but sometimes her vanity stopped her wearing her glasses.

'Cupboard door.' Jean dismissed Mary's question with a flick of her hand. 'Moods don't work with Patrick, though.'

'So what does?'

Jean shrugged. 'Not a lot. You were always the one to handle him, Mary.'

'Hardly. I've watched you with him over the years. You're perfectly capable of keeping a tight rein on him.'

'I don't know about that.' Jean fidgeted, looked uncomfortable. After a moment she nodded towards the window. 'I always think how lovely it is round here,' she said, 'but not home though, is it? Not home.'

'I know what you're getting at,' Mary said, 'and even with Tom – even with what's happened, I won't be coming back to Ashford.' She watched Jean. From her sister-in-law's frustrated expression it was obvious she was struggling not to argue.

Mary held her hand up. 'I'm glad you're here. And this little one.' She stroked Jacqueline's hair as she dozed against her shoulder.

'So am I.' Jean pushed at the bridge of her glasses with her forefinger and settled further into her seat, her hand on her daughter's knee. 'So am I. She's as exhausted as I am.'

'How's she been?' Mary whispered.

'Upset, not sleeping well. And she's wet the bed twice since I told her about Tom.' Jean hesitated, her voice quiet. 'But that's been going on a while now, thinking about it. Patrick and me – well, we've been arguing a lot lately. I'm hoping she'll be all right when we get to your house.'

Patrick would argue with the devil, Mary thought but instead only said, 'It'll help Linda being there.'

'Hmm.' Jean paused. 'Ellen shouldn't have come rushing down here. I'm sure it hasn't helped you.'

'I've got Peter.'

'Yes, well, that's the other thing I wanted to talk to you about.'

Whatever opinion Jean had about Peter Mary didn't want to hear. 'Look, here's our stop,' she interrupted, gathering Jacqueline into her arms. She reached up and pressed the bell on the nearby rail, waiting for the bus to slow down before standing.

Peter was at the gate watching for them. He took Jacqueline by one hand and the suitcase in the other, in spite of Jean's protests. When he bent to greet her, she stiffly offered her cheek and murmured, 'Hello,' before walking up the path to the cottage and adding, 'you smell of pipe tobacco. Mary said you'd taken up a pipe – revolting habit.'

Mary and Peter exchanged wry expressions. This was going to be a difficult visit.

Chapter 13

'You have to go back to your husband, my girl, that's what you need to do. Go back to your husband.'

'What's it got to do with you, you interfering old bag?'

'He needs you in the shop. Patrick says you—'

'Patrick says, Patrick says – he might rule your life but what makes you think I care what he says? The only brother whose opinion I cared about was—'

'Tom's? Well, m'lady, you kept that a good secret. From what I saw, you had no more time for him than the man on the moon. You've only ever done what you wanted. You've driven Mary mad in the past and here you are again. She's enough to cope with living with that man in there. She'll have the life of hell and all you can do is heap more trouble on her.'

'That's it!' Mary flung the bedclothes off and felt around in the dark for her dressing gown.

Peter held her arm. 'No, *Liebling,* it is of no matter.'

But it was. They'd listened to the strident voices of Jean and Ellen for the last five minutes and Mary sensed the growing tension in him.

'No matter?' The dreadful apathy that had protected her since Tom was killed was shattered by the triviality of Jean and Ellen's squabbles. As always she was being forced to be peacemaker between them. 'Of course it matters, Peter. They're in our home and I won't put up with it.'

The door opened and a ripple of light from the landing revealed the silhouettes of the two little girls. Although Linda was a few months older her head only just reached the shoulder of her cousin. She stood, thumb in her mouth, twiddling a lock of her hair around her finger of the other hand, cheeks wet with tears; the image of Ellen as a child, Jacqueline held on to her protectively, her solid square figure a miniature of Jean as she stood, feet placed firmly on the floor, fist on hip.

'Our mummies are falling out.' The words were accusing.

'I know.' Mary fastened her dressing gown. 'They're very naughty.' She picked up Linda, feeling the quivering sobs as she held her close. Her hand firmly on the flat of Jacqueline's back, she ushered them into their room. William, still asleep, looked so tiny in what had been Tom's bed and for a moment there was a catch in her throat. 'Come on now, settle down. Look after your brother, Linda. Jacqueline, I'm relying on you to see to both your cousins?'

Jacqueline nodded, her dark curls bobbing vigorously as she scrambled into bed. 'I will.' She stretched her plump little arms as far as she could past William and across the pillow, stroking the top of Linda's head with her fingertips.

Such an old-fashioned little thing, Mary thought, stopping by

48

the door to look back at the three children, so protective of Linda, always looking out for her. In spite of her anger she smiled. The two girls had their eyes screwed tightly as if in determined sleep.

Inside the other bedroom, where Ellen and Jean were forced to share the bed in Peter's old room, the quarrel continued. Mary held the palm of her hand against her chest and took a deep breath before lifting the latch.

'What the hell do you think you're doing?' Mary closed the door behind her, forcing herself to whisper.

The curlers in Jean's fringe wobbled as she lifted her head above the eiderdown. Her face glistened with the cold cream she used religiously each night.

'Oh do come in, why don't you?' Ellen raised her arms above her head, fingers spread wide. 'That's all we need, the bloody cavalry.' Grabbing the covers she flung herself over onto her side, her voice muffled when she next spoke. 'Whatever you have to say, our Mary, it'll have to wait till morning. I need my sleep.'

'And so do your children,' Mary said. 'You woke both girls with your stupid row. They heard everything you said and so did we.' She let that sink in. 'Now, you need to go and make sure they're all right.' She held out the copy of *My Naughty Little Sister* that she'd picked up from the children's room. 'Perhaps one of you could read to the girls for a bit. And if you can possibly bear to stop thinking about your own feelings, maybe you could also tell them you're sorry and explain how you had a silly little falling out?' There was no answer and no movement. 'As for your opinions about me and Peter, Jean, I'll thank you to keep them to yourselves or, if you can't do that, at least talk about it when we're not here to listen.' Jean didn't answer. Mary hesitated. From the minute her sister-in-law had stepped off the train, there had been a sense that she was holding something back. 'Jean?'

Jean turned her head away.

Mary opened the door. 'You might have forgotten,' she stifled the crack in her voice, 'but we have a funeral to go to on Monday.

So if you could keep off one another's throats for the next two days, I'd be grateful. If not, I promise you this – both of you – either of you cause any bother and you'll be sorry.' Cold fury made her fingers clench the door handle, her knuckles white under the skin.

'Sorry.' Ellen did sound contrite but Mary was in no mood to hear it.

'Just think on.'

Jean said nothing.

Mary left the overhead light on and the door open as she crossed the landing and went back into her room. 'I can't stand this,' she said, tight-lipped. 'I can't…'

'Try not to think about them, *Liebling*, try to sleep.'

'They're always the same. You'd think at their age…' She left it unsaid. Both women had brought their troubles to her door when she had enough of her own. Sooner or later they would expect her to help them. Nothing changes she thought, slipping under the covers and fitting her body to his.

Since Tom's death she'd dreaded night times. Mostly she just dozed, coming to with a sudden frightening start that jerked her whole body upright and covered her with sweat. And when she did finally sleep the dreams were horrific: broken bodies strewn across a road, blood running into gutters; Ellen, Peter, Jean, Jacqueline, all the members of her family, staring sightlessly at an ominous yellow and purple bruised sky, their arms somehow outstretched towards her. And then the road changed into a canal and she was pinned against a stone wall, unable to move, still helpless to help them. The same nightmare made her wake night after night.

'Peter?' She moved closer, his steady breathing calming her. She rested her hand on his shoulder and reached across to hold him, her fingers firm until she felt him throb and grow hard. He rolled over and gently lifted her nightdress over her head, wiped the tears with the pads of his thumbs. 'I love you,' she whispered, 'I need you.' She sat astride him, revelling in the closeness. From the dim slant of light under the door she saw him smile as he cupped her breasts.

'I love you too,' he said. 'My Mary, *ich liebe dich.*'

His hands slid from her breasts, settled for a moment on her stomach and hovered before gently grasping her hips. He let her take the initiative and she was grateful, she wanted to feel in control. Slowly, slowly, she started to rise and fall, keeping her eyes on his, a slight smile on her open lips. As she felt the urge in him she responded, rocking her hips, swaying from side to side. She tightened herself on him and they moved together, slowly at first, their breathing synchronised, and then with more urgency. '*Ich liebe dich, mein Schatz,*' Mary gasped. Then words became impossible.

Chapter 14

'Auntie Mary?'

Mary opened her eyes. 'Jacqueline?' The bedroom was in darkness, the little girl outlined in the doorway by the nightlight from the children's room.

'I can't sleep.'

Mary heard the sob in her voice. 'Okay.' She threw back the covers and fumbled around for her dressing gown. 'Okay, love, wait a minute.'

'Mary?' Peter lifted himself up on one elbow. 'What is wrong? What time is it?'

'Three o'clock,' Mary answered in a whisper. 'It's all right. It's Jacqueline. She can't sleep. I'm taking her downstairs.'

She peeped into the bedroom where the other children were sleeping and gently closed the door. Taking hold of Jacqueline's hand she said, 'Let's go and get a drink of warm milk.'

'Dad shouts a lot, Auntie Mary.' Jacqueline hiccupped after the long bout of sobbing. She rubbed the heel of her hand over her eyes. 'And Mum shouts back. I don't like it.'

'Grown-ups quarrel just like children do. Even you and Linda

51

fall out sometimes, huh?' Mary took the glass from her after she'd drained the last drops of milk.

'Sometimes.'

'And then you make up and everything's okay again. And that's what your Mum and Dad do. They love one another but they like a good squabble as well. You mustn't worry about it. They talk and laugh too, don't they?'

Jacqueline nodded.

'Well then!' Mary tucked the glass between the cushion at the side of her and the arm of the sofa and pulled Jacqueline closer. 'Let's have a *cwtch*.'

'What?' Jacqueline laughed, craning her head back to look at Mary.

'*Cwtch*, it's Welsh for a cuddle but it's better than a cuddle.' She gave her niece a squeeze. 'See? It magics nightmares and worries away.'

Jacqueline snuggled closer and closed her eyes. Mary wrapped the skirt of her blue quilted dressing gown over the little girl as best she could. The grandfather clock marked each minute with its plangent tick.

When Jacqueline spoke again, the chill rippled Mary's skin.

'Dad punched Mum,' she said.

Chapter 15

'Did you hear Jacqueline last night?'

Mary sprinkled a few flakes of Lux soap into the bowl of warm water in the sink and furiously swirled them around to make bubbles. She dropped a black cardigan into the bowl and pushed it under the surface.

'No. Why?' Ellen scraped the last of the boiled egg from the shell and put the spoon on the plate in front of her daughter. 'There you are, love, finish it off.'

Linda crammed the egg and the last of her toast in her mouth. 'Please may I leave the table?' She slid off the chair and gave Mary a tight squeeze around her waist.

Mary bent down and kissed the top of her head. 'Good girl.'

'Go in the parlour,' Ellen said. 'It'll be your programme in ten minutes.' She gave William the last spoonful of cake and walked over to the sink. Putting the plate and spoon down on the draining board, she peered over Mary's shoulder. 'Grief Mary,' she said, 'you've nearly put some soap in that.'

'Soap's still rationed.' Infuriated that Ellen hadn't noticed how angry she was, Mary started to knead and squeeze the cardigan. 'You should have washed this days ago. You knew you'd need it.'

'Soap rationing finishes in a couple of months, you didn't need to be so stingy with it.'

'Oh, for God's sake!' Mary slammed her hands into the water. It sloshed over the edge of the sink.

'What?' Ellen looked bewildered. 'What's wrong?'

Mary drew in a long breath. 'Patrick's hit Jean. And from what I can make out Jacqueline saw it.'

'What?' Ellen said. 'No.' She lowered her voice. 'The bastard.'

'Like father like son,' Mary spoke grimly. She'd been unable to sleep afterwards, angrily thinking about all the times Mam had been battered by their father, remembering the confrontations she'd had about it with him. She felt sick. 'He can't get away with it.'

'What will you do?'

'If it was any other time I'd go up there and tell him just what I thought of him.' Mary clenched her teeth. 'As it is I can only talk to Jean. Tell her what Jacqueline's said. And ask her what she is going to do. If it's true, I'll tell Jean to get out from there as soon as possible. Patrick can't just get away with it,' she repeated.

She knew that Tom would have had no hesitation in tackling Patrick. But he wasn't here anymore, and she had no choice but to deal with this on her own. Ellen would be no use.

'You don't think Jacqueline's making it up?'

'No! Why would she make something up something as horrible as that?'

'I just can't believe Jean would put up with it.'

'Well, no, nor me. That's why I need to talk to her, ask her why she's keeping it a secret.'

'Do you think it's just the once?'

'Just the once is once too often, don't you think?' Mary raised her eyebrows. 'Jean's my friend as well as our sister-in-law. I'm not just going to stand by and let Patrick think it's okay to hit his wife.'

Mary leant her hands on the edges of the bowl and breathed in deeply, trying to calm down. Eventually she asked, 'Where is Jean, anyway?'

'She said she needed a walk to clear her head.' Ellen rolled her eyes. 'Anything rather than stay in the same room as me, I think. She took Jacqueline with her.'

Mary looked out of the window. The greenhouse door was open and, beyond the line of washing, the potato patch where Peter was working was empty. For a moment she thought about asking him to help her but just as quickly appreciated it would make matters worse; Jean would hate him knowing. 'Did Peter say when he'd be back?'

'No, only that he had to see the minister about some arrangements for tomorrow.'

'Oh.' Mary drew in a ragged breath, guiltily realising that for a few hours she'd closed her mind to her grief. All at once she was consumed with hostility that Ellen and Jean had brought their troubles with them when they should be helping her; mourning the loss of Tom alongside her.

Not trusting herself to speak she rinsed the cardigan and rolled it in a towel to take off the excess water.

'Well, there's nothing you can do until she comes back,' Ellen said.

'No.' Mary resigned herself to the fact that her sister was accepting none of the responsibility of trying to help Jean. She obviously thought her own troubles with Ted more than enough.

When Mary came back from hanging out the cardigan, Ellen was trying to wipe William's hands as he dabbed at crumbs of cake on his tray and ate them.

Her sister was right on one thing. There was nothing Mary could do until Jean came back from her walk.

'What about you? You'll have to make some decisions, you know,' she said, in a low voice, keeping an eye on the little boy. 'The house for a start. You'll want Ted and Hannah to move out if you've decided to end the marriage. Do you want that?'

'Yes. No. I don't know.' It was as though the idea had only just occurred to Ellen. 'No, but why should he get away with it?'

'You don't know that there is anything he's getting away with, do you?'

'Something's going on,' Ellen whispered. 'I know it, I know Ted.'

Mary crossed her arms. 'Then stop stewing on it and talk to him. Find out what's going on. If anything.'

Ellen's face crumpled. 'I wish you'd come back to Ashford, our Mary.'

'Why? So I can sort out every little mess you get into? Even without our Tom...' The skin on the back of her neck tightened. She hated putting her loss into words. 'Even without Tom, I still have a life here. Peter, Gwyneth. This is where I belong now.'

'I miss you. I just wish...'

'What was it our Mam used to say? If wishes were horses—'

'Beggars would ride.' Ellen gave a faint smile.

'That's right,' Mary said, 'so think on.' Ignoring the clamour of worries in her head she took a small flat-sided bottle from a cupboard, measured thick syrupy orange juice onto a tablespoon and tipped it into a beaker. Letting the cold water run into the kitchen sink for a few seconds she topped up the drink. 'Come on, bring William, it's time for the kids' programme.'

In the parlour she switched on Tom's Alba wireless. 'Come on, love, sit down,' she said to Linda, 'it's nearly quarter to two.'

Linda kneeled on the rug, twirling a strand of her hair around her finger, faster and faster until it was a tight band.

Crouching, Mary slowly turned the dial until the red line covered the words 'LIGHT PROGRAMME.'

'This is the BBC Home Service for mothers and children at home. Are you ready for the music? When it stops, Catherine Edwards will be here to speak to you.'

There was a pause. 'Here you are.' Mary handed the orange juice to Linda. 'Careful with it.'

'Ta, Auntie Mary.' The little girl put her doll on the floor next to her and took the beaker with both hands, smiling her thanks.

Music crackled through the horizontal slats on the front of the wireless. *Ding-de-dong. Ding-de-dong, Ding, Ding!*

Linda wriggled excitedly.

'Are you sitting comfortably? Then I'll begin.'

There was a loud bang outside on the road. Ellen hitched the baby higher on her shoulder, twisted round in her chair by the window and peered around the curtain. 'Oh bugger, it's Ted. I thought I recognised the sound of that old banger. What the hell is he doing here?' She stood up, took the drink from Linda and grabbed hold of her hand. 'Come on, you, upstairs.' Carrying William, she led the complaining little girl through the kitchen. 'Obviously this is your doing, Mary,' she called over her shoulder. 'Well you can deal with him.'

Mary opened the front door as Ted, his raincoat crumpled and creased, climbed stiffly out of the cab of the baker's van, trilby perched on the back of his head. He stretched while gazing miserably at the vehicle. There was a whistling noise and steam escaped from under the bonnet, first a trickle of white vapour, then a noisy gush until both Ted and the van were enveloped. He appeared, flailing his hands and shaking his head. 'That's beggared it,' he said flatly.

Without speaking, Mary moved to one side to let him in.

She *had* telegrammed him to come to Llamroth. It had been a curt request: **ELLEN AND CHILDREN NEED YOU HERE STOP MARY**

He cleared his throat. 'I'm sorry I didn't come sooner, Mary.' He looked around the parlour, turning the rim of his trilby in his hands. 'Is Ellen okay?'

Oh, for goodness sake, Mary thought. 'No, she's not, Ted. How could you think she would be? Tom is – was – our brother. You let her come on the train with the two kids on her own. Didn't you realise what a state she was in?'

He coloured. 'She wouldn't wait.'

'For you to close the shop? Isn't your wife worth more than a few pounds takings?'

'It wasn't just that.' Ted protested. 'Mother…'

'Oh, yes, don't get me started on your mother.' Mary stopped. This really wasn't her business, however much her sister tried to drag her into it.

'What do you mean?' Ted stared at her. 'What has Ellen said?'

Mary walked away from him into the kitchen. She'd said too much.

He followed her. 'Mary?' He took off his raincoat and slung it over the back of one of the kitchen chairs, balancing his trilby on top.

'You need to talk to Ellen, Ted. All I can say is she's at the end of her tether with Hannah.' The hot tears were unexpected. Angrily, Mary brushed them away and turned, staring unseeingly out of the window. 'I can't deal with anybody else's problems at the moment,' she said huskily. 'Tom was my brother too. I saw what happened to him. It doesn't go away. I see it all the time.'

She felt Ted's hand on her shoulder. 'I'm sorry, Mary.' She heard him swallow hard. 'I'm sorry. I shouldn't have left you to cope with Ellen on your own. But I'm here now and I'll sort it. One way or the other.'

*

Chapter 16

'She won't listen to me.' Ted slumped onto one of the kitchen chairs when he eventually came downstairs.

'You'll just have to keep trying.' Mary studied him for the first time since he arrived. The flesh around his eyes was grey and puffy and she could see a thin dusting of flour around his hairline. He must have driven straight there from working overnight. No wonder he looked dreadful. 'You'll have to make her listen.'

'She's said she won't come home.' He rubbed at the red mark indented in his forehead from wearing the trilby. 'I know she's upset about Tom – I know you both are,' he added hastily as Mary flinched. 'But there's something else. It can't just be about my mother. What has she said?'

Mary leaned against the worktop. 'It's not up to me to tell you, Ted, it should come from Ellen.' She couldn't believe he was having an affair. He'd loved Ellen for as long as Mary could remember. But her sister obviously did believe he was unfaithful. And that fear needed to come out into the open and be sorted out before they could tackle the issue of Hannah Booth.

'If she won't talk to me what can I do?'

'You fight for her. Do you want to give up on your marriage that easily?'

'You think it's come to that?' Ted paled.

'I do.'

There was a querulous high-pitched complaining above their heads. They glanced at the ceiling.

'Linda's like her mum.' Mary gave him a small smile. 'Determined to get her own way. She wants to see you.'

'I love that little girl, Mary.'

'I know.'

'I've loved her from the day Ellen brought her home, the moment I opened the door and saw you both on the step.' He leant forward, his arms on his thighs. 'I knew already. Ages before

I'd found a small photograph of a baby on the floor of our room. Ellen must have dropped it. I left it there, didn't say anything.' He wiped his hand over his mouth. 'I don't mind telling you that was a blinkin' hard thing to do, Mary, waiting for her to tell me.'

'Did Hannah know?'

'Not until afterwards.'

'How was she about Linda?'

He moved his shoulders.

'Do you want me to be perfectly honest, Ted?'

He nodded.

'From what I can make out, it's Linda your mother has the most problem with. And Ellen's had as much as she can take from Hannah.' She watched him, head tilted to one side. 'Ellen loves you, I know that. And you love her.'

'Yes.'

'Then I think you and your mother have a bit of straight talking to do. If you don't make things right, somehow, I think Ellen will leave you. And then what will happen to the children?'

Chapter 17

The clump of the lavatory chain and the heavy splash of water filling the overhead cistern sounded throughout the cottage. Then there was a clatter on the stairs and Linda appeared, quickly followed by her mother trying to catch hold of her. 'I told you, madam. Stay upstairs.'

Linda took no notice. She ran to Ted. 'Daddy.' She scrambled onto his knee, her arm wound tight around his neck. 'Where've you been?' She grabbed his chin, pulled his face down to hers. 'I've missed you.'

'Sorry, love, I've been busy in the shop. Have you had a nice holiday?' Ted held her close.

'Yes. Uncle Peter takes us to the beach.'

Mary didn't miss the small automatic drawing in of Ted's eyebrows.

The little girl bobbed her head as she spoke. 'But we have to come home now, don't we?' She screwed her head round to look up at Ellen. 'Eh, Mummy, don't we have to go home?' There was anxiety in her voice. 'And I miss Beauty.'

'I've been feeding him and changing his water,' Ted reassured her. 'Her budgie. Got him for her birthday,' he said, answering Mary's look of enquiry.

'He's blue and he talks,' Linda said, 'nearly.'

'That's nice, love.' Mary smiled at her, standing up. She pointed to her chair. 'Sit down,' she said to her sister.

'No.' Ellen didn't take her eyes off Ted. 'I'm okay.'

Mary lifted William out of her sister's arms. 'Sit,' she said again and then wriggled her fingers at her neice. 'Come on, sweetheart, let's go and play in the garden.'

Obstinate, Linda clutched tighter to Ted. 'No.'

'Go on, love,' he said, 'go and do as Auntie Mary says, there's a good girl.' She wailed but let herself be put onto the floor and led away. 'Me and Mummy have things to talk about.' He glanced at Ellen. 'And then, soon, we'll all go home.'

Mary heard the sharp intake of breath and saw her sister fold her arms. 'Give him a chance,' she hissed, making for the back door.

Outside the sun had shifted around, casting the garden nearest the cottage in shadow. Mary shivered.

The children squirmed until she let go of them and they ran along the path into the sunshine. William's unsteady gait, a rolling from side to side, reminded Mary of her father's walk. They followed a large seagull that was strutting about and managing to stay a few feet away from them. She moved from the steps to the low wall to sit watching the children in case they went too near the greenhouse. She wrapped her cardigan around her and hunched over. Shadowed from the sun the back garden hadn't much warmth in it. Deliberately turning her back she realised that, even above the rhythmic sigh of the incoming tide, she could still hear Ted talking.

'Whatever's wrong, tell me and we can sort it. I can't live without you and the kids.'

'No.'

Nothing more was said. The minutes dragged by. Mary hesitated, not sure what to do. If it was true what Ellen said, life at Henshaw Street must be unbearable for her sister and Ted needed to know how bad things were. But was it only that? Was Ted having an affair? And would their marriage survive such betrayal?

Since Tom died, so much had happened; so many secrets rising to the surface, some still being kept. Mary covered her face with her hands. When she looked up the children were sitting on the path watching the seagulls circling around them. They were safe for the moment. And they needed to be safe in the future. If she couldn't be truthful to Peter about Tom, if she couldn't bring herself to ask him how he really felt about what Frank had done to her, she could at least do something about her sister and Ted.

She moved quickly, up the steps and into the kitchen. Ted was still at the table. Ellen, arms crossed, had her back to him and was leaning on the doorframe facing the parlour.

'Why don't you take the kids to the beach and let them have a run around?' Ellen refused to move. Mary raised her voice. 'So you can have a talk.'

Ellen glowered over her shoulder. 'I'll think about it.'

'You won't just think, you'll do it.' Mary caught her lower lip with her teeth. Ellen wouldn't like what she had to say next. 'I'll be honest with you. You can't stay here forever. This place is too small for all of us. You need to get things sorted.'

Chapter 18

'I wanted to be here for you, to be with you at the funeral.' Ted tried to take her hand.

There was a hot feeling in Ellen's chest. But now it wasn't guilt, and it wasn't for Tom – it was grief for her marriage. The simmering anger had turned into hurt; she was utterly bereft. Yet still she heard herself say, 'I don't need you.' She shook him away.

'I think you do.'

Ellen wandered further down the beach. 'I didn't want you to come here.' If he didn't touch her, she would stay strong. For years their marriage had been one-sided. Ted gave, she took, content in the knowledge he would do anything for her. But since she'd brought Linda home and seen how much affection he had for her daughter, how he made sure he was totally fair to each child, she'd felt the tables slowly turning. The only way she knew how to show her gratitude was to put up with Hannah's jibes. But lately she knew his mother was sensing the change between them and she was on the receiving end of more rancorous attacks.

Now she couldn't bear to be in the house with either of them.

'What have I done?' He looked genuinely upset but she wasn't fooled.

'You must think I'm daft.' Ellen watched Linda take William's hand as she searched for shells on the tideline. 'Not too far,' she called.

'What do you mean?'

She moved her shoulders, poised, ready to run. Nervousness made her restive.

'I don't know what you think I've done, Ellen, but you have to tell me.' Ted sat on a rock. 'Sit down here. Please.' He reached towards her. 'Tell me. Unless you do, I can't put things right.'

'No,' she said, making a performance of keeping an eye on the children. 'You know what you've done.' Tell me who you're having the affair with; tell me that, she silently pleaded.

'I don't.'

The light wind spiralled a veil of sand around their feet. A seabird, its feathers a white blaze reflecting the sun, rose from the nearby cliffs and then, closing its wings, arrowed into the sea. Ellen squinted looking for its re-emergence but failed. She felt another layer of sadness.

'Doreen Whittaker?' The words escaped her mouth before she could stop them.

There was a moment's pause before she slanted a look at him and saw the surprise on his face, saw him finger the jagged scar on his left cheek the way he always did when he was thinking. She waited to see how he'd squirm his way out of the accusation.

'What?'

'Doreen Whittaker.' Ellen spoke through clenched teeth.

'Doreen? You know?'

'I know.'

'I told him he was stupid. I said I didn't want us involved.'

'What? Who?'

'Patrick.'

'Patrick?' Ellen spoke slowly.

'Yes, Patrick.' Hurt understanding emerged on his face. 'It's not me having the affair, Ellen, it's Patrick. Do you really think I'd do that to you?'

Glancing back to check on the children, she took a step towards him but again wouldn't take his hand.

'The reason he keeps coming to the house is so he can slip out from the back yard to next door. I've told him I don't like it but your brother doesn't take no for an answer.'

Ellen took a few long breaths, searching his face for the truth. When she thought about it there were a couple of times she'd watched Patrick turn up the alleyway towards Greenacre Street, when it would have been quicker to go down towards Shaw Road if he'd been going home. And then she remembered something. 'Once,' she said, 'just after Christmas, that time he created hell because you wouldn't go to the Crown with him, I watched him hanging around at the back gate for ages, looking back at the house.' She held Ted's gaze. 'I was washing up. I kept looking at him. And then, suddenly, he'd gone, vanished.' She raised her eyes, cursing her stupidity. 'Obviously one of the times he'd gone next door … to see her.'

'Probably.' Ted was clearly shaken. 'You thought I was having an affair with her?'

'Yes,' she said simply. 'I did.'

Ted held out his hand. This time she took it.

'Listen Ellen. I've loved you since we were kids, you know that. I love you now and I will always love you. Whatever happens, whatever you do, I love you.'

The warmth that filled Ellen startled her. Somewhere, deep inside her, the tiny kernel of love that had grown began to spread until the overwhelming sensation almost made her dizzy. 'I love you too, Ted.' It was the first time she'd said it to him and she knew she really meant it.

In that moment of stillness she knew she needed to be honest. Her voice wobbled. 'Ted, there is something I need to tell you. I've kept something from you about Linda.'

He covered her mouth with his fingers. 'Frank Shuttleworth?'

She twisted her face away. 'You know?' Now it was her turn to say the words. What an idiot I've been, she thought. 'He used me to get back at Mary for chucking him.'

'I know. Patrick told me the first time I met him after I came home. I think he was trying to put me off. He felt I was too old for you.'

'He wouldn't care about that. He's just spiteful. You're a better man than he'll ever be. What's eight years anyway, it's never bothered me.' She enclosed his hand with both of hers. 'I'm sorry, Ted, I should have been the one to tell you.'

'I don't care who Linda's father was. I'm her Dad. I love her. I love both my kids.'

64

The seabird suddenly appeared again. Or perhaps it's a different bird, she thought. It rose and fell on the crest of each wave, drifting slowly away until she was unable to make it out against the horizon.

'I made such a mess of my life. I'm surprised you looked twice at me.'

'Well, I'm not. I love you, Ellen Booth, and don't ever forget that. You don't have to tell me anything. It was enough that when I came home you were there,' he said, shrugging off his jacket and dropping in onto the pebbles. 'Let's sit down.' Further along the beach the children were climbing small rocks. 'Don't fall,' he called. 'And watch you don't slip into the pools.'

Ellen sat by him, gradually aware Ted was staring at her. Self-consciously she tucked a loose strand of hair behind her ear, her cheeks hot.

'You're beautiful.'

'Don't look at me, I'm a right mess – no make-up.' She dipped her chin.

'You're beautiful to me, with or without.'

'Your mother said you don't like slap, as she calls it.'

'Ma?' Ted stared at her. 'I don't recall ever talking to her about anything like that. Anyway, whatever she put on her face it wouldn't improve it – unless it was a paper bag.'

Ellen laughed. He could always make her laugh. She sobered for a moment; pulling her knees up under her chin, she wrapped her full skirt around them. 'Your mother…' She was apprehensive. It was something she'd broached before, something they never resolved. She knew Ted felt beholden to his mother because of the money.

His face set. 'Mary told me some of it. How bad is it?'

'It's worse than ever. And it's driving me mad. She watches – and picks all the time. She's nasty and she's spiteful as soon as you've turned your back.' Her throat tightened with misery and she struggled for breath.

He pulled her close. 'That's okay, love. I get the picture and I'll make sure it stops.'

'How, Ted?' She pulled herself away from him. 'When you're not there? How can you do that?'

'I'll talk to her, tell her to stop.'

Ellen gave a small shake of her head. 'It's when she starts on about Linda that I really hate it.'

His face darkened. 'What does she say?'

'That I tricked you into keeping Linda, that she shouldn't be with us, that she'll grow up to be a whore like me.'

'Right!' A muscle in his jaw twitched as he clamped his teeth together.

For a moment Ellen was scared. She'd kept so much to herself for so long, thinking he wouldn't believe her. He was used to Hannah's whining but his mother kept the malevolence for when she was alone with Ellen. 'She calls Linda "the bastard", Ted.'

She heard his long muted breath. 'It won't happen again, Ellen. You'll not have to hear that ever again, I promise you.' He held her to him. She rested her head against his chest, relieved that at last she'd told him everything. He would make it all right. His voice echoed in her ear. 'Whatever it takes, I'll make sure she never speaks to you like that again. I love you more that I've loved anyone, ever. It's you, me and the kids from now on, believe me.'

Ellen swallowed; for the first time in her life she felt she belonged to someone, that she fitted just right into someone's life and she hugged that knowledge to herself.

Chapter 19

'So, Ted arrived then?' Jean stood by the parlour window looking out at the front garden.

'Yes, while you were out with Jacqueline.' Mary dried the last plate and piled it on top of the others in the wall cupboard.

Exhausted by the sleepless hours, the sick worry about the little girl's revelation, she pressed her fingers to her temples. Folding the tea towel she came out of the kitchen. 'Let's sit down. I need to talk to you.' How to start asking Jean about Patrick? She resented even having to think about him but she wasn't going to ignore what Jacqueline had said.

'What about?' Jean pushed the net curtain to one side and settled on the windowsill. 'Peter's drawn a game of hopscotch on the path for Jacqueline,' she said, filling in the pause. 'I have to say he's good with the kids.'

'What did you expect? He's the same man who looked after you when you lost your baby,' Mary said, immediately defensive. 'He's just a man, Jean.' She paused. 'No, actually, he's not *just* a man. He's the man I love and I'll thank you to remember that.' Just as Patrick's the one you've always loved, she thought, and Peter's worth a million times more than him.

'I was only saying.'

'Like you did last night? What was it? Oh yes, I remember. "She's enough to cope with living with that man. She'll have the life of hell." Something like that?' Frustrated by the diversion yet unable to ignore her hurt, she spoke sharply.

At least Jean was mortified enough to redden. 'I'm sorry. I'm only thinking of you.'

'Even after all these years you still think you're entitled to try to organise my life.'

'I'm trying to get you to think about what you're doing.'

'I know what I'm doing, thanks.'

'I doubt that. Look, there are plenty of jobs. Since Bevan opened the Park Hospital in Manchester they've been crying out for nurses. With your experience you'd have no trouble getting in.' Jean took off her glasses and cleaned each lens with her handkerchief. 'With Tom … gone there's nothing to stop you coming home now.'

'This is not what I want to talk about. Jacqueline—'

'Is really upset about Tom,' Jean butted in. Mary had a sense that she was being warned off. 'She's having all sorts of nightmares. Sometimes she's mixing bad dreams up with things that have actually happened.'

She knows what I'm going to say. Mary was determined to keep calm but her voice still trembled when she spoke. 'Is that what's she's doing when she tells me Patrick's hit you?'

There was a silent plea in Jean's eyes. 'Mary…'

'Is she mixing that up?' Mary stressed the words. 'Or has he actually hit you?'

Jean slid off the windowsill and stood motionless. 'Mary…'

'Has he?' She knew the answer, saw the humiliation in her friend's eyes. She moved swiftly from the sofa and grabbed Jean's arms. 'You have to tell me. Is it true?'

Jean lowered her head.

'Oh Jean.' The distress merged with the rush of rage. 'I am so sorry.' She gathered her in her arms, frightened by the ferocity of her friend's sobs. 'It'll be all right. We'll sort something out. You can stay here as long as you want.' Mary ignored the sudden vision of Peter's reaction; he'd understand when she explained. 'As long as you want,' she said again.

'I can't. I can't leave Mother.'

'Then move back in with her.' The solution came with a sense of relief that shamed Mary. 'You have to. You can't stay with him.'

Jean shrugged her away and turned back to the window. 'It's not that easy. Jacqueline…'

'Is frightened.'

'I'll make it right with her. Tell her she was mistaken.'

Mary gave a cry of derision. 'Mistaken?'

'It was only the once. He was upset about Tom.'

'He thumped you because of Tom? I don't believe that. He hated Tom.'

'He didn't. You should have seen him, Mary, he was heartbroken.'

'Huh!'

'He was.' Jean spun around to face her. 'I should have left him alone.' Her face crumpled. 'I should have left him alone but I didn't. I wanted to comfort him. I tried to hold him.'

'So he hit you.' Mary dragged out the words.

'It was the first time.'

'I don't believe you.'

Jean flushed. 'Then don't, but it's true.' She looked out of the corner of her eyes at Mary. 'Please don't tell the others.'

'Ellen already knows, I've told her.' Mary folded her arms, angry her friend wanted to cover up what Patrick had done.

'How could you? You know what she's like about me.'

'She has a right to know, he's her brother too.'

'She'll tell all and sundry,' Jean muttered, leaning on the windowsill.

'She won't … and if she did, it's not you who should be ashamed. It's him.'

'I pushed him into it. I should have left him alone,' Jean said again.

'Leave him, Jean. You have to.'

'No!'

'Then you're a bloody fool.'

Chapter 20

Hard rain splattered on the window. Mary drew the curtains against the night. 'Everything's okay then?' she said.

Sprawled on the sofa, holding a cushion to her, Ellen glanced up at Mary. 'Yeah, I'm going back with Ted on Wednesday. He's promised to tell Hannah to leave me alone. I'll be all right.'

'Let's hope she does then. And the other thing? What did he say about that?' Mary perched on the arm of the sofa. 'You did tell him what you thought was going on between him and that girl?'

69

'Yeah, of course. He's promised not to have Doreen in the shop ever again.'

'So it was true?' Mary looked incredulous. 'I wouldn't have believed it.'

'Course it wasn't true. I was being daft.'

Ellen wanted to tell Mary about Patrick but Ted had made her promise. 'For the time being, we'll keep out of it, wait to see what happens,' he'd said. 'Don't say anything to Mary, she has enough on her plate.'

'He's going to give the job to Evelyn Stott,' Ellen told Mary.

'Who?'

'Evelyn Stott. You know, lives in those old back-to-back houses on Church Road, due for demolition. Her granddad was that champion clog fighter in Bradlow, went round all the pubs. Remember, he once challenged Dad in the Crown. Little man with long straggly grey hair, big red nose, bow-legged…'

'I remember!' Mary exclaimed. 'The one our Mam always said—'

'Couldn't stop a pig in a ginnel,' Ellen laughed. 'That's the one.'

'Our Mam … all her sayings.'

Ellen rubbed her hands over her face. She felt odd, strangely emotional. Through the laughter she could feel the quiver of impending tears. 'She could be a right scream … until Dad came in the house.' She suddenly calmed. 'I do know what he was like you know, I wasn't that daft. It was just that he…'

'Let you get away with murder.'

'Until Linda.' Ellen would never forget her fear when their father found out she was pregnant.

'Don't.' Mary pulled her closer, their heads together. 'He didn't remember … at the end, he didn't remember. You were still his little girl.' She rocked Ellen. 'And, you know, our Mam, she loved him. I heard her once, at the end … just before he died. I heard her tell him she loved him. I didn't understand it at the time. I only ever knew him as a nasty old beggar.'

'Hmmm. Which reminds me.' Ellen snuggled closer, her arm across Mary's waist. 'Did you have a word with Jean about Patrick?'

'Yes.'

'And?' Ellen said. 'Did you get anywhere with her?'

'No, she won't leave him. She said he'd only hit her the once … as though that was okay.'

'Do you believe her?'

She felt Mary shrug. 'I don't know. I can't get her to say anything else about him. Except she's asked me not to tell anyone. You're not to either.'

Ellen admitted to herself she wasn't good at keeping secrets. She'd probably tell Ted. Avoiding having to promise she said, 'She's a fool.' In more ways than one, Ellen thought, really tempted to tell Mary about Patrick's messing about with Doreen Whittaker.

'I'm thinking I should go back with her after … after the funeral. Make sure she's all right.'

'And tell him exactly what we think of him, I hope.' Ellen pushed away the feeling that she should help Mary deal with Patrick. She sat back on the sofa pondering. If Mary was going to go back to Ashford, she was bound to find out about the affair anyway. 'I think you should know something,' she said, finally, 'that Ted told me this afternoon.' As soon as the words were out of her mouth she regretted it. Mary looked immediately concerned.

And yet she sounded irritated when she spoke. 'What now?' Mary got up and began to pace up and down in front of the fireplace. 'What's happened?'

Ellen pushed the cushion to one side and shuffled to the edge of the sofa. There was no going back now, and anyway, she persuaded herself, Mary should know. Jean wasn't only their sister-in-law; she was Mary's best friend. 'Don't tell Ted I've told you. Promise?'

Mary nodded resignedly. More secrets, she thought, more things to worry about.

'It's not him having the affair, it's Patrick.'

Chapter 21

'Will you be all right?'

'I'll be fine, *cariad*.' Gwyneth gave a finger of toast to William. 'Better here than there, see.' When she glanced up her eyes were blurred with tears. 'Can't be there today, I'm sorry.' She lifted the hem of her apron and dabbed at her face. 'I'll be thinking of you though.'

Mary nodded, pensive. 'I know, love.' They didn't touch. Mary thought that if they did, if they hugged, they would both give way to the enormous flood of grief that was just held at bay. 'Ellen, Jean and me should be back by three o'clock at the latest. The men are going to the pub afterwards. They've laid a spread on for them.' Gwyneth was following an old Welsh tradition, strange, she thought, that only men should go to funerals. As though only they were strong enough to stand the grief in public. Gwyneth hadn't even gone to Iori's, her only son's, funeral. How must she have felt that day? Mary felt a twinge of disbelief mixed with rebellion. No one could have kept her away from the service today. Tom was her brother. No one knew him as well as she did.

She stood at the back door, watching the two little girls skipping on Gwyneth's path. 'You'll come in to us then?' she said.

'I will.' Gwyneth sniffed loudly and forced a false smile at William. 'We'll have a little play, you and me, isn't it?' William laughed, arching his back in his high chair. She made a small wheezing noise as she lifted him out and set him on his feet.

'Let me.' Mary made a hasty move.

'I'm fine. We're fine.' Gwyneth straightened up. 'Now you'd better be off.'

This time Mary bent to kiss her. Gwyneth's cheek was powdery soft. She smelt of lavender and carbolic soap. It always reminded Mary of Mam. 'Don't let them run you ragged,' she said.

Gwyneth smiled. 'They won't.'

'I'll let myself out.' She went to the door. 'You two behave for Auntie Gwyneth.'

'We will.' Their voices subdued, the two girls stopped skipping and put their arms around each other. Linda's face suddenly distorted and she started to cry. Jacqueline's chin trembled as she fought against tears.

Oh no. Mary made to go to them but was stopped by Gwyneth's hand on her arm. 'I'll see to them, *cariad*. You go.'

Mary stopped at the front door, the image of the two small girls still with her. They were upset now, but how much more were they going to be hurt when they returned to Ashford. 'Oh Tom,' she murmured looking up at the grey blanket of cloud above her, 'it's all such a mess. What am I going to do?'

Chapter 22

The first heavy drops of rain fell onto the coffin with soft thuds. Mary watched as the beads of water shivered and spread, magnifying the grain of the waxed mahogany. Tom would have liked the sound. He didn't mind rain, he always said it was God's gift to the gardener – saved all the back-breaking carrying of watering cans. The corners of her mouth puckered into a half smile before she took in a shuddering breath. It felt wrong to be thinking of her brother in the past tense; it was too soon.

There was a shift of movement amongst the mourners as four burly men shuffled into position and, holding the braided gold cords, steadied themselves to lower the coffin into the ground.

'*For as much as it has pleased almighty God of his great mercy to receive unto himself the soul of our brother here departed we therefore commit his body...*'

Mary stiffened. His soul. If God existed, as Tom believed, then he had lived for years with the knowledge, that guilt, that he had committed the greatest sin. He had killed another human being and now he'd died with that sin on his soul. To protect her. She stared at the minister. Had Tom confided in him? Had this man of God managed to comfort her brother or had Tom kept his torment to himself?

Peter pulled Mary closer and she rested her head against him, trying to gain some comfort from the familiar smell of pipe tobacco and the soft wool of his jacket.

'Soon it will be over, *meine Geliebte*,' he breathed.

But Mary didn't want it to be over. It meant leaving Tom here in the cold earth and she couldn't bear the thought of that. Through the black veil on her hat she peered out of the corner of her eye at Ellen. She stood impassive, Ted's arm around her waist.

On the other side of him Jean shifted the weight from one foot to the other, her face hidden under the wide brim of her black sateen hat.

'*... earth to earth, ashes to ashes, dust to dust ...*'

Unwilling to see the coffin slowly disappear, Mary closed her eyes. But then all she saw was Tom lying so still with his blood slowly flowing towards her. She forced her lids open. Concentrating on the brass name plate, her lips moved silently as she read his name over and over again. Thomas Howarth 1912–1950, saying it faster and faster, as though by its repetition, she could hold on to her brother.

She heard Ellen take in a gulping breath. Glancing up she watched Ted tighten his hold on her sister's waist, supporting her. Heard her whisper, 'I'm okay.'

What would Ellen say if she told her what Tom had done? However relieved Mary was when Frank died, it was their lovely gentle brother who'd killed him; driven to protect her in a way that went totally against what he believed. Mary whimpered, moved her head from side to side on Peter's shoulder.

'Hush, *Liebling*.'

The rain increased. People huddled together, started to raise umbrellas and the drops bounced off the taut material in a pattern of sounds. The wet air carried the scent of the spray of yellow roses, the only flowers she'd allowed to be placed on the coffin.

She turned her face upwards, the rain washing away her tears.

'*... in sure and certain hope of the resurrection to eternal life, through Jesus Christ who shall change our body that it may be like his glorious body according to the mighty working whereby he is able to subdue all things to himself.*'

It was what Tom had believed. She hoped for his sake that, if He actually existed, his God was merciful. She hadn't held onto the religion she'd been taught as a child. Growing up in a household such as hers had driven that away. Perhaps if she had a faith it would help her now but she doubted it. Tom was a good man and the God he loved hadn't saved him.

She hated Frank Shuttleworth. But the sounds of him drowning in the canal hadn't diminished in her mind. Her conscience vied with the satisfaction that he'd got what he deserved and kept her awake at night.

She took an uneven breath. Peter tightened his hold on her. She wondered what he would say when, if, she told him. However much she loved Peter, did she trust him not to condemn Tom? Even as she thought it, she dismissed the doubt. Peter wouldn't judge Tom.

The undertaker dropped a few grains of earth onto the coffin.

'Mary?'

She flinched. The undertaker was holding out his hand, inviting her to take some earth. 'I can't.' She backed away, stumbling awkwardly against Peter. 'I'm sorry, I need to go now.'

As Peter led her away she looked over her shoulder at the long line of people filing past the edge of the grave. She didn't recognise many of them. She hadn't appreciated how many friends Tom had made over the last five years. She wished she'd known. And then she saw Tom's two best friends, Alwyn and Alun. The twin brothers stood for a moment, black bowlers in their hands, before moving on. They had also refused to fight in the war; their beliefs were the same as Tom's. She wondered how they would react if they knew what he had done. Even though it was to save her, would they would say there should have been another way? Surely they would believe their friendship was built on a falsehood.

That was something else to feel guilty about.

Chapter 23

'Another?' Ted lifted his glass.

'No.' Alwyn pushed the chair away from the table and stood up. 'Early start in the morning for us, eh, Alun? We've a lot on at the moment, see.'

'Indeed.' The other man nodded.

'But it was a fine turn-out for a fine man. Tom was a good friend to us when we came here from the Valleys. A good friend.' Alwyn looked towards the bar where a few black-suited stragglers from the funeral were huddled together consciously not looking their way. 'And take no notice of that lot. Live in the past, they do.'

Peter had noticed the way the four men ignored him on the way out of the churchyard. He hoped Mary hadn't seen. One of them had deliberately shouldered him in the pub doorway, even though he'd stood to one side to let him pass.

'It does not matter.' He pushed himself to his feet and held out his hand. 'Mary was glad to see you today. She said you also had been good friends to Tom. She said I must say that you always will be welcome to come to the house. Thank you.'

The handshakes were firm, friendly. For a moment Peter was overcome. Apart from Tom, the two brothers were the first men he could imagine as his friends since he arrived in Britain. He coughed, cleared his throat to cover the emotion and smiled as they turned to leave.

Ted nodded at the brothers. He'd sat silently watching throughout the exchange. Once they'd gone he held up his glass again. 'Another?'

'I will buy this one,' Peter said, but Ted had already slid along the faded red and gold *fleur de lis* patterned cushion on the bench. Using the wooden arm of the seat he pushed himself up, rocking slightly on the soles of his feet. He hadn't reached the stage where the room floated around him, but one more pint would tip him over. He wasn't used to drinking. Seeing the state Patrick got himself into and remembering Ellen's father's violent rages in drink, he'd promised himself he would never put her through that.

He looked back at Peter. The antipathy Ted nurtured towards the German who'd somehow managed to worm his way into Mary's life had started to dissolve earlier in the day, however much Ted tried to hold on to the hatred and fear he'd felt for his captors. At the bar he glanced over his shoulder. Peter was studying the dusty Victorian fireplace with the iron chains that hung across the collection of bottles at the end of the tap room. The thing needed a good clean as far as Ted could see, but there was no hint of distaste in Peter's expression, just curiosity.

Even so, carefully carrying the two gill glasses across the stone flagged floor, Ted tightened his resolve not to be won over by Peter. Not yet anyway. From what he'd heard, the bloke's time in captivity as a prisoner of the British army was nothing compared with his own horrendous experiences. Doctor at the prison hospital had been a cushy number for Mary's boyfriend as far as Ted could see.

Not for the first time he remembered Patrick's bitter words when they found out Peter had returned to Britain. 'Silly cow, she couldn't see he was buttering her up, trying to use her so he could escape.' But the man hadn't escaped. And anyway, he must have known it was impossible to get out of the Granville. The camp had a reputation for being the most secure in the country, with a record of not losing one prisoner. Ted assumed Patrick was mouthing off, holding on to his resentment about being forced down the mines during the war instead of being released to fight.

Still, he prided himself on not being a pushover. Even though Mary thought the chap could do no wrong, he'd make his own mind up about him.

He put the drinks on the table and sat directly opposite Peter, who waited, his face impassive as he took out his pipe and tobacco pouch.

'So, what do you think about warships and air squadrons being involved in the North Korea shindig then?' Ted took a sip of beer and wiped foam from his top lip with the back of his hand. 'Doubt it'll be long before the troops are sent in. Suppose it doesn't affect you?'

'Another war. It is sad.' Peter kept his voice neutral. He'd picked up on the resentment from Ted the minute he'd walked into the cottage at the beginning of the week and found Ellen and her husband 'going at it hammer and tongs', as Mary would say. The last thing he wanted was to cause more worry for her, especially today. Despite the sudden increased tension Ted's question caused between them, he held on to that thought.

Ted fidgeted. The man sitting across from him, leaning forward with his hands clasped around his glass, was difficult to understand. 'I know you were a POW.' Ted spoke harshly, loudly. The four men glanced over their shoulders and glowered before turning away.

Peter nodded. How could Ted not know? He pressed tobacco into the bowl of his pipe, concentrating on packing it closely.

'Did you ever try to escape?' Ted couldn't help himself; he couldn't prevent the challenging tone. He put his glass down

78

carefully on the drink-stained table top. He wouldn't drink any more.

Peter wasn't about to share his secret with Ted. 'No,' he said, and then, giving in to a forgotten pride, 'I couldn't, I was *Lagerführer* of the camp, what you would call, the leader of the prisoners.' Clamping the pipe between his teeth he struck a match and held it to the tobacco, sucking furiously. Waiting until the last second, just before the flame reached his fingers, he blew it out and dropped the charred remains into the ashtray.

Ted watched, and then shrugged, dismissing Peter's last words. He gave an almost imperceptible shake of his head. No, this man had never experienced anything like he had. He'd not spent hours terrified he would suffocate with his face pressed to the floor of a failed escape tunnel, the weight of tons of earth on his body, hearing the voices of his enemy joking and laughing while they made him wait until they decided to dig him out from the terrifying darkness. 'I did,' he said. It was becoming more difficult to concentrate. 'Eight times. Always got caught but I kept on trying. The Ferrets.' He belched. ''Scuse. The Ferrets, them that specialised in finding out about our escape plans, were sly buggers. Used to come into the compound whenever they felt like it and search any hut without warning, usually in the middle of the bloody night. They'd throw all our stuff in a bloody great pile in the middle of the room. Bastards.' He opened his eyes wide and blinked, searching Peter's face for a reaction but there was none.

Peter deliberately kept still. He knew Ted was trying to provoke him. And was quite drunk. But he also knew that he had to let the man speak. He repeated his earlier thought to himself, if the two of them quarrelled now it would cause more upset for Mary.

'Then I'd spend days cooped up in a tin shack, middle of the compound, sweating in the bloody heat of daytime, shivering in bone-numbing cold at night.' Ted took another drink and sat back, rolling his head from side to side. 'When I was first captured I was kept in what we called a sweatbox, a bloody awful little room where they turned the heating up. Left it on all night before the interrogation in the morning.' His voice was slurred now. 'Geneva Convention? They took no bloody notice of that, the bastards. They said we weren't governed by it, 'cos we were Air Force. They said we were what they called Luft gangsters, killers of women and children. It gave them the excuse to treat us just as they liked.'

Peter took his pipe out of his mouth and studied the burning embers in the bowl. Mary's brother-in-law was bringing back a lot of unwelcome memories.

Ted was restless. He sprawled his arms out on the surface of the table, spreading his fingers. 'Before I was captured … the last run we did, we'd dropped a few bombs around the mouth of the Gironde River and, on the way back, more bombs on an oil works off the shore.' He fixed Peter with a slightly unfocused stare. 'It was too bloody quiet for a bombing raid. We didn't see the flack coming and then all at once we were hit.' He stared down at his hands. 'I remember the pilot shouting, "One of you had better start praying."' He gave a short high-pitched laugh. 'Then, Jock, my mate, chanting, "For what we are about to receive may the Lord make us truly thankful," over and over again. I couldn't stop laughing.'

Peter shook his head. 'I am sorry?' Why was that so funny?

'It's a school dinner prayer,' Ted said, exasperated. 'It's what kids say before they have their school dinner.'

'Ah.' Peter moved his head, now grasping the meaning. Or at least partly understanding. Sometimes the British people perplexed him.

Ted's voice rose. 'The next thing, just a crunch and the aircraft started to rip apart. The order to bail out was given and I was gone. It seemed only a few seconds later there was a blinding flash.' He waved his arms in a wide arc. 'The whole plane was blazing as it fell. I didn't see any of my mates get out.' All at once he felt almost sober again. 'I think they were already dead.'

For a long time neither man spoke. The murmur of men's voices, the clink of glasses, the swoosh of the pub door as it opened, eddied around them. The smell of cigarette smoke and the whiff of urinals each time someone went in or out of the lavatory became stronger.

Eventually Ted's head drooped onto his arms, folded together on the table.

Peter glanced around, uncertain what to do. Before he could decide, Ted reared up, grinning, his mouth slack. 'We had a paper, you know, written by some of the Kriegies.' He flapped his hand weakly. 'Some other British POWs, you know?' Peter nodded. 'In one of the other camps. Telling us what was going on outside all that bloody barbed wire.' He couldn't keep the note of triumph from his voice. 'The Goons … we told them that Goons stood for German Officer or Non-com. They actually believed that for a long time.' He sniggered. 'They hadn't a clue; they even called themselves Goons sometimes.'

Peter's face tightened slightly. But when he spoke he kept his voice measured. '*Ja,* we too had a paper, the *Wochenpost.* It served the same purpose for me, *for my men.*'

Despite the emphasis of Peter's last words, Ted recognised in his expression the understanding of a shared experience. He was ashamed. He'd gone too far. 'Sorry,' he said, making himself sit up. 'Shouldn't have said that about Goons … bit too much of the old ale.' He pushed the glass from him. 'Not used to it, you know. I don't get out much and all this business today…' He rubbed his nose with the palm of his hand, embarrassed. He should have shut up ten minutes ago. The bloke'll think him soft.

'I was a doctor before the war.' Peter looked away, giving Ted a few moments to compose himself. He wasn't sure he was doing the right thing but he continued. 'I did not want to be involved. I was working in a hospital in Berlin. It was *mein Vater,* my father … *bestand darauf, dass ich in den Krieg ziehen sollte,* he insisted I go. He was a farmer, proud of me, but a man with strong

81

opinions. Proud of being German. He said I should do my duty; use my skills.' He met Ted's eyes. 'I killed no one.' He blocked out the old guilt. 'In the war, I killed no one.'

Ted inclined his head in acknowledgment.

'I think we should go home now,' Peter said.

Chapter 24

'He's a bit odd,' Ellen said, when the minister closed the front door and walked away from the cottage.

A few miles away thunder rumbled and through the net curtains Mary saw an occasional glimmer of lightning behind the distant banks of clouds. 'Shush. It was kind of Mr Willingham to come to see us,' she said, yet silently agreeing that the man made an eerie figure in his long black overcoat and Homburg hat. In the gloomy evening light the peculiar old-fashioned cream spats he wore over his shoes gave the impression that he floated along the dark ground. 'And he gave a lovely eulogy for Tom.'

'That hymn though,' Ellen said, querulous. 'I didn't understand one word.'

'That's because it's a Welsh hymn, *O fryniau Caersalem*,' Mary said, trying hard to be patient. 'It means *From the Hills of Jerusalem*, something like that. The minister chose it especially. It was one of Tom's favourites ever since he first went to that church.'

'Well, he still gives me the creeps.'

Mary rubbed her eyes with her thumb and forefinger. 'He was a good friend to Tom.'

'I thought he was nice.' Jean sipped her tea.

'You would.'

'Ellen!' Mary turned away from the window, frowning. 'It's been a long day.'

'Well, one good thing,' Jean said, clearly snubbing Ellen, 'it only rained a bit for the funeral.'

'It was enough for us to get drenched. Except for you in your big hat, of course.'

Mary tried to ignore the two women sniping at each other. She picked up the bowl of damask roses that Alun and Alwyn had sent from their garden, and held them to her face. 'I love these,' she said. 'Tom grew them for me. Do you remember when we were kids, Ellen, how we used to pinch these kind of roses out of the gardens of the posh houses on Manchester Road and put the petals into water to make scent?'

'It never worked,' Ellen said.

'Sometimes it did.'

'I remember doing that.' Jean bit into one of the biscuits Gwyneth had made.

'Not with us,' Ellen muttered, saying louder, 'and posh houses, our Mary? You mean where Patrick and Jean live now?'

Jean bristled, spluttered crumbs. 'He worked hard to buy that house for us.'

Mary stared at her, unable to believe she was still sticking up for Patrick. Red-faced, Jean refused to meet her eyes.

'Oh, yes, we know all about what Patrick does,' Ellen said.

As soon as the minister left, Ted had slouched in the chair. Now he roused himself, looking anxiously at Ellen. He sat up straight, taking the mug of tea Peter handed to him. 'Thanks mate.'

Mary saw him give Ellen a warning look. He doesn't know she's told me about Patrick's affair, she thought. She coughed to get her sister's attention.

Ellen looked towards her, pursing her mouth. Hesitated. 'Well, we all know he bought that place with all his wheeler-dealing.' She dragged her eyes away from Mary. 'And he's still showing off, buying this and that, while the rest of us have to put up with queuing.' She sniffed. 'Last time I went for tea I had to queue up for an hour for a packet of the stuff. Anyway,' she changed tack, 'what excuse did he have for not coming to the funeral?'

'Ellen! Stop it!'

But her sister hadn't finished. 'Can't be petrol rationing can it? Someone should tell him that finished in May.'

'He couldn't get away from his business.'

'His business? Two market stalls? He should be ashamed of himself.' Ellen stopped and took a breath. 'And that's not all he should be ashamed of, is it?'

'That's enough,' Mary interrupted. If Ellen carried on like this she was likely to blurt out about Patrick in front of them all and Jean would be mortified. Whatever she thought of the situation, Mary didn't want that for her friend. She'd tell Peter at the same time as she broke the news to him that she was going back to Ashford with Jean for a while. 'Not today, Ellen, please. I don't care that Patrick isn't here, in fact I'm glad.' Jean sat up, rigid. 'I'm sorry Jean but I am. You know what he was like with Tom. All the things he said about him. He hated Tom. He has no right to be here today.'

Mary hadn't forgotten Patrick had been the first to accuse Tom of killing Frank. She hated the idea that he'd been right all along.

'That's all old history,' Jean fired back.

'To you maybe but there are some things that just don't ever really go away.' The pulse in her throat was racing. 'We shouldn't be talking about all this. I'd have thought that for today at least, you two would stop this constant bitching at one another.' The combination of sorrow and anger settled like a hard stone in Mary's stomach. She flung her arms wide. 'Oh, I give up. I'm going next door to see Gwyneth and the kids.'

Peter had been silently watching, reluctant to be part of what was obviously familiar animosity. Now he stood and made to follow Mary. Before he left he turned and looked at the two women. 'It is to your shame you speak so to one another today.'

Chapter 25

The storm had left the air cooler and, even though it was late, Peter lit a fire.

'It is good we are on our own at last.' He stretched out on the sofa, relieved everyone else had gone to bed early. There was something wrong with Mary, had been for days now, and he had a feeling it wasn't only the grief. Perhaps now she would tell him what it was. 'Your family is ... how to say?' He lifted his stockinged feet to warm them against the flames.

'Hard work.' Mary sat down next to him, resting her arm along the high back of the sofa. She stroked his blond hair; it felt soft, thick under her fingers. 'I think Ellen and Jean have exhausted themselves with their quarrelling.'

They exhaust everyone around them, Peter thought, acknowledging how lucky he was to be with Mary. He didn't know how Ted managed to be so tolerant of Ellen. He seemed a steady man despite going through so much during the war. 'Ted is a good man.'

'Yes.'

'He has much patience with Ellen.' He felt her hand still on his head and wondered if he'd said the wrong thing.

'Yes,' Mary said after a beat, 'he does.'

Peter took a long suck at his pipe and blew a stream of sweet-smelling smoke into the air. 'Families can be sometimes difficult.'

'Yes.' She snuggled down, fitting her cheek into the slight hollow between his shoulder and chest. 'Do you miss your own family, your home, Peter?'

He didn't answer immediately. He thought about his father and brothers, all taciturn men, only Werner still alive, left to work the farm. 'No.' In the few short months he knew Mary's brother he'd grown closer to him than his own. 'No, but over the last few nights I have had recollections of days before the war,' he admitted. 'The pattern of the lines on the ice when I and my brothers skated on a local pond; long summer days, working on the farm.' His voice was pensive. 'Sitting by the Elbe, the water high on the banks, high over the boulders on the river bed; the mornings of autumn, harvesting, the cold winters and warm fires in our home. My work as a doctor.' He didn't mention his short marriage, the wife who left him for another man.

'I'm sorry,' Mary said. 'I've neglected you. With Tom and everything else that's happening—'

'No.' He stopped her words with gentle kisses. 'You have not,' he whispered against her mouth. 'I do think of home. But since the war, since the Soviets … Saxony is not a world I know anymore. There is nothing there for me now. I miss what there was, but it is not the same. And I do not miss that as much as I missed you all those years. We are family now?'

'We are,' she said. But Peter knew there would always be a space where Tom should be.

'It was a good funeral … one he deserved.' Peter said. He'd grown to admire her brother's quiet ways. 'Tom was well liked, I think.'

'I wonder if everyone would have thought so well of him if they'd found out he was with Gwyneth's Iori in prison. If they'd known he was a conscientious objector during the war?' And if they'd known that he had killed a man, despite his beliefs, she added silently.

'It would make no difference. They knew him as a worthy man. They are good people. After all, they show no quarrel with me, they have accepted me, and I was called the enemy.' The recollection of the four hostile men in the pub flashed through his mind. He wouldn't tell her.

They sat together, listening to the whistle of air through the sticks of wood in the fireplace, watching the changing patterns of the flames. For the first time in days Peter let the muscles in his shoulders relax.

'Peter?'

He felt the warmth of her hand through his shirt. He rested his chin on top of her head. 'Hmm?'

'I have to tell you something.'

There was a slight hesitation in her voice that alerted him. 'Of course, *Liebling*.'

'It's about Tom.' She sat up, looking into his face. 'And Frank Shuttleworth.'

'*Ja?*' Peter shifted, rubbed the side of his nose, reluctant to look at her. *Gott in Himmel,* how much longer would that bastard haunt them? Would the spectre of her former boyfriend always be there? 'I am listening, *mein Herz*.'

'We've never talked, you and me, about what Frank did to me?'

'I did not want to make you remember ... to upset you.' God forgive your cowardice, Peter Schormann.

'He raped me, Peter. On that canal bank, Frank Shuttleworth raped me.'

He flinched.

'And to stop him, to save me, someone threw him in the river and let him drown.'

Peter couldn't take his eyes from her. Did she know?

'The reason we moved down here was to get Tom away from Ashford, because I believed it was Tom. But he refused to talk about it. He said we should try to forget everything.'

'He was right, *Liebling*.' Peter lowered his head, willed her to let it go, let the past stay where it should be, in the past.

But she wouldn't be put off now. 'Then, one day, we did talk about it and we realised ... at least I thought we realised...' Mary rubbed her temples. 'That Patrick's constantly hinting that it was Tom who'd murdered him was to take attention from himself. He killed Frank.' She pressed her lips into a thin line. 'Or so I believed.'

Mary touched his cheek, moved his face so he had to look at her. 'The other day Gwyneth showed me a letter Tom wrote to her after Iori died.' She squeezed her eyes closed. 'He doesn't actually say… admit … he did it but I could tell that's what he meant.' She looked steadily at him. 'He always told me it wasn't him. Now I know it was. It couldn't have been anyone else. Oh, Peter, I thought Tom was incapable of killing anyone. I thought I knew him.'

Peter held her, rocked her in in his arms. Shame burned so deep inside him it hurt. But still he didn't speak.

Tom *wasn't* capable, he thought. But I was. I did that. For you. For us. He closed his eyes. And now I am too much of a coward to tell you.

Dead or not, Frank Shuttleworth still had the power to destroy them.

Chapter 26

'You are ready to leave?' Peter stood alongside Ted, hands in his pockets. He'd slept badly, the old wound in his shoulder was aching this morning and he'd spent the night going over and over what Mary had told him, reliving the shame of his cowardice, of his inability to confess. Instead he'd let her think the worst of Tom.

And yet still he knew he wouldn't tell her.

'Yeah.' Ted took a last drag on his cigarette and nipped the burning tobacco between finger and thumb before dropping the tab end into the top pocket of his jacket. 'Just waiting for Ellen to pack and get herself ready.' He cast an eye over the vegetables. 'Garden's looking good.'

'I follow what Tom started.' Peter bent down and pulled out an errant dandelion amongst the line of onions, a sudden stab of pain in his shoulder making him straighten up more carefully.

'I'm glad we finally met,' Ted said, feeling slightly uncomfortable, 'even under these circumstances. Happen you'll come to Ashford sometime?'

'Perhaps.' Peter had no intention of ever setting foot in that town again. Even so he smiled at Ted. 'It is good we understand one another.' He dropped the weed down onto the path and rubbed his palms together.

'And I'm sorry about Ellen's behaviour yesterday. She upset Mary, I know.'

'I am sure they have made friends again,' Peter said. 'Jean is also…' He halted, unable to find the words to describe Mary's difficult friend who obviously disliked him.

'Impossible.' Ted laughed and then frowned. 'She's having a hard time at the moment though.'

Peter cocked his head to one side. 'Oh?'

'Yeah, Patrick's getting handy with his fists by all accounts.'

'That is shameful.'

'Yeah.' Ted passed his hand over his mouth. 'There's other stuff going on as well.' He was almost tempted to confide in this quiet bloke, but then thought better of it. 'Ellen tells me Mary intends to go back with Jean.' He sensed the startled movement of Peter's head. 'You didn't know?'

'No.' The rush of anxiety unnerved Peter. 'I did not.' Why hadn't she told him?

'Personally, I don't think it'll do much good. Jean's been sweet on Patrick for as long as I can remember. She'll not leave him now, whatever he does.' Sensing Peter's unease, not sure why Mary hadn't told Peter, Ted focused on fumbling in his pocket for the cigarette end. 'Mary thinks she should have words with him. But I reckon he'll go mad and Jean'll resent it.'

'Mary should stay here.' Peter's voice was grim. 'She does not need more trouble, more worry. And also, she is to go back to work next week. The hospital, they have understood, but she said to me she has been away long enough. It is almost a month.'

'Mary's looked out for her family all her life. She's a strong woman.'

'Still, she has me now. I will look after her.'

'She's been especially good to Ellen. She's relied on Mary for a lot of things.' Ted nodded. 'I don't know how much you know about all the stuff that happened to Ellen during the war?' he said. 'She didn't have it easy ... and I know folk think I'm soft with her, that I let her get away with murder...'

Peter was barely listening, his mind furiously working on ways to persuade Mary not to go to Ashford.

Unaware he'd lost Peter's attention, Ted continued, 'I swore then if I got home and she'd have me I'd look after her if it killed me. When I found out everything that had happened with Linda and everything, I was so angry I wasn't there to protect her.'

So he knew about Shuttleworth? Peter didn't ask.

'It's hard,' Ted said, 'feeling guilty about something, when you know there wasn't anything you could do about it. I'd kill for her, you know.' Ted's spoke almost casually.

Peter tightened his lips before the guilty admission spilled out. Instead he moved his head, acknowledging what Ted had said.

'Ted, what are you doing? Come and drink this tea before we leave. The kids are getting fractious.' Ellen stood at the back door.

The two men grinned at one another in a shared moment of humour. Then, in an even tone, Ted said, 'You really don't want Mary to go to Ashford, do you?'

'No, it will do no good I think.'

'Let me have a talk with her. I think I can persuade her she's better off staying here.'

'Come on, we'll better get a wriggle on.' Ted stood on the doorstep, jingling the van keys. 'It'll take all day, the rate that old banger goes.'

'It'll get you home, though?' Mary imagined them stuck in the middle of nowhere. That would be sure to cause a row. She kissed both children, welcoming Linda's tight hug. 'Be good for your Mummy now.'

'Yep, radiator'll just need topping up every now and then.' Ted grinned. 'I'll get Ellen to do it if it's raining.'

'You won't.' Ellen gave him a light slap on the arm. 'Anyway,' she said, 'we'll be down again for the wedding, once you've set the date. We'll have a new car by then.' She gave her husband a mock warning look. 'Won't we?'

'Aye, I suppose so,' he said in feigned resignation. 'I doubt the nattering'll stop till we do.' He held out his hand to Peter, his grip warm. 'Thanks mate,' he said firmly, 'you make sure you look after our Mary.'

'I will.' Peter put his other hand over his and Ted's clasped ones. 'And thank you.'

'What for?'

'For the friendship you have offered to me.'

'And thank you for our chats.' Ted's voice affected casualness. 'And if ever you feel you can face Ashford, you'll always be welcome in our house.' He added sheepishly, 'And I'm sorry if I offended you yesterday. I was a bit bladdered – middle of the day as well – should be ashamed!'

'Not at all.' Peter smiled. Their conversation had broken down barriers that could have lasted years. 'As I said, thank you.'

Ted turned to usher the children out onto the path. 'Come on, wife,' he ordered in mock officiousness, laughing and staggering slightly as Ellen gave him an indignant shove.

She put her arms around Mary. 'I wish you were coming with us.'

There was something in her eyes that made Mary say, 'You'll be all right?'

'I'm fine.' Ellen crossed her eyes and grinned. 'Bright as a button, me. Right, no more yacking, let's get the show on the road.' As she turned away Mary saw she'd begun to cry; large beads of glistening tears. 'I'll miss Tom too, you know. It's easy to take things for granted, like I always knew he was here.' She gave a loud spluttering cough and shepherded Linda and William towards the gate. 'Come on, Ted, or it'll be dark before we get home.'

Mary lowered her voice. 'Look after her, Ted. She's not as hard as she pretends to be.'

'I know, don't worry.' He walked away. 'Tell Jean ta-ra for us, will you? We'll probably see her tomorrow when she gets home. Tell her I'm sorry there's no room in the van.'

'I will.'

'Course, she could have travelled in the back like you offered, Ted,' Ellen called over her shoulder as she ushered the children into the van. 'Bit of flour doesn't hurt anybody.'

Mary's lips twitched at the thought.

Ted turned back to hug Mary. 'Thanks Mary,' he said, 'I owe you.' He held her at arm's length.

'Give over.'

'You've got a good man there, lass,' he whispered.

'I know.' Mary smiled. 'And you're probably right about what you said. I should let Jean sort things out for herself. She wouldn't thank me for interfering in her marriage … and Patrick certainly wouldn't.'

Ted nodded. 'You have to look after yourself, love. You've gone through a hard time as well.'

They hugged one last time.

With Peter's arm over her shoulder she waved until the van disappeared round the corner. The loneliness the sudden loss of their noisy presence provoked was almost painful. Everything's changed, she thought. Oh Tom, I am really going to miss you too. Looking back at the cottage she felt that all at once she couldn't face going in.

Then Jean appeared at the door. 'Nice to have a bit of peace,' she called. 'Fancy another brew?'

Chapter 27

'I have to say the grounds have never looked so good.' The Minister pulled an apologetic smile. 'But that's all there is at the moment, I'm afraid. There doesn't seem to be anything else for you to do.' He handed a pound note to Peter. 'I'll let you know when ... as soon as ... something else crops up.' He beamed. 'Good job, good job, well done, well done – now must dash, a christening this morning. Yes, yes, a christening.' Muttering to himself he ambled back to the church, stopping now and again at various graves.

When he reached the last one before the porch, a grey headstone that was slightly sunken in the ground he turned back. 'Sam Jones,' he called in a bright voice, his hand resting on it, 'he was the church gardener for thirty years or so I'm told. Of course he did it for the love of his work – wouldn't take a penny, I believe.'

Peter pretended he hadn't heard. He picked up his shears and knelt down to trim around the graves. Tugging at a particular stubborn clump of weeds he studied his hands. There were cuts and calluses on his skin but he didn't mind. They were the hands of the gardener he'd become, not the doctor he once was.

But now he was worried. Would he get work with Tom gone? It didn't seem so. This was the only job he'd had since then. He shook his head, trying to shift the worry.

Packing away the tools in the old shed at the back of the church he pondered on what to do. He walked slowly along the path and perched on the stone wall by the lych-gate, folding the pound note into small squares. He looked up as two women passed by. The younger one's smile swiftly faded, vanquished by a dig in her ribs by the older woman.

Peter watched them until they turned the corner at the end of the church wall, his lower lip caught between his teeth. He needed to do something. Mary couldn't be the only one to bring in money, his pride wouldn't accept that.

He reluctantly acknowledged his only option: he must ask Alun and Alwyn if they could give him some gardening jobs. Tom had sometimes taken on work they hadn't time for. They were his only hope. For Mary's sake he had to try.

He jumped down from the wall and made his way to the outskirts of the village. Looking up towards the top of Ellex Hill he could just see the roof of the twins' house. He'd never been but Mary had once pointed it out to him.

The air was humid and difficult to breathe as he climbed slowly, back hunched, his knees bent against the steep gradient of the lane. When he reached the top he turned and looked out over the sea to the horizon. On fine days he supposed the views would be breath-taking. Today there was a heat mist rolling in shrouding the cliffs and the beach far below. He took off his cap and wiped his forehead with his arm before turning to face the path leading to the house. If he didn't know better he would have thought it was empty. No curtains hung in the widows, the framework and the door were badly in need of repair and paint, on the corner the drainpipe hung broken and grass sprouted from the guttering. Mary had told him the twins didn't bother about their home but still … he stared, a slight flicker of surprised humour in him.

He swallowed, his pride sticking in his throat like a piece of dried stollen. Begging for work wasn't something he'd done before and he resented it now.

For an instant he remembered the time he was revered as the doctor in his village in Germany. 'Dummkopf,' he muttered, twisting his cap in his hands. Those times had gone. He strode up the path and around the side of the house.

The plot of land at the back was immaculate. Canes steepled together were entwined by runner beans, the rows of dark red-veined leaves of beetroot gave way to the shoots of onions and inside the greenhouse was a mass of tomato plants. In the far corner, in the middle of lines of the ferny tops of carrots and the broad leaves of spring cabbage, a homemade scarecrow, wearing an old plaid shirt, black trousers and tattered brown trilby, leaned to one side, its clothes barely moving in the light breeze.

Peter looked around. The pitch roof of a large shed poked up from behind a trellis. 'Hello?'

Alun appeared first, his tangled black hair flopping over his eyes, a tray of small potatoes in his arms. 'Peter.' He grinned and Peter gave an inner sigh of relief. At least he was welcome here. Before Tom's funeral he'd been lulled into a false sense that he would be accepted by everyone in Llamroth. He'd learned since he was wrong.

Balancing the tray Alun shook his hand. 'Alwyn, come here, see. We have a visitor.'

Alwyn emerged from the shed wearing a trilby with more holes in it than the one the scarecrow wore. There was a piece of coarse string fastened through the loops of his trousers. He wiped his hand on his jacket and held it out for Peter to shake but said nothing.

'You are busy?' Peter shoved his cap inside his overall pocket and made a sweeping gesture with his arm. 'It is most impressive.'

The two men looked self-conscious and shuffled their boots on the gravelled path but he could tell they were pleased. Alwyn took out a large grubby handkerchief and blew his nose, peering over it at Peter.

'Just a visit, is it?' Alun asked.

'Yes. No.' Peter faltered. 'I was – I was hoping for some work?'

'We can have a chat about it?' Alun glanced at Alwyn who nodded, handkerchief still held to his face. 'We always like to have a chat about things first, don't we brother?'

Alwyn moved his head again.

'Hold on a minute.' Alun put the tray down. 'Mr Howells?' A burly man, in a tightly fastened dark blue suit and shirt and tie appeared at the back of Alwyn, his florid face devoid of expression. Peter smiled a greeting. The man snubbed him. Putting on his hat he glanced at Alun. 'How much?'

'Thruppence,' Alun said curtly. He'd noticed the snub.

'Bloody expensive.'

Alun bent down and picked the tray up. 'No then?' He tilted his head.

'You know I need them. Visitors have ordered them for their tea tonight.' Grumbling the man fumbled in his wallet. He dropped three coppers in Alun's outstretched hand and took the tray of potatoes.

Alun turned back to Peter. 'Perhaps you could cut the grass on the green in the village? It's a job we do for the Council.'

Peter felt gratitude run through him. '*Ja*, good. I will do that.'

'The Rushville?' Alwyn offered, his voice almost a whisper.

'The old folk's home? Yes,' Alun said, 'there's a few jobs you could do for them, like. We keep telling them we're better on the repairing side of things but they still keep asking us. Tom used to do all that for us. So if you…?'

'I will. Thank you.'

The man stopped before he turned the corner of the cottage. 'Don't send that Kraut to do any work for me. I don't want him anywhere near my place. Don't want my guests upset by the sight of him.'

The three men pretended not to have heard. Then Alwyn heaved a deep sigh. He walked along the path to the man and took hold of the tray. There was a short tussle before Alwyn jerked it out of the man's hands. 'Here's your money back, Mr Howells.' He pushed the coins into the man's palm. 'Get your tatties somewhere else.'

They waited until they heard the man's car start up.

'Tom was a good friend to us,' Alwyn said. 'He made us see how we felt about the war wasn't wrong. Not like our family back home.'

That was a surprise. 'I did not know. You were conscientious objectors also? Tom did not say…' His words trailed away. Uncertain how to continue, he said, 'It is of no concern to me but Tom told me you were his good friends.' He flapped the paper. 'And now, I see, you are also my good friends.'

'Aye, well, must get on.' Alwyn shifted sideways, embarrassed. He pushed his hair away from his forehead and giving Peter a wide grin which crinkled the skin around his dark eyes. 'Give us a shout if you need any help, see?'

'Aye, must get on,' Alun said in a low voice, his face mirroring his brother's and revealing a gap in his large teeth, into which he now fitted the empty pipe he'd been holding in his hands.

Peter swallowed. He was a proud man. Tormented since Tom's death that he would have to live on Mary's earnings he didn't know how to tell the twins what it meant to him. All he could say was, 'Thank you, thank you to both of you.' He shook hands with each of them.

Walking away from the house, self-respect flooded through him. It will be all right, he thought.

Chapter 28

The guard nonchalantly slammed each carriage door he passed. He turned and walked backwards, checking there were no latecomers. Then he blew his whistle and the train juddered, a rush of steam spurting out from under the engine.

Jean slid the window down. 'Let me know when you've decided on the date.' She didn't smile.

Mary was fully aware Jean still didn't approve of Peter. *At least he isn't a bully.* She instantly regretted the thought. 'We will,' she said. 'And you take care. Remember what we talked about.'

Jean didn't answer.

'Stay in touch.' Mary wondered for the tenth time that morning whether she should be going back with her. It was too late now.

They watched the train shunt slowly backwards on the rust-pitted iron rails; past the end of the platform and out of the station. Two hundred yards away, it connected with the main line opposite the red and cream signal box whose low line of windows flashed in the sun. Squinting, Mary could see the dark shadow of the man inside moving around, pulling on the levers. She dropped her gaze to watch the points sliding across the rails. The signalman appeared at the top of the wooden steps to lift a hand to the driver. It seemed to Mary that he also returned Jacqueline's frantic wave. The little girl's face was a pale blob now but Mary knew she was crying and she swallowed her own tears.

With a short burst from the whistle the train chugged away. As the sound grew muffled, others became more distinct: the signal clanged down, bouncing to a noisy stop; under the eaves of the wooden roof sparrows gave the occasional murmur, too lethargic to move; the porter shouted to someone inside the ticket office and a man replied with a laugh. The warm air carried a faint acrid smell of the funnel's smoke, growing less with each passing moment.

Peter squeezed Mary's hand. 'It is better you leave her to her own problems. You have much to do here.'

'I know.' He was right. There was nothing she could do. She could only hope Jean came to her senses and moved back in with her mother. She glanced up at the sky, almost translucent against the brilliance of the sun, and heaved a long sigh. Jean could be bossy and awkward but Patrick was a right chip of the old block, his father's son right enough. She might ask Ellen to keep an eye on Jacqueline.

She let her arm drop to her side, aware she'd been waving long after her niece would be able to see her.

Peter held her face between his palms, and kissed her forehead and then her lips. 'She and little Jacqueline will be fine. You must not worry.' He gave her one last quick kiss on the tip of her nose. Mary savoured the feeling of being cherished.

They climbed the steps to the bridge over the single track, their weight causing reverberations on the metal plates. An old memory returned to Mary, the sound of shuffling footsteps on the iron stairs from one landing to the next at Tom's prison. She closed her eyes for a second and stopped, holding on to the railing with one hand.

'Mary? What is it?'

'Sorry, Peter, I was thinking about Tom.' How can happiness and misery go so hand in hand? she thought. 'Take no notice of me.' She tried to laugh. The sound emerged as a sob. 'I feel so,' she spread her fingers, 'so mixed up.' It wasn't only the physical loss of Tom. She'd lost the need to protect him, and it left her bewildered. Ingrained in her since his release from prison, it was a role reversal she'd grown used to, repaying him for the way he'd safeguarded her from her father's temper all through her childhood. It was also the great sadness she felt that her brother and Peter had lost the chance to nurture the friendship they'd started to build.

'I know,' he said. 'I am sorry, *liebling*.'

'It's not your fault,' she said, threading her arm through his. 'Come on, let's go.'

They walked through the crowded waiting room to get to the main entrance of the station. The dusty, stale odour was overpowering and Mary held her breath until they were outside.

Strolling along the flagged pavement they stayed on the side of the road shaded by the three-storey stone buildings. Mary looked around, trying to see the town through Peter's eyes. This was only the third time he'd been to Pont yr Hafan. He'd been in no hurry to stray further than the village, and now he was saying nothing. The ground floors contained a variety of shops. The upper floors, some with windows blanked out with whitewash, others with grubby net curtains, seemed to be either flats or storerooms.

'It's a bit dingy, this place, I know,' she said. 'It's taking a while to recover from the war. But there are a few good shops, a Utility Furniture place, two second-hand clothes shops that sell really good stuff.' She smiled, fingering the lapel of his jacket. 'We could look for something for you if you wanted?'

He shook his head.

'Some other time then. Tom especially liked the ironmongers. He used to say there was nothing you couldn't get from there, or have ordered.' She pointed towards the end of the street. 'And there's a Woolworths on the High Street.'

She stopped outside a large window where blue and white checked curtains were held back by large blue bows. 'I thought we might splash out a bit, go in here for a cup of tea? We haven't done that before.' She waited, hoping she hadn't sprung this on him too suddenly. 'We can talk, like you said, make plans?' It wasn't fair to spoil Peter's mood. He'd been so good about everything.

Peter peered through the window. They could both see two or three small round tables from where they stood, and the outline of a few people. He pressed his lips together, ran a hand over his short blond hair and then pulled back his shoulders. 'That would be good,' he said finally. He held the door open for Mary and followed her into the café.

The middle-aged couple at the first table glanced up at them before resuming their conversation. An old man, wiping crumbs from his chin with a thin paper serviette, watched with no great interest. Mary led the way past a group of young women, giggling and chattering over frothy pink milkshakes, to a table in the alcove by the window.

The waitress, who was loading up a tray with used crockery, stopped to follow them. 'What can I get for you?' She smiled at Peter, arranging the frills on the shoulder straps of her apron.

'Oh, I think a pot of tea for two,' Mary said, seeing his reluctance to speak. 'And some Welsh cakes I think.'

'*Ja* … yes,' he muttered.

Taking a quick sideways peep at Peter the woman scribbled on her notepad. 'Two minutes,' she announced, picking up the tray and, carrying it above her head. Mary didn't miss the raised eyebrows and sideways movement of her head when she manoeuvred past the couple. She saw them twist around to look at Peter and stared back at them until the woman gave a slight cough and fiddled with her necklace, turning away and tugging at her husband's sleeve. Before long they left the café, followed by the old man who, clearing his throat, spat on the pavement in front of the window before shuffling away.

'This was a mistake.' Peter half rose.

'No!' Mary seized his hand. She smoothed the folds of her skirt, unfastened her cardigan and, taking it off, laid it across her knees. 'No, we stay.'

The waitress returned with the tray: brown teapot, milk jug, a plate of Welsh cakes, one cup, saucer and plate.

'You've forgotten something,' Mary said, placing the latter in front of Peter. '*My* cup and saucer? *My* plate?' The woman flushed and turned away towards the counter. When she returned, Mary took them without speaking.

One of the young women leaned towards them. 'Quite right.' She grinned. 'Snotty cow should realise who pays her wages.' Raising her voice she said, 'She'll not get a tip from us.' The others agreed. 'Should bloody realise the war's been over a long time.'

'Thanks.' Mary poured the tea, unable to say any more. She was trembling.

With a lot of clatter the girls shoved their chairs back and left.

Now, except for the glowering waitress, they were alone in the café.

'Thank you,' Peter said to Mary. 'Thank you for not caring, for being strong for the both of us, *meine Liebe*.' He leant his arms on the table, touching Mary with the tips of his fingers. 'I always think I do not know what I would do if I lost you.'

'Well that's not going to happen, ever, so don't worry about that.' The balance of sadness and joy tipped towards contentment. Tom would want her to be happy; he wouldn't want her moping around. And yet there was that small voice in her mind. She knew how ashamed he would be, knowing he had lied to her.

'You are fine now?'

'I'm fine.' Mary twisted the top flower-shaped button of her blouse.

He raised his hand dismissing the words. 'You must talk, tell me. Whatever worries you I must know. Perhaps help?'

Mary sipped her tea. There was no point in talking about Tom's part in Frank's death. She needed to put it all behind in the past; just as her brother had wanted her to. But there was something she could do. So when she replaced the cup on the saucer she said, 'I think it's just with seeing Ellen and Jean go back to Ashford. Seeing the children, Linda especially, growing so quickly. She's quieter than Jacqueline, more sensitive, I think, and such a lovable little girl. It set me thinking.' She hesitated, wondering if she should carry on. But he had told her to tell him anything. She took the plunge. 'There's something else I've mithered about for a long time. It's Nelly, Frank's mother, I feel sorry for. Sometimes, when I get letters from her, I feel bad that I'm keeping it all from her. She is Linda's grandmother after all.'

'Why is it today you are thinking of her, *liebling*?'

Was there slight impatience in his tone? 'I'm sorry, love,' she said, 'I didn't mean to upset you.' All they seemed to be doing today was apologising to one another.

'You have not. But Linda is happy, I think. What good would it be to have her to meet ... *diese Frau* ... this Nelly Shuttleworth?'

Again Mary thought she heard underlying irritation, so unlike him. 'Are you all right?' A movement of his head should have reassured her but didn't. Almost apologetically she said, 'I don't know really why it bothers me except I know she'd be a lovely grandmother – the only one for Linda since Mam died.'

'Do you think Ellen would want that? Have you said this to her?'

'No but...' He was looking down. Mary tried to see his expression. 'It's just something that bothers me. Especially now

I've found out how horrible Ted's mother is.' The thought of Hannah Booth saying or doing anything to hurt Linda angered Mary so much she was shocked by the depth of her hatred. 'Still, you're probably right. Ellen would hate Linda to be involved with Frank's family.' George Shuttleworth was a despicable man. He'd make Ellen's life unbearable. 'All hell could let loose.'

'That is probable.'

'Anyway, it's not my place to tell Nelly.' She put her hand over his. 'I hate secrets but this is one best kept, I think.'

Peter's voice sounded strained when he spoke. 'Yes, sometimes it is better that secrets are kept,' he said.

Chapter 29

'I've said nothing of the kind.' Hannah scratched at the bandages on her leg.

'You've called Linda,' Ted ground out his words, '*my* daughter, a bastard.'

'Never.' Hannah scratched harder. A small patch of brown discolouration from the infection had come through the dressings. 'One thing I will say though, your wife does neglect our William for the other one all the time. Poor little beggar can be screaming his head off and she just ignores him, when t'other just has to click her fingers.'

'You're lying.' Ted walked back and forth in front of Hannah. He swung round to face her, almost overbalancing on his weak ankle. 'All this nastiness about Ellen.' He steadied himself, rubbed his hands over his face. 'Why Mother?'

Hannah clamped her mouth together, pushing out her lips. The two metal rollers on her forehead quivered as she shook in indignation. 'I'm not the one who's lying to you. I'm not the one who's told that many lies about herself in the past she wouldn't know the truth if it smacked her in the face.'

'Shut up.'

'And you soaked them all up. You're a fool.'

'I won't have you talking about Ellen like that.' Ted turned away so he didn't have to see her. 'Ellen has been good to you. God above, she came to live with you, to help you, when you thought I was dead.'

'Don't give me that. She just knew which side her bread was buttered. She didn't want to be in Henshaw Street the way things were there.' Hannah's voice rose. 'You're too soft.'

'I'm too soft? I'm too soft?' The heat of his anger towards his mother, dormant for so long, boiled to the surface. 'I've listened to you, "Do this, do that, go here, go there," telling me how to live my life. And I let you. And why? Because I thought you'd had it rough being left on your own to bring me up. When I was a kid I felt guilty, thinking Dad had left because of something I'd done.' He pushed his face towards hers. 'But it wasn't, was it? I'd done nothing. It was you. With your nasty tongue and spiteful ways, your incessant carping and nagging. You drove him away.' His breathing was shallow and strained. He noticed a fleck of his spittle on her cheek but he didn't care. 'Just like you drove me away in the end. Why do you think I volunteered? To get away from you. Did you think I didn't know why you kept on and on about trying for the bakery at the Co-op? You knew it was a reserved occupation and if I got in you wouldn't have to be on your own.' He gulped in a quick breath. 'When I got accepted into the RAF Voluntary Reserve in Manchester and left here I felt free for the first time in my life. All because I was away from you.'

Her jowls trembled with an anger that equalled his but she stayed silent.

Ted flung himself onto one of the kitchen chairs but in his rage he couldn't keep still. His knee jerked up and down under the table, knocking against the drawer and jangling the cutlery inside. When he noticed what he was doing he swung himself around and faced her. 'This is how it's going to be from now on,' he said firmly. 'You'll leave Ellen alone and...'

'Oh, will I?' Hannah finally found her voice. She pushed the loose sleeves of her black cardigan up her forearms.

'Yes, you will.' Ted spoke harshly. 'And if I hear you've said anything else about Linda you'll be sorry.'

'Oh?'

'Yes, oh! Any more nastiness, Mother, and I'll have to ask you ... no, I'll tell you to leave and find somewhere else to live.'

'Then I won't be the only one who'll be sorry, Ted, will I?' his mother said. 'I just hope you'll be prepared to sell the shop and give me my money back.'

Chapter 30

Nelly Shuttleworth licked the point of her pencil and hunched over the table, holding the edge of the paper down with her thumb. She printed out the letter she'd been composing in her head for days. It wasn't easy; besides the physical effort of writing, she carried the burden of guilt for the way her eldest son had treated Mary. And the girl had been nothing but kind to her. In fact, Nelly thought, she'd treated her as a friend, keeping in touch all these years when she could just as easily, more easily, in fact, have refused to acknowledge any of Nelly's notes. There wasn't a day passed when she didn't think of the horrible thing Frank had done to Mary. It haunted her. And, sometimes, even though she knew he would despise her for it, she went to the canal to say a little prayer for his soul.

Nelly stared down at the note, struggling to concentrate. The noise of the paddle in the washing machine, the stew bubbling in the pan and the loud voices from George's wireless upstairs blocked her thoughts. Planting her stained worn-down slippers firmly on the floor and holding the tip of her tongue between her teeth, she formed each word with determination. She needed Mary to know how sorry she was that, yet again, she had grief in her life.

When she'd finished she sat back in her chair and, lifting up the hem of her skirt, she pulled back the elastic on the leg of her pink bloomers and scratched her knee, her lips moving silently as she read the letter in the pool of light from the bare bulb on the ceiling. When she'd finished she licked the pencil again and added a few more words:

… LIKE I SAID, THERES ALWAYS SOMEONE TO PASS ON BAD NEWS AROWND HERE. GEORGE SAW THAT BLOKE, ARTHUR BROWN, IN THE CROWN LAST NIGHT AND HE TOLD HIM ABOUT YOUR TOM BEING KILLED A MONTH OR SO BACK. I WERE THAT SORRY. WHY DINT YOU WRITE TO TELL ME. I WOULD AVE GOT IN TOUCH BEFORE. IM ALWAYS THINKING ABOWT YOU PET. TAKE CARE OF YOURSELF. DON'T FORGET WERE I LIVE WHEN YOU NEXT COME BACK HOME. ILL MAKE SURE YON BUGGER IS OUT.
YOUR FRIEND, NELLY SHUTTLEWORTH

The wireless upstairs became suddenly louder and heavy footsteps clattered on the stairs.

'What's for tea? I'm off out in ten minutes.' Nelly's son scowled at her. He squinted through his cigarette smoke as he stretched his neck to fasten the collar studs. 'I told you.' He ran a finger around his collar. 'I've got a date.' He smirked. 'Taking Gloria Grimstead to the flicks.'

'You want to watch yourself with that one. She's got a right reputation.'

'I'm not interested in her reputation, Ma.' He shot a look at her, trying to see what was on the paper hidden under her arm.

'What yer doing?' He clicked his fingers. 'Give us a look.'

'Mind your own.' But before Nelly could move he'd snatched the letter from her and ran his eyes over it.

His face flushed with anger. 'Why're you writing to that cow?'

'Why don't you mind your own business?'

'Our Frank's dead because of her.' George crumpled the paper and threw it towards the fireplace. 'She had him murdered.'

'He raped her.' Nelly closed her eyes, unable to believe she'd said the words to her youngest son.

'Crap. She asked for it.'

For a big woman Nelly could move fast. The chair crashed to the floor behind her.

With closed fist she hit the side of George's head. 'No woman,' she panted, 'asks for that.'

Didn't she know it? She wouldn't have been lumbered with a useless husband if that was the case. Four months pregnant she was when she married, her reputation in tatters. Hadn't she paid ten times over for Alec raping *her*, with the beatings and abuse from the day they were married? Hadn't he left her with two black eyes and a split lip when he walked out on her and her sons? And good riddance, she thought. She glared at George. 'Now get out.'

He'd raised his fists in retaliation, but the look in her eyes stilled him. 'Haven't had me tea.'

'I'll be making no tea.' Nelly picked up the chair and sat on it before her legs gave way under her.

He banged the front door after him, rattling the piled-up pots on the side of the sink. He'd left his wireless switched on; the voices droned to the empty room.

Nelly straightened her arms on the table in front of her. The muscles in her forearms bulged from the years of wringing clothes. Then she laid her head on them and dry sobs shook her whole body. She thought back to the days when her boys were little. If anyone had told her that they would turn out such cruel men she would have drowned them both at birth.

Chapter 31

'A stinking Kraut!'

The words hit Mary like a slap in the face as she passed the door of the laundry room. Two nurses had their backs to her as they pretended to arrange already folded towels piled on the shelves. Mary stopped, every impulse telling her to keep on walking, but she willed herself to stay, to refuse to creep away. Do nothing, she thought, and you might as well give in your notice to the Hospital Board.

'I presume Sister Davies knows you two are in here?' Without waiting for a reply from the two girls who spun around to face her, she continued, 'And when I go on to your ward I also presume I will find it spotless?'

'Yes Matron.' The one who spoke had blanched so much that Mary thought she would faint and she had to prevent herself from reaching out towards her.

'Good. Then I will tell her that, as you have carried out your duties so well on her ward, you will be continuing your training on Tudor Ward.' They barely suppressed their dismay. The geriatric ward was the least favourite amongst all the student nurses. 'I need not remind you that your role as nurses includes the hygiene and the social and psychological welfare of the patients, regardless of any difficulties you might encounter.' Their heads were lowered so she couldn't see their faces. 'Nurses?'

'Yes, Matron.'

'Good. However I do not think I will inflict you upon the patients on the ward there.' She didn't miss the look of relief they exchanged. 'No, you will be in the sluice room.' It wasn't relief on their faces now. 'You will take over from the students in there, dealing with the bedpans. Now get along. Report to Sister Rees on Tudor, tell her what I have said. I'll be checking on the two of you later.'

They glanced at one another. For a moment Mary thought they were going to challenge her. 'Now!' she snapped.

Waiting until she saw them go through the swing door to the geriatric ward she turned to go back to her office. She had a full afternoon of interviewing prospective student nurses and Bob Willis the Hospital Secretary would be waiting for her.

Vivienne Allott was standing at the side of the corridor, one foot flat against the wall, arms crossed.

Mary knew she must have been listening. 'What are you doing, Nurse Allott?'

'Nothing Matron.' The girl met Mary's stare.

'That's quite obvious, Nurse. I'll rephrase the question. What should you be doing?'

'I've just come off shift.' She didn't move.

'Then I suggest you go home.'

Still no movement.

'Stand up straight when I address you, Nurse.'

Vivienne Allott moved slowly. She straightened the front of her apron, adjusted her cap. Although she maintained the surly pout when she looked up to meet Mary's stare, there was apprehension in her eyes.

'You do realise I could report you to the Board for insubordination?' Even as she spoke, Mary knew she couldn't. She had no grounds other than Allott spreading rumours about her. And they weren't just rumours, were they, she said to herself. She *was* with Peter. There would be problems if it came to the Hospital Board's attention that she was living with him. They'd take a dim view of their Matron 'living in sin', let alone with a German. There were some mealy-mouthed old beggars on the Board.

And Nurse Allott knew it as well. 'But you won't, will you, Matron? I've done nothing wrong.'

Over the last week it had been one long line of sly remarks and outraged looks. The hospital had become a bedrock of gossip about her and Peter. Mary hated pretending to be oblivious to the atmosphere when all she wanted to do was lash out. Now, standing in front of her was the probable source of all the tittle-tattle. Mary folded her arms. She moved closer to the girl. 'I know it's you, you vicious little cow.' Shocked, Vivienne took a step back. Mary followed her. 'I know you're the blabbermouth, the one who is spreading your vindictive gossip. And I'm warning you, if I hear any more spiteful remarks – from anyone – I will hold you personally responsible.'

'That's not fair,' Vivienne Allott protested.

Unheeding, Mary continued, 'I will make sure you're so far up to your armpits with bedpans you don't come out of the sluice room for weeks. Now, do we understand one another?'

She nodded, barely moving her head.

'Nurse?' Mary wasn't going to let this go so easily.

'Yes Matron.' But even though her tone portrayed nothing but acceptance, the hostility in her gaze shook Mary. She forced herself to turn and stride away. She didn't trust herself not to hit the girl. Her lips twisted into wry self-condemnation. Perhaps there was more of her father in her than she appreciated.

Chapter 32

'Well, I have to say, Matron, this is a surprise. I knew nothing about your plans.' The Hospital Secretary glanced quizzically at Mary over the top of his half-moon spectacles.

'You're probably alone in that, Mr Willis. My fiancé is German. It's been quite a talking point in the hospital, I believe.' She scrutinised his face but there was no reaction.

'Well, goodness. I offer my sincere congratulations, Matron.' The colour rose from below his collar, reddened his cheeks and nose. He held out his hand. 'My good wishes to you … and to your fiancé. Umm?'

'Peter,' Mary said, 'and thank you, Bob.' She held his fingers for a brief moment. 'I'd be grateful if you would keep this to yourself for the time being. I have yet to inform the Board and I don't want to tell them until we have set a date for the wedding. But you and I have worked together very well for the last five years…'

'Yes, indeed, we've always worked hand in glove, so to speak.'

'Quite.' Mary smiled at him. 'Normally I wouldn't be able to continue my work here, as a married woman, but I think the system is slowly changing and I'm hopeful that, as this is a small hospital, the Board will be forward-thinking and allow me to stay. There are precedents I believe.'

'Let us hope so.' Bob pushed at the knot of his tie. 'I like to think the hospital runs as a team,' he blurted. 'All for one and one for all.' He fumbled with his spectacle case, eventually managing to fit in his glasses. 'Must dash, time and tide waits for no man.' Loading files into his arms, he held onto them with his chin. At the door he stood on one leg and balanced them on his knee so he could open the door. She crossed the room to help him. They stood just inside her office. He was sweating. 'I would miss working with you, Matron – Mary.' He held her gaze. There was no mistaking the expression of admiration in his eyes. 'And I really hope the Board have the foresight to see what damage they would do to the hospital if they let such a splendid Matron go.'

Mary closed the door after him and stood with her back to it, still holding on to the handle. She could hear the muted sound of trolley wheels and, further away, the faint clatter of metal trays. The copper fingers on the large round wall clock juddered to five o'clock with a loud clunk.

Deciding to go home, she picked up the telephone. When there was no answer she tried another number, listening to the ringing tone with increasing exasperation. She reached into one of the drawers, took out a couple of envelopes and some paper and scribbled two notes. Locking her desk and filing cabinet she unhooked her cloak from the hanger and looked around, checking all was in order. She slid the 'Out of Office' sign under her nameplate and, wrapping her cape around her, went into the typists' room. Two young women were putting on coats and tying headscarves, giggling and jostling to see themselves in a small mirror. They were immediately silenced when they saw her.

'Still here, ladies?' She smiled. 'I thought you might have left already. It's past your going home time.' Still they didn't speak. 'I've finished for the day…'

'We're just off. Did you want something?' The words were spoken boldly, the usual deference absent.

So, even the office staff were part of the gossip-mongering. Mary drew herself up and glared at the woman. 'Not from you,' she replied and looked across the room at a third woman who'd stopped typing and who, hands on keys, was waiting for Mary to leave before continuing. 'Please make sure the porter delivers these to the Home Sister and House Sister,' she said. 'Just to say I'm leaving early.'

'I'll do better than that, Matron,' the typist said, smiling, 'I'll take them myself.'

'Thank you.' Mary smiled back. Ignoring the others, she left and hurried along the corridors, avoiding eye contact with everyone she met, not stopping until she was standing outside the large blue doors of the hospital.

Breathing deeply she told herself to calm down. Why let a couple of silly women upset her? But she was upset. She'd gained a level of respect within Pont y Haven. Was it all going to disintegrate now?

Chapter 33

Jean had never been afraid of anyone in her life until Patrick had come at her, fist raised. Admittedly, in the end, it was more of a shove than a thump but she'd never forgive him that Jacqueline had seen it.

He'd gone down on his knees and begged for her forgiveness as soon as it happened but he wouldn't get away with it that easy, despite what Mary thought. She'd barely spoken to him since they'd got back from Wales. But she wouldn't leave him. It was as much her house as his and, anyway she wouldn't give her mother the pleasure of knowing she'd been right about Patrick all along. Jean could just see the look of triumph on her face if she turned up at Moss Terrace, tail between her legs. No, she'd too much pride for that.

The pulsing throb at her temple was threatening to turn into a headache. She couldn't think about it now. There was bedding to change before she went for Jacqueline. When Patrick offered to take her round to Ted's earlier she couldn't refuse. Jacqueline hadn't been to play at Linda's since they'd returned from Wales and she missed her cousin. But Jean hoped she'd keep quiet about what was happening at home. She'd seen the way their daughter watched her and Patrick all the time, worry in her face.

Pulling a duster out of her apron pocket Jean flicked specks off the mirror and blew out a short disapproving burst of air. Mary was a fool if she thought marrying a German wouldn't end in tears. Whatever she saw in him, that man could have ruined her life six years ago. She would have lost her job at the Granville, even been run out of Ashford and certainly would have brought shame on them all, if people had known.

'I would have thought she'd have learned, all the trouble it caused then,' she muttered, biting her lip. Patrick always swore that his Dad suffered the stroke because he found out about Mary's affair. Privately Jean agreed. She felt torn between her loyalties to him and to her best friend. But however fond she was of Mary, it didn't mean she had to agree that everything she did or said was right.

'Blast the man.' It was bad enough that Peter had returned. Jean had been speechless the day Mary told her he was in Wales with her, her joy unmistakable. But she'd hoped that once Mary saw him for what he was: a foreigner with no money, no job, no prospects – because surely there was no way he'd be allowed to practice as a doctor here – she'd come to her senses. But no. And when they married Mary would be well and truly trapped. She'd find out her friends would be few and far between. The war wasn't that far in the past.

Still, the small twinge of triumph when Mary asked her to be Matron of Honour at her wedding lingered. She wondered how Ellen would take that.

Stuffing the duster back into her pocket Jean willed the thumping in her head to stop. She studied herself in the hall mirror and wondered if she could lose half a stone before the wedding, whenever it was going to be. Fluffing up her short dark curls, she turned to consider both profiles, sucked in her cheeks. It didn't help the double chin. Taking off her spectacles, she deliberated whether she could manage without them on the day. But all she could see was a blurred image. She put her glasses back on. She was being vain. After all she'd worn them at her own wedding so what did it matter now?

And yet it did matter. Whatever Patrick had seen in her then had become elusive, just out of her reach to recapture. Most nights she lay for hour after hour listening to his breathing, deep in untroubled sleep, while she stared at the thin line of light under the bedroom door from the landing, hugging herself and unable to silence the relentless certainty that there was another floozy on the scene. Since coming back home the signs were all there: lipstick, face powder on Patrick's clothes, ineffectually wiped off and the smell of scent, cheap nasty scent, she judged. And that air about him, a restless anticipation when he wouldn't look her in the eye, an awkwardness. She could almost read his thoughts. And, of course, there were all the small gifts, a bottle of Jasmine perfume, her favourite scent (a much more sophisticated one than he stank of these days), a necklace, a new headscarf and, once, chrysanthemums from the allotment. What had brought those on?

The band of tension around her head tightened. She circled her index fingers over her temples.

She sensed he was almost relieved she wasn't speaking to him. At least he didn't have to answer any awkward questions. But she'd bide her time until she was sure.

Stripping off the crumpled sheets, she glanced out of the window. The driving rain gave the impression that the houses and gardens across the road were trembling. In the distance the North Country moors, pockmarked with black peat and patches of heather and rhododendrons, blended into the winter sky.

A gust of wind clattered the window and startled her. The bed creaked under her knees as she shuffled across it to run the palm of her hand around the edge of the frame. A draught whistled through the wood. The latch was loose and, grasping it, she released the casement.

At the same time she saw Patrick. Hunched against the weather, clutching his trilby to his head, he hurried along the road towards the house.

'Thought you said you were going to check on the allotment,' she murmured. But he wasn't dressed in his gardening clothes. She watched as he ran up the steps to the house, heard him unlocking the front door. Closing the window, she pushed herself off the bed.

'I'm back!'

She didn't answer him.

'Need to go again, finish off cleaning the greenhouse.'

I'll bet, Jean thought. Shaking out the starched white sheet, her mind worked furiously. When she'd suspected him before, it was always after some visit to a dealer or chasing the purchase of a particular car. But he hadn't been away lately; not that she knew, anyway. She finished making the bed, made sure the corners of the cover were taut and pleated, the eiderdown smooth. And then she stood with arms folded and listened. She couldn't hear Patrick moving around.

She was lonely. It was twelve months since they'd moved into Manchester Road and still she didn't know a soul. At least in Moss Terrace, she'd heard the neighbours. Here she felt cut off. The only sound was the traffic from the road. Once or twice she'd seen the woman from next door, hanging out the washing. The first time she'd waved but she wasn't acknowledged. No point in trying that again. She had her pride, after all.

The front door closed with a crash. Patrick on his way out again, still in his good clothes.

Jean caught her lower lip between her teeth. Where to this time?

'Has she been good?'

'She's always good.' Ellen closed the front door, balancing William against her side. 'They're upstairs.' Walking down the hall to the kitchen she didn't volunteer any more conversation.

Jean followed. 'All right if I go up?'

'Help yourself.' Ellen hitched William further up onto her hip.

Hannah Booth was sitting in the armchair by the range. Her eyes didn't leave Jean as she crossed the kitchen.

'Mrs Booth.' Jean nodded to her, half-smiled, uncomfortable under the fixed stare.

Ted's mother didn't acknowledge her. She sniffed and looked back down at the newspaper folded on her lap.

Upstairs there was no noise coming from Linda's room. The door was half-open. Jean put her hand on the handle and gently pushed. Kneeling on the bed by the window the two little girls had their backs to her and were peeping over the sill into the back yard, their arms over each other's shoulders. She smiled and was just about to speak when Linda whispered, 'Can you still see them?'

'No.' Jean watched Jacqueline straighten her legs and lean forward so her forehead was against the glass. 'No, they've gone.'

'Why was your daddy in next door's yard?' Linda said. 'Why was he kissing Mrs Whittaker?'

Jean's knees buckled. She stumbled backwards from the bedroom, crashing the door against the wall. Her chest was tight.

'Mum?' Jean felt her daughter's small hand slip into her own. 'Mum?'

Outside it began to rain again, slow, tentative drops.

Jean turned her head towards the window, as though listening to the uneven splatters on the panes. 'I'm fine, love. I slipped.'

Chapter 34

'I wouldn't normally marry a couple where one of them is divorced.' The minister lent forwards, his eyes closed, moving his head slowly up and down as though going over his decision again. 'But, I've prayed long and hard about this and I've decided I will.' Pressing his hands together as though in prayer, he clasped them between his knees and smiled. 'The good Lord is merciful and I feel it would be His wish to sanctify this marriage.'

His eyes snapped open and Mary gave a small start. The little man really was quite odd. But Tom had liked him and that was good enough for her. And she was grateful; it was important to both her and Peter that they were married here, where Tom had worshipped. It would feel as if he was with them on the day. For a moment the sadness overwhelmed her and she fixed her eyes on Mr Willingham's spats. There was a small black scuff on the left one.

'So, the service?'

'Will be simple.' Mary squeezed Peter's hand. 'There'll only be a few people.'

'Being so near to Christmas we must make preparations now. And make sure that I can fit it in with my other commitments.'

'It would have been Tom's birthday. I just wanted it to be a special memory for him.'

'I understand perfectly, Mary. Your brother was a staunch member of this church, and, speaking personally, a good friend.

I am more than happy to marry the two of you on that date. It is a fitting tribute to a man of exceptional qualities, a man whose tolerance and understanding spread in so many different ways.'

His words brought hot tears; she struggled to hold them back. 'Thank you.'

'I'll contact the Registrar, make sure the date is in his diary. We'll need him to be there to legalise the proceeding,' he explained, answering her look of enquiry. 'We're a Nonconformist church, we're not yet solemnised for marriages.' He leaned back in the pew. 'Nice chap – new to the area. Now, if we could go over a few details?'

An hour later Mary knelt in between the two graves, sharing chrysanthemums between each of the metal vases inserted in front of the identical headstones. The curled petals of the bronzed flowers tightly overlapped, trapping, here and there, drops of water that held tiny light reflections.

'There,' she said again, tracing the words chiselled on both graves with her fingers. '*Hedd perffaith hedd.*' Mary read it out as Gwyneth had taught her. She looked up at Peter. 'It means "peace perfect peace",' she said. 'Gwyneth wanted it on Iori's headstone and she asked if I minded having it on Tom's grave.' She gave him a small smile. 'I didn't, don't. It makes me feel they're together in their faith.'

Peter held out his hand and helped her to her feet. 'Walk?'

'Yes, please.' Mary patted the headstones, feeling for the first time a form of peace, of acceptance of Tom's death. 'You don't mind waiting until December to be married?'

'No, I think it is right for us. I believe Tom would like for us to be married on that day. He would have been my best man. And to have the *Brautlied* sung by Ellen will be wonderful.'

'It's a lovely suggestion, Peter.'

At the lychgate they turned to look back at the church. The diamonds of stained glass in the two large windows on either side of the arched door gleamed in a kaleidoscope of colours in the evening light. The yew trees at the corners of the small churchyard cast their long branched shadows across the paths and the irregular rows of headstones, some upright, some tilting.

'It is good, peaceful here,' Peter said.

'Yes.' Mary clasped his hand. It felt symbolic to be standing under the engraved wooden porch, as though they were being blessed. 'Let's walk back along the beach.'

They waited to let a couple pass by outside the entrance to the churchyard.

'Good afternoon.' Mary smiled at them.

'*Guten Tag*,' Peter said automatically. He dipped his head in greeting.

The woman glanced at them, looked away and then back at Mary. 'Dirty bitch!' she said, over her shoulder. 'Aren't our boys good enough for you?' The man tugged at her, urging her forward. She reluctantly yielded, still glaring at them. 'Bloody Nazi.'

Taken by surprise and angered, Mary stared after them. With a shock she saw the empty sleeve pinned to the side of the man's jacket. *Oh God.* In a way she understood the woman's viciousness, but she couldn't allow it to affect her and Peter.

'Come on,' she said, 'let's get home.'

His eyes were blank when he looked at her.

'It's fine,' she said, 'I don't care what anyone thinks about us, Peter. As long as we're together, I don't care.'

That night they sat on the low wall that separated the road from the beach. The sun was dropping behind the horizon, leaving behind streaks of pink and red. They watched in silence until there was only a domed sliver of gold resting on the dark skyline.

Peter lifted her hand to his mouth, a gesture he often did just to show he was thinking of her. 'It will be good,' he said.

'It will be wonderful,' Mary said.

Everything will work out. I'll be fine Mam, she thought.

Chapter 35

'Do you remember when you first came here to live?' Gwyneth held out her hand.

'I do.' Mary took hold of her fingers, noticing the freckled brown blotches on the skin, the flesh of an old woman, and the raised thin bones on the back of her hand. 'Coming here meant everything to us.'

She'd always known that Gwyneth's offer to rent the cottage wasn't only altruism. She also needed someone nearby who she could talk to about her son without worrying he'd be judged; who knew him as well, or better, than she did. That had been Tom. It hadn't made any difference to Mary. She was still grateful. Iori was buried in the graveyard in Llamroth so Tom had felt close to him. In an odd way it had saved her brother's sanity.

And Mam's. From the moment they arrived in Wales she stopped drinking, even at that first Christmas, even on the anniversary of her husband's death.

'And me, it meant everything to me.' There was a small smile on Gwyneth's lips. 'Ever since last week, after you told me you and Peter were getting married, I've had this thought in my head.' She crossed to the Welsh dresser and tugged at the copper handles of one of the drawers. 'And yesterday I decided to do something about it.'

The black metal box she pulled out looked heavy and Mary half-rose to take it from her. 'Here, let me.'

'No, I can manage.' Gwyneth carried the box the table and unlocked it. 'Put the lamp on, will you, *cariad*, I can't see what I'm doing in this light.'

'I'll pull the curtains back a bit as well.' Mary dragged the heavy blue velvet drapes as far as she could.

'I want to talk to you about the cottage.' Gwyneth rifled through some papers, peering myopically at first one and then another. Eventually she gave a small cry of triumph, flapping a

120

sheath of yellowed pages in the air. 'These are the deeds to your cottage. I've seen my solicitor and I have to take these to him.' She smiled broadly, showing the gap in her upper gum where two teeth had fallen out. 'And I want you to come with me.' She sat in her chair, the documents held loosely in her hands. 'Because I want to give you the cottage. It will be my wedding present to you.'

Mary watched the second finger on the face of the Welsh slate mantle clock turn a full circle before finally answering. She spoke steadily. 'You've always been so kind to Tom and me but this…' She held out her hands, palms upwards. 'This is too much.'

'I thought Iori would live there one day. During the war when he and Tom were in prison I hoped that they would come to live there.' Gwyneth glanced around, her gaze finally settling back on Mary. 'Tom and you coming to live in the cottage was the next best thing. The last few years have been better than I ever thought they could be after I lost Iori. I'm not getting any younger and I want you to have next door. It was *cartref mam a 'nhad* – my mother and father's place, and I want to know it'll be looked after when I'm gone.'

'I don't know what to say.'

'Then say yes, *cariad.*'

'If you're sure?'

Gwyneth waited, watching Mary steadily. 'I'm sure.'

'I still think it's too much.' Mary hugged her. 'But yes, Gwyneth, thank you, yes.'

Chapter 36

'Always thought she'd be famous, did that one.' Hannah Booth tipped her head towards Ellen, who was sitting at the kitchen table determinedly reading an article on Tyrone Power playing the leading role in *Mister Roberts* at the London Coliseum.

Hannah picked at her cuticles. After trying and failing to make eye contact with her daughter-in-law, she continued, 'Just because she's had a few jobs singing in the likes of back-street clubs she says she could have made a career of it. Caterwauling more like.'

Ellen mouthed the words along with Hannah. It was a comment she'd heard many times, one that used to hurt but not anymore. Now it made her want to scream. She forced herself to read against the background of Ted's mother's droning voice.

The District Nurse acted as though nobody had spoken. She'd learned months ago that this was the only thing to do. Keeping her head down, she concentrated on unwrapping the bandages from Hannah's leg and studying the varicose ulcer on her shin.

The stench was instantly noticeable and Ellen wrinkled her nose in disgust. God, she hated the sound, sight and smell of the fat cow.

Hannah poked the nurse on the shoulder. 'You'd think she'd know better, a wife and mother, wanting to gad about all the time.' She flicked away a small piece of cuticle with the pad of her thumb. 'Makes you think, huh?'

Ellen slapped her magazine on the table. 'Enough! I've heard it all before, Hannah, and I don't think Nurse Hampson wants to hear your vicious carping.'

The nurse bowed her head even lower over the wound.

Hannah smiled in satisfaction. 'Truth hurts, doesn't it?'

'Oh, just shut up!' Ellen stared at the pages of *Theatre World Magazine.* The words merged together. Outside, the tin bath scraped against the wall in the wind, rain rattled on the metal. She could hear Doreen in her kitchen next door, whistling to some tune on the radio. What was it their mam used say? *A whistling woman and a crowing hen brings the devil out of his den.* Yeah, that was it. She and Ted were living with the devil, that was for sure. Ellen scowled.

The nurse swabbed the ulcer with Red Lotion, but the sweet aroma of lavender and zinc did little to block out the reek of the slowly granulating flesh around the wound.

Ellen saw Hannah wince and for a brief moment felt some sympathy, recalling the very early days when they'd lived together in harmony and she'd helped her future mother-in-law to bandage the damaged varicose veins. It was impossible to believe they'd ever got on; now she sometimes wished Hannah dead.

'That's me done, Mrs Booth, I'll see you next week.' The nurse patted Hannah's arm. Packing her bag and closing it with one hand, she stood and fastened the buttons of her coat with the other.

'She'll see you out.' Hannah carefully took her leg off the small stool and lowered it to the floor, adjusted her long black dress over her knees.

Ellen led the way along the hall and opened the front door. She watched the nurse cycle, head bent against the rain, down the street, the black nurses' bag bouncing around in the wicker basket behind her. As she turned onto Shaw Street, Ellen saw Nurse Hampson wobble and grab hold of her hat with a shrill shriek, in danger of losing it in a sudden gust of wind. A man, hurrying down the street on the opposite side, swopped glances with Ellen and laughed before continuing on his way, taking long strides to avoid the streams of cream and yellow donkey-stone that was being washed off the door steps by the rain.

The smile faded when she closed the door and went back into the kitchen. Ted had told her he'd had a word with his mother about her constant picking. It hadn't made much difference.

'I'm at the end of my tether with you,' she said, sitting back at the table. 'This is my house and you'd better remember that before you start again with your nasty remarks in front of anybody else.'

'Aye and it's *my money* that paid for the shop that pays for the upkeep of *your house.*' Hannah's jowls shook with the force of her words. She wiped at the sweat on her forehead with a large white handkerchief. 'I speak as I find, my lady, and you've never been good enough for my Ted.'

'You didn't say that when you were so bloody lonely stuck up in that house of yours that you begged me to come and live with you.'

'You asked.'

'I didn't.'

'You did.'

Ellen rose and walked to stand over Hannah. 'You. Bloody. Asked,' she repeated. 'And, like I've said a thousand times, if I knew then what a selfish old cow you were I'd have run a mile.'

Even though she shrank slightly back in her chair the old woman raised a large pudgy fist and shook it at Ellen. 'If I'd known what kind of woman you were I wouldn't have let you within a hundred miles of my lad.' She sucked her lips into her toothless mouth and dabbed at her chin where she'd dribbled. 'You kept very quiet about her upstairs –' she paused to catch her breath in one loud intake, 'until it was too late for Ted to change his mind.' She pushed the handkerchief into her ample cleavage and wrapped her black cardigan tighter around her.

'Don't you ever again…' Ellen raised her hand and gritted her teeth. 'I've told you – and I know Ted's told you – leave Linda out of this. I'm warning you, Hannah, one word from me to Ted and you'll be gone, faster than a rat up a drainpipe. We'll both make sure of that.' She shoved her clenched hands into the pocket of her apron. She spun around and picking up the magazine, left the kitchen.

Upstairs, the two children were still napping. She checked the clock. She'd leave them for another half an hour.

In her room she flopped down on the bed and shuffled back against the headboard, pulling the eiderdown over her legs. The room was gloomy. Rain slapped on the window. She reached up and yanked on the lamp cord, intending to read in the pool of light. Instead she wrapped her arms around her waist and hugged herself, going over and over again what Hannah had said. She was trembling and a tight pain in her chest only allowed her to take shallow breaths. She'd had it a few days now and today it was worse. She couldn't take much more and she didn't know what to do. It was obvious Ted's talk to his mother had no effect, her nastiness had only increased. But up to today, she'd stopped the spiteful talk about Linda and directed all her venom at Ellen. Now she'd started again.

Gazing at the window against the dark sky all she could see was a reflection of the room. Except for Ted's bits and bobs strewn around, it hadn't changed much since she'd shared it with Mary, but that seemed ages ago. Sometimes she thought about how they used to snuggle up together, laughing and whispering until their father banged on the wall, yelling at them to shut up.

She began to cry. Once she started she couldn't stop. She tried but nothing halted the flood of tears, not even when Linda came into the room. Not even when she crawled onto the bed with Ellen and wrapped her thin arms around her.

Chapter 37

PRINCESS ANNE TO BALMORAL

Crowds gathered outside Clarence House as the young Princess Anne travelled with her mother and brother from their home to make their way north to Balmoral. Only the second outing since she was born.

Mary read the article with little interest and flicked through the pages. The resident columnist's by-line on page five jumped out at her.

Matron of the Pont y Haven hospital to marry German ex-POW Peter Schormann...

'Oh no!' Mary skimmed through the item:

... love thine (one-time) enemy ... my source at the hospital ... Mary Howarth, Matron at Pont y Haven will be one of the first in Wales

to marry a German ex POW … Peter Schormann, a former doctor and POW at a camp in the north of England … now an odd job man in the village of Llamroth where they live … fell in love at a time when it was totally forbidden … 'We are very happy,' says Miss Howarth, 'and don't see why others shouldn't be happy for us as well.' …will marry at Llamroth Church on Saturday 23rd December at 2 o'clock …

'Damn and blast.' Mary crumpled up the paper and threw it in the waste paper basket under her desk. Who would have talked to the *Clarion*? The answer was staring her in the face. She looked beyond the open door of her office and along the corridor filled with staff going about their business. Or my business, she thought, bitterly. 'Damn and blast "my source at the hospital",' she said, crossing the room and slamming the door.

Too angry to stay still she paced her office. She had a good mind to telephone the bloody newspaper, demand to know who they'd talked to, insist on speaking to whoever wrote the article. She couldn't remember the last time she'd been so furious.

An ambulance darkened the window as it passed, its bell shrill, insistent. At the same time the telephone rang. 'The Chairman would like to see you in the Conference Room, Matron.' The cool voice of his secretary held no hint of friendship.

Mary stood motionless, her hand still on the receiver, steadying her breathing. Pulling her shoulders back, she smoothed her hair away from her forehead, adjusted her cap and scrutinised herself in the mirror. Her blue eyes were resolute. 'All right,' she muttered, 'here we go.'

The corridor to the Conference Room had never seemed so long. Or so quiet. Mary was aware of the soft squeak of her heels on the tiles, the muffled sounds behind the closed doors of the wards, even the kitchens were quiet at this time, between breakfast and lunchtime. She had time to think as she strode, eyes fixed to the front. She needed to be ready to answer any questions if the hospital board members had seen the *Clarion*. She slowed to a halt. Or did she? Did she really have to defend herself? Was it any of their business? She kept this in mind as she settled in the chair opposite the six men and four women of the Board.

'We were aware of the rumours around the hospital about your – your domestic arrangements. And then, this morning, the *Clarion*…' Ivor Thomas almost spat out the words as though the name had left a bad taste in his mouth. 'Now I realise it is neither the business of the Board or of me as Chairman to make summary judgement without hearing your side of the situation—'

'No, it's not, Mr Thomas. And if you don't mind I will not be discussing my, as you call it, domestic situation,' Mary interrupted.

'Miss Howarth!' The remonstration came from Mrs Warburton-Thorpe, a tall, gaunt, very upright woman of about sixty with grey hair tightly scraped back from her face. She peered over her spectacles at Mary, clearly astounded. 'I don't think I've ever heard you be so rude.'

'Probably not, Mrs Warburton-Thorpe, but there again I have never been treated in such a fashion as I have lately. I realise you may have some concerns—'

'Indeed.' Mrs Warburton-Thorpe nodded. No one else said a word. Two of the men shuffled uncomfortably in their chairs.

'But I assume you concede that the hospital is functioning in an excellent manner, as it has over the last four years under my care.' Mary could hear the quiver in her voice and hoped they couldn't.

'Still, it's most unfortunate this has happened,' Ivor Thomas said. 'Dare I say even thoughtless and…'

'And?'

'Unprofessional.'

'In what way, Mr Thomas? Pont Y Haven has come on in leaps and bounds since I became Matron here and I pride myself that a great deal of the improvements were down to me.'

'Quite so.' This from a small woman at the other end of the table, new to the Board, who Mary only knew by sight. 'And I think we would be the first to acknowledge that.' Her large teeth gave her a lisp and when she smiled at Mary her lips didn't quite stretch over them.

Mary smiled in return before turning back to the Chairman who cleared his throat.

'We have convened the Board to discuss how this publicity affects the hospital.' With a flourish he produced a large blue handkerchief, took off his pince-nez and began to polish it vigorously. 'You are single but living with a man, consorting with…'

'Consorting!'

'With, I have to say, a person, er, a person, who could bring the hospital into disrepute.' He was sweating; the beads of perspiration bridged his nose.

'How?'

'I have no wish to discuss this further.'

'So you wish me to leave?' Mary kept her voice courteous but questioning. If they were going to sack her, he would have to say it. Through sheer stubbornness she would make him say it.

'You must appreciate our position, Miss Howarth, our reputation and that of the hospital.'

'And I have brought it into disrepute how exactly?'

'Well, I should think you would know how.'

'No.'

'Oh, this is getting us nowhere.' The interruption came from Mrs Warburton-Thorpe. 'Mr Chairman, we agreed with your proposal, it was seconded and passed by the Board even before Miss Howarth entered the room. We must ask Matron for her resignation.'

As though I have much choice, Mary thought.

'And wish her all success for the future.'

'Will you wish me to stay until you find a replacement?'

'That won't be necessary in the … er … in the circumstances.' The man folded his arms.

'Really, Mr Chairman, I must insist my objections are minuted. As I said before, this is a drastic action for the Board to take.' The small woman half rose in her seat.

'Thank you Miss Lewis, your, ah, your opinion has indeed been minuted.' He looked at Mrs Warburton-Thorpe who inclined her head. 'Now, please leave this to me.'

Miss Lewis subsided into her seat with a small murmur of protest.

Mary placed her hands on the arms of the leather chair and half stood. 'Will that be all, Mr Chairman?'

Flushed with annoyance, he was trying to keep his pince-nez on his nose. He gave up and pushed it into the top pocket of his jacket. 'It seems so, Miss Howarth, um, it seems so.' He almost appeared at a loss then said, 'I believe you have leave owing? Please feel free to take it as from today.'

'Thank you.'

As she closed the door she heard him say, 'Such a disappointment – quite the best Matron we ever had.'

'And such a shame you didn't feel able to tell her, Mr Chairman. Whatever I feel about her circumstances, that's the least we could do … thank her.' Mary recognised the clipped tones of Mrs Warburton-Thorpe and smiled; well, well, what a surprise. She lifted her chin and walked away.

'Miss Howarth?'

Mary turned. 'Miss Lewis?'

The small woman hurried forward, hand outstretched. 'I'd like to say good luck, my dear.' She blushed and said in hushed tones, 'My fiancé, he was Jewish and we were disowned by our families. I was only seventeen but I knew he was the only one for me. He died during the 'flu epidemic after the First War.' She spoke louder as two young nurses walked past with the heads down. 'I wish you and your fiancé all the luck in the world.'

129

'Thank you.' Mary had an almost overwhelming urge to cry. She turned on her heel.

Sitting at her desk, Mary laced her fingers together on the maroon leather pad set into the desktop and looked around her office. She felt strange, as though the last two hours were unreal and now she wasn't sure what to do. She'd emptied the drawer of all her personal things: her old copy of *Bailliere's Nurses' Complete Medical Dictionary*, a notepad and envelopes, gloves, a scarf, hairpins, pens; packed the blue vase from on top of the filing cabinet, her photographs of Tom and her mother, and the few books she liked to read whenever she had a quiet lunchtime, from the shelf under the window; straightened her blotter parallel to the edge of the writing pad, putting her pen and pencil pot neatly next to it.

She was afraid to stand, uncertain that her legs would take her weight.

This had been her place in the hospital for the last four years. She knew every inch of the room: the spidery cracks in the wall above the door, just visible under the cream paint; the stain on the carpet by the old green leather armchair where Bob had spilt his tea during a meeting, the subject of which she couldn't now recall; the green velvet curtains, worn along the hem. As her gaze moved slowly around the room it was as though she was distanced, watching herself taking it all in.

Through the panelled oak door of her office she could hear the muted sound of trolley wheels and, further away, the faint clatter of metal trays. A smell of cabbage and custard drifted in the air through the open window. It was odd to think that the everyday activities – the hustle and bustle of the wards, the coming and going of ambulances, the laughter and chatter in the staff canteen – were going on. Would carry on when she left.

The copper fingers on the wall clock juddered with a loud clunk to half past eleven and startled her into action. Removing her lacy cap and the white plastic cuffs that covered her sleeves, she looked at her face in the mirror above the small sink as she washed her hands. The whites of her eyes were bloodshot and she was very pale. Carefully applying powder and lipstick, unusual for her at work, she combed and pinned her hair back under the cap.

The sky was densely blue, so clear for September. A skewed spark of sunlight flashed across the glass, dazzling her. She was consumed with an overwhelming urge to go home, to find Peter, to hold him.

She stood, looped her handbag over her arm and picked up the cardboard box, balancing it against her chest. There was nothing else for her to do. Since the meeting, no one had been near her office. It was as though the whole place was holding its breath, waiting for her to leave.

The door clicked firmly behind her. She slid the sign to 'Out of Office', touched the shining brass plate with her name engraved on it and wondered how soon the caretaker would be told to take it down.

When she turned around Vivienne Allott was standing halfway along the corridor watching her.

Mary strode towards her, following her until Vivienne was backed against the wall. 'It was you, wasn't it? You went to the *Clarion* with your spiteful tales?'

Vivienne lifted her shoulders. 'If it wasn't me it would have been someone else. You're not as popular as you like to think.' She paused for a few seconds. 'Matron.'

Mary narrowed her eyes, meeting the girl's stare. She saw the glint of triumph. Don't, she told herself, don't rise to the bait. Without speaking she spun on her heels. She didn't look at Vivienne Allott but as she passed Mary heard the soft snigger. For a moment her step faltered, the urge to scream abuse at the girl almost irresistible.

Straightening her shoulders and lifting her chin, she quickened her pace and walked out of the hospital.

By the time Mary got off the bus it was mid afternoon. She sat on the wall, her back to the sea. The village, perched on the rising hill a few hundred yards away, surrounded the church where they would be married. The windows in the rows of cottages caught the low sun, the lustrous reflection thrown back towards the sea. From her vantage point Mary could see people going in and out of the post office and shop. She glanced to her left where the lane curved; to where Tom was killed.

She had the sudden urge to be home.

Peter wasn't there. She sat on the front steps. The wind carried with it the smell of the sea, a fishy, pungent seaweed smell that stung her nose. A group of squabbling seagulls, losing their battle against the wind, skidded along the water nearby. She watched them riding the scummed waves, dipping and shaking their heads.

Mary wondered if Vivienne Allott would ever realise or regret how much damage she'd caused by her vicious tongue. She doubted it. People like that never did; they just spread their poison and moved on, leaving people's lives destroyed. Well, she wouldn't let that happen. One way or another she and Peter had a good life in front of them. They had one another and that was how it would always be.

She began to cry.

However unfair it was, and however justified her anger, the shame and humiliation of being dismissed from her post and the fear of what the future held without her wages filled Mary with dread.

Chapter 38

'I need to talk to you.' Jean's scarf was flattened to her head by the rain.

Cold apprehension spread along Ellen's spine. Hell's bells, she

132

knows about Patrick. 'Come on in, it's tipping down.' She let Jean pass and forced the front door closed. It always bloody stuck. It was on Ted's list of 'things to do' that never got done. 'Go in the front room. You'll have to keep your coat on, it's always a bit chilly in there, but it'll be better than going in the kitchen.' From the looks of things the last thing Jean needed was Hannah Booth listening in. And the last thing Ellen wanted to do was give her mother-in-law another supply of gossip.

'Thanks.' Jean struggled to undo the wet knot of her scarf and gave up, pulling it over her head. She looked around the room. 'I don't think I've been in here since before Patrick and me were married. You've changed the three piece suite and the wallpaper,' she said, her voice flat. 'It's nice.'

Ellen switched on the standard lamp and drew the curtains. 'It needed doing. Ted did the hall as well. Got rid of that awful paper with the revolting cabbage roses.'

'I remember.' Twisting the scarf in her hands, Jean said again, 'I need to talk to you.'

'Mmm?' Ellen noticed the grate was full of dead ashes but couldn't remember when they'd last lit a fire in it. 'Sit down. Take the weight of your feet.' Her mouth was dry. Both knew they were edging towards Jean's reason for coming to the house, neither wanted to be the first to speak about it.

'I know we haven't always got on and I know I've been a bit of a cow in the past.'

'Still are, sometimes.' Ellen gave a burst of nervous laughter. Trust Jean to come when Ted was at the shop.

Jean forced her mouth into a smile but said nothing.

In the other room, Hannah coughed, a dry, hard, prolonged sound.

'Mrs Booth not well?'

'It's a heavy hint. She knows you're here and wonders why we've not gone into the kitchen.'

Jean nodded thoughtfully. 'I see.' She sat down on the sofa, winding the scarf around her hands until it was coiled tight and dripping water onto the carpet.

'That'll be an old rag by the time you've finished.' Ellen reached over and gently took it from her.

It was as though the gesture finally broke the barrier. The tears flowed silently. 'It's Patrick.' Jean hunched her shoulders under her coat, stuck her hands up the sleeves, and rocked back and forth. 'It's Patrick … he's…' She couldn't carry on.

'He's hit you again?'

'What? No…he's…'

There was no longer any use pretending she didn't understand what Jean meant. 'You've found out then,' Ellen said, almost relieved to be giving voice to the words.

'What do you mean?' Jean's voice was husky.

Ellen heard footsteps on the pavement outside. She watched the shadowy silhouettes pass the window before she spoke. She needed to be cautious. She could be jumping on the wrong bandwagon here.

'You said you wanted to talk?'

'It's about something our Jacqueline saw.' Jean lifted up her chin, steadied her voice as best she could. 'And from what you said, I think you know what that was.'

'No.'

'You said I'd found out. So you know something.'

Ellen bent her head, fiddled with the Kirby grips that held her French pleat together. Still looking at the floor she said, 'What exactly did she say she saw?'

'Patrick and her next door to you … kissing.' Jean waited for the reaction. There was none. 'How long have you known?'

Ellen prevaricated. 'Known?' She met Jean's eyes and sighed. 'Not long.'

'How long?' Jean leant forward, narrowing the gap between them. She had the urge to grasp Ellen by the shoulders and shake her.

'Since I came back home from Mary's.' Ellen shifted back in the chair.

'How?'

'How what?'

'How did you find out?'

Another pause. 'Ted told me.' Ellen smoothed the sleeves of her jumper along her arms. 'Look, all I know is that Patrick started calling round here months ago.' She glanced at Jean. 'I didn't know why at first, all I knew was he drove me mad talking politics – got Ted all worked up as well.'

'And?' Jean dismissed Ellen's last remarks with a shake of her head. 'What's that got to do with him and…?' She paused, began speaking again, slowly, working it out for herself. 'He went from here to next door, didn't he? In the front door and out the back? Very nice. And you're trying to tell me you didn't know anything about it?' She gave a derisive snort. 'I'm not a fool, please don't treat me like one.'

Ellen's protest was strident. 'We … I didn't know. Didn't realise what he was doing. Neither did Ted at first but he caught them at it in the backyard once.'

Jean flinched; the unwanted picture instantly conjured up.

'He didn't tell me though,' Ellen added hastily. 'Look, I'm sorry, Jean. I know you won't believe me but I didn't know anything about it until a few weeks ago. I only found out when Ted came for me from our Mary's. Honest.'

'Honest! You don't know the meaning of the word.'

'There's no need for petty insults,' Ellen retaliated. 'After all the flack you gave me at Mary's, do you really think it wouldn't have come out in one of the rows we had?' She stood, noticing for the first time how ill Jean looked. The sallowness of her skin emphasised the dark smudges under her eyes and the red swollen lids. The involuntary surge of concern for her sister-in-law was alien to Ellen.

Jean bowed her head. 'Sorry.'

'I'm trying to help you here.' Ellen paced from door to fireplace and back before she spoke again. 'I'll tell you what I know, shall I?'

135

'Go on.' Jean straightened her shoulders and ran her fingers across her forehead, wiping away the rain that still dripped from her hair.

'Right, and this is the truth, all I know is that Patrick used us as an excuse to see her next door. I didn't cotton on at all but, like I said, Ted found out and he told Patrick to pack it in. If he wants to play away from home, don't involve us.'

Jean moaned.

'I'm sorry.' Ellen put a hand on Jean's shoulder. She could feel her trembling under the wet raincoat. She must be frozen. 'I am sorry, really. Patrick can be a right bastard sometimes but this beats the lot.'

'It's not the first time, believe me,' Jean muttered.

'I'm sorry.'

Patrick had always thought he was God's gift but for some reason he'd also appeared to think the world of this plain, dumpy woman. And he idolised Jacqueline. Ellen couldn't believe he'd chance losing his daughter. 'Well, he's a bloody idiot!'

There was a slow heavy scuffling on the linoleum in the hall, a sound of breathless wheezing.

'Wait a minute.' Ellen crossed the room and quickly opened the door. 'What are you doing?'

'Just coming to tell you I'm off for a lie down, my leg's killing me.' Hannah moved her bulk from side to side, trying to peer over Ellen's shoulder.

I wish! Ellen thought. 'For your afternoon rest? Like you normally do, you mean?' The sarcasm wasn't missed.

'No need to be like that. I thought I'd see if there was anything I could do.'

Always good at the pretence, Ellen almost said, bitterly aware that few grasped how unpleasant Ted's mother could be. She made her skin crawl.

Hannah leaned against the doorframe for support, her arms, tightly encased in her cardigan sleeves crossed over her large bosom. Casually, as if accidently, she nudged Ellen, trying to get her to move.

Ellen stood her ground. 'No, everything's fine.'

Hannah puckered both lips and sniffed loudly. 'Right, then, I'll be off.' She pushed herself upright and made a great show of pulling her handkerchief out of her pocket and blowing her nose. 'Bye,' she called, trying one last time to see beyond Ellen.

Jean didn't answer.

Hannah used the doorframe to balance as she turned and moved slowly towards the kitchen, her hands splayed on the wall on both sides of her. At the bottom of the stairs she gave Ellen one last venomous look before pushing aside the velvet curtain and heaving herself onto the first step.

'Good riddance.' Ellen looked back into the front room. 'Come on, take that coat off and let's get you into the kitchen in front of the fire now she's gone.'

They could hear Hannah's slow ascent to her room, the stairs and floorboards groaning under her weight until, at last the door to what had been Patrick's room banged closed.

'Right, a brew?'

'Please, if it's no trouble.'

'Nope, none at all.' Ellen crossed the kitchen and shovelled more coal on the fire. Sullen smoke oozed through the lumps so she moved them about with the poker and flames popped up here and there. She glanced at the clock. Ted and the kids would be back from the shop in an hour. Hopefully Jean would have gone by then. 'Have you told our Mary?'

'No, I wanted to be sure.'

'You should. She'll know what to do.'

'I know what I'm going to do, thanks.' Jean rubbed her sodden handkerchief under her nose one final time.

From the set of her mouth and the unwavering look she gave her, Ellen knew as well. 'You're going to leave our Patrick, aren't you?'

'Certainly not – I'm going to kick him out.'

Well, there's not much to say to that, Ellen thought. And nothing she could do or wanted to do. She had enough on her plate. But no doubt, sooner or later, she'd get dragged kicking and screaming into it whether she wanted to or not.

But she wouldn't deal with it on her own. She was determined. Mary had to come and help. One way or another she'd make sure of that.

They drank their tea staring into the fire and listening to the rain splattering on the window.

'I've really missed Mary these last few years,' Jean said, not taking her eyes off the flames. 'She's the only real friend I've had.'

'Oh?'

'We made a good team on the ward, nursing together at the Granville during the war.' Now the decision was made; now she knew she would make him leave, Jean didn't want to say any more about her husband. It was rather a relief to talk about something else after two days of mourning her failing marriage. 'In a way I miss that too. Not the war, the nursing.' She rested the mug of tea against her mouth, glad of the warmth on her skin. She was just about thawing out. 'You know? The gratitude of the patients?' She turned to Ellen. 'Even though half the time we couldn't understand what they said, we could still tell they were grateful.' She frowned. 'Mary said it changed at the end of the war, after I left, when the Granville was made into a transit camp for the Germans coming back from Canada. But I didn't see any of that. By then I was married and had Jacqueline.' The thought brought her back to the present and she frowned.

'Another brew?'

'No, I must be going. I've a lot to do.' Jean sucked in her lips. 'And I need to do it before tonight.'

She stood and fumbled with her coat. Fastening it she noticed, for the first time, the photograph almost hidden behind a large glass vase on the sideboard. The picture lay crooked in the frame where the corner was loose. It was of her and Patrick on their wedding day.

Ellen saw her looking. 'Mam left it behind when they moved. She said they had two copies.'

'It was a lovely day,' Jean said. The memory hurt. 'We went from the Registry Office to the Crown on the bus. You should have seen the driver's face.' She stopped. 'Of course you did see, you were there.' And tried to spoil things in a fit of jealousy, if I remember rightly. But she kept that thought to herself.

They stood staring at the photograph, lost in their own thoughts.

Jean closed her eyes. Patrick could have run a mile after she lost the first baby but he hadn't. The flash of love and gratitude was deadened by what he was doing now, what he had done since they were married. He seemed incapable of keeping his hands off other women. Of course her mother was relieved they'd married, probably less worried about her daughter being ruined in front of the neighbours than of being terrified of losing her meal ticket on the black market. At the time, Patrick had his fingers in many pies. Still had, she supposed. These days she didn't bother to ask.

She looked around for her scarf.

'It must be still in the front room. I'll get it.' Ellen hurried off.

Jean looked in the age-spotted mirror by the back door, fluffed up her now dried curls. She chose not to look at her face, shiny and flushed from the tears. 'I've still got my wedding outfit, you know,' she called, 'back of the wardrobe.' Ellen came back into the kitchen, scarf in hand. It was obvious she wasn't listening. 'Doesn't fit now, of course,' Jean said, more to herself than the other woman. 'Thanks.' She took the scarf from Ellen and pushed it into her coat pocket. 'No point in putting it on, it's wet through.'

'Borrow Hannah's old umbrella.' Ellen went into the scullery and came out unfurling a brown umbrella covered in mould marks. 'Chuck it when you get home, it's had its day.'

She'd hardly finished speaking when the gate to the yard crashed open and they could hear someone whistling. Ellen groaned. 'Oh my God.'

Jean looked at her in bewilderment. 'What?'

The latch on the back door snapped down, the door opened and a young woman poked her head around it. 'Wonder if I can borrow…'

'Doreen,' Ellen said.

Chapter 39

Ellen looked from one woman to the other, she saw both faces drain of colour.

'Fuckin 'ell.' The woman held on to the door, the rain splashing in off the doorstep onto the linoleum, but no one noticed.

Jean's mouth twisted. She drew herself up. 'Quite,' she said.

Doreen Whittaker flushed. Chin raised high and with a defiant set to her mouth she stepped inside and leaned against the wall, arms folded.

Jean's legs buckled. Ellen moved quickly, catching hold of her elbow. 'Here, sit down.' She lowered Jean onto one of the chairs and stood behind her, her hands on her shoulders. 'You're all right,' she said.

Jean stared at Doreen.

'I'll get you a drink.' Ellen crossed to the scullery, passing Doreen. 'What?' she said curtly.

'Some sugar?' Doreen Whittaker raised a bowl. Composed, she stood, back arched to emphasise her swollen belly under the maternity smock, meeting Jean's scrutiny calmly.

'None to spare, sorry,' Ellen said. 'What's up? Mrs Miles decided she's not going to be a soft touch anymore?'

Doreen glowered. 'She's not in, and anyway she's not a soft touch, she's a good neighbour.'

Jean couldn't believe she was listening to them talking about sugar when her whole world was crumbling. She opened her mouth but no words came out. She was afraid.

Ellen let the water run for a minute, rinsing a cup under the tap and finally running water into it. 'You still here?' Ellen glanced over her shoulder. 'Can't you take a hint?'

'No,' Jean said, 'I want to hear what she has to say for herself.' Her head spun. The kitchen whirled in a stream of colours.

Ellen moved to her side. 'Drink this.'

Jean glanced at her, gratefully, and took the cup.

'Say for myself? What are you talking about?' Doreen flicked her fringe back, a slight smile on her face. But there was trepidation in her eyes and it was obvious to Ellen she was as alarmed as Jean with the encounter.

'You know who I am?' Jean said.

Doreen lifted her shoulders. 'Seen you around, I suppose. What's the matter? I only came to borrow some sugar.'

'Shut up about the sugar,' Jean said calmly. 'You know I'm Patrick's wife.'

'Who?'

Jean saw the change in her face at the mention of his name. 'Don't play games with me, lady, I'm not stupid.' She sipped the water, took in and held her breath slightly before letting it go. The room stilled, the colours faded, the rain slowed to an occasional splash on the window. 'Whose baby is it?' she said, almost casually.

'What do you mean? I'm a married woman.'

'Whose baby?' Jean said again.

'My business, I think,' Doreen said, smoothing the flowered top over her stomach and resting her hand on it.

The boldness wasn't lost on Jean. She wanted to leap at the woman, tear clumps of her hair out, to scratch and destroy the beauty. Because there was no doubt she was beautiful, she thought bitterly. Trust Patrick to go for a lovely face however vacuous the mind – or how coarse the voice.

'My husband's?' Jean hadn't expected to be so forthright. And now she was terrified of the answer. Her world was falling apart.

Doreen shrugged but then said, 'Course not.' Then, as though she understood she'd given herself away, she said, 'Who did you say your husband was?'

'You know full well who he is.' Jean jumped up. 'Is that…' She pointed with a shaking finger at Doreen's stomach. 'Is that his?'

Doreen looked Jean up and down. 'Could be … yes,' she said finally.

Chapter 40

'I'm going bloody nowhere.' Patrick emptied out his clothes from the suitcase onto the bed. 'We can sort this out.'

'Sort out what?' Jean grabbed the handle and tugged it away from him, her face flushed with temper. 'What's there to sort out?' She began shoving his things back into it. 'You've had an affair. Again. But this time you've gone one better and you've made your floozy pregnant.' She stumbled over the word; the desperation she felt each month, knowing yet again she wasn't pregnant, fuelled her rage. She made an impatient sound as she tried to close the case and couldn't. A sleeve from one of his jumpers snagged in the lock.

'You're fucking ruining that.' Patrick dragged the suitcase towards him.

The anger flashed through Jean and she pushed him. He overbalanced and when he steadied himself he raised his hands, the veins standing out at his temples.

Jean backed away. For one awful moment she thought he was going to hit her again. Her heart thumped, sweat prickled her scalp. 'Go on,' she said, 'and it'll be the last time, Patrick Howarth.' The fear was intermingled with sudden, almost physical hatred.

Patrick froze. Gazing straight at her he said, 'I'm sorry, Jean, I'm so sorry.'

'Once was more than enough.' The relief hardened her voice. 'I was a fool. I should have left you then.' She knew now she'd got the upper hand. 'I want you to leave, Patrick.' She stepped towards him, more confident now. 'I want you to go.'

'No.' He was almost pleading. 'I've been bloody stupid. I've made a bad mistake.'

'Just the one?' She crossed her arms, rubbing her damp palms on the sleeves of her cardigan. The pounding in her chest was slowing. 'Is that how you see all your tarts ... as mistakes? You've got a bloody nerve. And this one? This one that's pregnant?'

'Doesn't make any difference. It might not be mine. Doreen's admitted—'

'Don't you say her name in this house,' Jean hissed. She flung out an arm. 'In this room, in our bedroom, you bastard.'

'I'm sorry. I don't want to lose you.'

'And Jacqueline,' Jean said. 'Don't forget your daughter. You're losing her too.'

'I'm sorry.'

'You've already said that. I've heard it all before,' Jean jeered. She couldn't help herself.

'I mean it. I don't know how it started ... how any of it started.' Patrick paused and then began speaking again. 'It's always been the same – one minute we're okay and then the next you're in a mood and I don't even know what I've done. I'm not explaining myself well. I'm not good with words, not like you anyway.' He ran his hands over his head, held them there. His eyes glistened. 'Put me in front of a market stall or a load of blokes at a union meeting and I'm off. I can sell sand to the Arabs. But with you, with anything to do with you, I make a bollocks of it. You can run rings round me.'

'So it's my fault is it? You can't keep your trousers buttoned up because I have moods? Is that what you tell yourself? Don't you

143

even try to blame me for all your … your gallivanting, you sod.'
Jean breathed deeply. He was unbelievable. Yet, even as she spoke
she struggled to maintain the disgust she'd felt. She'd not seen him
so cowed before and she didn't like it. What do you want? she
asked herself. The answer came quickly – she wanted him to love
her as much as she wanted to punish him. She waited.

'No, it's me, it's all me.' Patrick straightened. 'It's always been
me. I've never treated you right.' His voice was strong. 'And I
promise I'll make everything okay. Whatever it takes.'

'It's too late.' Jean moved her head, dismissing him. She
dragged the suitcase towards her again, pushed the sleeve inside
and clicked the lock.

'What's happening?' Jacqueline stood in the doorway,
uncertainty on her face. 'Are we going on holiday?' Her eyes were
fixed on the suitcase. 'Are we going somewhere?'

'No.' Patrick spoke calmly, meeting Jean's eyes. 'Nobody's going
anywhere.'

Chapter 41

Ellen cursed softly under her breath. She'd known that one way
or the other she'd get dragged into Jean and Patrick's mess. She'd
telephone Mary as soon as the children's breakfast things were
cleared away; Mary would have to come to Ashford, help sort it
all out. It wasn't fair she had to do this on her own. It wasn't her
problem.

Ellen swished the last of the cutlery around in the water, her
thoughts skittering back half an hour to when Jean had arrived
unexpectedly with Jacqueline to take Linda to school. It was a
shock when Jean had told her Patrick had refused to leave so she
and Jacqueline were staying at her mother's. Linda's giggles of
excitement at the unexpected treat of having her cousin living so
close again had stopped when Jacqueline cried. Ellen couldn't stop

herself thinking that the house on Moss Terrace would seem pokey to her sister-in-law after the one on Manchester Road.

She took the pot towel off the hook. Without turning round she knew Hannah was standing on the last step of the stairs, holding back the curtain. She heard the wheezing breaths, the rustle of her shapeless black dress. 'Ted's not home yet from the bakery,' she said, 'but I've made porridge for when he gets back. You can have some of that.'

'No eggs?'

'None in the corner shop. They hadn't delivered. Didn't deliver yesterday either, something to do with a shortage of hen food – apparently it's still rationed.' Ellen swirled the little mop head round in a cup, trying to get the tea stain off. 'Mrs Cox's hens aren't laying.'

Hannah snorted and shuffled towards the scullery. Holding on to the table and chairs, her movements were more side to side than forward.

Ellen watched her from the corner of her eye, noticing with distaste the folds of her red-veined ankles settling over the sides of her slippers each time she stopped to take in a wheezing breath.

At the sink Hannah took the bottle of milk out of the basin of cold water and carried it dripping to the kitchen table. She groaned as she lifted one leg after the other off the buffet her feet were resting on. She saw the look on Ellen's face. 'If you had to put up with my legs you'd have summat to moan about.'

'I have you to put up with,' Ellen said, 'that's worse than varicose ulcers any day.'

Hannah carefully peeled off the silver cap and poured the milk into a bowl.

'You've taken all the cream off the top,' Ellen said. 'You could have shaken it.'

The woman turned her back to her.

'It's just that Ted likes cream on his porridge as well.'

Silence. Then, 'So, that's another bastard what's going to be born into your family.'

Ellen was stunned by the cruel baldness of the statement. Hannah had obviously overheard the row between Jean and Doreen.

'Your brother's got her next door up the tub, then?' Hannah dragged a chair out from under the table with a screech, setting Ellen's teeth on edge. 'Seems these things run in the family eh? Happen it's a good job there's one brother less.' She grinned, showing red wet gums. 'Oh no, I forgot, from what I heard, women weren't his thing, right?'

Hannah was hunched over the porridge stirring it when Ellen slapped her. Her head whipped round with the force and the spoon clattered across the kitchen floor. Hannah balanced herself by flattening her palms on the table on either side of the bowl. When she heaved herself up with a hoarse roar, Ellen left, the back door vibrating with the slam.

Ellen steadied herself against the dustbin in the backyard and leant forward, folded her arms over her head. She felt winded by the hatred inside her. She wouldn't go back inside until Ted came back from his night shift. 'I'll kill her, so help me God, before long I'll kill her.' She took in a long shuddering gulp of air and even though the yard retained the warmth of the morning sun, a chill shook her. When the tears, held back by anger, brimmed and poured down her face, they fell unheeded on the frills at the neck of her apron.

Further along the alleyway someone banged a gate, a pram trundled past, and Ellen heard the bouncy squeak of springs as it was pushed over the cobbles. Pins and needles prickled in her arms. She lowered them, rubbing hard at the skin. She glanced up at the open bedroom window. Still no sound. William was a good little sleeper and Linda was in school, so at least there were no worries about either of them.

From the kitchen Ellen heard the mantle clock strike ten

o'clock. Ted was late. He must have waited until Evelyn Stott arrived to open the shop. She'd been in the yard for almost an hour, just sitting and trying not to think. Now she felt just about calm enough to go back inside. Pushing herself off the dustbin and stretching, the tingling in her arms subsided but her backside was numb. She rubbed her buttocks and circled the yard stamping her feet, stopping when she heard the lavatory next door flush and Doreen's husband cough. A whiff of Harpic floated over the wall; a bit different from the stench from the lavvy when old Ma Jagger lived next door.

She wondered how Doreen's husband would react when he found out that the baby might be Patrick's.

Chapter 42

Jean's head ached. She poked one finger behind her glasses and rubbed her eyes, swollen and itchy from crying. She watched the two little girls run across the concrete playground to join the line of children already outside the main door. Linda's grey socks had already slipped down, her thin legs encircled by red lines from the knotted elastic bands that were supposed to hold them up to her knees.

She was worried about Jacqueline. She'd hardly answered Linda's chatter all the way to school. She knew her daughter was upset, both about the quarrel and that they were staying with her Granny Winterbottom. She'd almost had to drag Jacqueline to Moss Terrace. But Patrick wouldn't leave and Jean couldn't be around him so she had no choice. She'd try to explain everything to Jacqueline after school.

Relieved there were no other mothers about to ask awkward questions, she leaned against the low wall that surrounded the small building. The stone was cold against her legs but not as cold as she felt inside. She couldn't remember the last time she was as unhappy as this.

The Headmistress, holding the large brass bell by its wooden handle, frowned at the restless children, inspecting them. A scuffle broke out between two boys hitting one another with their school caps, promptly brought to a halt by a quick cuff from one of the teachers who paced up and down the lines.

'Mrs Howarth?' The Headmistress was waving at her. What now? Jean saw all the children turn round to look. 'We have the nit nurse coming this afternoon. We haven't had Jacqueline's permission form back. Do you have it with you?'

'No but it's fine.' Jacqueline would be mortified, she thought, seeing the others giggling. She was glad to see Linda's arm slip around her daughter's waist.

Unwilling to move, to carry on with the pretence of a normal day, she stood for a long time staring up at the tiny bell tower on the school roof that hadn't held a bell since the early days of the war. When she was small, that bell announced the beginning and end of the school day.

Soon she heard the singing in assembly. It was an old familiar hymn, *'I'll be a sunbeam for Him'*, and she listened until the last notes of the piano died away. Jacqueline's favourite. Perhaps she should have kept her home after all. It wasn't the first argument she'd heard since she was little but it was the worst. And if *she* didn't know if things would ever be the same again between her and Patrick, how must their daughter be feeling?

She walked slowly along the short lane from the school, past the old air raid shelter, now bricked up, and onto Huddersfield Road, reluctant to go back to her mother's. At the entrance to Skirm Park she walked in. At the first bench she sat down. The fragrance of the low spreading red rose bushes wafted around her. She bent down and picked up a couple of fallen petals, crushed them in her hand and lifted them to her nose. Patrick had bought a red rose as a surprise to give to her on the first night of their honeymoon. She remembered being horrified at the thought of the price. Months afterwards he confessed he'd done a deal on the black market.

Yet, despite that, it was those gestures which endeared him to her. However angry she was with him he always managed to charm her round somehow. But not this time. Yesterday had been the final straw.

She brushed her palms together, ridding them of the last of the crushed rose petals, and rubbed the red stain from her skin.

What would happen next Jean didn't know. She tried to forget the gloating expression on her mother's face when they'd walked through the door with suitcases. Elsie Winterbottom had left Jean in no doubt that she'd never expected her marriage to last. And, for once Jean bitterly agreed with her. Marrying Patrick had been the worst mistake of her life.

Chapter 43

Ellen braced herself to go back into the house. Things had gone too far. Ted would have to tell his mother to go, whatever else happened. Her nerves wouldn't take any more. He had to find her somewhere else to live. Anything as long as it meant Hannah left Henshaw Street.

With her thumb on the latch Ellen listened at the door. There were no sounds. With a bit of luck her mother-in-law had gone to her bedroom.

She ran her hands over the front of her pinny, pulling the frills straight. Tucking her blond hair behind her ears she lifted her chin, pushed the door open and went in, crossing her arms.

Hannah was lying on the floor, her eyes open and blank. It seemed to Ellen they were fixed on her. Other than letting her arms drop, Ellen didn't move. The sudden whooshing sound in her ears blocked out all but one thought. She'd killed Ted's mother.

Just as quickly, the noise went and she heard the dripping of the scullery tap, simmering water murmuring in the Ascot above the sink, the clock softly ticking, a bluebottle that droned and patted on the window.

Acid bile rose in Ellen's mouth and she swallowed. Skirting around the body on tiptoe as though the movement would bring life back into the shapeless mound sprawled in front of the armchair, she ran upstairs. In the children's room William was still asleep. Ellen leant over him watching the way his breath quivered his lower lip and lifted his chest under his pyjamas. She felt her own body taking in air to match the same rhythmic movement and it calmed her. He murmured but didn't wake when she lifted him and held him close, his skin warmly damp against her neck. The nearness comforted her. Creeping downstairs she avoided looking at the body, moving swiftly out of the kitchen and through the yard, leaving the back door and gate open. Her need to be with Ted became more urgent with each step.

Skidding on the cobbles in her slippers she ran to the top of the alleyway. She stopped and looked along Greenacre Street. The quivering that took over her whole body was unexpected. Her back to the end house wall, she slid to the ground with William in her lap.

And then she acknowledged the emotion that flooded through her.

It was relief.

Chapter 44

'I'm sorry Mary, I didn't know who else to turn to.'

'No, I understand Ted, you were right to call me. I'll get the earliest train I can tomorrow.' Mary slowly replaced the receiver. She put her hand to her throat as though to press away the lump that seemed to be choking her.

'What is it?' Gwyneth was still slightly breathless from running to fetch Mary to her telephone. She stood by Mary's side, her brow furrowed with anxiety.

'It's Ellen. She's had some sort of breakdown. And Ted's mother's had a heart attack. She's dead. Ted wants me to go up there to help with the children while he sorts everything out.' She moved her head in bewilderment. 'Ellen telephoned me last week to tell me Jean had left Patrick. I was worried but I was glad at the same time. I'd said to leave him when she was here.' Gwyneth nodded. 'I told Ellen they just had to get on with it.' Mary's hand moved to her mouth. 'I asked her how she was managing with Ted's mother and she said it was hard so I said she should tell Ted again. Oh Gwyneth, I was so angry, because when they were here, all they seemed to be bothered about was how losing Tom affected them. They both thought I should go back to Ashford, but only because it was best for them. And now this has happened.'

Gwyneth took Mary's hand between hers. 'Ellen has cried wolf so often, *cariad,* how were you to know?'

'I should have.' Mary bent down to kiss Gwyneth. 'Thanks for trying to make me feel better, love, but Ellen's my little sister and I should have seen some of this coming. She's always relied on me and now I've let her down. I need to tell Peter what's happening. I'll see you before I go in the morning.'

'No.' Peter followed her across the room as she opened the wardrobe door and shook two dresses off their hangers, throwing them into the suitcase on the bed. 'No Mary, you cannot go.'

She lifted a jumper and cardigan from the shelf in the wardrobe. 'Why not?' She folded the woollens and the dresses without looking at him.

'Your work. They may yet need you.'

'They don't. I've been sacked.' Her words were clipped. The devastation of losing her job so suddenly, her vocation, a calling she'd worked so hard for all her adult life, was still raw.

'You think it my fault?' he said. 'That is why you are going.' It was a flat statement.

'No, of course not.' Startled, she stopped what she was doing and stared at him, clutching a jumper to her chest.

'I feel it is as though you blame me.'

'No.' She shook her head. 'Of course I don't. We've talked about this, Peter.'

He wasn't listening. He moved restlessly around the room. 'Yes.' He nodded emphatically. 'Yes, that is what you think.'

'No, that's not true. Honestly, love, it was my choice. I would probably have left eventually, once we were married anyway.' She smiled. 'You know, when we started a family?' It didn't help with the memory of her humiliation in front of the Board, or the loss of her self-respect, but it was something to hold onto.

He didn't return her smile. What was wrong with him? Standing still he crossed his arms. 'The wedding?'

So that's what it was. 'Isn't until December, two months away. I'll be back long before then.' Mary opened a drawer and rifled through, choosing nightgowns and underwear. 'And, if I'm not, if we have to put it off until everything's sorted, that's what we'll do.' She folded her woolly dressing gown. The Henshaw Street house could be freezing in the mornings at this time of year. 'But I will be back, don't worry.'

'No!'

'What do you mean, no?' She was stunned. 'They need me, Peter.'

'I need you.' He sounded infuriated.

'Peter—' She stopped, wondering how she else could describe the catastrophe that had happened. 'Things are in turmoil up there. We can't just ignore it. We have a future together, you and me. I love you and I will love being your wife. But for now I have to put the others before what I want.'

When he didn't answer she assumed he'd come to terms with what she said. 'Look,' she said, continuing to pack, 'come with me. You got on well with Ted, you could talk to him, help him.'

'I cannot. My work here. I cannot take the chance that I will lose my customers.' He caught hold of Mary's arm so she was forced to stop and straighten up.

'Yes, I see that. But you need to see what I'm saying as well.' She gave him a quick hug before turning to look around the room, murmuring, 'I must take some soap with me, it's still difficult to get. So, scarves, gloves, stockings, suspender belt, spare shoes.' She halted, fingers to her chin. 'What else?'

She looked up, saw him pacing the room again. She thought she knew what was really wrong. 'I'll never expect you to go back there if you don't want to. I realise there are too many bad memories for you,' she said quietly.

'No, it is not that,' he said. 'I am only thinking, why?'

'Why what?' She studied him. He was pale, agitated. 'Peter?' The silence stretched between them before she said again. 'Why what?'

'Why do you feel you have to be the one to do this?'

'Because Ellen's my sister.' She flipped the lid of the suitcase down. 'And there is only me.' Her heart clenched when she thought how frightened Linda must be. William wouldn't understand, he was too young, but Linda would. She'd be taking everything in. 'I told you, the children need me, Peter.'

'And I told you.' He stood still but she saw he was shaking. 'I need you with me. They always call for you. It is not fair ... to you ... to me. It is not right they do this all the time. Since I came here we have had no time with just the two of us.'

She looked at him intently, trying to make sense of what he was saying, why he was saying it. His lips were thin, pressed so tightly a white line bordered them. For the first time she saw how cold his pale blue eyes were in anger.

She felt her own corresponding fury begin to build deep inside her. But still she reached out to him, aware of how much had happened since he first arrived in Llamroth. 'I know it must seem unfair, love. And there's really nothing I want more than to be here with you. But they're my family.' She stopped, remembering

153

the day she'd said almost the same words to Jean. But that time she'd meant her and Peter and, all at once, she saw how it must seem to him, how insignificant he must feel. She opened her arms to him, beseeching. 'I'm sorry.'

He jerked away from her.

'Peter!'

'*Nein.*' He held his hand to stop her speaking. 'I left my family to find you, to be with you.' He turned his back to her. 'I thought I was your family?' Peter raised his eyebrows, his voice haughty. 'That is what you have told me. I believed you. Yet now you leave.'

'Yes.' Mary raised her voice against his stubbornness. 'Now I leave. To help *my* family. I didn't ask you to come here. I didn't ask you to leave Germany. I was…' She stopped. She wouldn't lie, she hadn't been happy, but she'd learned to live with the sadness. 'I was okay before you came back.'

'So? Now we have the truth.' His proud upright stance was once something that had antagonised her, which she'd grown to love. Now it was as if she saw the old arrogance in the way he straightened his broad shoulders, in the emotionless gaze.

Mary felt suddenly sickened. 'I grew up with a bully,' she said. 'Two bullies actually. I thought you were different.'

'I am not the bully. The war showed me what is a bully.'

Mary thought of Frank and knew that Peter was thinking of him too. But his next words made no sense.

'I saved you from a bully.'

The room was still. They waited, watching one another.

Mary turned away from him and stared through the window. Across the road the blackthorn hedge shivered in the late afternoon breeze. Her mind worked feverishly. She blinked rapidly trying to work out what he was saying. 'Saved me?' she said finally, stressing her words. 'What do you mean, you saved me? When did you save me?' She sensed him move closer, heard his shallow rapid breathing.

'Mary.' This time he sounded more like the Peter she knew.

But she was angry. 'What do you mean, you saved me?' Her voice was harsh, because an unwelcome understanding was hovering at the back of her mind. How? How could it have been him? It was Tom. Perspiration trickled down the nape of her neck. Yet she was so cold.

She felt the touch of his fingers on the bare skin of her arm. This time she pulled away.

'What are you saying, Peter?'

'I should have told you before.' Now he was almost pleading. 'It would have been better if I had told you the day I came back.'

'Told me what?' Mary faced him.

'I did it for you.'

Oh God, no. She saw him swallow. Forcing out the words she whispered, 'Are you saying what I think you're saying?'

He nodded, his face slackened.

'Say it.'

He looked away, towards the window.

Mary grabbed the sleeve of his shirt. 'Say it.'

'It was I … I was the one … I killed Shuttleworth.'

She moaned and pushed him away from her. He stumbled back a couple of steps but kept his gaze on her.

She couldn't bear to look at him. Her voice trembled. 'You let me think it was Tom.'

'Tom, he knew, Mary, I swear he knew. He did not want me to tell you. That day, the day I arrived, we spoke about it. He told me it was all in the past and that I must not mention it again.' He tried to make her turn to him but she knocked his arm away. 'But I had to. Only a month before he was … he died … we talked. He was reluctant but he knew I needed to speak with him about it. We were working in the war memorial garden. On part of the plaque there were the names of four brothers, four sons from the same family.' Peter followed her around the room as she walked away from him. 'It made me think of the devastation of the war. And then of my part in it.' She stood still by the side of the bed. He stopped behind her. 'I told Tom, I said that for years I had saved lives and yet I do not think of that. I think of the one life I took. And I think of another man being blamed for my action, of Tom being blamed for what I had done. And I am ashamed.' She could barely hear him for the loud rushing noise in her ears but she felt the warmth of his breath on the back of her neck and it revolted her. 'Tom said he forgave me, Mary.'

She twisted away from him. 'I don't believe you.'

'He said he forgave me,' Peter insisted. 'I am not sorry I killed Shuttleworth. But I am sorry your brother was blamed. And I am sorry I kept the truth from you.'

'I told you about the letter he sent to Gwyneth.' She spun on her heel to face him and raised her voice. 'You let me think it was Tom,' she screamed at him, her eyes wild. 'No!' She stretched out her arm. 'Don't come near me. Don't ever come near me again.' The rage strengthened her. 'I hate you.'

All night she lay, silent and inflexible, by his side, knowing there was a gulf between them that had been inconceivable yesterday; one that grew with every hour that passed. She didn't sleep. The fear of saying goodbye to him in the morning, and the awareness in her heart of hearts that she wouldn't be coming back, kept her awake. Five years ago she had run away from Ashford to the safety of Wales. Now she would be escaping from the very place she'd felt protected, away from a man she loved yet couldn't abide being near.

In the morning she turned her head towards him. He was awake, watching her.

'It's over,' she said. 'You've ruined everything. I'll never forgive you.'

She left without speaking again.

Peter wanted to reach out, to touch her, to take the few strides it would need to get to the gate and to kiss her. In the end his guilt and his pride wouldn't let him.

He should have stopped her. But he didn't. He watched her walk away.

Chapter 45

Mary didn't remember much about the journey to Ashford. Her quarrel with Peter, the reality of Frank Shuttleworth's death, the horrifying memory of Tom flung into the air, melded into a confusion of images she couldn't escape. She stared at the passing scenery through the window. A thick low mist covered the ground, leaving only the bare branches of trees reaching skyward like skeletal arms. As the train moved northward, the shapes above the fog changed to the oblong mills or tall black-rimmed chimney stacks.

When she stepped out of the carriage, Ted was waiting. He wore only a jacket and his overalls, his shoulders hunched against the cold. Drizzle from the mist glistened on his flat cap and the metal studs on his boots clinked on the concrete flags as he stamped his feet. When Mary kissed his cheek his skin was damp and icily cold.

'How long have you been here?' she said. 'You look frozen.' She fastened the knot of her headscarf under her chin.

'I'm fine.' His tone was grim but he managed a smile and a hug as he took her case from her. 'Peter all right? He didn't mind you coming?'

'I'm here now,' she said, avoiding the question. 'Let's get home.' She gave an inward start; how easily she'd thought of Henshaw Street as home, even after all these years.

They walked quickly, Mary barely giving a glance towards the derelict mill. The Granville belonged in the past, just as she was determined Peter did. The hurt and bitterness increased each time she thought about the last years with Tom. She knew Tom was quite capable of forgiving Peter for all the years of suspicion and Mary persuaded herself she would have as well, if only he had confessed as soon as he realised Tom was blamed. On the train she'd been determined to concentrate on what was happening in Ashford but it was impossible. Worried her face had given her away she glanced at Ted but he just gave her a brief smile, concentrating on getting back to Henshaw Street as soon as they could.

They passed St John's church, the serried rows of gravestones behind the wide stone. Mary automatically looked towards the middle of the cemetery where Frank was buried. She shoved her hands deep into her pockets, drawing her coat closer and shutting out her thoughts. 'How's Ellen?'

'Won't get up.'

They crossed the road and hurried through Skirm Park. Mary had avoided the place each time she'd returned to Ashford, since they moved to Wales. There were too many memories of childhood, of Tom, of being separated from Peter, of the time she thought happiness was an elusive memory. And now it seemed that was finally, irrevocably true.

'Who's with her now?'

'Jean. She's been brilliant. But she's got more than enough on her plate without us.'

'How are things between her and Patrick?'

'Same.'

'Well, I can stay as long as you need me to.'

In the centre of the park the grey surface of the lake was ruffled by the wind that stung her cheeks.

'The wedding?'

'We've put it off for now.'

'Not because of us?'

'It doesn't matter.'

'Aw, Mary.'

They'd reached the other side of the park before a thought struck her. 'Ted, I'm sorry, I should have asked. How are you? With your mother…?'

He brushed her concern away.

She knew not to say any more. 'How are the children?' she said instead.

'Linda hasn't said anything. I think she knows my mother didn't like her and now she doesn't know how she's supposed to feel.'

'I'll talk to her.'

'Thanks. William doesn't understand. He's been coming with me to the bakery, thinks it's great.' He looked anxiously at Mary. 'I had to keep the shop open. We can't afford to shut up, even for a few days.'

'I know.'

'It'll be shut for the funeral, of course.'

'When is it?'

'Friday.'

'Everything's arranged?'

'Yes.'

They walked along Greenacre Street and down the alleyway to the back gate of number twenty-seven, soaked through and breathless. It was obvious Ted couldn't bear to be away from Ellen any longer than necessary.

Linda was skipping in the backyard, Jacqueline holding one end of the rope, the other fastened to the joint of the drainpipe.

> *Jelly on a plate*
> *Jelly on a plate*
> *Wibble-wobble*
> *Wibble-wobble*
> *Jelly on the plate*

Custard in a jug
Custard in a ...

Their voices were quiet, subdued. They stopped and rushed at Mary, wrapping their arms tight around her waist. When Linda raised her face it was pale and wet with tears.

Mary kissed her. 'Let me go in and see Mummy,' she said, 'then I'll come back down. You too, Jacqueline.' She gave her a kiss as well. 'Be good girls.' She pushed open the door.

Jean was sitting with William on her knee. She put her finger to her lips and then pointed to the ceiling. 'She's asleep. Got a bit upset when she found out you weren't here,' she said to Ted, 'but quietened down when I told her you were meeting Mary.'

Mary bent over to first hug Jean and then stroke William's cheek. 'Hello sweetheart.' The little boy dipped his head, all at once shy of her. 'Jean?' Mary didn't know what else to say. Jean's eyes were difficult to see against the reflection of light from the window on her spectacles but her face was flushed and her voice trembled.

'We can talk later. One thing at a time. I'll get off with these three. You go up and see Ellen.'

'Thanks.' Mary smiled her gratitude. 'I'll pop over and pick Linda and William up later. You're still at your mum's?'

'For my sins.' Jean started to put the little boy's coat on. He didn't resist. 'Little chap doesn't know what's hit him,' she said, with a grimace.

'I know.' Mary stroked William's head. She looked at Ted. 'I won't be a minute if she's asleep.'

Ellen was curled in a tight foetal position. Soft snores moved the strands of hair that had fallen across her face.

Mary smoothed them back and let her hand rest on her sister's forehead. It felt cold and clammy. 'It's going to be okay, sis,' she whispered. 'I'm here now.'

*

Ellen didn't move until Mary left the bedroom and she heard the top stair give the familiar squeak. The nail marks dented into her skin stung. She unclenched her hands and rolled to face the wall, hunching the covers over her head. She wouldn't talk, not yet. If she even tried to open her mouth the scream would escape. And she knew it wouldn't stop.

She wasn't sure what had happened, why she was in bed when it was light, when it was obviously the middle of the day. All she knew, all she felt, was the sense of relief that Mary's presence brought. It would be okay now. Mary would sort it, whatever 'it' was. With a long sigh she curled her hand against her cheek and relaxed.

But a moment later a kaleidoscope of recollections and emotions gathered and splintered. Ted's mother; the slap, the dead gaze, the panic; Frank Shuttleworth; that quick coupling years ago, his contempt. Mary, guilt; Ted, guilt; Linda, guilt. Ellen hurled herself from one side of the bed to the other, pushing and pulling at the covers, trying to escape the darkness of the memories crashing around her. At last she forced her eyes open, afraid that if they closed it would start again. She stared up at the jagged crack on the ceiling that split the whitewash just above her, drawing air into her lungs in short shallow breaths.

Selfishness came at a price, she realised. And the people Ellen most loved had paid the price for hers in the past: Mary, Ted, Linda. Her thoughts were jumbled but the shame, disintegrating and assembling, finally came together in the one image – Linda. One emotion – guilt, for leaving her daughter with the foster carer when she was six weeks old; the memory of walking out of that grubby terraced house and moving faster and faster down the street until she was running. Running away.

For the next two years she'd kept on running.

So much to feel bad about, she thought. So many things she'd done wrong, so much fodder for Ted's mother to torment her with and the old cow had made the most of it. Ellen turned onto her side, exhausted, and focussed on the photograph of her and Mary taken years ago. But it would all be all right now. Mary was here, she would help make everything be okay. Ellen was sure of that.

Perhaps, with Mary nearby, she would be strong enough to acknowledge the mistakes, the regrets in her life. It wouldn't be easy but she'd try.

Yet Hannah's face, eyes blank but accusing, still stared into hers.

Chapter 46

'She's asleep.' Mary sat on the kitchen chair. 'She looks awful, Ted, what the hell happened?'

'I don't rightly know. I think when Mother had her heart attack, she panicked. And it's been rough for her over the last couple of years. I told Mother when we got back from your place to leave Ellen be. I even threatened that she'd have to leave if she didn't. But she had a hold over us, the money, I suppose you know that?' Mary nodded. 'I should have had more guts, told her to get out but I didn't. I just thought she be scared enough to stop being so vicious.' He sighed. 'And then there was the business with Patrick playing about with that woman. As far as I can work out, it'd played on Ellen's mind for months that it was me messing about,' he said. 'I should have told her the truth but I'd no idea that's what she was thinking. I wouldn't do that to her, Mary.' He flushed. 'I love her too much.'

'You can't blame yourself.' Mary remembered how she'd dismissed Ellen's complaints about Hannah, how she'd scoffed at the idea of Ted having an affair. All that time Ellen was driving herself mad with worry, and she hadn't helped.

'I do though,' he said. 'I swore the day Ellen said she'd be my wife that I'd look after her.' He paused, looking straight into Mary's eyes. 'I haven't.' Ted rubbed his palms over his face. 'I was the proudest man in the world the day she said she'd marry me. I was in a black hole when I came home from the war. She made me come alive again. But I've been selfish. Building up the business has taken a lot of my time.' He stared into the fire. 'And I know I get a bit moody sometimes.' He placed his hand on his chest. 'Like in here it's all bottled up, what happened in the war. Ellen doesn't want me talking about it so I don't…'

How could two sisters be so different, Mary thought? I wanted so much for Peter to talk to me about what happened to us, yet Ellen refuses to listen to Ted.

'But it still haunts me, Mary.' There was agonised pain in his eyes. 'It's only five years since it ended but everyone's like, "It's gone … so forget it." You only have to listen to the news these days. It's all about Korea now, as though what happened to all the men who fought, all the men and women who suffered, who died in our war are forgotten.' He licked his lips, his mouth working, a habit Mary knew he had when he was trying to form what he wanted to say. 'Don't get me wrong, I know there are horrible things going on. Now China's joined in the Korean War, God only knows when it'll stop.' His voice was harsh, bitter. 'Six bloody years of hell, Mary, and still men are killing one another.'

And some too cowardly to own up to it and only too happy to let others take the blame, Mary thought, her anger quick to bubble up against Peter.

Ted leaned forward in his chair, forearms on his knees, hands clasped together. 'All the time I was a prisoner, I told myself that when, if, I got home, I would woo Ellen and I wouldn't give up till she agreed to marry me. I couldn't do anything about what other people did to one another, but I could protect her. I knew it hadn't been easy for her, what with having Linda and all the other stuff. She's gone through a lot.' He blinked hard. 'I promised I'd look after her. I've failed.'

'No you haven't. She loves you, Ted.'

'I shouldn't have been so tied up with myself.'

163

'You've done your best. That's all any of us can do.' We all have images that haunt us, she thought: seeing that van swerve towards Tom, seeing his crumpled body, his blood staining the road, the coffin going into the ground forever. Mary widened her eyes, knowing if she closed them, it would all be there, vivid against her eyelids. And we all bury things inside us, memories that turn into nightmares, returning when least expected. How many nights had she woken, sweating and fighting against the twisted sheets, with the sounds of her clothes being ripped from her body still in her ears, the taste of her own blood and tears in her mouth, the revolting sensation of a man viciously pushing himself into her, unwelcome, unwanted? How many times had she stared into the darkness hearing the heavy sounds of footsteps, of a brutal fight, the splashing of water, the screams of a dying man? How many times had she remembered and hoped for the relief of oblivion?

'It's hard,' he said, 'feeling guilty about something, when you know there wasn't anything you could do about it.'

'I know.' Oh how I know, she thought, shuddering.

She realised Ted was watching her. 'Like I said, I'm here now.' She gave him what she hoped was a reassuring smile. 'And I'll stay until it's all sorted out.' There was no point in telling him that she and Peter had separated. That she wasn't going back to Wales. She hadn't even told Gwyneth yet. She hadn't plucked up enough courage to tell the old woman that she was throwing the gift of the cottage right back in her face. Because that's how it would seem, Mary was sure. But she would have to eventually. She was dreading that.

Chapter 47

'Come on Jackie.' Linda put her arm around her cousin's neck. 'You like hopscotch. It's fun.'

Jacqueline was shivering. 'Don't want to.' She scowled.

'You will.' Linda jumped up from her cousin's Granny Winterbottom's front doorstep. She windmilled her arms, wishing she could make her cousin smile. She usually felt safe with Jacqueline, but lately it was as though she had to look after her and she didn't know how to make things better.

Jacqueline saw the yellow donkey stone on the back of Linda's kilt but said nothing. She was feeling odd, sort of wanting to cry because she thought her dad might be lonely back home and because, try as she might, she didn't like Granny with her scraggy arms, bony hands and a voice that hurt your ears. 'Don't you miss your Grandma Booth?' she said.

'No. She was horrid,' Linda said airily. She twirled round, admiring the way her kilt swirled into a circle.

Jacqueline's lower lip trembled. She glanced behind her, making sure the door was closed. 'I don't think my granny wants us here. She shouts.' She pulled her knees up under her chin.

'Come to live with us.' Linda crouched down to draw the squares for the game of hopscotch with a small piece of brick. 'Your mummy could make our dinners with mine being poorly?' Her face brightened when she looked up at Jacqueline. 'That'd be good. Daddy makes yummy bread but he's no good at tater hash.'

'I think they'd still fall out.' Jacqueline wrapped her arms around her legs. She wished she could make herself as small as William.

'Hmm, you're right.'

The two girls looked at one another, cohorts in their opinions of the adult world.

'Anyway, we might go home soon, we've been here a long time.' Jacqueline tilted her head to think. 'Two whole weeks.'

Linda twiddled a piece of her hair around her finger, her mouth turned down. 'I like you living close. I can come here whenever I want. At your house I'm not allowed. It's too far.' She stood up.

'Well, we'll be big soon and then they can't stop us.'

'I don't know about that. Mummy's very old and Grandma Booth used to boss her all the time.' Linda put her hands on her hips. 'I hated her and I'm glad she's dead. And I don't think she's gone to Heaven either. I don't think Jesus wants her there.' When she spoke again she was nonchalant. 'I think Grandma Booth is in Hell.'

'Oh, our Linda!' Jacqueline stood up with her back to the wall of the house. 'God will hear you.'

'I don't care. He knows she was a nasty lady.' Linda threw the flat piece of red brick on the first square and hopped onto it. 'Anyway, you used to laugh at her as well.' She jumped, two-footed onto squares two and three, glancing at Jacqueline. 'We both did, remember, last Christmas?'

'When we had to wait for her to come for dinner?'

'S'right.' Linda hopped and jumped to the last square. As she turned she said, 'Cos she was in the lavvy.' She balanced on one leg, hopped up and down. 'Then she just sat at the table and started eating without talking to anybody. And she made horrid sloppy noises.'

'And her chin and nose bumped together when she chewed.'

They giggled and Linda wobbled, her heel turning on the uneven stone flag. 'Your mummy shouted at us. But I saw my mummy smile. She put her hand over her mouth but I did, I saw her smiling.' She was glad she'd made Jacqueline laugh, it made her feel good.

'It was a shame we missed our pudding though.'

'Yeah.' Linda made her way back to the start of the hopscotch. 'Your turn.' She handed the piece of brick to Jacqueline and flopped down on the step. She wet her finger and rubbed at the donkey stone and then examined her finger. It was satisfyingly yellow. 'So I'm glad she's dead. They're going to put her in a hole in the ground today.'

'In somebody's garden?'

'No, in some gravy yard or something.' Linda paused. 'I heard Auntie Mary say. She told the milkman they were burying her this afternoon. So, see, she can't hurt Mummy anymore.'

166

Chapter 48

'I've arrived, and to prove it, I'm here!'

'Turn that bloody rubbish off.'

Jean twisted the knob of the radio. 'I like it … and it's not your house.' The volume of the banter between Max Bygraves and the clipped high-pitched tone of Peter Brough's ventriloquist's dummy increased. *'Well Archie…'*

Patrick reached past her and switched the wireless off.

'Do you mind?' Jean banged the iron down onto the board, holding it steady when it rocked. She much preferred to iron on a table but her mother insisted on 'being modern.' Her scalp was still prickling from the dismay of seeing her husband. She'd forgotten he had a key to the front door.

'When're you going to stop being stupid?' he said. 'It's daft when you've got a bloody good home of your own.'

Jean pulled her lips into a tight line. 'I prefer it here at the moment, thank you. And I don't take kindly to being called stupid. I'm not in the wrong. Remember?'

Patrick ran his fingers through his thinning hair, the two carefully arranged waves instantly in disarray. Impatiently he brushed the strands from his eyes. 'I've said I'm sorry, Jean. I've said it a hundred times.'

'You could say it a thousand times and the situation will still be the same.' Jean wouldn't look at him. She arranged the pleats on Jacqueline's kilt and started to press each one slowly. 'You had an affair.' She pushed the point of the iron into the waistband, trying to keep her voice calm, wishing she could say to her husband she forgave him, she just wanted all this to go away. But she knew she had to be strong. She stressed her next words. 'Another affair, Patrick. That is one thing I have been stupid about. Turning a blind eye to all your shenanigans. I should have left you the first time.' The kilt blurred. Jean lifted her glasses with her forefinger and flicked the tears away. Some fell onto the material, the tiny patch of tartan became a brighter red and green and she dabbed at it with the edge of a tea towel off the pile of ironing. When she spoke her words were too loud but she couldn't do anything about that. 'I didn't. But this time it's different. This time there's going to be a baby.' She didn't trust herself to say any more.

Patrick's fingers twitched on the brim of his trilby he held to his chest. 'Please, Jean. You know I love you.'

She moved her head in denial, noticing the way his face darkened with anger.

The bright sunlight angled across the linoleum through the opened backdoor. 'It's dried this lot already.' Jean's mother peered over the top of the pile of washing. 'That backyard's a suntrap. You wouldn't think it's nearly November and—' She stopped mid-sentence. 'What are you doing here?' Her features set. 'Get out of my house.'

Patrick's fury found a different target. 'I think you'll find it's Jean's house. Her father put it in her name when he left. Remember?' Patrick pushed his face at her, his brown eyes narrowing. 'Jean, my wife? Therefore my house too. You're just the tenant we let stay here.'

'Patrick!' Jean protested. She'd seen the fear in her mother's face and, realised, for the first time, she was the stronger of the two women. She took the clothes from her. 'It's all right Mother, go into the front room and I'll bring you a cup of tea in a minute.'

Seeing Jean had the upper hand, Elsie Winterbottom tossed her head. The metal curlers under her hairnet rattled. Giving him one last glare she went out, leaving the door ajar.

Through the crack they could see her lingering in the hallway. 'You didn't complain when you were getting all that stuff for nowt, did you?' Patrick shouted. 'I was the bee's knees then, eh? Kow-towing all that time just so you could get stuff from me … must have bloody killed you, you old crow.'

Jean picked up the iron again. 'You really are spoiling for a fight, aren't you? If you think that's going to make things better you've another think coming.'

'Bloody old bat.' Patrick sprawled on the kitchen chair. He stretched his leg and pushed the door shut with his foot. 'I just wanted to know if you were going to the bonfire on the old Rec on Sam Booth Street?'

'I am,' Jean said. 'I'm taking Jacqueline and we're going with Mary, Ted, Ellen and the kids and a few others off the street.'

'What's Mary doing here without her Nazi boyfriend anyway?'

'You've not seen her yet?'

'No.'

'Think she might want to talk to you.'

'Well, I don't want to talk to her.'

Jean shrugged. 'It's a free country, suit yourself.'

He ignored what she'd said about Mary. 'Thought I might tag along to the bonfire. That okay?'

'It's a free country,' Jean said again.

'With you? Thought I might tag along with you?'

'After that little episode with Mother?' Jean scoffed.

'She's a fucking stupid old bitch.' He just couldn't help himself.

'There's no need for language like that.'

'And I still don't see why you had to come here.'

'Because I didn't want to be in the house with you and you wouldn't leave.'

'It's my…' Patrick stopped. 'I want you at home. I want us to sort things out.' He stood, took a couple of steps closer to her.

She hung Jacqueline's kilt on a hanger, unplugged the iron and put it on the worktop to cool down, folded the ironing board and let him carry it to the cupboard under the stairs. When he turned towards her, the question in his eyes, she let him wait a full minute.

'Go home, Patrick,' she said. 'Go home, there's nothing for you here.'

Chapter 49

The house was silent when Patrick closed the door behind him. He stood for a moment staring at himself in the hall mirror, for once oblivious to his good looks, seeing only the grey pallor of his skin, the dark shadows under his eyes.

There was no getting away from the fact that he was missing Jean and his daughter. And that he'd been a fool. Like all the other times with other women, those few weeks with Doreen Whittaker were just a bit of fun. She wasn't even a challenge with that soft lad of a husband of hers being away most of the time and her having a reputation for being easy from the minute she had moved into old Ma Jagger's house. Being next door to Ellen's made it all the more simple. 'Stupid bastard,' he said to his reflection, 'always chancing your arm. Always thinking what the wife doesn't know won't hurt.' But he had hurt her and he was sorry, because the bottom line was that he loved Jean. He was just weak when it came to other women. It had to stop.

He scowled, picturing the look of triumph on her mother's face when he pushed past her on his way out. 'Bloody old cow.' How he'd kept his hands to himself he didn't know. The spite showed in his face as he glanced again in the mirror and all at once he was uneasy. It was like he was looking at his father, the tight-lipped scowl, the narrowed eyes. He suddenly pictured his mother cowering against the sideboard in the kitchen at Henshaw Street.

He'd despised his father. The only time they'd ever got on was when they were both drunk. 'I'm not like him,' he mumbled. And yet here he was, alone, a man who'd hit his own wife.

The surge of self-recrimination and remorse made him turn away. Taking off his overcoat he flung it in the direction of the newel post at the foot of the stairs. Ignoring it as it fell to the floor, he stumbled into the kitchen and flung himself onto one of the chairs, running his fingers through his hair. For the first time in days he became aware of the mess: the fireplace overflowing with ashes, cigarette packets and charred newspaper, the table cluttered with dirty cups and plates, butter-smeared knives and sticky lumps of jam and crumbs. He was sick of toast.

He scraped back the chair, grabbed the ash bucket by the back door and knelt in front of the hearth, feverishly emptying the grate. Standing up, he added the crockery to the pile in the sink and turned on the tap. The water was cold; with no fire lit since yesterday, the boiler in the back of the fireplace had no chance to heat up. With an exclamation of impatience and a promise to himself that he'd wash up later, Patrick grabbed a bottle of beer from the sideboard. Lifting the top off with his teeth, he headed upstairs.

It was icily cold in the bedroom. He'd opened the window to let the smell of cigarettes out before he'd stormed out that morning, determined to bring Jean home where she belonged. Closing it, he gazed out of the window. The woman next door was in the garden, calling for her cat. Patrick watched as it appeared from under the bushes and slunk across the lawn. As she turned to go back into the house she stared up at the bedroom window.

Patrick swore. 'Nosy bitch,' he added and hid behind the curtain. He remembered Jean once saying the woman had yet to speak to her, but he bet she knew every bloody thing that happened for miles around. She looked that sort.

He leant against the wall holding the bottle to his mouth, wavering for a couple of seconds before taking a gulp. He didn't know how to make things right between him and Jean. She'd left him because he was messing about with Doreen, but in his mind hitting Jean was far worse than having a bit on the side. He'd known what he'd done was horribly wrong the moment it happened. What was it his father used to say after he'd given their mother a beating? Something about cutting off his right arm before he'd do it again? Of course he always did do it again. Now he was no better. How could Jean forgive him when he couldn't forgive himself?

But he was better than his father. *He* wouldn't say those words but he'd promised himself that he would never be violent to her again. And he'd never look at another woman. He'd learned his lesson.

The same thoughts went over and over in his head. He'd messed up badly, with the women, with Doreen Whittaker being pregnant, especially with what he'd done to Jean the night Tom was killed.

Tom. A sob as he took another gulp of beer turned into a hiccup. He pushed himself away from the wall and stood next to the bed. It was a crumpled mess. He'd meant to change the sheets. He couldn't remember doing it in the six weeks since she'd gone, but then when she'd first left a lot of his days had passed in a drunken fog. Lately he'd made sure he worked all hours on his stalls so that by the time he got home he was so exhausted he fell asleep as soon as he dropped onto the mattress.

Now he sat, piling the pillows behind him and shuffling up to the headboard. Twisting sideways he put down the beer onto the bedside table, slid open a drawer and emptied out the contents until he finally found what he was looking for.

Although the date on the letter was years ago, the paper was still crisp. Until the day of Tom's funeral he hadn't read it for a long time. It was the only time he'd ever written to him.

Dear Patrick,
You will probably be surprised to hear from me but there is something I need to say to you. Mary and me have been talking and I've realised something that hadn't occurred to me before you tried to put the blame on me, even knowing how I feel about the war and all the killing. You know what I'm talking about. I was angry at first but I'm not now. And after I've written this, I'll be able to forget it. Or at least get on with my life as best I can.

Patrick remembered how he'd felt the first time he'd read those words. He'd always been so bloody ashamed of his brother and his weird ways, the first to mock him before anybody else did. It had taken him a few minutes to cotton on that somehow Tom was cutting him out of his life.

You and I have never been close, Patrick. Perhaps it was the difference in our ages, more likely it is because we have never thought the same about life, about all sorts of things. And I know you don't understand me any more than I understand you. But it doesn't mean I don't care about you. I do. I need to tell you that as my brother, I'll always care.

Patrick sniffed, wiped the back of his hand across his nose.

And I want you to know that I understood why you did what you did on that day. I would have done the same to save Mary. I would have done exactly the same.

'But it wasn't me.' Since getting the letter all those years ago he'd gone over and over this in his mind. If it wasn't either of them, then who? It had to be his brother. The one and only time he'd gone to visit him in the Scrubs he'd almost admitted it. Hadn't he?

He should have chucked the letter away as soon as he'd got it but he'd always intended to tackle Tom, ask him what sort of sly game did he think he was playing? He didn't get the chance. Tom never came back to Ashford and he'd vowed he sure as hell wasn't traipsing all the way to Wales.

Between us we both know what really happened. I pray to God that the truth will never come out but if it does I hope you have the strength to face the consequences. I will never betray you but you have to live with your conscience.
Your brother, Tom

Patrick let the letter drop from his fingers. He died believing I'd killed Shuttleworth … that I'd tried to pin it on him. The thought hadn't gone away since the night he heard his brother had been killed. If he believed in God, that Tom was in Heaven, he'd ask his forgiveness. But he didn't. And now there was nothing he could do to make things right.

Curling up on the bed he pressed the pillow to his face. The tears were hot and painful.

Chapter 50

By the time they arrived on the Rec, Patrick was there anyway, helping some other men to hoist the Guy Fawkes onto an old wooden chair on top of the bonfire. Brushing his hands together he came towards them grinning. 'Looks good eh? Good size bonfire this year.' Jean noticed he barely acknowledged Mary. When he came to stand next to her she moved to the other side of the family group.

'Smashing, Dad.' Jacqueline leaned against him. Jean blinked hard. She knew her daughter loved it when they were all together like this. But she felt distanced from all the cheerful babble and laughter. Last year Patrick had bought a huge box of fireworks and set them off in the back garden. She'd made treacle toffee, using up a whole week's worth of sugar ration, Linda had stayed over and the girls had a wonderful time. An unwelcome thought came into her mind. Patrick had woken her up in the middle of that night and made love to her.

She glanced up and saw him watching her with a strange expression. She felt her face grow hot and looked away, wishing she'd stayed in at Moss Terrace.

'There isn't one star out tonight,' Ellen said, shivering. 'I don't like nights like this.'

Jean looked past the growing crowd around them at the shells of the bombed-out terraced house on Sam Booth Street, still to be demolished, and then upwards. There were no stars, but here and there were faint blurs of orange and grey smoke rising into the blackness. 'There're a few other fires already lit,' she said.

Mary pulled the collar of Ellen's coat around the back of her neck. 'You warm enough.'

'I'm fine.'

Ted leaned towards Ellen. 'The fire will soon warm you up.'

There was a murmur through the crowd. A huddle of men were striking matches and holding them to twisted-up newspaper. Jacqueline grabbed Linda's hand. 'Let's watch.'

They moved forward.

'Be careful,' Ellen said, 'no closer.'

Without acknowledging either of them, Patrick leaned past Mary and Ellen. 'Ted, how's the new van running?'

'Fine.'

Ted kept his eyes on the three men moving around the fire with the burning makeshift torches, touching the pieces of cardboard at the edges.

'What's she do to the gallon?'

'She?' Jean muttered.

'Don't know properly yet, haven't really had a good run in her,' Ted said.

Jean saw him get hold of Ellen's hand between both of his. She felt a stab of envy.

Patrick looked past Ted at Jean. She pretended she hadn't noticed but out of the corner of her eye she watched him sidle round the back of Mary to stand next to her. Aware that he was edging closer, Jean threw him a sideways glare. When the cuff of his overcoat brushed the back of her fingers, she stuffed both hands into her pockets and gazed intently at the bonfire.

'Really getting going now,' Patrick whispered.

'What?' She didn't look at him.

'The fire. It's taken hold. Flames will be leaping sky-high in a minute.' He pushed his thumb into her coat pocket alongside her hand and stroked her palm. He didn't take his eyes off the Guy Fawkes, now obscured by the swirling smoke. 'It's going to be a good night.'

Jean didn't move. Her reaction to the sensation of his warm skin on hers threw her. She didn't trust herself – any more than she trusted him. She didn't want him, she told herself, while a small voice at the back of her mind reminded her she didn't want to lose him either.

The touch-paper smouldered, filling the milk bottle with smoke. Then, with a loud whoosh the rocket flew into the sky, splitting the darkness with a trail of golden sparks. The two Roman Candles that followed fired a series of red, green and blue flares into the air, colouring the faces of the crowd watching and there was a exhalation of delight when the Catherine Wheel began to spin, shooting out stars of white light from the post on a slab of old concrete near the entrance of the site. Above the laughter and the chatter there were cries of disappointment when the last firework died out.

'We'll have a break now.' Ronald Turnbull from Atkinson Terrace had appointed himself in charge of the celebrations.

'He's enjoying himself.' Ted grinned, his arm protectively around Ellen.

'Mind,' said Jean, 'his wife looks none too pleased.' She nodded towards a woman standing on her own by one of the ruined walls, all that was left of one of the bombed houses on the cleared ground.

'Face like a lemon,' Patrick joked. He'd taken Jean's hand out of her pocket a while ago and was now openly holding it.

Mary raised her eyebrows at Jean.

Jean shrugged, pulled her hand away from Patrick and crossed her arms.

'Should we ask Mrs Turnbull over?' Mary said.

'Oh no, please,' Ellen said. 'She works as the receptionist at the doctor's, thinks she's above everyone.' She glanced around. 'Where are the girls? I don't want Linda wandering off. There're a lot more strangers round here these days.'

'There they are.' Jean pointed to the two girls who were prising the used Catherine Wheel from the wooden stump. 'They're fine. Our Jacqueline knows how to look after herself. And she'll keep an eye on Linda.'

But still she saw that Ellen nudged Ted, tipping her head towards her daughter. He hitched William further up onto his shoulder. 'Linda, come away,' he called above the babble of noise. 'You'll get burned.'

'Oh for goodness sake.' Jean pulled a face. 'Stop mithering.'

She exchanged glances with Mary, who frowned at her and shook her head. 'Leave Ellen alone,' she whispered. 'It's taken me and Ted ages to persuade her to come out.'

Jean sucked in her breath, irritated, and turned away. To her mind Ellen was making the most of all the fuss, so much so that Mary barely had any time for her best friend these days.

Patrick's arm found its way around her waist. This time she didn't move away.

Linda ran towards the group, her face rosy in the light of the bonfire, the green balaclava pushed back from her forehead. 'I'm hot,' she said.

'Yes, well, keep that on, and your scarf,' Ellen said, 'it's bitter tonight.'

'Linda, come on,' Jacqueline shouted. 'Guy Fawkes is going to fall.'

'Watch where you stand, stay where we can see you.' Ellen held on to Linda's coat. 'There's sparks flying and there'll be more in a minute.'

When Linda managed to pull herself free from her mother's grasp she ran towards her cousin, shoving the balaclava off her head. They wrapped their arms around each other and, peeking surreptitiously at the adults, moved around the back of the bonfire out of sight, where they went closer to watch the stuffed figure, slumped in an old school chair, sink into the flames to loud applause.

'His hat will be last,' Linda confidently predicted.

'How do you know?' Jacqueline squinted up through the heat. The Guy's head was an old pillow case. Someone had drawn a face on it and a big smile. Jacqueline couldn't see herself looking that happy if she'd been shoved on a fire. The hat was black and squashy and had fallen over one of the pretend eyes.

'Because it's an old one of Granny Booth's and I heard Mummy tell Auntie Mary that Granny's hat was made of stone.' She rested her head against Jacqueline's and together they stared into the fire.

'Well, she was wrong,' Jacqueline said, as the hat was engulfed in a blaze. 'See? Its trousers and jacket are still there and the hat's gone.' She gave Linda a playful push. 'Come on, let's buy a potato.' Clutching their pennies, they raced to where a large, sweating, red-faced woman was standing behind a table. She wore a checked turban that was knotted at the front and had slipped low on her forehead. Nearby a man was knocking potatoes out of the red embers of the fire where it had already died down. He had a very long iron poker and held his hand in front of his face, but Jacqueline could see that he'd still managed to singe the front of his hair. They waited at the end of the queue watching the woman carefully wrap newspaper around each of the blackened potatoes piled up in an old tin bucket.

'Yummy!' Jacqueline said.

By the time they returned to where the adults stood, Jacqueline's face was smeared with black soot and newspaper print. 'Timmy Powell let a Rip-Rap off behind Mr Turnbull and he jumped a mile and then chased Timmy off the Rec.' She laughed. 'You should have seen it, Mum.'

'You were wrong, Mummy,' Linda said, 'the hat got burned first.'

'What do you mean, love?' Mary looked from Linda to Ellen.

'The Guy Fawkes,' Linda said, impatiently hopping from one foot to the other, her wellingtons making small squeaking sounds. 'It had one of Grandma Booth's hats on and Mummy told you it was a stone one.' She stood still, crossed her arms, her face stubborn. 'I heard her: "a hat of stone".'

Mary's face cleared. She smiled. 'I think she means a heart of stone,' she said in a low voice to Ellen and Jean.

Patrick let out a laugh and hugged Jean who exchanged smiles with him; it felt good to share the amusement.

Ellen put her fingers to her mouth. She looked apologetically at Ted. 'I'm sorry, love.'

'Oh, give over.' He grinned. 'I think you're spot on. Never one for sentiment, my mother. As we both know,' he added in answer to her expression of faked astonishment.

Jacqueline spit on her hands and rubbed them together.

'Jacqueline,' Jean protested.

'Cleaning them.'

'Looks as if you're having a good time.' Patrick studied her with a grin.

'Smashing! I've just had a tater.'

'I can see that. Didn't you want one, Linda?'

'It was messy. I didn't want it on my hands.' She looked towards Ellen for approval.

Ellen smiled. 'Good girl.'

'Anyway, Jacqueline said it was raw in the middle.'

'Didn't matter,' Jacqueline said, wiping her mouth across her coat sleeve, 'it was good.'

'Here, I have something for you.' Patrick took a white packet from his overcoat pocket. He tore the top open and took out a thin metal rod. 'Sparklers. That okay with you, love?' he asked Jean.

'As long as they're careful,' Jean said, surprised but pleased he'd asked in front of everyone.

The two girls laughed, excited. 'Let's light them now.'

'Put your gloves on,' Ellen said. 'Hold it well away from you.'

Patrick moved behind both girls and held their arms straight. 'Right.' He nodded at Ted.

Ted struck a match and held it to the grey end of Jacqueline's sparkler.

'It's not working.'

'Give it a chance,' Jean said, 'your dad wouldn't buy duff ones.'

Patrick frowned, glanced up at her as if unsure whether she was being sarcastic, but she smiled at him and he visibly relaxed and grinned back.

Suddenly there was a shower of tiny sparks lighting up the darkness around them.

'Light yours from mine,' Jacqueline urged Linda, 'light yours from mine.'

Patrick helped Linda to hold the sticks together.

'Now we'll write our names,' Jacqueline laughed.

Holding hands they waved the burning metal rods, spelling out their names in golden lines against the blackness.

As the last flashes fizzled out, Ellen shivered. 'I think I'd like to go home now.'

'Me too,' Jean said. The front of her body was hot but, despite the thick woollen trousers, the back of her legs were frozen. Besides she was conscious that Mary and Ellen had been watching her and Patrick all night and she was sick of it. They'd had their say about him, it was up to her what she did now. For Jacqueline's sake, she told herself, feeling a thrill of anticipation when his hand brushed hers again.

'Okay,' Ted said. 'Are you ready?' he said to Linda.

'Aw, no,' Linda protested, 'there'll be more fireworks in a minute.' Her bottom lip jutted out and she swung around so her back was to them.

'Don't be awkward, love.' Ted put his hand on her shoulder. 'Your Mum's cold and we can't leave you here.'

'I'm going anyway,' Jean said. 'Jacqueline?'

'I'll come with you? See you back safely?' Patrick said. 'Here give me those.'

Jacqueline went with him to drop the burned-out sparklers in the bin nearby. When they came back he said, 'Jacqueline wants to stay on for a bit as well.'

'Please Mum?' Jacqueline put her arm across Linda's shoulder. 'And Dad says I can sleep at Linda's tonight?'

'You asked,' Patrick said hastily when his daughter looked from him to Jean. 'You know I said only if your mum says yes.'

'Well…' Jean dithered, the warmth of Patrick's fingers stroking the back of her neck completely unsettling her.

She shot a swift look at Mary to see if she'd noticed, but it was obvious she hadn't when Mary said, 'I'll stay with them. They'll be fine.'

'Can Jacqueline sleep at our house, Mummy?' Linda looked anxiously at Ellen. 'It's been ages.'

'If that's all right with Auntie Mary? She's in the room next to yours. I don't want you keeping her awake all night with your giggling.'

Mary smiled at the girls. 'Or your snoring.'

They laughed.

'If you're sure?' Jean said.

'I am. You get back.' Mary glared at Patrick. 'To your mother's.'

The fireworks in the distance were like coloured stars, flickering, sharp bursts of colour that rose and died in the sky. Far away dogs howled against the bangs and crashes. The faint light glowed intermittently on Peter's face. He'd counted four bonfires along the coastline. It seemed as though almost every village had their own.

He pulled his jacket tighter around him and folded his arms, tucking his hands under his armpits.

He'd never felt so alone.

Chapter 51

'Mother will wonder where I am,' Jean murmured.

Patrick turned the key and pushed the door with his foot, his arms around her. 'I'll take you back there afterwards, if you insist.' He traced the shape of her ear with his tongue. 'It'll be just like when we were courting.' His warm breath rippled on her skin.

Barely waiting until Jean closed the front door, he put both hands flat on the wall on either side of her and covered her face with kisses, finally finding her mouth. The smell of the bonfire lingered between them when he pressed against her, unbuttoning and sliding her coat from her shoulders. He held his hand over her breast, gently squeezed until she felt her nipple hardening under his touch. When his kisses became more urgent, she curved her back, returning the pressure with her own mouth, pushing off his jacket and holding him closer to her. With a small whimper she let him raise her skirt to her waist and quickly helped him to pull her roll-on down over her hips and thighs, self-consciously aware for a moment that he would feel the indented marks left by it on her buttocks.

He didn't hesitate. Wrapping his arm around the back of her waist he lifted her, unbuckling his trousers at the same time. She felt the rush of moist heat inside her, the coldness of the wall on her lower back, the rough coarseness of hair on the insides of her thighs and the one sudden ecstatic thrill as he entered her. Kissing him, searching for his lips with her own and finding them, she flicked her tongue rhythmically between them, feeling the urgent response in him and matching his movements.

For once he waited; only shuddering against her after the quivering warmth exploded within her and she tightened around him.

Afterwards, breathless, she was embarrassed. They'd never done anything like that before and, for a second, she let herself wonder who else he'd made love to like that. But, without a word, he picked her up and carried her upstairs. Laying her on the bed he made love to her again, this time slowly, tenderly.

When she woke, he was already awake. Propped up on one elbow he grinned down at her. 'So?' he said. 'We okay now?' He put his hand on her shoulder and pulled her to face him.

She pressed her lips together, irritated by his self-assurance. She wanted so badly to say yes, to forget every affair, forget every quarrel. She'd done it before. But this time was different; this time she needed to forget the fear and pain of his fist. And this time there would be a baby, a child, always there, in the background. Once the gossips got hold of that juicy little titbit she'd never be able to hold her head up again, especially around where they lived.

'I don't know, Patrick, I don't know.'

Chapter 52

Stepping onto the pavement on Shaw Street, Mary shivered. A bank of cloud covered the weak winter sun letting through only a silvery wash of light and, after the oppressive heat of bodies squashed together in the bus, the chilly wind seemed to go right through her.

She was glad of the fresh air though. On the way back from Manchester she'd started to feel nauseous. It was having to go on the top deck, she told herself, all that cigarette smoke and the rolling motion of the bus. Yet, always there, the anxiety that in the middle of the night magnified itself into panic. She'd missed one monthly and was three days overdue on the second. In the daytime, like now, she could convince herself it was all the turmoil, all the upset she'd been through. She'd begun to dread going to bed.

'You all right, m'dear?' The old woman who'd got off the bus behind her put her arm around her. Mary nodded, her lips compressed into a forced smile. The woman stank of damp and her black coat was spotted with greenish splodges. Mary watched the bus move away, a funnel of shimmering exhaust fumes distorting the air. She held her breath, not wanting to take in either smell.

'Dirty bugger, that.' The woman followed her gaze. 'You'd think there'd be a law against it – belching all that bleeding muck out. You crossing?'

'Yes.'

'Come on, then.' They crossed the road. On the other side the woman said, 'I'm going that way. I live on Huddersfield Road. Been to a funeral,' she said inconsequentially. 'Now you look after yourself, you need to take care.' She tipped her head to one side. 'Especially now.'

Mary's heart missed a beat. But before she could ask what the woman meant she'd hurried away, moving quickly for such an old woman, her black hat bobbing on her head. Her mother would have been around the same age now. 'Oh Mam,' she whispered, 'I need you so much.' She put a hand to her stomach.

The wretchedness was overwhelming. First Mum, then Tom. And, in her mind, losing Tom was now intermingled with losing her job. Sometimes she could almost persuade herself both were waiting for her in Llamroth. Then the loss came back with an unrelenting rush. And she blamed Peter for everything. So why hadn't she told any of the family that she'd finished with him? That she wasn't going back to Llamroth? What was stopping her from clearing Tom's name at least, from telling Ellen and Ted, Jean and Patrick … especially Patrick … that it was Peter who killed Frank, not Tom? She didn't know. All she knew was that she wasn't ever going back to Wales. And she didn't know how to break that news to Gwyneth.

'Sorry, miss.' A man knocked into her. He raised his trilby and hurried on.

'My fault.' Mary managed a small smile.

'Too cold to be standing around,' he called back to her.

'You're right.' Pull yourself together, she thought. It's all the worry, you're not… She couldn't even form the word in her mind. She pulled back her shoulders and took in a long breath. She'd be glad to get back to the house. The Saturday market was a good place for bargains but it was as though all of Ashford and Bradlow had the same idea and she'd been pushed from pillar to post. Still, it was worth it. The three skeins of parrot wool she'd bought were a bargain and more than enough for jumpers for all three children. She was sure they'd like all the random mix of colours in the wool and knitting would be a good excuse for sitting down. Running about after Ellen was hard work.

Quickening her step, she disregarded the sensation of the heels of her shoes, hard on the pavement, jolting through her body as she wound her way past the straggle of people who seemed in no hurry to go anywhere, despite the cold.

The tops of the trees in Skirm Park shivered with each gust of wind, flinging the last of the dead leaves around the sky. The year is almost over, she thought. So much has happened but it was as though she'd never moved away from Ashford, as though the last five years had not happened.

The van didn't stop at the top of Newroyd Street before turning onto Shaw Street. The noise of the brakes and the squeal of the tyres as the driver took the corner too quickly brought Mary out of her reverie. Her fingers loosened on the handle of the shopping basket and it fell to the ground, the brown packages of wool scattering.

The van was white with an orange oblong painted on the side as though blotting something out. White and orange. The same colours as the van that killed Tom.

It was that van.

And the driver, turned towards her grinning, as it sped past, was George Shuttleworth.

Chapter 53

'I'm sorry miss, we've investigated your allegation and the man you think you saw…'

'The man I saw,' Mary interrupted.

'The man you *think* you saw driving the van that killed your brother has denied being in Wales on that day.' The police sergeant rose up and down on his heels in front of the tiled fireplace, his hands behind his back as he looked at Mary over the top of his glasses. 'And he has an alibi.'

A plump woman sitting at a long wooden table jabbed rhythmically at the keys of a large typewriter. She stared, unwavering, at Mary as a small bell pinged and the carriage skidded back before she carried on hitting the keys.

Mary discounted her and looked to a young police officer who was standing by a four drawer metal cabinet balancing a large pile of folders under one arm. 'He can't have an alibi. I told you, I saw him, I saw the van.'

'You saw a van,' the sergeant stressed.

'It was his van, white with orange on the side … like the orange had been painted on to cover something up.'

His eyebrows rose.

'Like it was covering up words. Oh, that's not important…' Mary flushed, the anger rising quickly. 'It was the same van. I saw the driver and I recognised him. I know it was him.' Her voice was hard. It was impossible George Shuttleworth could get away with killing Tom. The police had to believe her. 'He's someone I know.'

'So I understand, miss.' The sergeant cocked his head to one side. 'We found the report of a previous altercation between your families.'

Oh no! Mary swallowed hard against the sickening lurch of her stomach. How could she have been so stupid? Why hadn't she realised their investigations would uncover all the stuff from before? Stupid woman, she told herself. She gripped the edge of the counter. Pull yourself together, she thought. There was nothing else to do but brazen it out. 'Altercation, sergeant? If you've read the report, you will know full well what kind of altercation it was.'

His face mottled.

'This man's brother assaulted me.' She couldn't bring herself to say the word.

'And was subsequently murdered, according to records.'

'Nothing to do with me or any of my family,' Mary said. She went cold, a wave of uncertainty flooding through her. Now was the time to tell him that it was Peter who'd killed Frank Shuttleworth. But she couldn't. Why? Confused thoughts raced around in her head. Her bitterness that he'd let her think it was Tom was still there but, right now, standing in front of this policeman, something held her back from blurting out the truth.

'Hmmm. That's as maybe. The case was not solved.' He raised his eyebrows. 'But neither was it closed.'

Oh God. Mary stayed as still as she could and maintained eye contact with him. Stay calm, stay calm. She was here to persuade them that it was George Shuttleworth driving the van that killed Tom. Nothing else mattered.

'However …' He stopped rocking on his heels and clapped his hands. 'That's for another time, perhaps.' He glared at the young policeman. 'Find the file on Miss Howarth's complaint, Roberts,' he said bluntly. 'Read out the results of our investigations.'

The officer pulled out a file from the top drawer and, giving Mary an apologetic smile, placed it on the large table.

The typist twisted the end wheel of the carriage with a flourish and removed the paper. She rose, adjusted the hem of her black cardigan and went through an opaque-glass partition in one corner of the charge room. Mary heard the click of metal covers on the switchboard, the slide of extension plugs and the low voice of a man but she kept her eyes on the young officer.

187

He coughed slightly before reading. 'According to this, there is a witness to say he was at home that day.' He paused. His gaze on Mary was almost sympathetic before, lowering his head, he read the next sentence. 'There was no chance he could have travelled to Wales and then back to Manchester on the day the victim was killed.'

'And those are your investigations? After only three weeks you're giving up?' Mary couldn't help herself. 'A witness? Who? Who said he was home on that day?'

'We're not at liberty to tell you that, miss.' The sergeant walked across the room.

Mary spoke slowly. 'You said the witness said George Shuttleworth was at home. There's only one other person who lives in that house with him as far as I know and that's his mother, Nelly. Was it Nelly Shuttleworth?' She looked past the sergeant to the other man, who cleared his throat again and coloured but didn't answer her.

Behind her the door of the vestibule opened and a man was pushed against the counter next to Mary. The smell of alcohol filled the air as he blinked slowly at her before being shoved again by a constable holding him up.

'I suggest you leave the investigations to us, miss.' The sergeant turned to pick up a large leather-bound book from the table and placed it on the counter. He studied the drunken man. 'Right Lewis,' he said to the constable, 'charge?' Without looking at Mary, he added, 'And you'd better think twice, miss, before making any more false accusations.'

Without another word Mary left of the police station, shaking with fear and anger.

Standing on the steps outside, she glanced up at the stone letters engraved above the door. *BRADLOW STATION*. Alongside it, the blue lamp flickered. A black car drew up and an officer in full uniform crossed the pavement and got into the back.

She was unable to move. A few people passed by, looking up at her with curiosity but she was indifferent to them. Her only thoughts were, The man has an alibi.

It was a lie. Nelly, because it had to be her, had lied. Why? After everything Frank did? Mary knew the answer even as she formed the question. Nelly would do anything to protect the one son she had left.

And then she thought of the other thing the sergeant said. 'The case was not solved … but neither was it closed.'

Mary put her hand to her stomach. If there was a life beginning inside, however much the thought terrified her, how could she tell the police what she knew? Peter might even own up if confronted. She'd made it clear she would never go back to him. Knowing she hated him, knowing there was little to go back to in Germany, would he care what happened to him?

If she was having his baby, whether she ever saw him again or not, she couldn't be the one to tell the authorities. How would she ever tell his child it was her fault its father was hanged?

Chapter 54

Barnes Street didn't look much different from the last time she'd been there. The houses still had that air of prosperity long since departed. One or two of the small walled gardens now sported a shrub or two, some of the old bay windows had been replaced by sash ones that looked out of place against the faded red brick, but the street was still as quiet as she remembered. Unlike Henshaw Street, no children played football on the road, no neighbours gossiped on the doorsteps. Further along a black Ford car was parked outside one of the houses and a man and a young boy, wielding buckets and sponges, were cleaning it despite the cold drizzle of rain.

There was no van outside Nelly's house. Mary breathed a sigh of relief but still hesitated. She hadn't prepared what she wanted to ask and she was nervous. If Nelly wouldn't help she didn't know what else to do.

The corroded metal number four was missing now, only the imprint remained on the door. Red paint barely concealed the burst bubbles and flakes of the black paint that Mary remembered used to be there. She grasped the dull brass knocker and banged it down.

She heard the soft shuffle of feet and then the door shifted slightly in the frame. A woman's voice cursed. 'Bloody thing.' The door was tugged again. And then, 'Can you give it a shove?'

Despite her anxiety Mary grinned and put her shoulder to the door. It opened with a screech.

Nelly's blue turban flopped, as usual, over one eye. She squinted at Mary, pushing out her large lips in concentration. The recognition came all at once. 'Mary, pet,' she exclaimed. 'Well, I'm blowed. Mary.' She brushed floury hands on her apron and engulfed her in large soft arms. 'Come in, come in.' She peeped out of the doorway at the overcast sky. 'Another storm, I shouldn't wonder. Let's get in. I'm just doin' a bit of baking.'

'I can see that.' Mary smiled, closing the door and surreptitiously wiping the white marks from her sleeves.

The grey strands of hair that had escaped from the turban were covered in flour and she had a streak across her nose. She waddled along the hall, her bare feet spread at angles. ''Scuse, the old trotters,' she said, over her shoulder, 'bunions playing up.' Her backside bounced from side to side with each step. 'I was sorry to hear about your brother, Mary. You got my letter?'

'I did, Nelly, and thank you, it meant a lot.' Now was the time to tell her why she was here. But Nelly was talking again.

'Sorry it was a bit crumpled. It got screwed up by mistake and I had to iron it flat again. It'd taken me that long to write it I hadn't the heart to copy it out again.'

'No, don't worry, it was a lovely thought. It meant a lot to me,' Mary said again.

'And I was sorry to hear about your Mam, she was a good woman,' Nelly carried on. She took a tray of unbaked scones from the kitchen table and, opening the oven door, pushed them carelessly onto a shelf. 'I liked what I saw of her.'

'Thanks, Nelly.' Mary left it at that. The feelings hadn't been reciprocated. Winifred couldn't stand Nelly, mainly because Frank was her son.

'And loyal to her family.' Nelly sounded breathless from bending forward. 'Loyal to you, pet. I respected that.'

Her words made Mary uncomfortable. 'How are you keeping?'

'Fair to middling.' Nelly clapped her hands together and a puff of flour rose around her. She turned and studied Mary for a few moments. Then she sighed and gave a guarded smile. 'Hope you don't mind me coming right out with it, pet.' She put her fists on her hips. 'This isn't a social call, is it?'

Straight to the point, Mary thought, deciding to give the old woman the same courtesy. 'No, Nelly, not totally. Is your George in?'

'George?' Nelly put her head to one side. 'No, there's no need to worry, pet, he's out. I would have warned you at the door if he was here, knowing what he's like about you.'

'Yes, of course. I just wanted to make sure. I want to talk to you.' This was going to be worse than Mary had expected.

'About?'

'It's awkward, Nelly.'

'About what, Mary?' Her tone was wary. She folded her arms and leant against the table.

'Can I sit down?'

The woman nodded but when Mary sat at the table she didn't follow suit.

'We've been friends for a long time.' Mary put her palms flat on the worn surface, rubbing them back and forth, covering her fingers with a dusting of flour that she barely noticed. 'And what I want to ask you isn't easy. I …' She stopped.

'Go on.'

Her words came out in a rush. 'The night Tom was killed, I saw the van.'

'And?'

'I've seen the van again, here, in Ashford. It's white with orange markings on the side. Do you understand what I'm saying?'

'I'm not thick. But I still don't know where you're going with this.'

It was obvious to Mary. Nelly knew exactly what she was saying. 'Please don't be like this.' Mary's eyes prickled with hot tears. 'This is as awful for me.'

'Just spit it out.' The words were harsh but the fear was unmistakeable.

'You gave him an alibi. You know it was George…'

'One son.' Nelly pleaded. 'That's all I have now.'

The two women stared at each other. Nelly was the first to blink.

'What do you want me to do, Mary?'

'You know what I want you to do. Tell the truth.' The agony in Nelly's eyes was painful to see but still Mary urged, 'Please Nelly. I just want you to tell the police the truth.'

'I can't help you, pet.' Nelly's voice was weary. 'You know I would if I could … but I can't.'

Mary caught her lower lip between her teeth. She had one thing she could bargain with, but Ellen would be furious with her if – when she found out. 'I need to tell you something else, Nelly.' She rushed on before she could change her mind. 'But you must promise to keep it a secret, for now anyway.'

'What is it?' There was relief in Nelly's voice, as though she thought Mary was changing the subject.

'Please, promise me.'

Nelly closed her eyes slowly in agreement.

'We, you and me, are more than friends. In a way we're related.' Mary waited. Nelly looked baffled. 'My sister, Ellen, has a little girl, she's beautiful.' She spoke quickly. 'She's Frank's child too – your granddaughter.'

'Frank's?' Nelly's ruddy face drained of colour. 'How?' She flopped down on the chair nearest Mary.

'They were together … once. It was a mistake on Ellen's part. No.' She saw Nelly close her eyes in despair. She held up her hand. 'Please, don't fret. It wasn't like what happened to me.' She swallowed hard. 'Ellen was as much to blame as Frank. I'll tell you all about it some other time. For now I just want you to know.' Mary reached over and took Nelly's hand. 'I wanted you to know because I'm frightened what George will do next. I want to protect my family, my niece, your granddaughter.'

Nelly pulled her hand away. 'I don't understand why you haven't told me this before? Frank's? What's she called? How old?' She moved from side to side in bewilderment, tears brimmed. 'I don't understand,' she whispered.

'She's called Linda. She'll be six next May.' Mary could hear her voice tremble. It was a big risk she was taking, one she wasn't entitled to, but she carried on. 'If you stop George, if you tell the police the truth, I'll try to persuade Ellen to let you see Linda, get to know her. Eventually.'

She waited. The only sound was Nelly laboured breathing.

'Nelly?'

The older woman lifted her hand. 'I can't.' She looked at Mary, despair in her eyes. 'I can't.'

'But…'

'I need you to go now. Please.'

The door slammed behind Mary almost before she left the step. Aware that the net curtain shifted to one side in the sash window, she lifted her chin and walked purposefully towards the gate and along the street. She'd just made things worse.

Nelly watched her walk away. Her hand trembled as she let go of the curtain. 'Linda.' She tested the name on her tongue. 'Linda.'

There was a strange feeling inside her. She put her hands to her throat. 'I've got a granddaughter,' she breathed.

Chapter 55

'I've been waiting for you.'

'Why?' George ran his fingers through his hair, fastened the top button of his shirt and straightened his tie. 'I told you I was going to the pub.'

Nelly made herself concentrate. She was keeping the knowledge that she had a granddaughter to herself for now. She'd had too many disappointments in her life and trusting Mary to keep her promise didn't mean she would ever be able to talk to Linda. She gave herself a shake and said, 'Mary Howarth's been here.'

His mouth tightened. 'What about it?'

'I think you know.' He was perfectly capable of doing what Mary had said. He had his father's temper. How had she raised such a monster? With a sickening jolt she remembered that it was the same thought she'd had about Frank, all those years ago.

'No.'

'Yes.' Watching the man, her son, it was as though she'd never seen him properly before. 'When you asked me to tell the police you were home that night, when you went missing those couple of days, you said you'd just been moving stuff for that wide boy mate of yours.' She waited for him to answer.

He lifted his shoulders.

The cold inside Nelly unfolded and grew. 'She said you killed her brother. She saw the van. She saw it then and she saw it again here with you in it. She said you ran him down.'

His expression was all the confirmation she needed. He twisted his head, running his finger round his collar. 'You don't want to believe everything you hear, Ma.'

She looked into his eyes, saw the strange mixture of contempt and barely concealed fear. She didn't know she was going to voice her next words until she heard herself. 'You'll hang.' Oh God. The horrific image made her scalp crawl. She lurched towards the sink and retched.

In the long hiatus that followed, she listened to George's shallow breathing, the slight clearing of the throat he did when he was agitated.

'Ma?'

'I want you to leave.' Her throat was raw, the words hoarse. He had to go. She couldn't stand the sight of him anymore. Her legs shook so violently she thought they wouldn't hold her much longer. Blindly she felt around behind her for a chair.

He caught hold of her hand. 'You don't mean that.'

She pulled away, furious. 'Get off.'

'Ma? Please?'

Nelly fell onto the kitchen chair, banging her elbow on the table. She moaned, almost glad of the physical pain instead of the searing agony that tore at her insides.

'What are you going to do?'

She hated the pleading whine. She'd heard it too many times in his lifetime.

'Tom Howarth murdered our Frank, Ma.'

'You don't know that. Nobody knows who did it.'

'I do. I was told. Her own bloody mother's old boyfriend told me when I was in the Crown.' George knelt down at the side of her. 'That's why they moved to Wales. They ran away to save that coward's skin, to stop the coppers getting him.'

'I don't believe you.' Nelly looked him full in the face. The fear was openly there for her to see now. 'Tom Howarth was a conscientious objector, he went to prison for it. We talked once, Mary and me. She told me all about him. He didn't believe in killing anyone. He didn't kill our Frank.' Nelly couldn't prevent the cold hostility. 'But I do believe you ran him down.' She spoke slowly, firmly. 'I want you to leave.'

He changed then. He challenged her. 'Or what, Ma?'

'I'll go to the police.'

'You wouldn't.' He moved quickly, standing over her.

'I will.' Nelly waited for the blow. It wouldn't be the first time.

Instead he leaned closer to her. 'I'm telling you – Tom Howarth murdered our Frank. You have to believe me.'

Nelly turned her head, shifted in the chair until she couldn't feel his warm breath on her ear. 'I don't. Just go, George. I don't want you here anymore.'

He gave a short laugh and straightened up but still crowded over her. 'Fine. I don't know why I moved to this godforsaken hole in the first place.'

'You'd lost your job and you'd nowhere else to go. No one else to sponge off,' Nelly said softly. 'You're a murderer. You're no better than your brother was. Now get out.'

'You'll give me time to pack my things though, Ma?' he jeered even as he stumbled backwards towards the door. 'You'll do me that favour, like?'

'I'm not your mother. You're not my son. Not anymore.'

She saw the shock register on his face. 'You don't mean that.'

'I do. Now leave me alone.'

The scones had burned. The kitchen filled with swirling blue smoke that stung her eyes. Taking them from the oven and ignoring their scorching heat she crumbled them one by one at the back door and chucked them into the yard. She took off her turban and wiped her hands on it. A pigeon swooped down and snatched at the scattered crumbs, now melting in the puddles on the flags. Breathing in the fresh air, she watched the last threads of smoke float over her head from the kitchen.

Chapter 56

George stayed in his room until it was dark. He didn't care what his mother said. He'd leave when he was ready.

Now, sidling along the wall of the alleyway behind Henshaw Street, he was in half a mind to chuck a brick through Ted Booth's kitchen window on his way to Arthur Brown's house.

'If it wasn't for that stupid cow, Mary Howarth, I'd be in bed with a few pints under my belt by now.' George said in answer to the questioning angle of Arthur's head as he let him in. He looked around in distaste. There were dirty dishes piled high in the sink. A cat sat on the draining board licking its arse.

Arthur, obviously noticing George's face, swiped the cat off with the back of his hand. 'Get down, you bugger.' He gathered a pile of old newspapers off a chair, its arms black and shiny with grease. 'Sit here?' he said, fumbling in his jacket pocket and producing a crumpled packet of Woodbines.

'I'm okay here, thanks.' George picked up Arthur's jacket off the seat of the hard wooden chair by the door and slung it on the back. He sat down, dropping his rucksack to the floor. God what a stinking mess. How the hell can the bloke live like this? Could he stay here? He could catch anything in this fleapit.

'I don't understand why the Howarth girl's back 'ere anyway.' Arthur pleated a piece of newspaper and lit it from the small pile of smouldering coals in the grate before holding it to the end of his cigarette. 'I've a lot to blame on that one. Buggering off with the mother. If she'd not taken 'er off to bloody Wales we would 'ave been wed, Winnie and me.' He sucked furiously on the cigarette in between talking. 'Didn't find out where they'd gone for bloody ages. They made a right fool of me. Sodding laughing stock in the pub I were. Then I 'eard she'd died – my Winnie. If she'd cocked her toes up 'ere, if we'd been wed, I'd be sitting pretty in that house of 'ers instead of this dump.'

George noted Arthur hadn't offered him a fag. Watching the

man, he carefully felt inside one of the pockets of Arthur's jacket and slid out a pound note between two fingers and crumpled it in his palm.

'Last I 'eard, 'er Nazi boyfriend 'ad come back to look for 'er,' Arthur said, letting go of the cinderised paper with a yelp. He examined the skin on his thumb. ''Eard some bugger told him where they'd gone, 'er and 'er bloody mother. I wouldn't 'ave told the bastard. I wouldn't have 'elped 'im – no bloody way. Bloody Kraut.'

George couldn't prevent the smirk.

'Don't you start bloody laughing at me.' Arthur squinted at him. 'What you grinning at, you silly sod?' He scowled. 'Sometimes I think you're bloody mad.'

'Aye, happen you're right,' George said softly, 'happen you're right.'

Arthur shook his head. He sat down on a small wooden stool by the fireplace and tipped his head back against the wall to blow smoke rings before saying, 'Thought I was on my feet there with the mother, you know, mate, 'till that one interfered.'

'Yeah, yeah.'

'So? What 'as she done to you, then?'

'Nowt for you to worry about.' George said, 'Just wondering if I can kip here a few days?'

''Ere!' Arthur sat up, a startled look on his face. 'Why?'

'Had a bust-up with the old lady.'

'What about?'

'Summat and nowt.' George's foot drummed impatiently on the floor.

'She's a fine looking woman, your ma.'

'Yeah, well, you can keep your mitts off her, she's not interested.' George wanted to thump the old bugger but, keeping in mind he needed a favour, he let it go. 'Well? Will you put us up or not?'

'I would if I could.' Arthur's voice took on a whining tone.

'What's stopping you?' George was confused. He'd believed the sad old sod would leap at the chance of a bit of company. Looking around at the shithole, he would have thought Arthur Brown would offer to pay him to stay here. 'What's the problem?'

'Just the one.' Arthur's hand shook as he lit one cigarette from the tab end of the first. 'Howarth's sisters live four doors down. If you've 'ad trouble with the eldest, that means 'e'll be on the war path.' He stood up and moved towards the back door. 'Sorry, that Patrick Howarth's a nasty piece and I'm too bloody old for a fight.'

'Some soddin' mate you are.' George shouldered him as he left. 'Thanks for nothing.'

He'd barely stepped outside when the door crashed behind him. At least he had the pound note. He shoved it into his trouser pocket. Do for a rainy day.

And there might be a lot of those. He frowned. There was no one else in Ashford he could ask tonight. In fact there was no one else in this sodding town he could ask at all. He'd have to sleep in his van. The van – a thought struck him. He'd have to get shot of it, and quick. No home, no van, no work. Danny Arkwright would be mad. He was supposed to be getting rid of that last batch of fags, taking it to Manchester. He thought quickly. He could still do that and get shot of the van at the same time.

What a fucking mess. Bastards, all bastards, the lot of them.

He slung his bag onto his back and, still walking, scooped up a broken half brick out of the weeds at the side of the alleyway. When he stood outside Ted Booth's he bounced the brick in the palm of his hand and peered over the gate. Swinging one arm back he lobbed it at the kitchen window.

For a moment there was silence, then the glass smashed, a woman screamed, a man shouted, an angry yell and the back door to number twenty-seven was flung open.

George didn't wait. As soon as the brick left his hand he started running and didn't stop until he'd crossed Shaw Street and down a passageway to Scott Street. For a few split seconds he savoured the glee. Then, scowling, he looked around. The damp streets were deserted; he was the only bugger out on this miserable night.

Chapter 57

'I don't understand, Mary. Why can't you come home for Christmas?'

'It's just not possible, Gwyneth. Ellen still isn't well and there are other things I need to see to here.' Mary watched Ted angrily sweep the last of the glass onto the shovel. She knew he was furious with himself that he hadn't moved fast enough to catch whoever had thrown the brick. Ellen was only relieved the children were safely tucked up in bed. The window was covered with cardboard. Replacing the glass was an expense they could do without.

A thought suddenly struck her. I couldn't afford the train fare to Wales if I wanted to go. She'd been secretly worrying about money for weeks. With no job, no chance of getting a job with a baby on the way, because she was convinced she *was* pregnant, she didn't know what she was going to do.

'Peter misses you as well, *cariad.*' There was a distressing break in Gwyneth's voice that made Mary close her eyes against the tears. 'Mary?'

'I'm here, love. What has he said?' Had he dared to tell Gwyneth what he'd done? Had he told her that she wasn't going back to Wales, that they'd finished?

'Nothing, *cariad,* that's just it, he won't talk. I know you've had a quarrel of some sort, isn't it. I can tell. But I don't understand.' There was silence between them. The line crackled and hummed. When Gwyneth spoke again her voice was tentative. 'What about the wedding, *cariad?* I thought it was all sorted but then the minister told me on Sunday that Peter had said it wasn't happening until next spring? That you'd set a date when you came back?'

How dare he? A flash of anger almost made her say, I'm not coming back, but she couldn't do that to Gwyneth, not yet anyway. She waited.

'You didn't say anything about that to me.'

'No. I'm sorry, Gwyneth, it was all such a rush to get here and then so much has been happening. I should have kept in touch more.' Mary leant her head against the wall. The back door was open and Ted was in the yard. She could hear him shovelling the glass into the dustbin.

When Mary looked up, Ellen was watching her from the kitchen with a worried look on her face. 'Are you okay?' her sister mouthed at her.

Mary nodded, smiled reassuringly. But she wasn't. By rights she should now be in a frenzy getting ready for the wedding, her days full of excitement and anticipation, instead of this gaping emptiness. If she could just get through the next few days, get past the twenty-third, she'd be all right. Who are you kidding? she thought. That day would be doubly hard, the day she should have married and Tom's birthday. She wondered when that stab of grief, that he wasn't here anymore, would lessen. She forced a smile into her voice. 'Your lovely outfit will keep,' she said.

'I'm not bothered about that, *cariad,* I'm worried about you.'

'Don't be. Please, Gwyneth.'

'When I asked him if he was coming to you for Christmas, he said he had too much work to do in the village.'

Mary fielded the hidden question in her neighbour's voice. 'Will you be all right, Gwyneth? What will you do at Christmas?'

'*O, iawn,* I'll be fine. Ivy Morris at the fish shop is on her own. She's asked me to go to her for the day.'

'Good.' There was a clamour of voices in the kitchen. Mary looked down the hall again. Linda had brought William downstairs. Now she was walking backwards holding onto him and leading him across the room. He was chuckling which was making her laugh as well.

'Listen, Gwyneth, I need to go and help with the children's breakfast. I'll ring soon, I promise. Just look after yourself, eh?'

'Shall I ask Peter to telephone you?' Gwyneth spoke quickly. 'He's always welcome to use my telephone.'

'No, it's all right, love,' Mary butted in, 'he telephones from Alun and Alwyn's place sometimes.' She forced a smile into her voice. 'I'm sorry, Gwyneth, I really must go. Like I've said, don't you worry, everything will be okay.'

It wouldn't. Mary slowly put the receiver down. She placed both palms on her stomach, feeling a slight roundness where before she'd been flat. The cold apprehension that tightened her skin made her feel sick. She was pregnant. And there was no father on the scene.

Chapter 58

Christmas Day

'Here we are.' Jacqueline was excited and relieved to be at Henshaw Street. When she'd woken, there'd been an odd light in her room. Peeping through the curtains, she saw it was snowing and she worried that they wouldn't be able to get to Linda's. She really, really wanted to be with her cousin because, even though Mum and her had moved back with Dad this week, they were still being funny with one another sometimes. And she didn't like Mum sleeping in her room with her because she snored. Dad was sleeping on his own. She always thought mums and dads slept together because they had the biggest bed.

Even opening her presents hadn't been fun. They were so quiet watching her, instead of laughing and teasing like they used to.

In the end she'd left some gifts unwrapped and sat on the bottom step of the stairs for the best part of an hour in her balaclava, coat and wellington boots, waiting to go, unsure if

Mum would agree to going, even though Uncle Ted and Auntie Mary had asked them last week. So she was happy when they finally closed the front door and left, carefully walking along the spade-sized path that Dad had made through the snow.

Kicking off her wellingtons and throwing her balaclava and coat in the direction of the clothes stand in the hall, she ran into the kitchen to find Linda.

'What did you get?' she said, kneeling and hugging her cousin who was on the rug in front of the fire.

'A new doll from Father Christmas, this spinning top from Mummy and Daddy and a toy piano from Auntie Mary. Look.' Linda held up the small, pink, wooden instrument. 'It plays too.'

'I know. Auntie Mary bought one for me as well.' Jacqueline lifted the lid and poked at the keys.

'And she bought William a tambourine.' Linda picked it up and shook it in the little boy's direction. Sitting in his high-chair he leaned over and she handed it to him. Laughing, he banged it on the tray.

'Father Christmas got me a Kaleidoscope and a kit of some moulds and Plaster of Paris. I'll be able to make all the seven dwarfs and Snow White.' Jacqueline pressed down quickly a few times on the handle of the spinning top and it spun off the rug. She scuttled after it. 'And a Rupert Annual.'

'We can swop. I got a Noddy Annual.'

Jean and Patrick crowded in at the door, looking awkward. They were still wearing their coats.

'We nearly didn't get here did we, Mum?' Jacqueline said. 'And look, Linda's got her parrot jumper on that Auntie Mary knitted, like me. Oh and William. See? All the colours all mixed up like mine?'

She gazed up at the Christmas decorations. Mum had only let her fasten some balloons to the ceiling in her bedroom but here they were all over the house; crinkled paper rolls pinned with drawing pins near the light bulb in the centre of the room were twisted round and round, blue then yellow, red then green, and fastened to all the corners. And the lametta draped over each line looked like a sparkling curtain; the short heavy strands of silvery lead balanced precariously, falling off when anyone touched them. Perhaps she and Linda could smuggle some upstairs later, to put over the metal rail on Linda's bed.

'Parrot wool,' Jean corrected, with a tight smile. 'We certainly had a job on the streets,' she agreed.

Jacqueline laughed. 'Dad threw snowballs and Mum threw one back.' Of course the fun stopped after they'd called for Granny Winterbottom. Mum had said she had to come too. Dad almost had to carry her over the snow. He'd pulled some really funny faces behind her back though. 'We had to jump over all these lines of snow that the milkman made with his float. We followed it all along Manchester Road and up your street.'

'Working on Christmas Day, poor sod,' Patrick said.

Jean frowned at him. 'Some of the tracks were none too straight, either,' she said, 'I think he'd already had a tipple or two at some of the houses.'

'Well good for him.' Ted laughed, picking up William and the highchair together and carrying them down the hall to the parlour.

Patrick looked towards the window. 'You find out who chucked the brick?' he asked Ted as he passed him.

'No, they'd gone by the time I got to the alley,' Ted said, his voice tight with renewed anger.

'Probably some drunk. I could ask around?'

'No point. Didn't take long to put new glass in.'

'Bloody cheek, though.'

Jean glared again at Patrick.

'Yeah, well, done now,' Ted said, coming back into the kitchen and glancing at the window, at the same time calling: 'Back in a minute, son,' to William who, objecting to being left on his own, was wailing.

The thought occurred to Mary that it could have been George Shuttleworth but she kept quiet.

'Anything I can do?' Jean asked Mary, taking off her coat and glancing over at Ellen who was sitting in the armchair reading the *Radio Times*.

Ellen saw her; she flapped the magazine. 'Want to read the King's Christmas message ... got his picture in as well?'

'No, thanks. Mary?'

'No, it's all ready. I've set up the table in the parlour and Ted's carried everything in except the chicken.' Mary was flushed, her forehead and nose shining from the heat in the kitchen and scullery and she'd spent most of the morning heaving against the smell of the roasting chicken and boiling sprouts.

And it wasn't just being pregnant or worrying all the time about money that was churning her stomach. Every day she waited for the knock on the door, hoping Nelly had second thoughts and had spoken to the police. Afraid she'd warned her son.

'Bird okay, then?' Patrick said, as Ted passed them it on a large serving dish. 'Got a good deal from the butchers for that and the sausages.'

'First time for everything.' Jean pressed her lips together. He was only trying to get in their good books. It hadn't done him any harm putting his hand in his pocket for once.

'Come on then, don't let it get cold.' Ellen ushered the girls out of the kitchen.

'I'll be with you in a minute. I just need to make some more gravy,' Mary said.

When everyone left she closed the door to the hall and went to the back door for a breath of fresh air. Ted had cleared a path through the snow to the lavvy and thrown some bits of bacon rind down for the birds. Now a cluster of sparrows scattered and lined up on the wall, squabbling. Above them the sky was clear blue and, when she looked higher, she saw the full moon, still visible from the night before, a pale, tissue-paper thinness.

Mary automatically covered her stomach with her hands as though to protect the tiny life inside. Fear for the future mixed with a bleak sadness. And guilt. She shouldn't have told Nelly about Linda without asking Ellen. What she'd say if, or when, she found out, Mary didn't want to think about.

She stretched her neck from side to side to try to release the tension. Closing the back door she pulled her pinny over her head. Looking in the mirror she tidied her hair. She couldn't be bothered with lipstick and face powder.

At the parlour door she listened to the chatter and laughter, the clinking of cutlery and dishes. She took in a long breath, fixed a smile on her face and went in.

The last thing she felt like doing was pretending to enjoy a family day.

'Good scram that, our kid.' Patrick tipped his chair back on two legs. 'If I say so myself. Can't beat a good bird.'

Jean sighed with impatience.

'Glad you enjoyed it,' Mary said, starting to pile the plates together.

'Ask your dad to play his harmonica.' Jacqueline gave Linda a nudge. 'Go on, ask him,' she urged.

'Okay.' Linda went to sit on Ted's knees. Arms around his neck she burrowed her face into his shoulder and whispered to him.

He nodded and went through to the kitchen, returning seconds later holding the harmonica and waving a trail of Izal toilet paper and two combs.

Sitting on the sofa, the two girls next to him, he helped them to wrap the Izal around the combs. 'Right,' he said, '*The Grand Old Duke of York.*' The girls put their lips to their makeshift instruments and hummed. The comb and paper made a rasping sound.

'Makes your lips tingle,' Linda giggled.

Mary forced a smile. Feeling sudden loneliness amongst her family was unbearable. 'I'll clear up,' she said.

'I'll help.' Jean moved her chair back. 'Ted, you and Patrick have some of that rum he brought with him.'

They didn't need telling twice. Ted put the harmonica in his trouser pocket and went to get two glasses from the sideboard. 'Come on, then kids,' he said to appease their protests at the ending of the music, 'who wants a game of Ludo?'

'Are we having a cup of tea?' Peeved at being left out Elsie Winterbottom followed the women into the kitchen. She belched loudly. 'That Christmas pudding has given me indigestion.'

'I thought it was tasty, Mother.' Jean put the large dishes of leftover food on the kitchen table and covered them with plates. 'I thought you did too. You had two helpings. And you got the sixpence.'

'Which she bloody pocketed,' Ellen whispered to Mary. She raised her voice. 'I'll make a brew.'

'I'll make soup with the leftovers later.' Mary ran hot water from the Ascot heater into the sink, ready to tackle the mountain of dirty pots on the draining board.

'That new?' Jean asked.

'The Ascot?' Mary lathered up the bubbles. 'Yes, Ted put it in last week. The other one was on its last legs and this is bigger, holds more water so we're not having to wait for it to heat up all of a piece.'

The window clouded over with the steam, melting the snow that had settled in the corners of the frame. The top panes were still clear and showed a few flakes swirling against the greyness of the late afternoon sky. 'It's started up again,' Jean said, 'I'm going to ask Patrick to take Mother home.'

'Right.' Mary listened to the children's laughter coming from the front room. Any other time it would have made her believe they had a happy carefree childhood. But how many times did she and the others laugh when they were kids, though their house was filled with trouble and anger? Lots, she supposed. Nothing is ever like it seems, she thought, never.

All of a sudden, she knew what she had to do.

The logs in the fire shifted, sending a spark of flames up the chimney and changing the pattern of the shadows on the back wall of the parlour. For once the five adults were comfortable in one another's company. The two men dozed after the half bottle of rum, Ted with his arm around Ellen on the sofa, Patrick slumped in one of the armchairs, his hand on Jean's shoulder as she sat on the floor between his knees. Nobody spoke, nothing contentious had been brought up in the conversation, and general chatter had gradually drifted away.

The children had been in bed for the last hour, worn out by all the day's activities.

Mary held her lower lip between her teeth, sucked on it for a moment. She straightened up in her chair, aware of being the one solitary figure in the room. 'I've got something I need to tell you all.' Her voice was too loud – the men jumped. Jean and Ellen turned quickly to look at her. 'Sorry,' she said.

As one they shook their heads, their eyes fixed on her.

Her heart was thumping. She clasped her hands in her lap to stop them shaking.

The logs shunted again, louder this time, and everyone glanced at the fire before returning to Mary. It gave her a second to calm down. 'I thought I should tell you I'm not going back to Wales. I'm staying in Ashford.' She didn't miss the delight in Ellen's eyes.

'What are you—' Jean started to ask.

'Going to do?' Mary pre-empted her. She turned to Ted. 'If it's okay with you I'll stay here for the time being?'

'Of course, you know you're more than welcome.' He was puzzled. 'But what about Peter?'

'I'll come to him in a minute.'

'You could go for one of the jobs I told you about,' Jean said, immediately enthusiastic.

'I couldn't … I can't. Because I'm pregnant.'

There was a stunned silence.

She hurried on. Better to get it all out into the open while she felt brave enough. 'I'm about three months as far as I can work out. But I'm not with Peter anymore.' She warned Jean to keep quiet with a look. 'And that's not something I'll discuss just now. Which means, Ted, that for the time being I won't be able to pay my way. I won't be able to contribute anything to the housekeeping. I'm sorry.'

'That doesn't matter.' He looked extremely upset. She knew he'd grown to like Peter. 'You've done more than enough these last three months.'

'There's something else.' Her stomach muscles tensed and she threw a cautioning look at Patrick. 'But I need all of you to promise me that you won't tell anyone else.'

'If that's what you want, Mary.' Ted spoke firmly. 'Me and Ellen promise. Don't we, love?'

She moved her head. 'Of course.'

'Jean?'

'Yes, yes.' Mary could tell she was bursting with curiosity.

'Patrick?'

'It depends.'

'Then I can't tell you.'

'Patrick,' Ted said, 'for God's sake man.'

'All right, all right,' Patrick growled, 'I'll say nowt.'

Mary sat back. It was now or never. 'I've seen the van that killed our Tom,' she said. 'Here in Ashford.'

'What!'

'Be quiet, Patrick.' It was Ellen. 'Go on.'

'I went to the police.'

'You did what? Fucking hell, Mary, why?'

'Patrick!' This time it was all three of them who shouted at him.

'I thought they'd believe me,' Mary said. Patrick gave a snort of derision but kept quiet. 'They didn't.' Mary stared down at her folded hand; her knuckles were white. 'I saw the van coming out of Newroyd Street.' She took a deep breath. 'As soon as I did I knew it was the one that ran our Tom down. Same colours, same markings on the side.' Watching Patrick fling himself from his chair she still didn't know if she was doing the right thing. 'George Shuttleworth was driving it.'

Patrick paced the rug in front of the fire. 'Right!'

'You're not to do anything Patrick, you promised.' Mary watched him, anxious.

'I don't understand.' Ellen twisted her fingers together. 'Ted?'

'It's obvious,' he said. 'After all these years Shuttleworth somehow found out where Mary and Tom lived. He drove down there and ran him down because he knew Tom was the one who saved Mary and killed his brother. That's what you're saying, isn't it Mary?' His voice was gentle.

'Yes … but he was wrong.'

Except for the low crackle of the fire and a sudden creak of springs through the ceiling as one of the children turned in their bed, the room was silent.

'You all thought Tom killed Frank. I did too.' She waited a moment. 'But it wasn't Tom, it was Peter.' She kept very still, willing herself to stay calm. 'We had a row the day you asked me to come here. He didn't want me to come to Ashford. I didn't understand why. Then it all came out. He said … he told me … he told me … I'm sorry, I can't.' The tears, held back for so long spilled over. Jean came towards her. Mary flapped a hand at her friend. 'No.' She stumbled from the room.

The icy air, streaming in from outside, stung her throat but still she took in great mouthfuls of it, clinging to the handle of the back door. Her whole body shook. But she'd done it; she'd told them everything. Nothing was hidden now and she felt an enormous relief. Whatever else now happened she wasn't carrying that burden of secrets anymore.

Gradually Mary's head stopped spinning and she began to focus. The yellow light from the kitchen doorframe was a slanted elongated shape on the snow in the yard. A paler blurred shape from the children's bedroom window covered the back gate. The yard walls and lavvy roof were outlined with layers of white. Further away, over the houses on Bridge Terrace, the sky was indecipherable from the surroundings; no moon or stars tonight, just a dark covering of cloud. And all around a smothering silence.

When she heard the footsteps on the kitchen linoleum she knew it was Patrick.

'I'll kill him.'

'Who?' She didn't turn.

'The Kraut.'

'You won't.' She blew her nose.

'Our Tom's dead because of him.'

'No, Tom's dead because George Shuttleworth believed he'd killed Frank.' Mary glanced at Patrick's profile. In the light from the kitchen his face glistened with tears. Impatiently, he wiped them away on the cuff of his shirt sleeve. She pretended she hadn't seen. 'He wanted revenge. But it was on the wrong man.' She scrubbed the handkerchief under her nose again. 'I'm warning you, Patrick, keep away from Peter. Whatever I feel about him, and all I feel at the moment is contempt, you leave him alone.' Still holding onto the handle she twisted around to face Patrick. 'You know why George Shuttleworth believed it was our Tom?' He shook his head, refusing to look at her. 'Because somebody told him that's what happened.'

'Not me,' Patrick protested.

'No, I didn't think that. But who was the one who first pointed their finger at our brother? Who was convinced it was our Tom and didn't waste any time telling us? You.'

Patrick moaned. He rolled against the doorframe, stumbling out into the yard. He crumpled against the wall, shoulders heaving with dry sobs.

Perhaps she'd been too harsh? 'There's nothing we can do now.'

The tears were hot on her cold cheeks. 'And I'm carrying Peter's baby. I couldn't live with myself if anything happened to him.'

Patrick gave a muffled howl. Of anger? Of despair?

'We all share some of the blame for what's happened.' She touched him on the shoulder. 'This all started years ago.' When I first got involved with Frank Shuttleworth, she thought. She stepped into the snow, ready to take him into her arms, to comfort him. 'Shuttleworth might leave us alone now.'

His next words stopped her moving any closer. 'I'll sort it, once and for all.'

'No, Patrick.'

'For Tom. I'll sort it for Tom.'

'No. Leave it alone, Patrick. George Shuttleworth is dangerous.'

'I'm dangerous.' He turned his tear-stained face towards her. 'I'm fuckin' dangerous. He'll find that out soon enough.'

Chapter 59

By the time George Shuttleworth staggered down Barnes Street to the shabby front door of number four, Patrick was surrounded by cigarette butts and memories, and rage.

He resisted rushing up to the man. Instead he watched, biding his time as George stood swaying, mumbling to himself and slapping his hands against first his jacket and then his trouser pockets, looking for keys.

Patrick waited.

George gave up searching and banged on the door before peering through the bay window, shouting and swearing. When there was no reply he gave up and weaved his way to the gate and turned to walk along the road.

Patrick followed him to the narrow lane at the back of the houses. Casting a glance around to make sure they were on their own he shouted, 'Oi!'

'What the hell are you doing here?' George swayed and squinted at Patrick through his cigarette smoke. He took off his cap and rolled it up, smacking it against his thigh.

'I've been looking for you,' Patrick said. 'Someone told me you'd buggered off but here you are.'

'So? I'm back. What's it to you where I've been?'

Patrick shrugged. 'Remember our Tom?' He saw the almost imperceptible flicker of nervousness, the innate aggression falter for a second before re-establishing itself and he knew Mary was right. This was the bastard that killed Tom. 'Tom Howarth,' he said again, his tone soft, 'my brother. Remember him?'

'Huh?'

'You deaf?'

George moved his shoulders. 'Heard about him. Wasn't he the conchie? The bloke too fucking scared to fight? And, from what I hear, a dirty poof?'

Patrick's neck reddened. 'Shut your mouth.'

Since Mary told him about George Shuttleworth, he'd searched all around town for the bastard. He'd no other plan but to beat the living daylights out of the man. To make him pay for what he'd done and to hell with the police. They were no bloody good. He needed to sort this for himself. For Tom.

Now he looked beyond the man and glanced over his shoulder. There was still no one in sight.

'Come on, then.' George appeared to have sobered up rapidly. Shrugging off his jacket, he threw it and the cap on the ground and raised his fists. 'Come on… You want a fight, so come on.'

Patrick noticed the heavy square signet ring on his right hand. Shuttleworth could do some damage with that given half a chance. But he wouldn't get it. He showed all the signs of a heavy drinker, the purple veins on the nose, the rolls of fat under his chin, the tight press of stomach against his shirt. Shuttleworth's movements as he circled in front of him were lumbering and slow. Patrick knew he could play for time, make sure the man knew

213

just why he was going to get the beating of his life. He straightened up, dropped his arms to his sides.

Shuttleworth stopped. 'What you doing?' Uncertainty flickered and then he grinned. 'What's the matter? Bitten off more than you can chew, huh?' He stepped forward, jabbing his finger at Patrick's chest. 'Runs in the family eh, being a coward?'

Spittle hit Patrick in the face with each word. He turned his head away, his lips thinning. Let the fucker talk. He'd talk himself into an early grave.

'Like a rabbit in the headlights, he was.' The man tittered, still prodding at Patrick. 'Couldn't believe my luck when I saw him. Took me the best part of the day to find the place. Never have found him in a month of Sundays if that Nazi hadn't come back to look for his tart.'

That was it. Patrick stopped trying to control himself. He grabbed the man's finger and viciously snapped it backwards. 'What did you say?'

George yelped. 'Sodding hell.' He staggered and lost his balance. He tried to hold on to Patrick's arm but was viciously shaken off.

'What did you say?'

George dropped to the ground and Patrick brought his knee up. There was a loud crack as Shuttleworth's nose broke, splattering blood and mucus. He screamed, rolled over, his hands over his face. Blood poured through his fingers. Patrick studied him for a moment. Then, looking around again to make sure they were still alone, he adjusted his jacket, pulled at the cuffs of his sleeves and, with great concentration, kicked him.

'I'll. Teach. You. To. Fucking. Mess. With. Me.' He ground the words out each time his foot came into contact with the other man's body.

Building up the force behind each attack, he took his time, taking in gulps of air to steady his breathing, pushing back the strands of hair that fell over his face.

The man's screams faded into grunts with each assault.

Patrick gave him one last kick, straining for breath. 'Arsehole.' Then he walked away, his legs faltering.

'Bastard!' The word was slurred but loud enough for Patrick to hear.

In two strides he stood over George, grabbed him by his jacket and hauled him within inches of his face. The man's eyes were swollen and closed.

'What?' Patrick spoke through clenched teeth.

'Bastard.' The man spat two teeth out, flecks of blood landed on Patrick's hand.

Patrick threw him back onto the ground, wiped his fingers on Shuttleworth's shirt. He placed his boot on the man's chest, pressing down, emphasising each word. 'Every fucking time I see you, this is what you'll get.'

Shuttleworth moaned, pushed ineffectually at Patrick's foot.

'We'll keep the coppers out of it but you remember – I know. I know you ran my brother down. I know you murdered him.'

He gave one last kick. The man gave out a long winded breath and lay still.

'So, like I said, you see me anywhere, anytime, you give me a wide berth. You cross the road and you run.'

Chapter 60

'You do know her next door's had the baby, don't you? Day before yesterday. A little lad.' Mary hunched over the fire trying to keep warm. It was freezing outside.

Pulling off her gloves and scarf and unbuttoning her coat, Jean was conscious her friend was watching her with concern. She moved her shoulders in an effort to look nonchalant. Even though she'd prepared herself for it, the news still made her scalp crawl.

'I didn't, no,' she said. 'Nothing to do with me.' But a sickly watery feeling churned inside her. When Jacqueline was born, she'd known Patrick was badly disappointed that she wasn't a boy. He hadn't said anything and he loved their daughter, but, at the time, standing by the hospital bed, she'd seen it. Then the doctor had said no more children after Jacqueline. She'd already had one miscarriage and the birth was difficult. Well, he's got a son now, she thought, that bitch next door managed that for him. Did he know? Had he somehow already sneaked off to see the boy?

Sitting on the arm of Mary's chair she said, 'You haven't seen Patrick today, have you?' She couldn't help asking and, as soon as she had, she was sorry. She saw the way Mary looked at her, as though pitying me, she thought, angry.

'No, love, her husband's there.' So Mary knew exactly what she was getting at.

'I couldn't care less anyway.' She gave Mary a thin smile.

But what about the husband? Wouldn't he know? Hadn't Ellen once told her he was away most of the time, something to do with the TA? Didn't he realise the dates didn't work out? Would it make him think twice? Or had Doreen Whittaker pretended the baby had come early … or late … whichever suited the cow more. The thoughts tumbled around in her head. She didn't want them to but they wouldn't go away.

Mary leaned back and put her hand on Jean's arm. 'You're shaking,' she said. 'Are you sure you're okay, you and Patrick? You're sure it was for the best, you moving back?'

Jean knew all along she'd go back to Patrick. She wouldn't give him the opportunity to get involved with Doreen permanently. She brushed Mary's hand away and stood up. 'It's better for Jacqueline.'

'Is it? You sure about that, Jean? She's still upset. She saw our Patrick with that woman, she sees the way the two of you blow hot and cold. Worst of all she saw him hit you.' Mary twisted around so she could see Jean as she stood in front of the kitchen window. 'She thinks you might leave her dad again. She knows

216

there's something still going on. And if there is any chance you'll split up with him, surely she needs to know.'

Jean flushed. 'And leave the field open for that cow next door? You must think I'm soft.' Hadn't Mary enough to worry about, single, pregnant and virtually homeless? 'I'll deal with it my own way, thank you, and you can be sure he'll not get away with all this scot-free.' But would this baby make a difference?

'Anyway.' She tilted her head towards next door's wall. 'I didn't come here to talk about that.' Even though it plagued her day and night. 'I came to tell you Patrick's been in a fight.' The horror of seeing his face when he walked through the door the day before suddenly returned. 'His face is a right mess.'

'Oh no.' Mary suddenly looked scared.

'A right mess but he says he's all right.' She grimaced. 'He tells me the other bloke looks worse.' A thought flashed into her head – suppose it was Dennis Whittaker? What if he'd confronted Patrick? She looked fearfully at Mary. 'You don't think it was *her* husband, do you?' That would open up a whole new can of worms.

'What?' Mary opened her eyes wide. 'No, definitely not. I saw him pass the back gate this morning and he looked fine.'

'So it can only be something to do with George Shuttleworth?'

'I don't know.' Mary held her hands over her stomach.

There was nothing they could say to make one another feel easier. There was trouble brewing from all directions.

Chapter 61

'I can't keep him.' Doreen Whittaker stood on the doorstep, shabby in an old grey raincoat. She was shivering, her face pinched and white and the hair escaping from her headscarf was lank and greasy. 'We're leaving. Dennis won't let me keep him.'

If only Patrick could see her now, Jean thought, adjusting the paisley scarf on her head. 'What do you want me to do?' She glared at Doreen. Rage closed her throat, made it difficult to breathe. Trust him to be out. 'It's nothing to do with me.'

One of the cotton-padded wire pipe cleaners which she used to curl up her hair overnight was sticking in her neck. She surreptitiously pushed it back under the scarf.

'If you don't take him, he'll go into care or something.' Doreen's shoulders slumped. 'I can't…' She took a huge gulp, still refusing to meet Jean's eyes. 'I can't keep him, I have to be with my husband.' She held out the baby. 'Please.'

'Shame you didn't think of that before you threw yourself at mine.' Jean ignored the desperation in the woman's dark-ringed eyes; hardened her heart to the tiny bundle inches away from her. She looked to see if any of the neighbours were witnessing this debacle. There was no one around but who knew how many were hiding behind their curtains. She hunched her shoulders against the bitter cold. 'I want you to leave.' She nodded towards the gate. There was still a sparkling of frost on the path that the sun wasn't strong enough to shift.

She repeated her earlier words and tried to ignore the baby's whimpering. 'Look, this is nothing to do with me, nothing at all.' She stepped back into the hallway. 'I'm shutting the door now. You'd better get that child home.' Why say that? It wasn't as if she cared what happened to the brat. Even as she thought it, she knew it wasn't the baby's fault he'd been born into all this. He was innocent, an unwanted child. Without looking at the woman she began to close the door.

'Please?' Doreen stopped it from shutting with the flat of her hand. The baby cried louder.

Angry, Jean swung the door open. The woman fell forwards and was only stopped by Jean catching hold of her. In an instant the baby was thrust into her arms and Doreen had half turned away.

'Whoa there, madam.' Holding the child to her, Jean clutched at the woman's coat. 'Just one minute. Where the hell do you think you're going?'

'I have to do this. Dennis says if I've still got him when I get home he'll leave on his own.' Doreen yanked herself away and hurried to the gate.

'I've told you, this is not my problem.' Jean raised her voice above the baby's cries. She was beginning to panic. It really looked as if the woman would leave. Still in her slippers she ran after her, slithering and sliding on the icy path. As Doreen quickened her steps Jean faltered to a stop. 'I'm putting him down,' she yelled, oblivious to the next door neighbour who, stooping to pick up the milk bottle from her doorstep, had stopped in surprise and now, still half bent, was staring at Jean. 'Do you hear me? I'm putting your baby on the ground.'

'Do what you want.' Doreen didn't look back.

Jean watched until she'd disappeared around the corner.

'Mum, come in.' Jacqueline was at the front door. 'Bring it in.' She made a gesture, indicating the house. 'Bring it in, we'll look after it.'

Oh God, Jacqueline had heard everything. Jean cursed her husband.

'We'll have it if she doesn't want him. She's nasty. You should have just taken it and told her to bugger off, Mum.'

Jean heard the neighbour make a tutting sound and turned to glare at her before hurrying into the house, holding the baby at arm's length.

Jacqueline was arranging the eiderdown off her bed on the rug in front of the fire in the living room. 'Let's put it here,' she said, leaning back on her haunches and holding out her arms.

Jean knelt down next to her, relieved she didn't have to hold the baby any longer than necessary. 'We can't keep him.' He began to scream again, a thin helpless wail interspersed with quivering silence, as though he was listening for a response.

'Isn't he my brother like William is Linda's?' Intent on

unfolding the blanket wrapped around the little boy, Jacqueline didn't see Jean flinch. 'Pooh!' She held her nose. The stench from his dirty nappy immediately filled the room. But when she saw her mother's look of disgust she said, 'It can't help it. It's only a baby. It doesn't know how to use the lavvy yet.'

Ignoring the protest Jean pushed herself off her knees. 'I'll find some rags, clean him up.'

Undressed, the little boy was pitifully thin, his lower body caked in excrement. Jean concentrated on cleaning him, pushing away the compassion which vied in equal measure with anger towards her husband, towards the child's mother.

'What's he called?' Jacqueline was sitting back watching with interest and excitement, her arms folded across her knees which she'd pulled up under her chin.

'I don't know.' It struck her. She didn't even know the kid's name. She stood again. 'I'll find something to make into nappies.' She looked around the room. A feeling of helplessness prevented her from moving. This was her worst nightmare. 'Towels,' she said at last. 'I'll cut a towel up, that'll do.' She nodded, agreeing with herself. 'Nappies and starch.'

'Starch?'

'Reckitts' starch. It's good for nappy rash. I used it on you.'

When she came back into the room Jacqueline had wrapped the now-sleeping baby in her cardigan and was cuddling him as she rocked from side to side. When she looked up at her mother she beamed. 'See, I've got him to sleep.'

Damn you, Patrick, you'll pay for this, Jean thought. You'll bloody pay.

220

Chapter 62

'Where's Doreen?'

'They've gone.' Ellen didn't look up at Patrick. Her arms were aching but she was determined to finish sweeping the yard. She banged the head of the brush on the wall to clean it. Brick dust fell off and she swept it onto the shovel with the rest of the debris. 'Left last night, and good riddance.'

She put the brush behind the door of the lavatory and closed it, folding her coat closer around her, suddenly cold and tired again. 'Why do you want to know? I would have thought you'd have learned your lesson, Patrick, you got your fingers well and truly burnt there.'

When he didn't answer she glanced towards him. He stood in the gateway, the baby in his arms swaddled in a grey Army blanket. She looked swiftly from him to the house next door. 'No!' Her hands on her hips, she said, 'What have you done?'

He scowled. 'Wasn't me. Stupid tart came round yesterday and dumped it on Jean. I've had a right soddin' earful, I can tell you.' The baby started to cry. He hugged it closer to him, jiggling his arms up and down and then said, 'Can I come in a minute?'

It wasn't like him to sound so unsure. 'Course.' Mary was right when she said it was one thing after another in this family. She led the way to the back door and held it open. 'Get in front of the fire, you look frozen. That child shouldn't be out without proper clothes on.' Undoing her scarf, she pulled it off and shook her hair free.

'It's all he's got. The stupid cow left him at our place like this.'

'I'll find some old stuff of William's in a minute.'

She went to the bottom of the stairs. She avoided the spot where Hannah had lain. She always avoided walking there. What happened that morning was something she'd have to live with for the rest of her life.

'Mary?' Anxiously, she threaded her fingers together. 'Can you come down a minute?' Ellen glanced at Patrick, noticed how he gently uncovered the baby to let the flames warm him. She wouldn't have believed how sensitive he could be. 'Mary?'

'What is it? For goodness sake I'll be down in a minute.'

Ellen nodded. She stood still watching the baby. He wore a grey woollen romper suit. His little legs were rosy as he gradually warmed up. 'I'll get those clothes in a minute,' she said.

The voice from the wireless filled the silence: *Labour politician Herbert Morrison sees the Festival as a means of giving the British people a symbolic pat on the back for their postwar achievements and sacrifices. And Gerald Barry, the Festival's director general, claims that the Festival will prove a 'tonic to the nation'.*

'Must be bloody joking.' Patrick glowered at the wireless. 'Pompous bugger. Here they go again, getting it all wrong. We need a festival like a hole in the bloody head, state the country's in.'

'State you're in, more like.' Ellen looked anxiously towards the bottom of the stairs. Come on, Mary, she urged silently. 'You've enough to worry about without griping about the bloody Government, Patrick.' She turned the wireless off. 'Mary!'

'God only knows what I'll do.' He clumsily arranged the baby in his arms. 'You any ideas?'

'No.' She watched him struggle. 'There's only one thing you can do, you know that,' she said. 'You're going to have to throw yourself on Jean's mercy and ask her if she'll look after him. You've no choice.'

'What's going on?' Mary stepped down from the last tread. She stopped when she saw Patrick with the baby.

Ellen swept her arm around. 'See?'

'I can see.' Mary buttoned her thick cardigan over her wraparound pinny. 'I just don't believe it.'

'I don't need a soddin' lecture.'

'Then you'd better leave,' Mary said sharply. 'You've a talent for bringing trouble on yourself, Patrick, but this time it seems you've dragged us all in it. Is that what I think it is?'

222

'Doreen's baby,' Ellen said. 'She's dumped him on him.'

'But they've gone.' Mary looked bewildered. 'They left yesterday.'

'So I bloody hear.'

'I'll look for those clothes.' Ellen almost ran up the stairs, glad to get away from the row that seemed to be brewing.

Mary fixed him with a stare. 'How's Jean taking this?'

'Like I said to Ellen, I've had a right ear-bashing.'

'Poor you.' She didn't even try to cover up the sarcasm. 'Better than another kind of bashing, I guess.'

'Okay, okay. You're having a right dig today, aren't you?' Patrick flushed, uneasy under her stare.

'First chance I've really had.'

'I've said I'm sorry to her. Right?'

'You know what I'm talking about then?'

'Come on, sis, I know I was wrong. It'll not happen again.'

'If I remember rightly, Dad used to say the same thing.'

'I'd cut my right arm—'

'Don't.' Mary's voice was cold. 'Don't say it. I told her to leave you for good, you know.'

'I know.'

'Next time you raise a hand to her, I'll make sure she does.'

'I've told you, there won't be a next time.'

'Good.'

The baby began to cry.

Mary moved towards the two of them, her arms instinctively held out. Then she lowered them. Patrick had to deal with this on his own. 'Has he been fed?'

'I fed him this morning. I got a bottle and some Ostermilk stuff from the chemist. He said that's what's used these days. But I haven't got it with me.' Patrick jerked his head towards the wall. 'I thought she'd be there. I was going to give him back. Poor little blighter should be with his mother.' He wiped his palm over his face. 'Not with me.'

'We've got some evaporated milk I can water down and there's an old bottle of William's in one of the cupboards, I think.' Mary knelt down and opened one of the sideboard doors. She gave a small sound of triumph. 'Here it is. I'll rinse it out. I think there's still some hot water in the kettle.'

When she came out of the scullery with the bottle and the evaporated milk he looked up at her. 'What am I going to do with a bloody kid, sis?'

What am *I* going to do? she thought. I shouldn't be drifting along not making any plans, but what else can I do? She flipped a look at him, opening the drawer under the table to find the can opener. 'You should have thought of that ... and no, I won't,' she said in answer to the unspoken question of his face. 'I'm not taking him on. In case you've forgotten I'll have a baby of my own soon and for now I have enough to do looking after Ellen's two until she's properly on her feet.' She struggled with the can opener and the tin of evaporated milk.

'One more thing – Jean said the other day you'd been in a fight? Shuttleworth?' She kept her voice down, looking over her shoulder at the stairs.

'He won't bother us again.'

'I asked you not to do anything. I asked you to leave well alone.' She forced the blade of the can opener through the last bit of tin and prised open the top. 'I should have known you wouldn't be able to keep your hands to yourself.'

'Well, you going to old Ma Shuttleworth didn't work, did it?' Patrick stood and patted the whimpering baby.

'It might have, if you'd given it some time.' Mary poured the evaporated milk and some of the warm water into the glass baby bottle and forced the rubber teat on.

'She wouldn't drop him in it with the police and I'm damn sure he wouldn't have given himself up.'

'You can't solve everything with your fists. One day you'll come across somebody who gives as good as they get.' Shaking the

224

mixture, Mary perched on the arm of the chair next to Patrick. 'No, you do it,' she said as he tried to pass the little boy to her. She gave him the bottle. 'You'll need the practice.' She watched the little boy suck greedily on the teat. 'God, he is hungry, poor little beggar.' She lowered her voice. 'I'm worried, Patrick. George Shuttleworth?'

'I told you, I sorted him.'

'No you didn't, you had a fight with him. He won't leave it at that, you know. He's no different than his brother was. He'll want his revenge.'

'Then I'll be fuckin' ready for him. But I'm telling you, Mary, he's learned his lesson. There's no way he'll bother us again.'

Chapter 63

'Where is she?' The woman stood in front of Peter, hatred etched on her face under a broad-brimmed brown hat, which had darkened on one side from the earlier rain. 'What have you done with her?' He tried to sidestep her but she thrust her furled umbrella across his path. 'I've known Mary from the first week they moved here and I'm not shifting until you tell me where she is.' She stood toe to toe with him, her mud-caked wellingtons pushed against his own.

Peter looked around, helplessly aware they had attracted some attention from a few passers-by. He wished he'd gone straight back to the cottage instead of offering to wait for Gwyneth, to carry her shopping for her. 'I am sorry—' he began.

'You will be.' In the light from the shop window, her weather-beaten cheeks developed an unsightly red flush.

'What's all this, Mair Bevans?' Gwyneth came out of the butcher's shop. 'Bullying again? What's the matter? Had another row with your Ryan, is it?'

'I just want to know what this one has done with Mary. Not seen her for months on my rounds.'

'Just because he cancelled the milk doesn't mean anything. Don't be so bloody *twp*, woman. Mary's looking after her family in England, see? Now, if you don't mind?' Gwyneth handed her shopping bags to Peter, who took them in one hand. 'We'll be on our way.' She glanced around at the small group of people who had gathered, fixing them with a scathing glare. She linked arms with Peter as they walked away.

'You know, Peter, that sister of hers must be better by now. She's one for always wanting attention, see,' she said. 'I knew it from the minute I saw her years ago. Not bad, just spoiled. And, from what I saw, nobody has babied her more than Mary.'

He didn't answer. He didn't feel he had the right to judge Ellen but he couldn't help the resentment. If it wasn't for her he and Mary wouldn't have quarrelled. Instantly he was fiercely ashamed of himself. If he'd told the truth as soon as he arrived in Llamroth they might have had a chance of happiness. As it was he'd been *ein Feigling* – a coward. It wasn't Ellen's fault. It wasn't anybody else's fault but his own.

Gwyneth was watching him. 'Mary's grieving,' she said eventually, 'that's what it is. She and Tom were very close. They looked after one another and it's only a few months since he went … and in such a horrible way.' Her voice choked. 'No,' she said as Peter stopped walking. 'I'm all right, keep going.' She gave a small cough before saying, 'She's grieving for him. It's all part of life. So she's gone away from where it happened, just for the time being.' She gave his arm a little shake. 'But not for too long, see. Now, I know there's something you've not told me … and that's fine. But I also know how much you mean to one another. So, when you think the time is right, will you go after her?'

Peter thought for a moment. He couldn't tell her the truth; what he'd done, how he'd hidden behind the lies, how he'd ruined Mary's life by coming back to find her. He shook his head. 'She does not want me to go there. I must wait for her here.'

Other than making a small noise of exasperation, Gwyneth was quiet as they walked along the road. In the gathering darkness Peter heard the sea moving sluggishly between tides, a damp film of mist glistened in the gas street lights, hovering above the beach. His pressed his thumb and forefinger against his eyes, ashamed to show that tears threatened. His skin was cold and clammy.

'Oh!' Gwyneth gave a shudder. 'Someone's just walked over my grave.'

'What is it?' Peter was concerned. She looked frightened for a moment.

She gave him a small smile. 'Just a shiver,' she said, still looking at him pensively. They'd reached the cottages. Peter walked with her to her front door.

'Come in for a cup of tea?'

'No, thank you, no.' He gestured to his clothes and boots. 'I have had a long day working with Alun and Alwyn in their garden. They are putting a new shed there,' he said, by way of explanation.

'Have you eaten today?' Gwyneth studied him.

'I have.' He hadn't. But all he wanted was to go into the cottage next door. All he wanted was to lie down on the bed; the bed where he and Mary had slept and made love. To wrap himself in the covers and sleep, to escape the misery that walked alongside him all the time.

Chapter 64

The air carried a fine drizzle that landed bead-like on Jean's raincoat as she hurried towards Skirm Park. The two girls were swinging on the new gates at the entrance oblivious to the rain.

'Get down, you two,' she said, brusquely, 'you'll be wet and filthy before we start.'

She was so tired. The baby had cried for most of the night. She'd heard Patrick walking about in the spare room with him.

Once, Jacqueline had gone in to them. Jean forced herself to stay in bed. She'd lain on her back, listening, arms by her side, her teeth clenched so hard her jaw ached.

'Go on, get down.'

Linda jumped onto the ground and, tucking her doll under her arm, held her hands out. Making an impatient noise Jean pulled a handkerchief out of her pocket and wiped the grime off her niece's fingers. 'There, all clean.' She smiled at Linda and gave her a quick hug before raising her voice in annoyance. 'Jacqueline, get down. I won't tell you again.'

Jacqueline leapt from the gate and raced towards the lake, wiping her hands on her dress before holding out her arms and twirling around, faster and faster, then she stood with her eyes closed until she began to topple over.

'Jacqueline, stop it, if you fall over you'll get grass stains all over your dress.' Her daughter laughed, staggering towards them and crossing her eyes.

Linda giggled.

'If the wind changes you'll stay like that,' Jean warned, but forced a laugh. She didn't want her daughter to see how tired and upset she was.

'Look up at the trees, our Linda,' Jacqueline shouted. 'Remember when it snowed and you said it looked like that crotchy thingy mat your Mum has on her sideboard?'

'Crocheted,' Jean corrected. 'Crocheted.' She rummaged in her handbag for her cigarettes and matches and then changed her mind. She only smoked to annoy Patrick because he hated seeing it. He wasn't here now, so there was no point.

'Yeah, well, Linda said the snow on the trees looked like a piece of that and she was right.' Linda looked smug. Jacqueline grabbed her cousin's hand. 'Now, all the leaves are coming out like little fans.' She looked around. 'Can we go on a boat?'

'Not today.' Jean walked towards the bandstand. 'Too wet. Play on the swings.' This whole park thing was a bad idea but she'd had to get out of the house before she went mad. The whole place was littered with the baby's things. 'Far too wet,' she said again.

'Slide then.' Jacqueline dragged Linda to the playground. 'Let's go on the slide.'

'I won't be able to hold on to my dolly.' Linda hung back. 'I don't like it. It's too high.' The metal sheet glittered with blobs of golden rain in the weak sun. 'And I'd get my knickers wet,' she said.

'Don't be a mardy. Put it down. It's not as though it's a real baby,' Jacqueline said. 'Not like ours. He's a real baby.'

Hearing what her daughter said brought a frown to Jean's face.

'Come on.' Jacqueline climbed the steps. 'The wet'll make us go faster, be more fun.' She stopped, held out her hand. 'Come on, I'm with you. I'll make sure you're okay.' She moved to one side to let Linda pass and then grabbed the rails just in front of her so her own arms encompassed her. 'See? You're safe, you can't fall back,' she said. 'When we get to the top, wait until I sit down and then sit on my lap. That way I've got you and you won't get your knickers wet.'

Linda clutched Jacqueline's knees as they hurtled down the slide, both of them screaming. When they reached the bottom they were tangled together and it took a while before they could stand up. 'Again.' Linda laughed. 'Again.' She gave Jacqueline a kiss.

'Yuk, what was that for, you daft brush?'

'Cos,' Linda said, 'just cos.'

They ran round to the steps again.

'Hello, love.' Patrick stood next to Jean who was absently watching the girls and listening to the bell ringers practise at St John's church. 'Mind if I join you?'

Jean shrugged, not looking at him. He must have followed them from the house. She reached inside her handbag for her cigarettes.

Patrick unstrapped the baby and took him out of the pushchair.

229

Jean looked at the child, recognising the blue knitted hat and coat. Ellen appeared to have donated most of her son's old clothes to Patrick's by-blow. Well, she was showing whose side she was on, no doubt about that. She blinked hard.

'Can we talk?' Patrick sat on the iron bench, his knees only inches from hers. He put his hand on her sleeve.

Jean felt the tingle in her stomach from his nearness. They hadn't made love since Bonfire Night and, although she wouldn't admit it, she missed him.

'Jean?' She didn't respond. 'Love, look at me.' He moved his fingers down until he was gently stroking the back of her clenched hand. 'Love?'

'Dad!' The shriek came from Jacqueline. 'Have you come to take us on the boats? Will you, Dad? Will you take us on the boats?' She galloped up to him turning her pleas in her mother's direction. 'It stopped raining ages ago.' She made a wide arc with her arms towards the sky. 'Please, Mum?'

Patrick leaned forward, only inches from her. 'I can't sweetheart. I've got Jack to see to.'

Jack? Jean grimaced. Where the hell had he got that name from? I'd have chosen Adam, after my granddad, if I'd been asked. What was she thinking? She had no interest whatsoever in the child. But she'd furtively watched her husband struggle to cope with the baby over the last month. She hadn't even offered to help him when he'd gone to one of the stalls to check the stock or cover for someone who was absent. He'd just fastened the boy into a makeshift cot on the backseat of the car and left. To give him his due, she thought, he hadn't moaned once about it and he'd never asked for her help. Until now. The implication was there. She sniffed, aware both Patrick and Jacqueline were looking at her. She knew they were waiting for her to offer to hold the baby while he took the girls on a boat. He knew there was little she'd refuse her daughter if it were possible.

'Mum? You take him,' Jacqueline demanded.

Silently Jean held out her arms. Patrick passed Jack over to her. 'He should stay asleep. He's only just had a bottle.'

She nodded stiffly, looking straight ahead.

Patrick and Jacqueline ran down to Linda, who was waiting by the lakeside, thumb in her mouth and holding her doll to her face, its clay head against her cheek.

Clutching one another, the girls stepped into the middle of the wobbling rowing boat, while Patrick paid the hire fee to the attendant sitting inside the small green ticket box. He took off his flat cap, shoving it into the pocket of his coat which he folded so that the lining was to the outside. Then he doubled it up and handed it to Jacqueline. The girls waited in excited impatience as he sat down on the seat, turned his shirtsleeves up his arms and stuck his thumbs under his braces to adjust them. 'Right,' he said at last, 'let's go.'

Spitting on his hands and rubbing them together with a flourish, Patrick grasped the oars, delicately turning the left one in small circles to spin the boat around before heaving on them both and heading for the middle of the lake. The clunk of the oar in the stirrup and slap of water on the paddle were the only sounds as his muscles bulged and relaxed in his arms.

Jean felt the warmth of the small body against hers. She'd opened her raincoat so the baby wouldn't get wet against it and wrapped it around both of them. He was taking small open-mouthed breaths. She glanced across at the lake, making sure no one was watching before looking down at the little boy's face. Barely five months old his features were as yet not fully formed but with a start she saw the shape of his eyebrows, the curve of his earlobe, both so familiar. There was no doubt she was holding her husband's child by another woman. She registered the knowledge with an acceptance that surprised her and tried to work out why the anger against the boy, which had flared since his birth, had burned itself out. She was holding the answer in her arms. He was so small, so vulnerable. Whatever the circumstances of his conception, it wasn't his fault.

Yet, stubbornly, as she knew she would, when they finally climbed out of the boat and stumbled up the wooden ramp, when Patrick walked towards her, hand in hand with the girls, she set her face and held the baby out to him saying, 'It wants changing.'

'He's called Jack,' Jacqueline said, 'like the beginning of my name. Call him Jack, Mum.'

It hadn't occurred to Jean. She looked up at Patrick. He grinned sheepishly, in the way that usually melted any animosity towards him. 'Seemed the obvious thing.' He moved his shoulders.

'Not to me,' Jean interrupted. 'Not to me.' He'd even stolen that from her. He'd chosen Jacqueline's name and now he'd shared it with another woman's bastard. How could he? However irrational a thought, and she knew it was, she couldn't stop the anger. But this time it was different. This time there was a deep hurt threaded through the resentment that didn't include the boy. In the thirty minutes she had held him close to her something had changed. What she felt about him was completely different from how she felt about Patrick. What she felt for the boy – for Jack – was a tiny flame of compassion, of a need to protect this defenceless human being, born into such turmoil.

But she'd be damned if she'd let anyone know how she felt.

Chapter 65

George pushed his way through the white sheets and pillowcases propped up on washing lines strung from the outside lavatory to the house. His hands left smears of grime.

'Ma?'

Nelly was at the kitchen table ironing. The back of her neck was red and sweaty. She stiffened. 'What do you want?' She didn't turn to look at him.

'Well, that's a nice way to greet your son.' George dropped his duffle bag on the floor and slung his jacket on top of it. He wiped his nose with the back of his hand and sniffed, hoping she'd notice he had a cold. When she still didn't look at him he shrugged and glanced around. 'Mind if I make a brew? I'm parched.'

'Aye, I do.' This time Nelly banged the iron down onto the asbestos trivet and swung round to stare at him. 'I told you, you're no son of mine. Get out.'

'Oh for fuck's sake, Ma, look at the state of me.'

'Not my problem anymore.' Determined not to ask where he'd been, Nelly forced down the pity she felt at the sight of him. His hair needed a good cut and he was filthy. She noticed the frightening scars and the puffiness around his red-rimmed eyes. 'Still drinking, though, I see.' She took the iron and crossed the kitchen to put it on top of the range. Picking up a smaller, second one she spit on the flat of it. The saliva hissed and bubbled and she nodded, satisfied.

'Piss off,' he said.

It hadn't taken long for his temper to show, Nelly thought. 'You bugger off, George. Now! You'll get nothing more from me. Ever.' A second later she felt the blow in the middle of her back. She fell against the hard back of the chair and then onto the floor. She rolled onto her back, fighting for breath, one arm covering her face as he bent over her.

'I'm back,' he said, 'whether you like it or not.' He grabbed the front of her apron and pulled her closer. 'Now, sort me a bath out and then get me some grub.'

She didn't think what she was doing. As though by itself her arm swung in an arc, the hot iron still in her hand.

'Bloody cow!' George staggered back holding his cheek, his skin reddening.

Taking advantage of his shock, Nelly got on all fours and, still clutching the iron in one hand, heaved on the edge of the table to pull herself upright. The pain in her back was almost unbearable but she lumbered towards him, erratically swinging the iron. 'Out!' she shouted, 'Out!'

'You're mad, you stupid bitch,' he yelled, backing away. 'You want locking up.'

'It's not me that'll up be locked up if you come near me again,' Nelly panted. 'I'm warning you for the last time.' She gave him a shove. 'If I see you … or even hear you're still in Ashford I'll go to the police. And don't think I won't.'

He fell through the open back door into the yard. Throwing his bag and jacket after him, she slammed the door and bolted it.

'You'll be fuckin' sorry you've done that,' he yelled.

Nelly covered her ears. 'Go away,' she mumbled, 'leave me alone.'

He carried on cursing and shouting. Then stopped. Nelly stayed leaning against the door for a few minutes before straightening up. She peered through the net curtains at the window. He'd gone. She was shaking. She stumbled towards the armchair by the range, sinking onto it. He'd gone. But she knew it hadn't ended. She didn't dare to think what he'd do next.

Chapter 66

'I should have stayed in Manchester with my mates.' He tipped back on the chair, balancing on two legs. 'We've had such a blindin' time they begged me to stay.' His mouth twisted. They hadn't, not the last lot he'd dossed at; kicked him out like his sodding mother had, like they all had in the end, just because his money had gone. With no one else to sponge off, he'd had to come back to Ashford.

He pinched his nostrils together and sniffed before spitting out into the empty fireplace.

'Hey up, yer dirty bugger,' Arthur Brown said, 'don't do that.'

'Got a cold.' George sniffed again.

'Well, use your sodding 'anky,' Arthur grumbled.

George noticed an opened bottle of Arthur's homemade potato wine on the sideboard. 'I could do with a drink. Bloody landlord in the Crown wouldn't serve me.'

'That's my last bottle.' Arthur reached over and, opening one of the doors, put it in the cupboard.

George stood up to leave. 'You're a miserable bastard, Brown. Always have been, always will be. A proper bloody tight-arse.'

George hung around in Skirm Park until it was almost dark and the park-keeper kicked him out and locked the gates. There was only one place left to go.

He sidled through alleyways and side streets in a circuitous route, resentment and anger rising as he passed the terraced houses with the lit windows and the sounds of voices, muffled by curtains.

Once, hearing footsteps, he waited in the shadow of one of the Corinthian columns outside the Roxy. The cinema was closed, the crowds dispersed over an hour ago, and behind the mullioned windows the building was in darkness. A couple, arm in arm, hurried past, their voices loud and echoing as they walked under the glass canopy. He gave them a few minutes before moving off again, slipping past the backs of the houses to come out near the camp.

There were no street lamps at this end of Shaw Street. The cloud-shaded half-moon gave just enough light for him to check there was no one around. He crossed the road and pushed his way through the undergrowth beside the high fence. After a few minutes he stopped. The culvert was hidden by shrubbery and rubble, but he knew exactly where it was. Tucking his jacket into his large duffle bag and pushing the two blankets he'd dragged off his bed in front of him, he worked for a few minutes clearing the entrance before crawling inside.

The smell hit him instantly, a rank dampness; the culvert angled upwards and a thin trickle of slimy water trailed sluggishly downwards under him. He clutched the blankets to him and wiped first one hand and then the other on his jacket lapel, thinking of his mother sitting in the warmth at their house. 'Bitch!'

The curse resounded around him, and he heard a tiny rattle of claws and high-pitched squeals somewhere in the darkness. He stopped, swallowed the sob in his throat and tried to hold his breath against the stench. When he pressed the switch on his chrome torch, the bulb flickered and went out.

'Shit!' He shook the torch hard. It suddenly lit, filling the culvert with a harsh yellow beam. And then went out. In his frustration he banged it on the side of the metal tunnel. The dull thud was followed by the tinkle of glass and a sudden pain in his thumb. 'Shit,' he muttered again, sucking at the skin. He tasted blood.

The smell of the tunnel, the dampness seeping into his clothes, the sharp pain, and the darkness prevented him moving forwards. In that moment, the self-pity, the hatred gnawing at his insides was overwhelming. He covered his head with the blankets and howled.

The noise stilled him. He crouched, knees under his chin, waiting for any sense of courage to return. Eventually, gagging, he scrambled up, avoiding the slow moving slime under his arms and knees. Taking short breaths through his mouth helped to shut off the stink.

It took a long time. The rats' squeaks stayed just ahead of him, stopping every time he did. The tunnel was wide but it was long and he struggled against the instinctive panic of being trapped.

At last, he felt a change in the air. Wedging his knees against the sides of the culvert he pulled himself upwards, laughing with relief. Hooking his fingers around the edge, he fell out onto the ground.

He stood for a moment gulping in the fresh air. Then he bent over and retched, vomit splashing over his boots.

Trembling, he waited until the heaving subsided before feeling his way around the crumbling brick walls that enclosed the duct.

Years ago, the first time he found his way into the camp, just to have a nose around after a long session in the Crown, he'd realised this small building housed some sort of drainage system. There were channels leading to other culverts covered by metal grids and bits of pipes. Frank used to say the hospital was like a warren, full of places where he and the other guards could stash beer for the long boring night shifts. From the sight of the dusty old broken bottles scattered around, this was obviously one of them.

Relying on the pale moon to find his way, George slowly crossed a narrow path towards the hospital and felt down the side of the building until he came to some steps leading up to a small door. He fumbled in his pocket for matches. In the small pool of light he moved cautiously along the dark corridors. The air was fetid. He'd seen rats here as well, before now.

The flame crept along the match. Spitting on his fingers he turned it and held onto the blackened end until that too burned. He'd need to be careful and limit his cigarettes; he only had the one box of matches.

The boiler room felt damp when he forced open the heavy door. And cold. There was little light from the air vents near the ceiling.

He threw the blankets on the floor and knelt down to rummage blindly inside his duffle bag for a bottle of beer. There was enough food filched from home to last a few days but the beer had been his first thought.

'Fuckin' shithole. Fuckin' Ma. Fuckin' Brown. Fuckin' Howarths.'

Because of them he was stuck here. Because of them he would have to run, to hide somewhere where no one knew him.

But sooner or later he'd make sure they were sorry they'd ever crossed him.

Chapter 67

'Have you been to the doctor's yet?'

'No, there's no need. I'm fit and healthy.' Mary was making a pastry crust for the meat and potato pie that was cooling on the table. 'A bit like you these days. It's good to see you getting more like your old self.' She studied Ellen. 'You're feeling better?'

'I'm sleeping better, not having as many nightmares,' Ellen said, 'and I don't get as tired so quickly.'

'Good, I'm glad.' Mary smiled. She shook the last of the flour through the sieve and banged it on the side of the mixing bowl. 'Look, there's something I need to say, well, ask really.' She rested her hands flat on the table. She hadn't slept well herself over the last week. However she lay, she couldn't get comfortable and she couldn't stop the fears for the future. Now, knowing what depended on Ellen's answer, she felt sick. 'And be honest, love. Do you think you could manage on your own now? Without me being here?'

'No! Why are you asking that?' Her voice rose immediately. 'I don't. I can't.'

'You don't mind my staying on here, at least for the time being?'

'This is as much your house as mine, Mary. Mam left it to us all.' Ellen sat forward on the edge of her chair and rested her arms on the table.

'But it's your home,' Mary insisted. 'I know at Christmas Ted said I could stay, but I have been here quite a while now and I'm not helping moneywise at all.'

'You brought your ration books.' Ellen put her hand over Mary's. 'Don't go.'

'It's just that Ted's been so quiet lately. I wondered if he thought I was in the way?'

'Don't be daft. No, he says he feels guilty he doesn't miss his mother.'

'Is that what it is?' Relieved Mary slid her fingers from under

Ellen's and straightened up to rub at the ache in the small of her back. 'His mother? I'd be surprised if either of you thought twice about his mother, knowing how vile she was to you.'

'She was a nasty cow.' Ellen's gaze slid towards the bottom of the stairs. 'She did her best to split us up. And I think Ted's glad she's gone. But he feels guilty…' Mary waited. 'That and the shop. He worries when he can't get stuff for the shop. He's struggled to get decent flour this last month.' Ellen wafted that worry away. 'We have talked about it … you and the baby.'

'What's he said?'

'Nothing. Except to suggest I do a bit more round the house.' Despite the ache spreading further up her back Mary smiled. Her sister couldn't have sounded more disgruntled if she'd tried. 'We want you to stay. And the children love having you here, especially Linda. She worships the ground you walk on, you know that.'

'And I love her … and William.'

'So that's settled? You'll stay?' Ellen unwrapped the greaseproof paper off the square of lard next to the mixing bowl. 'Here you are.'

'Thanks. I just wanted to make sure, you know. With the baby and everything.' The relief made Mary's fingers shake. She cut the fat into small pieces, narrowly missing the top of her thumb.

'We'll manage,' Ellen said. 'Do you know how far on you are?'

'About six months, I think.' It was that long since Ted's telephone call; the night her whole world came crashing down around her head.

'Have you told Peter?'

'No, and *you* won't either.' In her weekly telephone calls Gwyneth insisted on telling her what Peter was doing, how unhappy he seemed. Her voice was becoming more and more anxious, her questions more probing. To hide the shaking, Mary dipped her hands into the flour, feeling the fat slide through her fingertips, separating and combining to turn it all into bread-like crumbs.

239

'Will you ever forgive him?'

'No, he lied to me.' Mary slapped her palms together, shaking off the last of the mixture. 'And I don't want to talk about it.' She could feel panic rising.

'But…'

'But nothing.'

'Okay.' Ellen watched Mary drip cold water from a jug into the bowl and work the mixture with her hands until it formed into a pale smooth lump. 'I was just thinking, with you talking to Gwyneth, won't he find out anyway? And then what will you do?'

A trickle of trepidation ran down Mary's arms to her fingers at the same time as a stab of pain in her groin caused her to gasp.

'Mary?' Ellen jumped up and, putting her arms around her, lowered Mary onto a chair.

'I'm fine.' Mary held her breath until the pain receded. She swallowed. 'I'm fine, it's gone.'

'You've gone deathly white.' Ellen stood back, frowning. 'I think a day in bed wouldn't do any harm.' She paused. 'And, as our Mam would say, it's time I picked up the reins again and stopped leaving everything to you.'

Chapter 68

George scratched his itchy head. He lifted his arm and sniffed. He stank. He'd have to go into Bradlow, if he could sneak on the train, to see if he could find a way into the public baths for a wash and brush up without paying.

Standing behind the gates of the camp he stared past the sycamores at the allotments across the road. He wondered if there was anything fit to eat over there. He hadn't eaten since yesterday morning. Walking from Bradlow, he'd worked up an appetite, looked forward to some of his mother's cooking. He'd been so sure she'd have calmed down. Even surer she wouldn't have gone to the cops. After all she'd lost one son. He scowled. He and Frank might have fought like cat and dog but he'd still been his brother. And blood's thicker than water. Or should be. Bloody old cow.

He looked to the top of the gates. It would be easier if he could just climb over and get in and out of the camp that way. Anything would be better than that bloody awful culvert. But he was too short; there was no way he could even reach the first crossbar. Besides, all the new sodding barbed wire the Council had stuck on up there made it impossible.

What a bloody mess he was in. Howarth and his bloody meddling sister had ruined his life between them. He tried to work out how to get his own back, to wipe the whole lot of them off the face of the earth. He was too hungry to think straight.

But he'd got rid of one of the buggers. He thought back to the satisfaction of seeing Tom Howarth flying over his van bonnet. He'd do it again. If not the girl, then Howarth himself. He'd nothing to lose now; hung for a sheep as a lamb. He gave a short gulp of laughter but shivered. Pack it in, he told himself. His hands balled into tight fists at the memory of the beating he'd taken from the man.

He started at the sound of someone on the allotments shouting out and he fell back behind the stone post. Peering round he saw two men on adjoining plots. One, rolling his sleeves up, a spade propped against his waist, gazed upwards at the cloudless sky. 'Always summat to do,' he shouted and, grabbing hold of the handle, started to dig.

The other man gave a small uplifting movement of his head. 'Aye, there is that.'

George was stuck now. He didn't dare cross behind the gates in case he was seen. The old bitch might have changed her mind and grassed on him to the cops. Besides, just being seen inside the camp would bring some bugger over to see what he was doing there. He'd have to sit it out.

The sun was hot on his head. He'd left his cap with his other stuff in the basement. He pressed his fingers over his eyes. Christ, he was turning soft.

He must have fallen asleep. His neck ached as though he'd been stuck in the same position for hours. He rubbed the back of it, kneading the muscles in his shoulders and slowly, painfully, stood.

He looked for his watch before remembering he'd pawned it, then up at the sun. Late afternoon? The allotments looked empty.

His stomach rumbled reminding him he hadn't eaten. He ran his tongue around the inside of his mouth, searching for saliva. He was thirsty as well – he could murder a pint.

It wasn't the only thing he could murder, given half a chance.

Slowly, limping slightly because a nail had come through the sole of his boot, George made his way across the long stretch of concrete towards the old hospital building.

Less than ten minutes later he was sliding down the banking of grass between the sycamores and climbing over the fence into the allotment. One greenhouse door was only held by a small bolt. In no time George was breathing in the warm muggy air and the smell of tomato plants. He touched the leaves, feeling the softness between his fingers, and looked around. At the far end there was a small bed of soil with a few lettuces of varying sizes. But it was a half-eaten sandwich and what looked like homemade biscuits on an old wooden chair that caught his eye. He pulled up two of the lettuces and tore off the roots. Then he sat down to eat.

A light, high-pitched laugh cut into the quiet.

George ducked down below the wooden staging and waited until a group of people passed. When he peered over the edge of the greenhouse door he saw a small chubby girl running between the allotments followed by a blonde child clutching a doll under her arm. Their voices floated towards him.

'First one there.'

242

'Wait for me.'

A bloke passed manoeuvring a big blue pram along the narrow path. Looks a right soft arse, George thought.

There was a thud and then a wail. George shuffled forward so he could see. One of the kids had fallen over. He ducked down as the man looked around.

Patrick Howarth.

George watched as Howarth left the pram and went to pick up the blonde girl who buried her face against him, crying. The other kid jigged from one foot to the other in front of them. 'She all right? She all right?'

He'd got kids! Of course. He'd got a family. George had forgotten that. A sodding family. And here he was, on his bloody own, with nowt to look forward to. Fingering the scar on his cheek, he could almost taste the bitterness. Overwhelmed by the fierce rush of hatred, his legs gave way and he slid helplessly down until he was sitting on the dirt, struggling to take in air. Gradually the weakness subsided and he was left with just the loathing coursing through him.

He raised his head.

Howarth had put the girl down and was rubbing her knees. A few moments later they set off along the path again, the two kids holding hands, stopping at one of the other greenhouses.

He heard Howarth call out, 'Wait here, watch the pram!' before going inside, reappearing with a bunch of lettuce and some newspaper. Wrapping the leaves up and putting them in the tray underneath the pram, he came back along the path. 'No running this time.'

George waited until he was sure there was no one else around. He strode over to Howarth's greenhouse, grinning. Once inside, he ripped up all the tomato plants and lettuces, smashed the wooden staging that held pots of geraniums and emptied every tray of seedlings into the metal tub of rainwater outside the greenhouse door.

They'd know it was him, at least he hoped they would. And he hoped it would put the fear of God in Howarth, wondering what else he would do.

Chapter 69

Whitsunday

Linda prodded her last chip into the cone, searching for any grains of salt. Screwing the paper up she glanced around to check no adults were watching before she pushed the wad through the bars of the grid in the gutter. She almost wiped the grease off her hands onto her dress before remembering she was in her new Whitsuntide clothes. Mummy would go mad if she went home with them mucky.

Peeping through the door of the pub at the noisy mass of drinkers she knew she'd never get through to the backyard where the outside tap was; where her Mummy and Auntie Jean had gone to the lavvy. Damn. Mouthing the word, she relished the click of the first letter against her teeth.

Carefully holding her arms away from her side, she ducked under the elbows of the men lounging against the wall of the Crown holding their pints of beer. She pushed past the crowds waiting at the top of Newroyd Street for the next band to arrive and stood, looking around for Jacqueline.

The final notes from the outgoing band ended in a discordant jangle as the men jostled to get onto the charabanc, eager to get to as many venues as possible before the contest's ten o'clock deadline. The old man who carried the board announcing the name of each band, Grimetown, Blackthorpe, Boarshill, tipsy after an evening of free pints, directed the bus in a haphazard fashion as it manoeuvred to reverse. He lurched away and, attempting to step onto the pavement, lifted one foot high in exaggeration above the kerb. Linda giggled.

Straining her neck to see past the charabanc steering around groups of people in the road, she heard the high-pitched, tuneless chant.

Teddy Bear, Teddy Bear, turn around,
Teddy Bear, Teddy Bear, touch the ground...

Jacqueline was skipping with two other girls. Without a word she'd found someone else to play with. Her cousin had forgotten about her, left her. Dipping her head to hide her face she turned and weaved her way through the crush of spectators until, suddenly, the road held only a few stragglers and she was able to run. When she stopped she was alongside the allotments. Today there was no one working in them. Breathing heavily she flopped down on the bank of grass at the side of the road. The ground was still warm from the long day of sun, and pulling at a blade of grass she carefully stretched it between her thumbs. Putting it to her mouth she blew; the screech was satisfying.

She avoided looking along the road towards the old mill with its new barbed wire which glinted in the sun. Once upon a time, a long time ago, before she was even born, it was a prison. Linda knew this because her Mummy had told her once that it was where they'd kept Uncle Peter. Not because he'd done anything wrong, she'd said, but because a lot of men were fighting about something and it was better for Uncle Peter not to get in the way. Still, it wasn't a nice place. When she was really little she used to imagine that the wooden platform near the big locked gates, overgrown with tall pink-flowering weeds, was hiding someone. And she still believed that the mill beyond, with its black and empty windows, was the home of ghosts. But it was all right. Being there when it was still light was all right, because everybody knew ghosts only came out at night.

A band started playing. Linda leant forward to watch the men marching past Newroyd Street into Skirm Park where the adjudicators, locked in the boating lake shed, judged their performance against the other bands. They were playing *Marching Through Georgia,* one of her dad's favourites and she could see their instruments flashing in the sun even from this distance. Next year, when she was seven, she was going to start learning the cornet. One day she'd be there, helping to win the contests. And all those people lining the streets would be clapping for her.

Still listening, she lay back, her hands pressed together under her head and stared up at the sky. Sparrows darted back and forth from the sycamore trees. She tipped her chin to watch them, heard them squabbling. Then she closed her eyes and thought back over the day.

One of the worst things was the church parade, having to carry the little basket of flowers while still trying to hold on to the ribbon attached to the banner. On the whole she didn't mind Whitsunday but wearing the new clothes worried her. When she'd woken up they were already laid out on the chair: pale blue cotton gloves that matched the dress with the tiny sprigs of forget-me-knots, and the blue crocheted cardigan. She'd had to stand up and lean forward to eat her toast so she didn't get any crumbs on her front. Worst of all were the itchy new knickers. She grimaced and pulled at the crotch until she was more comfortable and then snuggled into the dip she'd made in the grass.

The best thing about Whitsunday was the afternoon races. Today she'd won every one despite Geoffrey Fry trying to push her over. But then after the sports and the potato pie tea in the church hall, she'd had to get out of her shorts and t-shirt and back into her dress. She pulled the sleeves of her blue cardigan down over her hands, making fists. She supposed there were some good things about new clothes, such as that morning when Auntie Jean gave her a penny and said she looked beautiful. Daft really because then her Mummy had given Jacqueline a penny for showing off her new dress, which Jacqueline hated because she'd rather wear trousers.

Grown-ups do funny things.

Sometimes they said odd things as well. She'd heard her Mummy and Auntie Jean talking about Auntie Mary, saying she was having a baby, when everybody knew that it needed a mummy and a daddy to find the baby under the gooseberry bush. And Auntie Mary hadn't got a daddy, not yet anyhow because Uncle Peter and her hadn't had a wedding so they couldn't be a mummy and a daddy. It was too hard to think about.

When William was born she and Jacqueline had gone into the backyard and searched the alley for a gooseberry bush but there wasn't one, only a patch of dandelions that next door's cat had pooed on.

She plucked another piece of grass and chewed the end. The sweet taste filled her mouth and she had a sudden thought. Perhaps it was magic. For as long as she could remember, everybody in her class had been having little brothers or sisters and not once had she seen a gooseberry bush. She smiled, satisfied, that was it, it was magic. She closed her eyes.

When she woke there were no sounds and she lay still, listening. Then a band struck up in the distance and she relaxed. But the sun was lower in the sky and she jumped to her feet. She was always nervous of this time of day. Dad said there was nothing to be afraid of, it was called dusk, but she didn't even like the sound of that.

She flinched when the hand grasped her shoulder.

'Hello.' The large man was pale, like he'd never been in the sun and his curly hair was an orangey colour. There was an old cut on his cheek, like a half moon, and his nose, spread wide between his eyes, was bent to one side so that he looked sideways at her. His clothes looked like he'd got them off the rag and bone man.

She wanted to run. Instead she shrugged his hand away. It was dirty.

247

'Don't be like that,' he said. 'I'm a friend of your Daddy's.' He smiled. Large yellow teeth, not a nice smile, like the wolf in Red Riding Hood. And he smelled. He smelled really bad.

'I've got to get back to Mummy,' she said, and then, 'she knows where I am.' She watched a couple pass, arms linked, on their way to the railway station at the end of Shaw Street. The woman glanced at her as though she might speak but didn't, and the words that Linda wanted to say were muddled in her head and the moment was lost.

The man laughed. 'Now that's where you're wrong. She doesn't and she's worried.' He bent his head to one side, frowning so his bushy eyebrows almost met and his voice was stern when he next spoke. 'She's not too happy with you, young lady.' He sniffed and tilted his head even more, studying her. 'She's pretty mad you've wandered off. She told you to stay outside the Crown, didn't she?'

Linda nodded, anxiety knotted in her stomach. She hated it when Mummy got cross. The man must have been talking to her if he knew what she'd said. 'I'll run back now,' she said, but the man already had hold of her hand. It was horrible, cold but sweaty at the same time.

'I'm going back to the pub myself,' he said. 'I'll walk with you. Don't forget your hat, then.'

Linda picked up her hat. It had got squashed on one side. She pulled the thin elastic under her chin.

In an odd voice, the man said, 'Look at me, walking out with such a pretty young lady.'

She twisted her hand against his but he was holding too tightly and the fancy ring he wore hurt her fingers so she let him lead her.

She looked down at her feet. The black patent leather was scuffed and there were grass stains on her socks. Something else to make her Mummy cross.

Chapter 70

'How is Mary now?' Jean asked.

'Better for a rest.' Ellen threw the end of her cigarette on the flag stones of the pub's backyard and ground it out with her foot. She was feeling quite virtuous, insisting Mary stayed in bed for the last two days, and being back in charge of everything was good. And today was her reward to herself. 'But she doesn't want to overdo it again. She's had a fright. So she's kept her feet up today.'

'I'll call in later and see her.'

'Best you don't. No need to mither her.'

'I won't be mithering her.' Jean looked affronted. 'She's my friend and I want to make sure she's well.'

'I've just told you.'

'Yes, well, I'll see for myself, won't I?'

For a few minutes neither spoke.

Jean looked sideways at Ellen. 'Do you think she'll ever get back with *him*?'

'Peter, you mean?' God, Patrick's bigotry really has rubbed off on her. 'No, which, actually, I think is a shame.' Put that in your pipe and smoke it, Ellen thought.

'When I think what could have happened if they'd been found out during the war. And they put me in a dangerous position. They seem to have forgotten that.' Jean folded her arms and pulled her chin in.

'This isn't about you, Jean.' Ellen put one foot against the wall of the pub and leaned back, balancing. Chafing her arms to warm them she looked up at the sky. The sun had moved off the yard, only the roof of the little building at the end, housing the two lavatories, had a sliver of weak evening sun on it. She should have brought a cardigan with her. 'She doesn't want to talk about it. You have to go along with her.'

'She can't have the baby without being married. There's enough gossip about this family as it is.'

'She doesn't care about that.' Ellen took her cigarettes and matches from her skirt pocket and lit up.

'Well, she should.'

'Why?' Ellen picked a piece of tobacco off her lower lip. 'She doesn't care what people think.' She took a long drag and flicked the match away. 'Anyway, she's says she's not going back.'

'She's so big now. They were talking about her in the Post Office.'

'I hope you told them to mind their own business?'

'I walked out.'

'Oh, I'm sure that told them.' Ellen inspected her fingernails, not even trying to keep her sarcasm under control.

Jean flushed. 'Anyway, I'm going to call in on her later.'

Hell's bells, why wouldn't the woman take the hint? 'She's resting, I told you. Ted's gone to work so she offered to stop in with William once we'd got him to bed.' If he hadn't insisted he had to go, she wouldn't be stuck on her own with Jean. 'He's run off his feet getting ready for tomorrow. Where's Patrick anyway?'

'With the boy.'

'Jack,' Ellen said. Jean's callous tone and the way she was refusing to say his name upset her. It was too much like listening to Hannah talking about Linda. 'He's called Jack. It's a nice name. And it's not his fault what's happened, poor little bugger. You know what I went through with Ted's mother, how she made sure I knew exactly what she thought of Linda, how I worried that Linda would hear her ... understand. Do you really want to hurt a child like that?'

'I'm nothing like Ted's mother.' Jean was indignant.

'You should hear yourself.'

'I wouldn't hurt a child.' Jean stopped, looked uncomfortable. 'I wouldn't...'

'Look,' Ellen said, 'we've managed to go the whole day without bitching at one another but I can't stand hearing you go on about the baby like that. What's wrong with just calling him by his name?'

'Patrick chose it.' Jean pulled a face. 'It … he,' she said hastily seeing Ellen glare at her, 'was called something else before.'

'What?'

'I don't know. What I do know is he thought it clever to call some other woman's kid nearly the same as our Jacqueline.' Ellen looked blank. 'Jacqueline … Jack?'

'You don't know what he was called before? Haven't you seen the birth certificate?'

'No, why should I have? I'm not interested.'

Ellen glanced indifferently at the large woman who stepped out of the pub's back door, moved to one side to let her pass and was rewarded by a toothless smile.

'Thanks pet.' The woman shuffled across the yard. Her stout figure made the hem of her skirt uneven, showing more of her swollen calves from the back than the front. Her shoes, worn down at the heels, slapped against her feet.

Jean and Ellen stood in silence. The noise from inside the pub had risen steadily over the last hour and now the voices and the clink of glass vied with the bands making their way to the park.

Inside the lavatory there was a squeal of the chain being pulled, a pause and then another attempt. There was no following gushing of water. The door opened. 'Bloody thing won't flush.' The woman hitched up her skirt and adjusted her large pair of white bloomers. 'Sorry, no room to swing a cat in there, I couldn't move my arms.' She walked towards them. 'I wouldn't go in there if I were you,' she said, tilting her head backwards. 'Old Green's ale's right off today.' She sucked her lips inwards. 'Pretty bad, if I say so myself. Th'owd sod must be making a mint, he's mixed it with summat and it's not only water.'

She stopped in front of Jean and the two women stared at each other. Jean raised an eyebrow. 'Yes?'

'Don't I know you from somewhere?'

'I don't think so.' Jean wrinkled her nose.

Ellen lowered her foot and pushed herself off the wall. This was interesting. She knew Jean enough to know she was uneasy. Come to think of it, the old woman did look a bit familiar. There was something about her: her eyes, the way she lifted one bushy grey eyebrow, almost in comic imitation of Jean.

'I'm Nelly Shuttleworth. I live on Barnes Street. You're a friend of Mary Howarth, aren't you?'

'Yes, I remember you now. Frank Shuttleworth's mother.' Jean didn't bother to hide her contempt.

Ellen's mouth slackened. Frank's mother? Oh God.

'That's right.' Ellen saw the old woman pull her shoulders back and look straight at Jean. When she turned towards her and said, 'You Mary's sister?' Ellen felt sick. It was the first time she'd spoken to her daughter's grandmother.

'Yes,' she said.

'You look alike. Well, except she's got dark hair, of course. You got children?'

'A girl and a boy.' Ellen clenched her jaw. 'Why do you ask?'

Nelly shrugged. 'No reason. Does the little girl look like you?'

Oh God. Goose-bumps rose on Ellen's skin. 'Suppose so.'

'That's nice. I only had lads myself.' She stopped. 'Sorry, I suppose you know that already, don't you?' She looked long and hard at Jean. 'Now, if I could just get past?'

Jean stepped aside.

Ellen stood inside the door, watching the woman push her way through the crowded tap room before speaking. 'Nelly Shuttleworth.'

Jean moved her head in acknowledgement.

Linda's grandmother. The words repeated in Ellen's head. Why had she never thought about her before? 'I need a pee.' She made herself laugh. 'I'll have to hold my nose while I'm at it.'

Sitting in the semi-darkness, her head tilted back against the smoke of the cigarette in her mouth, Ellen's mind worked furiously. Linda was Frank's child. That woman, that dreadful woman was her grandmother. Stop it, she told herself, stop thinking about it. She felt quite ill.

When she came out she dropped her cigarette end onto the flags and screwed her foot on it. 'We'd better find the girls,' she said.

Chapter 71

It was so cold. The dampness of the stone floor seeped through the rough material Linda was lying on and every now and then her body moved in spasmodic jerks that shook her from head to toe.

And it was dark. Even when she opened her eyes as wide as she could there was nothing, only blackness, and it took all of her courage not to panic. If she did she'd start screaming again and her throat hurt so much already.

When the man picked her up and ran towards the scary old mill she'd shouted for her daddy but he'd put his smelly hands over her mouth and called her a little gobshite. She couldn't breathe. The sound bounced around her as she screamed and fought all the time he dragged her up through that horrible wet stinky pipe. The tops of her arms burned from him pulling at her, and her elbows and knees smarted and were sticky with blood. Once, she'd rolled on her back and pressed her feet on the top of the tunnel to stop herself from being moved but then something ran over her face and the man said it was a rat and if she didn't shut up others would come. So she'd let him heave her to the top, even though she could hear her frock being torn. When he dropped her to the hard ground she curled into a ball and couldn't stop shaking. It was a long time before she opened her eyes. All she could hear was the man coughing and wheezing.

Then he'd carried her under his arm to this room. She'd lost one of her shoes.

There was a noise. Her stomach jerked. Lifting her head she whispered, 'Hello?' And then louder, 'Hello?'

Silence.

A scraping noise above. Footsteps.

She felt warm wetness between her legs; she'd peed herself. She hadn't done that in years. The shame she felt was soon lost in the fear. She shuffled away from the rapidly cooling cloth.

The footsteps stopped. Linda heard the crunch of grit under boots. Then there was the snap of a bolt being pulled back, the scraping of a key turning. The sob in her throat stuck. She saw the outline of the man against the faint light from the open door. She could hear him breathing. She held her own breath, hoping he couldn't see her, but then he walked towards her and even though she knew he was there, right in front of her, she jumped when the toe of his heavy boot nudged her and couldn't stop a small quivering cry.

'How about I get you some fish and chips?' The man leant over her, his breath sour, smelling of cigarettes.

She shrank back, twisting her head away from him. 'Please,' she said, 'please let me go home.'

'I said how about I get you some fish and chips?'

'I'm thirsty.' There was a salty taste on her lips from her tears.

The man moved away from her. He was still in the room. She heard him clear his throat. Water running somewhere.

The cup, shoved against her teeth, cut her gum. The blood mixed with the water and made her feel sick.

Suddenly, she was being covered by something, the material harsh and prickly. She screamed, kicking out and squirming backward. The rough flags scraped the skin on her wet thighs and buttocks. 'Get off, get away.'

'Don't be bloody stupid,' the man shouted, 'shut the fuck up.' His voice echoed around her. The room was bigger that she thought and empty sounding. 'It's only a sodding blanket, for God's sake.'

'I want my mummy,' she pleaded, 'please.' He didn't answer. She tried to be brave, to scare him. 'If you don't I'll tell my daddy about you.' That was a mistake. The blow to the side of her head hurt her ears. No one had ever hit her before. It left a buzzing sound in her head and sick rose in her mouth. She swallowed.

The door closed, she heard the key turn and he was gone, his footsteps a clink of metal studs on concrete.

'Mummy,' she whispered.

The darkness closed in on her, the air was thick and damp, cloying to breathe in. There was a scratching sound, a scuffling of soft noises.

Linda screamed.

Chapter 72

Let her scream all she liked. She deserved that clout, the little bitch, threatening him with that bastard.

George stood outside the boiler room flexing his fingers.

What the hell was he thinking? It was a fucking stupid idea, bringing her here. The vague plan he'd thought of when he watched Howarth's missus leave her and the other kid outside the Crown – shutting her in one of the sheds on the allotment – went to pot the minute she started screaming.

He hit the wall with his fist. The pain stopped the rising panic but he needed a drink.

No he didn't, it was bloody drink that had got him in this sodding mess. As soon as he'd done it he knew it was stupid. Too bloody late by then. Never thought anything through... It was only supposed to give the bastards a fright for a couple of hours. He walked back and forth, trying to decide what to do.

He couldn't keep her here forever.

He took a deep breath and went back into the boiler room, leaving the door slightly open. There was a sour smell of urine.

The kid had obviously pissed herself. He waited for his eyes to adjust to the gloom before he spoke. 'Look,' he said, 'I can tell you don't like this game. Me, I thought it would be fun but I don't think you're enjoying playing, are you?'

She shook her head.

'Right. Well then, how about we get out of here and I buy you some chips, eh?'

She nodded slowly.

'But you have to do something for me as well.'

She took in a quivering breath.

'I mean it. Understand?'

She moved her head again. 'Yes,' she whispered.

'Right. You have to promise you'll keep your mouth shut. You won't tell anybody where you've been.' He stopped, waiting to see if she said anything. She didn't.

Congratulating himself that he might be able to get out of this mess, he carried on, 'I want you to pretend you got lost. You went exploring and you got lost. Okay?'

'Yes.'

'Promise?'

'Yes.' Linda drew her knees close to her chest and put her arms around them.

'Right.' He had to make sure she'd stick to what she said. He squatted down.

'Because if you don't, I'll have to come and get you again. Understand?' He shuffled nearer. 'And don't forget your mummy was cross with you for running off.' He reached out to touch her cheek. 'If you tell her you got lost, she won't be mad anymore.'

She grabbed his fingers and bit him.

He yelled, yanking his hand away, falling backwards.

On her hands and knees she scrambled past him.

'Bitch.' He was breathing heavily.

She was at the door.

He flung himself across the floor, grabbed her ankle.

She yelled, kicked out at him.

Pain shot through his jaw. 'Bitch.'

He twisted over onto his stomach, grasped her other ankle and tugged.

She fell.

He heard the crack of bone on the stone flags. And then silence. 'Kid?' He still had hold of her ankles. He gave one of them a shake. 'Come on, kid.' No answer. The girl was pretending. She had to be pretending. He couldn't see enough in the shadows behind the door. Fear churned inside his guts. He crawled alongside her, feeling for her face, her mouth. She wasn't breathing. 'Oh God, no, please, no.' He felt for the pulse in her neck, an almost forgotten automatic gesture from the first aid training he'd done in the Fire Brigade years ago, before he was kicked out. He couldn't tell if there was any movement but when he took his hand away it was sticky. Blood, oh God, it was blood.

He had to get away. He should never have come back to Ashford. He ran blindly, bouncing off the walls, until he was stumbling down the steps into the fresh air.

He stopped once to look back towards the old hospital before plunging headfirst into the culvert.

Chapter 73

'Ted.' Starlings, squabbling over breadcrumbs behind the bakery, scattered when Ellen burst into the yard. 'Ted!'

The shed door was open, bits of coke spilled over the wooden barrier inside and Archie, the man Ted employed, was washing down the yard. The black liquid left its mark on the flags as it streamed towards the grid in the middle. Oblivious to the mess, Ellen splashed through it as Ted appeared at the door.

'What?'

257

'Linda's missing.' Ellen sobbed, gasping for air, her hands on her knees. A mop and bucket, stinking of ammonia, was on the doorstep. The smell stung Ellen's nose and made it run, mucus mixed with the tears.

Ted pulled his white apron over his head, his cap falling to the flagged floor. 'What do you mean, she's missing?'

'She's missing.' Doubled over, Ellen saw his boots, dusty with flour, in front of her and a rage erupted. One hand still on her knee, she lashed upwards, swinging wildly. Her fist connected with the side of his head.

Stunned, he rocked on his feet. 'Ellen!'

Straightening up she drew back and hit out again. She knew, she hoped, it would hurt. She couldn't stop. 'Your fault.' The words came out at first as a low growl. The harder, the faster, she thumped, the louder the words until it was a howl. 'Your fault.'

At first Ted tried to catch hold of her then dropped his arms to his sides and waited.

Eventually she stilled.

'You're right,' he said gently. 'I'm sorry, I should have been with you.'

'No.' Ellen fell against him. She knew she was to blame. 'It's all my fault.'

'Tell me exactly what's happened, love?'

'At the band contest,' Ellen whispered, 'one minute she was there, the next she'd gone. Oh God!'

Why lie? Why not tell him she was with Jean in the backyard of the pub? Because you never stand on your own two feet, she told herself bitterly; because you always expect someone else to pick up the pieces of whatever mess you get yourself in.

'She can't have gone far.' Ted pulled off his large cotton gloves and threw them onto the curved metal bars of the oven. 'You know our Linda, she's a dreamer, she'll have wandered off.'

'So many people, Ted. Strangers.'

'It's all right, we'll find her.' Kicking off his plimsolls Ted overbalanced, his flailing hand hit a shelf. Rolling pins and stacked pie trays clattered to the floor. 'Archie! Get in here!'

Archie was already peering around the door, fear and uncertainty on his normally placid face. 'Boss?'

Ted shoved his feet into his outdoor shoes. He thrust the keys at the man. 'Lock up.'

'Go in, see if she's home.' Ted waited by the back gate.

In a few seconds Ellen came back to the back door, holding onto the frame, her face whiter than ever. 'She's not here. I've been upstairs. Mary hasn't seen her.'

Mary appeared behind her, hand over her mouth, eyes wide. 'She's not been here.'

'She's probably just wandered off and got lost.' He spoke loudly and slowly to Ellen, as though to a child. 'Stay with Mary. I'll round some of the neighbours up and we'll go and look for her.'

'No, I'm coming with you.' Ellen shoved her arms into a cardigan. 'You'll keep an eye on William?' she said to Mary. 'Stay here, in case she comes home?'

'Course I will.'

'I'm better off on my own, love.'

'I'm coming with you.' Ellen was holding on to Mary and hopping on one leg, changing from her high-heeled shoes to a flat pair. 'I can run as fast as you.'

She didn't wait for a reply. After a quick hug from Mary she crossed the yard. 'I can't stay here, Ted, I have to do something.' Pushing past him she ran along the alleyway.

Crashing through the last gate at the end of the row, Ted shouted, 'Bert? Bert?' A man appeared at the back door, smoking a pipe. 'Our Linda's gone missing, round some of the blokes up, ask them to look around, will you?' Ellen watched the man grab his jacket from behind the door. Then she and Ted spun on their heels. Swinging around the corner of the end house they stopped, looking both ways along Shaw Street.

259

'Which way?' Ellen said. 'We've already looked all along Shaw Street and Huddersfield Road.' She didn't know where to look for her daughter but it was important to be moving, to be going somewhere.

'The park?' Ted took a few hesitant steps along the pavement and then lengthened his strides. Ellen followed. That's where she and Jean should have looked in the first place. They paid no attention to the few cars that passed or the groups of revellers catcalling and laughing. Ellen forced herself to go faster, to keep up with Ted's limping run.

Outside Skirm Park they stopped. It was closed. Ellen leaned against the gates, straining to take in air. Ted sank to his knees, his head slumped between his shoulders.

'What are we going to do, Ted? What if something's happened to her?'

'It won't have.'

'I couldn't bear it if—'

'We'll find her. And she'll be safe.' His face was unreadable. 'Come on, I'll give you a leg up.'

They struggled over the gates and slid down the other side. The path was arched by trees. They walked, listening all the time but the only sounds were the hushed giggle of lovers hidden by the bushes, the grumbling squawk of nesting birds, and the rustle of leaves in the light breeze.

'Linda!' Ellen turned in a circle, shouting her name. 'Linda…'

She'd never been so afraid.

Chapter 74

'Linda's missing!' Jean burst into the kitchen, dragging a weeping Jacqueline behind her.

'What?' Startled, Patrick threw his newspaper onto the floor and jumped up from his chair. 'What's wrong with Jacqueline?

Why is she crying?'

'It's Linda, we can't find her,' she shrieked at him, furious he just stood there and didn't listen.

'What the hell are you talking about?' Patrick picked Jacqueline up. 'You okay, love?'

'She's fine. Didn't you hear what I said?' Dear God, she'd hit him in a minute. 'It's Linda who's missing.'

'Where were you? When she went missing?'

'Does that matter?' Jean screamed, pushing her face into his. 'Just for once, in these last six months, try concentrating on your family – instead of that.' She flung an arm towards the ceiling.

'Whoa!' Patrick reddened in anger. 'Back off. Just where were you and Ellen when she went missing?' he repeated.

Jean suddenly calmed. Breathing heavily she didn't speak.

'Pub?' he said sarcastically.

Jacqueline buried her face into her father's shoulder.

'Where was your cousin when you last saw her, sweetheart?' Patrick held Jacqueline's chin, made her look at him. 'Did she say she was going somewhere? Did she say anything at all?'

She should tell them it was her fault, that she'd seen Shirley and Anne Taylor skipping and she hadn't waited for Linda coming back from the chippy. 'No,' she gulped. 'She ran off and left me.'

'Right. I'll go and see what's happening. Get Jack dressed and get the three of you to Henshaw Street.'

Then he'd gone.

Jacqueline clutched hold of Jean's skirt. Her face was red, screwed up with the effort of not crying, not showing how frightened she was.

Jean forced a smile. 'Tell you what we'll do. We'll get Jack dressed, like Dad said … you'll help me, won't you?' Jacqueline sniffed and wiped her nose with the heel of her hand, but she nodded. 'Then we'll all go to Linda's house and I'll bet, by the time we arrive, she'll be there, waiting to tell you all about her adventures.'

261

Chapter 75

'Bloody hell man. Look at the state of you.' Arthur Brown slurred his words. He'd not long been back from the Crown. George was waiting in the shadows of the backyard when he arrived home.

'Been in a bit of a scrap, that's all.' George was sweating, his heart thumping. What in God's name was he going to do now? Stupid kid. What a sodding mess. He wished to God he hadn't seen the kid outside the allotments, that he hadn't had the stupid idea of taking her to give Howarth a fucking fright. He pushed his way into the house.

'Hey, hey!' Arthur held his hands up and backed off. 'Steady on. What's happened?'

'Told you.' George held onto the chair to stop himself from falling. His legs shook so much his whole body trembled. 'Been in a fight.' He tried the usual joke. 'You should see the other bugger.' But the rasp in his voice gave him away.

'You in trouble? I want no trouble.'

George cursed. 'All I want is a bit of a wash.'

'You'll need more than that. Just look at your togs.'

'Okay then, a bath – and I'll wash my clothes in the water once I've done.'

'Well, I'll have to put the Ascot on. I've used up all the hot water for today.' Arthur paused, looked expectantly at him. 'Difficult managing on the pittance I have coming in, you know.' He stood back to let George in. 'And this bloody National Grid thing is a bloody con – state-bloody-owned, my arse,' he grumbled. 'It's us poor bloody suckers who cop it – price of gas. Festival of Britain? It's a bloody joke.'

'Okay, okay.' George cut him off. Once Arthur started there was no stopping him and he'd had more than enough. He pulled some coins out of his trouser pocket. 'This do it?'

*

George sat in front of the fire, a tin bath full of cold scummy water nearby; his clothes steamed over the back of a chair to one side of the hearth. He tilted the glass of beer and took a long swallow and belched loudly.

'I missed the contest later on.' He held out his glass. 'Who won in the end?'

'West Riding Home Guard Band, I think.'

'How come you missed it?'

'Had to see somebody.'

'Who?'

George lifted his shoulders.

'Another?' Arthur poured the beer from a jug into a glass. 'That'll be a shilling you owe me now,' he reminded George, 'besides that bob for the ciggies you've borrowed.'

'Okay, you tight bugger.'

'Hey, I forgot.' Arthur straightened in his chair. 'You missed all the excitement earlier.'

'What?' George took a swig of beer. He tried to block out the man's voice.

'Ted Booth's kid's missing.'

George's stomach jerked. 'Ted Booth's kid?'

'Aye.' Arthur looked puzzled. 'Called Linda … summat like that.'

Fucking hell! George felt the shudder run along his skin. He'd taken the wrong girl.

'Well, I say Ted Booth's kid. He took her on, like adopted her or summat. You must know that, you being you?'

George stared. 'What d'you mean, me being me?'

'The girl that's been took. Well you know, it's her … that kid…' Arthur spoke slowly.

'Haven't got a clue what you're talking about,' George interrupted.

'She were that younger sister's by-blow.'

George tapped out an impatient rhythm with his foot. 'If you don't tell me what you mean I'll sodding thump you.'

'All right, all right.' Arthur was enjoying himself. 'One time, when she'd had a few, Winnie told me that her youngest … that Ellen what's married to Ted Booth … once had a bit of a fling with your brother. And Winnie told me that the kid she was 'aving was your Frank's. You must 'ave known that. So that means…' Arthur paused for the greatest effect and then said triumphantly, 'That means the kid's your niece.'

Chapter 76

'Mary, come back inside, it's pitch black out there.'

'I can't breathe.' Mary stood on the back doorstep. These days it felt as though her lungs were being squashed upwards by her stomach. She turned her face up as the rain started; fat slow drops at first and then faster until they hurt as they hit her face, plastering her hair to her scalp, her dress to her heavy body. For a few minutes she revelled in it, the sensation on her hot skin almost stilling the dreadful fear that had engulfed her from the moment Ellen had burst through the door. Then it came back in a wave of anguish. 'Do you think she's out in this? Do you think she's hiding, frightened in the dark?' Her voice caught in her throat. 'She hates the dark, Jean.'

'I think you'll catch your death out there.' Jean pulled her back into the kitchen. 'And it's helping nothing and nobody, you getting in a state.' She spoke briskly, hiding her own anxiety and self-reproach. 'Here, dry yourself off.' She handed Mary a towel. 'Go and get into your nightie and dressing gown. We'll have a brew. And try not to wake the children. I've put them all into the one bed in Ellen and Ted's room for now.'

Mary dragged herself upstairs. She was sure they got steeper every day. Her calves ached. She tried to ignore the nagging pain in her groin. On the landing she stopped to get her breath and looked across into the bedroom, watching the sleeping children.

264

Three where there should be four, she thought, a lump in her throat. Jacqueline had both arms around the two boys. William had his thumb in his mouth, his curled forefinger pressed against his nose. Jack was on his back, his mouth slightly open. But there was something wrong. She took a step towards the bed. Jacqueline was very still but her eyelids flickered.

'Jacqueline,' Mary whispered, 'are you awake, love?'

There was no reply but her mouth turned downwards. Suddenly her chest heaved and she sat up. The two babies rolled together to the middle of the bed behind her as she held out her arms to Mary.

'Auntie Mary, it's my fault Linda's gone,' she wailed. 'I should have gone to the chippie but I was cross 'cos I didn't have any pennies left. If I hadn't bought that ice cream, I would have had enough for chips.'

'Shush love, come here.' Mary reached over and lifted Jacqueline from the bed. She felt the pull on her stomach as the sturdy little arms clung around her. 'Come on, come with me while I get changed.'

'Sit there on my bed,' she said, after they'd crossed the landing, stepping out of her dress and reaching for her dressing gown. 'Now…' She sat next to her niece. 'Tell me what happened.'

'None of this is your fault,' Mary said, when Jacqueline had sobbed out her story, 'and Linda will be back before we know it. Now, I want you to close your eyes, it's been a long day. You can sleep with me tonight, if that's what you'd like?' Jacqueline nodded, her face blotched with crying.

It didn't take long. Mary lay alongside her, stroking the little girl's hair until her breathing became slow and steady. Despite her words, the thought of Linda out there, alone, filled Mary with dread. She rolled onto her back and closed her eyes. Come back to us, sweetheart, she thought. Dear God let her be safe, don't let anything happen to her.

'Mary? What are you doing?' Jean stood by the bed, her outline against the landing light. 'I thought you were coming downstairs. I've been waiting.' She clasped and unclasped her hands. 'What's Jacqueline doing in here?'

'She was upset but she's okay now.'

'I hope so. She was in such a state earlier.' Jean looked around the room. 'Are you staying up here, then?'

'I might as well.' Mary didn't tell her friend about the dull ache in her abdomen. 'I can keep an eye on the children.' She watched Jean move restlessly from one foot to the other.

'Look,' Jean said all at once, 'I can't stand this. Do you mind if I go out as well? The kids are asleep, they're no bother and I'm going mad sitting around waiting for news.'

Mary glanced at the clock; the green luminous hands showed two o'clock. 'It's the middle of the night. Patrick wouldn't want you going out on your own at this time.' It was the only thing she could think of but as soon as she'd spoken she knew it was the wrong thing to say.

'The time's gone when I worried about what Patrick wants.'

'You don't mean that, love.'

'Jack?' It was more an answer than a question.

'I know.' Keeping an eye on the sleeping girl Mary inched her way into a sitting position, pushing up the pillows behind her. 'But I've seen you with Jack.'

Jean pushed her glasses further up on the bridge of her nose. 'Hmm.' Behind the frames her eyes were swollen.

Even married to Patrick, with all his shenanigans, over the years, it struck Mary that she hadn't seen her friend cry so much as she had tonight. Being partly responsible for losing Linda must be soul-destroying for Jean. But Mary couldn't bring herself to say that. So instead she persisted. 'I've seen how good you are with him when you think no one's watching.' Mary squeezed Jean's hand. 'I know how much you love Patrick and I do think he's learned his lesson, you know.'

Jean gave a sniff.

'And I think,' Mary hesitated, 'I think, if you want to stay with him, if you want to try to make your marriage work, you'll have to accept that Jack's here to stay.'

'It's hard.' Jean sat next to Mary and hunched forward, her hands, palm to palm, pressed between her knees. Jacqueline murmured in her sleep and turned onto her side. They waited a couple of minutes, watching her, before Jean said, 'She loves him, the baby, you know.'

'I know. What will you do?' Mary saw Jean's shoulders hunch.

'I don't know. Take things day by day, I suppose, see how things go.' She sighed. 'But to be honest, Mary, I can't think about that now. I have got to look for Linda. It's as much my fault as Ellen's and she's still out there in all this weather. We should have been watching the girls but we just got talking in the yard at the back of the pub.'

Mary leaned back on the pillows. She felt incredibly tired. 'If you must go, take that torch in the sideboard. And, please, just stick to the main streets. After yesterday there're bound to be some drunks still lurking around.'

Jean bent over and kissed Mary's cheek. 'I will, don't worry. And try not to fret about Linda, it will be fine.'

How many times had that been said over the last few hours?

Chapter 77

Whit Monday morning 3 am

'Mary?' Mary shifted her head from side to side on the pillow trying to shut out the voice. 'Mary.' A more urgent tone – forcing her to listen.

She'd slept fitfully, a few minutes at a time. Now she was struggling from a nightmare: she was running along the canal path, a sharp stinging rain hitting her in the face, Linda floating away from her on oily water. As she was swept under the bridge the little girl raised one arm slowly, fingers spread, reaching out towards her.

'Mary!'

'No!' Mary hit out at the hands holding her.

'Mary, it's Ted. Wake up, you're dreaming.'

She was sweating. Something was wrong. 'Ted?'

'Yes. Jean found us and she's still looking with the others ... except for Ellen. I persuaded her to lie down on the sofa and she's flat out, so I'm leaving her down there. I've just come up to check you and the kids are all right. Are you okay?'

'Yes. No.' She quietened. She felt odd, wrong. Putting a hand under the sheets she touched her legs. 'No. I'm not. I'm bleeding.'

He'd rung the doctor. He paused, rested his hand on the receiver before picking it up again. 'Is that Gwyneth? It's Ted, Mary's brother-in-law. I'm sorry it's the middle of the night – could you get Peter to the telephone please?'

Chapter 78

The room was warm from the day's sun. Mary heard the ripple of the curtains wafting with the light breeze that had risen. The open window allowed noises from the street: a man whistling, a child's cry, the rumble of some sort of a cart. She frowned, reluctant to open her eyes, savouring the effects of the sedative given to her by the doctor. She wasn't sure how long she'd been cocooned in this small world but she knew she felt safe. Out there, there was something terrible waiting to pounce; something she needed to face.

She was drifting again, back into the protection of the soft sheets that smelled of lavender. Then it was there again, the horror. Eyes still closed she flung the covers to one side, tried to sit up. 'Linda.'

'Hush now, *Liebling*, it will be all right.'

'Peter?'

'I am here, *mein Geliebter*, I am here. Ted, he telephoned me.' She felt the warmth of his fingers on hers.

'I will always be here, *Liebling*.'

The relief that he'd returned to her was instant but fleeting. The anger and resentment rose up again, vying with the fear of what was happening to Linda. The image of her niece somewhere, lonely and frightened, consumed her, tortured her. But she wouldn't let him comfort her. She pulled her fingers from under his and turned away. Tracks of tears slowly slid from the outer corners of her eyes and down to her hairline.

Peter waited until he was sure she was sleeping. He smoothed her hair away from her face, stroked her forehead. She was very pale. He looked at the shape of her under the covers, unable to believe she was carrying his child and he hadn't known. There should have been some instinctive awareness. The combination of happiness and trepidation made him lightheaded, had done since he'd put the telephone down in Gwyneth's and looked down into her anxious eyes. 'Go to her,' she'd said, 'go and bring her home. And don't take no for an answer.'

Waiting for the milk train on the platform at Pont y Haven, he'd known he was taking one of the biggest gambles of his life.

Had he lost?

Chapter 79

'That'll be them now,' Ted said, when the heavy thumping on the front door rattled the letter box.

Patrick pulled his face. 'Fat lot of bloody good they'll be. We should be out there looking for her.'

'Do you think I don't know that?' Ted whirled on him. 'Just shut the fuck up.'

The three others in the room stared at him. Neither Ellen nor Jean had ever heard him swear before.

'Sorry.' Ted locked his fingers on top of his head, watching Patrick stalk off in a temper to answer the door. 'It's just that I said we'd all be here when they came.' He slid his hands down to the back of his neck and stretched. 'The others are still searching,' he answered Ellen's distress, 'and, as soon as the police have gone, we can get out there again.'

She reached up and touched him. 'As soon as they've gone,' she said, nodding. Her eyes were almost closed by her constant crying. 'We have to.'

They listened to the muttered conversation at the door.

'Detective Hardcastle, Mr Booth.'

'Well?' Patrick demanded.

John Hardcastle shook his head. 'Sorry, no news yet. My boss has asked me to go over a few things with you.'

'What more can we tell you?' Patrick cut in, reluctantly moving to one side to let him into the hall before poking his head out into the street. Outside almost every house women stood watching, arms crossed under aproned bosoms, collective expressions of nosy sympathy on their faces. Patrick scowled but then realised there wasn't a man in sight; they must all still be out looking for Linda. He raised a hand to the women, acknowledging them.

The detective followed Patrick into the kitchen, taking off his trilby. 'Just making sure we got all the information last night, Mr

Booth, Mrs Booth. So we know everything that'll help us to find your daughter.' The man paused, looked beyond them at Jean. 'Miss?'

'Mrs – Mrs Howarth. I'm Linda's aunt.' She rocked Jack in her arms as he slept. His closeness comforted her and she felt a certain satisfaction that she could settle him better than Patrick could these last few days. Though she certainly wouldn't tell her husband that.

The detective nodded, coughed and turned again to Ted.

'There is something I need to ask, Mr Booth.' The detective held the brim of his hat, constantly running it through his fingers. 'Is it possible Linda has run away?'

Ellen buried her face in her hands. 'No.'

'No, she's a happy child.' Ted was grey with fatigue. He'd spent the last thirty-six hours searching the streets.

'She's seven years old, for God's sake,' Patrick shouted. 'She wouldn't know where to run to. Bloody idiot!'

The man overlooked his outburst. The uniformed policeman standing by his side raised a warning hand to Patrick.

'It's happened in the past,' Detective Hardcastle said. 'Children can get very disturbed by things that are happening at home.'

'Nothing's happened. Not in this house anyway.' Jean spoke slowly and deliberately. As she fixed Patrick with a stare, she instinctively stroked Jack's head. Patrick's expression softened as he returned her look. He'd noticed how close she was getting to the little boy.

When the detective looked around inquiringly, no one spoke. He shrugged. Without being asked he sat down, adjusting the creases of his trousers. 'Now I need to clarify a few details from you. Go over what you told us at the station, Mr Booth.' He took a notebook from his pocket. 'As I understand it, on Sunday, Mrs Booth was at the band contest with…?' He looked up.

'With me,' Jean said. She lifted her chin in the direction of Patrick. 'And our daughter, but she knows nothing either. She was playing with some other girls when Linda went to the chip shop.'

'Perhaps if Jacqueline had stayed with her…' Ellen gave her an angry look.

'Now Ellen.' Ted laid his hand on her shoulder. 'There are so many ways we could all blame ourselves.' His voice cracked. 'If I hadn't worked…' He didn't finish.

Ellen covered his hand with hers. 'Sorry,' she said to Jean, 'sorry.'

'Don't worry about it.' Jean said to her, shaking her head. 'My husband wasn't with us,' she told the detective. 'He was home looking after this one.' She rested her cheek on top of Jack's head. He snuggled closer.

'Ah, giving you some time off then?' He smiled at her first and then at Patrick. 'Not many men would do that, especially on a Whitsunday. Good turn-out too, I hear.'

No one answered.

He cleared his throat. 'So, if I'm right, the first time you noticed Linda missing was when you'd been to the lavatory at the back of the Crown?'

Both women nodded, avoiding one another's eyes.

'And that was about five o'clock?'

'Yes.' Ellen whispered, rubbing at her nose with a wet, bunched up handkerchief.

'And you've been searching since then?' This to Ted.

'We have.' Ted nodded. 'All of us.' He indicated the three others. 'And half the street. Nothing.'

'Right. And it's just you and Mrs Booth and Linda live here?'

'We have another child, William. He's with one of the neighbours. And Jacqueline, she's there too.'

'I might have to talk to Jacqueline.'

'No,' Jean protested. 'I don't want her frightened. I told you, she doesn't know anything.'

'We can leave it for now. Perhaps in a few days if Linda hasn't turned up?'

'Oh!' Ellen folded, her head on her knees. She rocked on the chair.

'She'll be back. We'll … someone will find her.' Jean spoke more to herself.

Ted crouched by Ellen, held her. He looked across at the detective. 'You asked if there was anybody else living here?'

'Yes?'

'My sister-in-law, Mary, is here. My wife hasn't been well. Mary came to give us a hand with the kids.'

'Can I speak to her?'

'She's in bed, not well herself today. The doctor came this morning and gave her something to make her sleep.'

'Right, but I'll have to speak to her sometime.' It was obvious the detective wasn't satisfied but he stood up to leave. 'We've got men out searching as we speak. I suggest you leave it to us now.'

'Not bloody likely,' Patrick muttered.

'It would be better if you did, Mr Howarth.'

They looked at one another, both remembering the few times they'd met before. Patrick was no stranger to the police. He gave a mirthless snort.

'I'll leave you my details,' Detective Hardcastle said. 'Any news, please contact me. Rest assured we'll do the same. Try to stay calm.' He looked around at them, his eyes resting last on Patrick. 'It's still early in the investigation. She could have wandered off and not known how to get back home. It wouldn't be the first time a kiddie's done that.' He stood. 'I've seen a few in my time in the force.'

Ellen and Ted didn't move when the policemen left the room.

'Investigation! Bloody heartless sod.' Patrick rubbed at the bristles on his chin.

After a moment's hesitation, still carrying Jack, Jean followed the policemen to the front door.

'I'll be in touch,' the detective said to her. 'And we'll carry on searching, Mrs Howarth. I'm sure we'll find Linda in no time. But we're going to have to look further afield. I think we've covered everywhere around here and there's been no sighting of your niece. We have to consider all the options.' He tipped the front of his trilby.

Jean nodded. She watched them get into the black car before closing the door. Heaving a deep sigh she went into the kitchen.

Ellen and Ted were sitting silently at the table. Patrick was smoking at the back door.

'Are you okay?' Jean asked. 'You didn't say Peter was upstairs as well?'

'Why complicate things?' Ted said. Ellen didn't respond.

Patrick motioned with his head towards the yard and walked outside. Jean frowned and went after him.

'What?'

'Bert Rowe told me last night there was a young lad went missing two months ago the other side of Bradlow. They found his body last week near Chester.'

Dear God. Jean put her hand on Jack's head. Not that, she begged silently, not that.

Chapter 80

'Well, I don't care what he said. I say we carry on looking for her,' Patrick said.

'Yes.' Ted laced his fingers again behind his aching neck and flexed his elbows as he walked around the furniture. He couldn't stay still. 'But where? We've searched the park, the old quarry, all along the canal.' He looked at them all in turn. 'We looked in all the sheds on the allotment, the bombsite on Clayton Street and Huddersfield Street, the derelict shop on Tatton Terrace. Anywhere we could think of. Where else is there?'

Peter stepped down from the stairs. He'd stayed out of the way while the police were there – he was still apprehensive around British authorities.

Since his arrival in Britain he'd thought his place within this family was with Mary. Now he wasn't sure and he felt like an outsider intruding on a desperate situation that had nothing to do with him.

But he didn't need to feel like that, he told himself. Ted asked him to be here. He'd grown fond of Linda when she was in Llamroth and he knew how much Mary loved the child. He must help all he could. 'The police, they found nothing?' he said. 'No clue where Linda might be?'

Ted grimaced. 'They're no further forward than us.'

'Mary?' Jean glanced up at Peter.

'Asleep.' He moved to stand at the back of the room.

'Good.'

Ted noticed the stiff way he walked. 'Did you manage any sleep?'

'It was fine. Thank you.'

'I don't know what else we can do,' Ted said. 'Where else we can look?'

'There is nowhere else around here,' Patrick said.

Ted shook his head. The silence held all their thoughts.

Peter stayed quiet. He didn't know the town at all. The only time he'd spent in Ashford was at the camp. And the only way he'd arrived was by train. He spoke softly. 'The railway? Beyond the platform there are wagons? On a line that leads to nowhere?'

'The sidings … where they keep the old wagons,' Ted exclaimed, eager to clutch at any hope. 'Did the police say they'd searched there?'

'I don't know.' Jean thought for a moment. 'Ellen?'

'No.' There was sudden renewed hope in her eyes. 'No!'

'Nobody's said anything about the railways. Keep an eye on him?' Patrick gestured to Jack who lay sleeping in Jean's arms.

'You go.'

'Ellen? Will you stay here?' Ted was already putting his jacket on. 'You look tired out?'

'I'm all right.'

'Please?'

'Okay, then.' She was reluctant. 'But let me know as soon as you can?'

'We will.' Ted looked at Peter. 'Ready?'

It would mean going past the camp. Peter's pulse quickened with dread. 'Ready,' he said.

Chapter 81

They drove without speaking to the railway station in Patrick's car, Peter sitting in the back seat, and when they got there, Patrick parked at the gates of the Granville.

'Here's as good as anywhere,' he said when Ted, glancing at Peter's tense expression, protested. 'The road gets crappy further up.'

Neither of the other two men missed the malicious glitter in Patrick's eyes.

Peter forced himself to look towards the old mill; the long rows of broken windows flashed, disparate shapes in the high glare of the sun. His eyes wandered along each storey of the building. The place still looked as intimidating as before. He shivered, thankful he would never have to set foot in the place ever again.

'Let's go.' Ted nudged him. They ran, the old, ridged concrete crunching under their boots, the wooden platform hollow.

The sound of their footsteps brought the ticket inspector to the entrance of the station. 'What the heck? What's going on?'

None of them stopped to explain. Jumping down onto the line, they crossed over to the sidings, pushing through the brambles and weeds tangled around the couplings and wheels of the wagons.

'Here, you can't do that.' The man waved his copy of the *Bradlow Gazette* at them as each of them chose a wagon and hoisted themselves up the side. 'I'll call the coppers.'

Ted stopped for a moment. 'We're looking for my daughter.

She's missing,' he shouted, ready to leap into the next wagon. 'Have you seen anyone hanging around here with a little girl?'

'No, mate, I haven't.' The ticket inspector folded the newspaper and pushed it into his pocket. 'I'm sorry. I'll go round the buildings and check while you're doing that. Forget the cops. I'll pretend I haven't seen you.' He adjusted the peak of his cap and squinted, looking up and down the railway lines. 'Watch out though, there's a train due in twenty minutes.' He disappeared into the waiting room.

'Anything?' Ted shouted to Peter who'd just emerged from the last truck in the line.

'No.' For a few seconds when he'd climbed into the wagon, Peter thought his heart would stop. A pile of clothes were bundled in one corner. But when he reached down to move them, he saw they were damp and mildewed and obviously untouched for a while. '*Vagabund* ... a tramp ... he must have slept here,' he muttered, not knowing if he was thankful or disheartened. 'Nothing.'

'Patrick?'

'Nah.'

As they climbed back onto the platform the ticket inspector appeared at one of the doors. 'Sorry. No sign of anybody being in that shouldn't.'

'Thanks anyway.' Ted stood, arms dangling by his side, shoulders drooping. 'Best get back to the house then.'

They walked slowly back to the car.

'I am sorry,' Peter said. 'I should not have raised your hopes. It was only an idea.'

'Stupid idea,' Patrick scoffed.

'We had to try,' Ted said. 'Anything's better than doing nothing.' Slumping against the car, both arms on the roof, the sobs erupted.

The two other men stared at each other. Peter knew the turmoil on Patrick's face, the uncertainty, must be reflected in his own. He stepped forward and rested a hand on Ted's back. Ted turned and held onto him, desperate tears shaking his whole body.

The last time Peter had held a man in his arms was when he was leaving the farm and he'd hugged his brother. The contact had been brief, cursory, both men relieved when it finished. This time he tightened his grip, wanting to put strength into Ted.

Patrick turned away, unwilling to show his own misery. He blinked rapidly.

Eventually Ted's sobs subsided. Peter let his arms drop to his sides. 'Sorry about that.'

Peter lifted his shoulders, careful not to show his embarrassment. 'It is fine,' he said.

Patrick was staring at the old mill. 'What about the camp?' he said and then contradicted himself. 'Stupid idea, the mill's closed up tight as a duck's arse.' He spoke rapidly, covering up his wretchedness. 'Those gates must be ten foot high. And with all that fucking barbed wired on top ... daft idea.'

'They mended all the fences last year,' Ted said. 'Linda wouldn't have been able to get in there.'

A train rattled past on the line with a whoop of its whistle, leaving behind a thick trail of grey smoke. In the long silence that followed they stood dejected. 'Unless,' Peter said, 'someone has taken her in there.'

Ted cried out in despair.

The blood pounded in Peter's ears. He twisted around to look at his old prison. All that was left of the look-outs were wooden platforms interwoven with ivy and pink-flowered weeds. If he didn't know what was behind them he could almost think they looked attractive. But beyond he could see the mill with the crumbling roof and broken jagged glass in the windows and it resurrected the fear that still lurked in him, the stuff of his nightmares. Bad memories rushed through his mind: the bullying from the guards, the intimidation of the Nazis and the cruelties

278

used to dominate the other prisoners. One would live with him forever. The time Frank Shuttleworth shot him.

But then he remembered a summer day, leaning against the wall of the mill, eyes half closed, the rugged line of the high moors in the distance shimmering in the heat. That was the day when he'd become conscious that he loved Mary.

And she loved Linda.

He stared at the gates. Only a few moments ago, he thought he would never have to go in that place again. Now he knew he had to. 'We must look,' he said.

Chapter 82

Ted held the padlock in his palm. The men looked at one another and then at the iron gates. The chain fastening them was new, the thick strong links looped twice around the bars, glittered silver in the sunlight.

Peter cleared his throat. 'So,' he said, 'how will this be done?'

'Well, we're not going to break this,' Ted said, looking hopelessly around.

Patrick weighed up the height of the gate. 'If I stood on your shoulders I could shimmy up.'

'The barbed wire?' Peter pointed.

'Chuck my jacket over it.'

It took him a few minutes to work out footholds, oblivious to the painful shuffling of his heavy studded boots on the other man's back. Giving one push against Peter, he wedged his toes in the crosspieces of the gate and, when close enough, threw the jacket over the top. The heavy tweed clung to the spikes of the wire. 'Got it,' he gasped. 'Come on, get a bloody move on.' He swung himself over to the other side and dangled, one arm outstretched. 'Come on, these bloody things are sticking in my guts.'

Peter took a few steps back and took a run. He leapt at the gates and grabbed one of the rails. It felt as though his arm was on fire as it took his whole weight. Then he pivoted, making his body rotate until the sheer force crashed him against iron and he hung on. He wouldn't have been able to do this a year ago and thanked fortune for the muscles he'd built up through his gardening work. Scrabbling upwards he grasped Patrick's hand and gained enough leverage to join the other man.

For a few seconds they were suspended, the air wheezing and whistling in their chests. Then Peter slid down the other side.

'Ted?' Patrick motioned to him. 'Come on, man.' He clicked his fingers impatiently.

Ted bit his lip. 'I don't think I can.' Reaching up he could just touch the first cross. Frustrated he looked around.

A man on the allotments was leaning on his spade and staring at them. When he saw Ted a look of recognition flashed across his face and he raised a hand.

'For fuck's sake, man, I can't hang on much longer.' Patrick tried to tuck more of the thickness of his jacket under him.

'Well, get down then, but leave the jacket there.' Ted crossed the road towards the man.

'It's Ted Booth, ain't it?' The man jabbed his spade into bed of soil. 'Heard your little un is missing.'

'Yeah, thought we might look in there.' Ted gestured with his thumb towards the old mill. Peter and Patrick stood watching behind the gate.

The man looked doubtful. 'How'd she get in?'

Ted ignored the question. 'I need help to get over the gate.' He looked over at the greenhouse. There was an old dustbin by the door. 'Can I use that?'

'Hmm – my burning bin? I'd want it back.'

'I only want to use it to climb over.' Without waiting for the man's permission, Ted slid down the bank and climbed over the allotment fence. Emptying ashes and bits of burnt wood out of it he heaved it onto his shoulder. 'I'll bring it back.'

At the gates Patrick had once again clambered onto Peter's back and was waiting to hoist Ted over.

When they were all three inside the camp, Patrick said, 'Stick together or split up?'

'Together.' A tremor ran through Peter.

'Separate,' Patrick decided. 'Where first? Ted?'

'Top floors of the mill?'

'You?' Patrick glanced at Peter.

'I know the hospital buildings,' Peter said. He would avoid going into the compound if he could.

'Right, you do those and we'll start in the mill.'

Peter watched Ted and Patrick as they ran across the crumbling concrete of the large yard and up the ramp where lorries used to load up those prisoners sent to work on farms. Two large doors hung crookedly on their hinges. He heard the echoing voices of both men as they shouted for Linda, saw their pale silhouettes against the dark of the windows on each landing.

Peter walked towards the narrow entrance where the guardroom used to be. With the toe of his shoe he traced the outline of the foundations. There was an ashen taste in his mouth. This was no good, recollections did him no good.

He whirled around to face the building that had been the hospital. He crossed the path and ran up the steps to the entrance. The doors were stiff but, with a little persuasion, gave way, scraping years of rubble with them. His footsteps were a hollow click on the floor. He took the stairs two at a time, stopping on each floor to shout Linda's name, until he reached the top.

Walking through the long wards he stared at the disarranged iron bedsteads, some missing springs, some head rails, and the moulding mattresses piled up in corners, now the homes of mice. Or rats, he thought seeing the large lumps of stuffing pulled out and arranged into nests and the size of the droppings everywhere. His mouth made an involuntary repulsed shape as he moved the mattresses with his foot.

He only touched what he had to, the door handles, rotting blankets, cupboards large enough to hold a little girl. At each of those he instinctively held his breath, letting the air out in relief when he found nothing.

And then he was in the ward where he'd worked with Mary. *'Mein Gott,'* he whispered, *'Gott in Himmel.'* Flies lay thick on the windowsills, bluebottles buzzed around his head. He flapped at them, cursing. Disturbed dust motes floated around him, shimmering in the gleam of yellow sunshine that forced its way through the grimed windows and lay in slanted rectangles on the floor. He heard water and crossed to the back of the ward to the small wash hand basin. A long green stain from beneath the tap to the plughole gave evidence to the years of wasted water. Peter tried to tighten it but it wouldn't budge and he left it to drip.

Finally he stood in the entrance again, marking off in his mind where he had been, making sure he'd missed nowhere. Two steps and he was outside, gratefully taking in the clean air. A train passed through the station without stopping, the thick smoke curling as it rose. He looked across at the mill. Ted was disappearing through the door to the officers' quarters. Patrick was nowhere to be seen.

There was still the boiler house to check. He felt his way along the dark corridors, the walls rough under his fingertips. Always dimly lit, now it was pitch black. When he came to the stone steps there was a slight glimmer of light from the air vents near the ceiling. He shouted, 'Linda?' The name bounced off the walls.

A whistling flutter of wings made him stoop quickly as two pigeons brushed past his head and flew along the corridor. For a moment he thought his heart was going to burst out of his chest. Steadying himself he made his way down the steps until he was standing outside the heavy door. Running his hands over the surface he found a bolt. It was rough with rust but moved quite easily when he tugged it. The door still didn't open. As he dropped his hand away his knuckles hit a large key. It took both hands to grasp and turn in the lock. A scraping of metal on metal.

Standing in the doorway, he let his eyes get used to the gloom. Here, in this dismal place, he and Mary had first made love, desperate in their need for each other. They'd taken such chances to be together in those days, jeopardised so much, especially Mary. He remembered casting aside the terror of discovery, overwhelmed by his love for a woman he thought could never be truly his. He knew how lucky he was to have found her again.

He shivered. At least then this room had been warm. The furnace, which covered most of the far wall, was always lit. Now it was cold, rusty and disintegrated. The wall was damp when he placed his hand against it. Grit crunched under his shoes, but became tacky as he took a couple of strides and stopped.

He bent down and felt the ground. It was sticky. He lifted his fingers to his nose. Blood. Still fresh. His skin tingled with fear. '*Oh mein Gott, kein.*' He squatted down, peered into the darkness and then shuffled forward holding one hand in front of him and one on the ground, brushing aside the years of dirt and grime until his fingers touched something. Stunned, he held the air in his lungs as he moved trembling fingers over a small foot. 'Linda,' he breathed.

There she was; a small bundle of clothes, seemingly thrown into a crumpled heap. His heart stopped, silence all around him. 'Linda?' His hands hovered. And then his years of training came back with a rush. He held the pad of his thumb to the cold frail wrist and waited. It was there, the pulse. Relief flooded through him. He didn't try to stop the sob that burst out.

At his touch she stirred, moaned, began to cry.

'It is all right, *meine Kleine.*' He spoke softly. '*Du bist jetzt in Sicherheit.* You are safe now.' Hooking his arms under her he rose, almost stumbling in his haste, out through the door, running along the corridors, his footsteps echoing in the emptiness.

Outside the air was clean and fresh, the sky a brilliant blue as they emerged into the sunlight. Peter shrugged off the years of fear. 'She is here,' he shouted, 'she is here!'

They didn't see George Shuttleworth watching them from the behind the wall of the bridge over the canal path. They didn't see him turn and stumble down the steps. As they passed by they didn't see him hiding under the bridge.

And, late that night, no one saw him catch the last bus into Manchester.

Chapter 83

'How is she? Is she okay?' Mary's eyes were sore with crying but relief had dissolved the hard lump that had been in her throat.

'She is well … she will be well,' Peter said. 'The hospital has told Ted she is dehydrated. It must be so. She was in that place for two days.'

'Alone.' Mary's voice wavered. 'She will have been so frightened.'

'She is safe now.' Peter didn't tell Mary he'd found the little girl in the basement. Somehow, however awful the place, it held a precious memory of the first time they made love. He wouldn't destroy that. 'There is some shock,' he added. 'But they have done the X-rays on her head and on her ankle. Sadly, poor little girl, the ankle is broken but there is no problem through the bump on her head.'

'Was there…?' Mary faltered. 'Was anything else, was anything else done to her?'

The unspoken question hung between them.

'No,' Peter said. 'Ted said there was nothing else.' Although every instinct in him wanted to enfold Mary in his arms Peter carefully kept his distance. He would wait until she was ready, until she forgave him. If she ever did. The unwelcome thought forced itself into his brain. And then he couldn't stand being so close to her yet not touching. He got up and walked to the window resting his head against the window pane and looking out onto the street. 'The worst is over, *Liebling.*'

Is it? Mary wondered. She kept her eyes on his back. He'd grown thinner in the months they'd been apart. The weight of unsaid words separated them. Neither of them had mentioned the previous night when she'd turned from him. Now, from the stiff set of his shoulders she knew he was waiting for her to say what she wanted. But the turmoil in her froze any decision. Whatever Peter needed, whatever she needed from him, would have to wait. She was exhausted and too weak to face up to what could be; that everything they had between them had now gone, destroyed by a dreadful secret. And she knew if she started to cry again she might not be able to stop. Because, now she was safe, it wouldn't be for Linda. It would be for what she and Peter had lost. She wrapped her arms over the mound that held her … *their* baby.

There was so much pain between them.

Chapter 84

'Can you tell us what the man looked like, Linda?' Detective Hardcastle sat on the chair by the bed and leaned back, crossing his legs.

Linda didn't want to think about the nasty man. It made all the horrible feelings come back. She slid further down under the covers, shook her head and winced – the large bump on her head hurt. Her ankle, raised on a hard pillow, was bound in brown calico. 'My foot's hot,' she whispered to her mother.

'Nurse?' Ellen looked up at the young woman next to her.

'It's a simple sprain but the ankle requires support so it needs the bandage on and must be kept still and raised up for now.' The nurse smiled sympathetically at Linda.

Her daughter looked so tiny. Ellen see-sawed between relief that she'd been found and rage at the person who'd done this to her. She clung on to Linda's hand. She never wanted to let her out of her sight again. This was how she felt the first time she'd brought her home, she remembered; the journey on the train with Mary by their side, as always, she acknowledged. Mary. Always there when needed.

How many chances in life were possible? Ellen realised that, for the last two days, she'd unconsciously convinced herself that her luck had run out. That she'd gambled once too often with her daughter's life.

Now she felt fiercely protective. When the policeman leaned towards Linda and said, 'Okay, let's try again,' Ellen interrupted.

'Do we have to do this now?'

'Yes, the sooner we know what the man looks like, the sooner we can concentrate on who we're looking for.'

'You can leave this to us.' Patrick slapped his clenched fist into the palm of his other hand.

'We can't.' Detective Hardcastle exchanged angry looks with Patrick. 'We have other reasons to find this man, as you may know.' Turning slightly away from Linda he moved his eyes towards her with a small tilt of his head. 'I just wonder when you were going to tell us you'd found her. And where.' He waited, his eyes wandering over the three of them. They refused to meet his gaze. 'If someone hadn't reported seeing you going into the old camp we wouldn't have known anything about it.'

Ellen shivered. The thought of the murdered boy had haunted her from the moment she'd heard about him. Her heart went out to the mother and she was almost ashamed of the relief that it was him and not her daughter; almost, but not quite.

'Look, the description of this man could be the nearest lead we've had so far. I've got some men in the old camp now, looking for anything they can find that might identify this chap. In the meantime…' He swung back in his chair and smiled at Linda, leaning on the bed. 'Let's start with his hair, eh sweetheart. Try to think what that looked like.'

Linda held her lower lip between the tips of her finger and thumb. It was cut and swollen from when the man had pushed the cup at her mouth. She reluctantly made the picture of the man in her head. 'Like the curly horns of the big goat in the Billy Goats Gruff story, Mummy,' Linda said. 'Funny colour, like your blouse.' It frightened her to think about him but that was how she remembered the man's hair the first time she saw him, frizzing up around his head in the sunlight.

'Hey, cheeky monkey, leave the colour of my blouse alone.' Ellen leant over to tickle Linda's chin.

Everyone laughed. It lightened the atmosphere for a second.

'Orange? Ginger!' A note of triumph in the policeman's voice. 'Good girl.' He looked at each of them in turn. 'Ring any bells?'

Ellen and Ted shook their heads.

Loud as a bloody church bell, Patrick thought. But he'd keep the information to himself. He'd be the one to kill the bastard.

'Anything else?'

'Funny nose.' Linda pushed her nose to one side.

'Broken nose?' Again his gaze swept over them.

No response.

Linda touched her cheek. 'His face was really red … here … bumpy.' She touched the other cheek. 'But not on this side.' She thought for a moment. 'No.' She swopped sides again with her hand. 'Just this side.'

'Like a burn?'

She shrugged. 'Mummy?'

'She doesn't understand,' Ellen said.

'That's fine. Anything else?'

'He had a ring on his finger.' Linda held up her right hand. 'This one.' She pointed to her finger. 'Big. And like this.' She drew a square on the sheet. 'Big,' she repeated. 'Dirty nails.' Now she felt safe, now everyone was looking and smiling at her, as

287

though they were all pleased with her, she felt braver. 'And he was very smelly – stinky,' Linda added.

She was beginning to enjoy herself and was a bit disappointed when the policeman said, 'Well, I think that's enough for now.' He stood and smiled down at her. 'You've done really well, Linda. I wish all our witnesses were as good.' He patted her head. 'See you again sometime, eh?'

'Yes.' She snuggled down under the covers and closed her eyes in pretend sleep.

The men moved away.

'You sure this doesn't ring any bells?' Detective Hardcastle asked.

Again Ted shook his head.

'Mr Howarth?' He stared steadily at Patrick.

'Nope, no bugger I know.'

The policeman looked as if he didn't believe him. Nowt he can do, Patrick thought, but a hell of a lot I fucking can, if I ever manage to find him. He repeated his earlier thought to himself. I can kill the bastard.

Chapter 85

'He's got good sturdy legs.' Ellen stroked Jack's head.

'He has.' Jean laughed softly, struggling to change his nappy as he wriggled. She coughed, fully aware that she'd been caught out in her growing fondness for the little boy. Putting her hand between the nappy and his stomach she pushed and fastened the large pin through the towelling cloth.

'Loving him isn't something to be ashamed of, Jean.' Ellen picked Jack up from the table and held him close. He grasped a lock of her hair and pushed his face next to hers, making small murmuring sounds. 'He's gorgeous.'

'And he's not mine.' Jean rinsed the wet nappy under the tap and dropped it into a bucket by the back door. 'Mother doesn't think I should be looking after him but what choice have I had this week?' Instantly mortified, she said, 'I'm sorry, I didn't mean that the way it sounded. I would have done anything to help find Linda.'

'I know.' Ellen's old antagonism towards Jean had vanished over the last few days.

She knew Jean had been surprised to see her on the doorstep. But, as Ted had said when he dropped her off at the end of Moss Terrace, 'If that's what you feel you need to say, now is as good a time as ever, before Patrick comes back from the market. And it'll give me a bit of time with William … so two stones and all that.'

'If you don't mind my saying, I think you should ignore your mother.' Elsie Winterbottom was a hateful old cow – the thought was automatic. 'Where is she by the way?'

'Next door. She's spent a lot of time there lately, while I've had Jack. Like I said…' Jean shrugged.

'Then I'm sorry, but I think she's mean. Mean and unkind.' She kissed Jack on the nose. 'And I think you're lovely with him.'

'Do you?'

'Yes.' Ellen was firm.

'You don't think I'm being too soft with Patrick?'

'Well, he needs bringing into line, but I'm sure you're more than capable of doing that. Anyway is it about him?'

After Jean dried her hands, Ellen gave her the little boy and went to sit on the back doorstep. It would be easier for her to speak if she didn't have to face Jean. 'When I brought Linda home, I didn't know how Ted would take it. I didn't even consider his mother.' She looked at the line of baby clothes, now dried from the day's sun. 'But she was hateful almost from the beginning. She'd wait until he wasn't there … and then she'd start.' Ellen hugged her knees up to her chin. 'She'd say the most vile things.' She glanced over her shoulder at Jean. 'Oh, I told Ted at first but she denied it, said I'd misunderstood or something. He was good about it, told her to think before she said anything, but he didn't really understand and I'm obstinate, you know?'

Jean gave an ironic chuckle. 'Never?'

Ellen managed a smile herself. 'I thought I could deal with her on my own.' She turned back to look at the yard, spoke thoughtfully. 'In the end, I couldn't. I'll tell you something, shall I?'

'If you want to.' Jean put Jack into his pram and covered him up. She squashed up to Ellen on the step. The yard was partly in shade now as the sun dropped. The pitch of the roofs of the next row of terraced houses made pointed shadows on the flags.

'I think I killed Hannah.' Ellen swallowed. 'It wasn't any better after we came back from Mary's. Ted told her she'd have to leave if she didn't stop but it made her worse. I knew I couldn't take much more. I couldn't sleep. I cried most of the time. She used to laugh at me. We'd had the most awful argument and I hit her.' She heard the intake of breath. 'I know. I was wrong but I can't remember a lot of what was said, my head was spinning. She came back at me. I ran … I stayed in the yard for ages. When I went back into the kitchen she was lying dead on the floor.

'It doesn't matter how many times Ted tells me the doctor said her blood pressure was sky high, that she could have died anytime. I think I'll always blame myself.' She straightened her back, her voice determined. 'But I'm going to change, Jean. What happened to Linda's made sure of that. And I'm ashamed of how I've behaved since Tom died, being so selfish, expecting Mary to fuss over me, despite everything she's gone – is going – through. I have to grow up.'

There was something else she'd decided as well. She'd heard two nurses talking at the hospital. Nelly Shuttleworth had been to the police, told them that she was mistaken, her son hadn't been home the day of Tom's death, wasn't actually home for over two days at that time. Ellen remembered the sickly heave of her stomach as she eavesdropped on the nurses' casual conversation. So she'd decided she was going to let Nelly meet Linda. Not at her house, only at Henshaw Street, but it would be a start for Linda to get to know her grandmother.

She felt Jean's arm around her shoulder and leant against her plump figure. 'And I'm sorry. I've always been jealous of you.'

'Have you?' Jean sounded amazed. 'I didn't know that.' There was a hesitation in her next words. 'Well I'll let you into a secret now, Ellen. I've always envied you being beautiful and slim. So I think we're quits there, eh?'

'I think we are.' Ellen lifted her head and smiled at Jean. 'I know you're a kind woman, Jean. You've always been good with Linda … and you knew what her father was, but that it wasn't her fault. Any more than it's Jack's fault how he was conceived.'

Jean flinched.

'Try to forget where he came from, Jean. Just think of him as a baby you've been given to love. Like Ted loves Linda.'

Chapter 86

'Okay, this is what's going to happen.' Jean sat opposite Patrick. They'd been going around in circles for the last hour. She was sure he was sorry for everything that had happened. She was sure he wanted their lives to go back as they were. But not quite as they were, she told herself. She was even sure that, in his own way, he loved her.

'Ellen told me tonight that the police know George Shuttleworth killed Tom. So get all thoughts of going to look for him right out of your mind.'

He didn't answer. He kept his eyes on Jack who was sleeping in his arms.

'Patrick! If you can't even promise that, we might as well give up now.'

'Right, right.' He kept his voice low.

'Promise.'

'I promise.'

'Look at me.'

He lifted his head. 'I'll leave it to the police. All right?'

Jean nodded. 'Good. We've had enough grief to last us a lifetime, you don't need to go looking for more.' She watched him caress the baby's head in the palm of his hand. For a second her whole body cried out at the wrongness of him holding another woman's child when it should have been hers. She forced the jealousy away. 'And if you ever raise your hand to me again, Patrick, you'll never see me or Jacqueline again.'

This time there was a catch in his voice. 'I know. I always swore I would never be like Dad. I know I've fought men before … loads of times…'

'Which needs to stop.'

He moved his head in agreement. 'But I didn't think I would ever hit a woman, any woman, but especially the woman I love.' He choked on the words. 'Not after I saw how it made Mam. I'm ashamed, Jean.'

He looked it, she conceded. 'And you know the last thing I'm going to say, don't you?'

'No more playing around.'

'Or I'll go, and I'll take Jacqueline with me. I won't be humiliated again. I wouldn't do it to you.' She saw his face darken. The thought had never occurred to him, obviously. 'And don't think I haven't had the opportunity.' Did the butcher's boy flirting count? She hid her smile. No harm in giving him something to ponder on. 'But I wouldn't do it,' she emphasised.

'And neither will I from now on.' He looked at her. 'I've been stupid, chancing throwing away everything we've got.'

That was enough for now. 'Fresh start?'

He smiled tentatively at her. 'Fresh start.'

She heard her mother's key in the front door.

Holding out her hands, she gestured towards the baby. 'Now, give Jack to me.'

Chapter 87

Mary put both hands flat on the mattress and hoisted herself higher, the wire springs of the bedframe moving with the old familiar twang. The sheet under her was hot and she felt sweaty and clammy; her nightie stuck to her buttocks and the back of her legs.

'What time is it?'

'Only five o'clock. I was looking to see if you were settled. I am sorry to wake you.' Peter's voice was cautious.

She hadn't slept well. She'd lain awake staring into the darkness, trying to work out what she was feeling. She knew she still loved Peter, it was obvious he loved her, but there was a distance between them that seemed intractable. She knew it was one she had created, but there'd been a reason for that: he'd lied to her and she wasn't sure she would ever forgive him. And if she was unable to do that, how could she share the rest of her life with him?

But then there was the baby. Although she had been prepared to, when she was angry with Peter, she knew now it was unfair to keep the baby from him. She'd no right. From the moment she'd looked into his eyes as he sat at her bedside almost a week ago, she'd known the agony he was going through; the fear of losing the life he'd hoped to build with her. But still, even though she was terrified that something awful had happened to Linda and she'd needed his comfort, still she'd rejected him.

She noticed now that he was looking at her, his head tilted to one side as though he'd asked her a question and was waiting for an answer. When she didn't speak he moved away from her.

'You didn't wake me,' she said eventually. 'Where is everyone?'

'Ellen could not sleep. Ted took her back to the hospital to be with Linda.'

'They must be exhausted.'

'They know it is for the best that the hospital keeps Linda there. They need to be sure she is totally well. It has only been four days. She has had a dreadful experience.'

She watched him moving about the room, hanging her dressing gown on the nail at the back of the door, straightening the mirror on top of the tallboy, running his hands up and down the blue curtains as he pulled them back. He stood, peering through the folds of the patterned net curtain at the street below. The heat from the early morning sun already shimmered on the glass. A bluebottle buzzed, whirling around on its back on the windowsill. Peter scooped it into his hand, lifted the sash and tipped it out. Rubbing his palm on his trousers he came to the end of the bed and said, 'When you were sleeping Ted telephoned to see if you are all right and to say that Linda is fine. They will be home later.'

'Will they be able to bring her home today?'

'He said another one or two days – to make sure.'

'Right.' Mary pulled at the pillows behind her, trying to give her back some support.

'May I help?' Peter moved forward.

'No, thanks, I'm fine.' She settled back. 'Where's everybody else?'

'Patrick has just left for the market in Bradlow,' Peter said. 'He said he must go to see if "those bloody women have ... er ... fleeced him"? I think that is what he said.'

'Stolen money from him,' Mary said. 'Yes, he would say that. Typical Patrick.'

It made a lighter moment between them; they exchanged smiles.

'He and Jean seem to be making the best of things, don't you think?' Is that what we're trying to do right now, Mary thought, make the best of things?

'Yes, I think you are right. I think all will be well there.' His eyes lit up. 'She is also being nice to me.' His grin was infectious.

'Well, make the most of it. It won't last.' Mary gave a small laugh. 'Where is she?'

'She is still at her mother's house with Jacqueline and William. She thinks it will be for the best at the moment. Give you a chance to rest.'

A slight frown creased Mary's forehead. 'What about Jack?'

'Oh, Jack is with her also.'

'My goodness, I wonder how Elsie Winterbottom's taking to that.' Not too well, if she knew anything about that woman. Jean must have well and truly put her foot down. 'I've been really worried about Jean, but it seems she'll be okay with that little boy.'

'Children only need to be loved,' Peter said simply. 'I think Jean is learning to do that.' He hesitated. 'I did not mean to ... but I heard her say to your brother that she would take care of Jack, but only if Patrick promised to change his ways. He said that he would promise if she could forgive him.'

'I hope it works out for them, Peter, I really do. Jean has had a lot to put up with. I hope she can forgive him but it might not be that easy.'

They exchanged glances.

If Peter asked for her forgiveness now she didn't know if she could reject him again.

He didn't. He left the room in silence.

She couldn't let him go. 'Peter,' she whispered.

He must have been standing just outside the door because he appeared immediately. *'Liebling?'*

'I love you,' Mary said simply. 'I love you.'

He stood for a second, shock etched on his face. Then he crossed the room in slow steps and knelt by her bedside. *'Ich liebe dich auch Schatz.* I always will.' Slow tears rose and fell. Peter brushed them away with his arm.

'Don't, love,' Mary said, 'don't cry. It will be okay.' He lay face to face with her on her pillow. She closed her eyes, listening to his breathing. It matched her own, almost as if he'd done it on purpose, as though they were breathing as one.

There was no noise through the open sash window. They were alone in their own world.

'It will be all right?' Peter kept his voice low.

'It will.' Mary gently ran the tips of her fingers through his blond hair, longer now than the last time they were together in Llamroth. She quickly closed her mind to the memory. If they were going to move on, if they were going to make a success of their lives together she had to shut away those feelings. Forgive, she told herself, if not easily forget.

'Now, will you help me to get up? If I stay in this bed much longer I'll go mad.'

'*Nein Leibling.* Please.'

'I want to sit out in the yard in the sun. I have to get up. I'm hot, I need a wash and I'm bored. If I have to read any more of Ellen's Penny Dreadfuls I'll scream. They're absolute tripe.'

'You must promise to rest?'

'I will.'

He helped her to shuffle to the edge of the mattress and stand. Her stomach pressed against him, firm and unyielding and she was glad of the comfort, of the baby safe between them. He put his palm under her chin, lifted her face and kissed her. 'I have missed you so much, Mary Howarth.'

'Me too … oh me too.' She revelled in the taste of his lips, again felt the stirring of desire for him. Even at this stage, she smiled inwardly, even being a fat lump, you're still fancying him. She gently pulled at his hair at the back. 'You could do with a haircut.' It felt so good for them to be back on such easy terms.

'Ted has said there is a barber shop on a street in town … Yorkshire Street?'

Mary grinned. 'I believe so. It's called *Herr Cutz.*'

'At first I did not understand but then Ted explained it to me.' Peter looked thoughtful. 'Ted says the man was a prisoner at the camp at the end of the war, was the barber there for a short while, that I might know of him. Perhaps he is the one I remember.'

'You should go to see him?'

'*Ja.*' He rested his forehead against hers. 'Mary?' His voice sounded too loud in the quiet room. He faltered, opened his mouth and then closed it again. He shook his head as if to clear his thoughts. 'About Shuttleworth. About Tom.'

'Hush.' She stopped him. Now wasn't the right time.

'We should talk.' He watched her anxiously.

'No. Not here, not now. When we go home.' She saw it all in his face, the sudden odd mix of apprehension and happiness.

'We will go home?'

'Yes. I think I've been away long enough, don't you?' Mary took hold of his hand and placed it over her breast.

'Too long.' He took his hand away from her, laughing. 'And I think you are the wanton woman, Miss Howarth.'

'Soon to be Mrs Schormann?' She looked quizzically at him.

'*Ja, Liebling.* I would like that; I would be a proud man if you were to be Mrs Schormann.'

She saw the relief on his face. Mary pointed at the mound of her stomach. 'And I think we should hurry up, don't you?'

'As soon as we are home we will go to see the minister.'

'I should think we're in his bad books already for cancelling the wedding. What he'll say when he sees the size of me now I dread to think.'

'He is a nice man, Mr Willingham, he will not judge. See how kind he has been to me already.'

'I know, love. It was my idea of a bad joke.'

'Ah.' Peter gave her a wry smile. 'But still, we will go home soon?'

'Hmmm.' Mary pretended solemn consideration. 'Yes, I think everybody can manage without us now. So, perhaps by next week we'll be back in Llamroth. But for now…' She turned him around and rested her hands on his shoulders. 'For now, you can get me down those stairs.'

Peter walked in front of her, her stomach bumping gently on his back.

In the kitchen he encircled her waist, his hands just about reaching around her, and lowered her onto one of the kitchen chairs. 'Sit here, I will carry the armchair out to the yard and then you can relax outside in the fresh air.'

'No, I'll be fine on one of these.' She patted the edge of the seat she sat on. 'Put me in that thing.' She wafted her hand at the armchair. 'And I'll never get up.'

'Stay a moment.'

She waited while he decided where the best place was in the yard. 'It is good here?' he asked, looking up towards the sun and rearranging the chair for the tenth time.

'It's perfect.' Mary hauled herself up. 'Perfect.'

'You must rest.'

'I will.' Mary sat on the wooden chair and shifted uncomfortably. Now she was out of bed she realised how exhausted she actually was. 'Thanks.'

'Do not move,' Peter added sternly. In the kitchen the clock struck six times.

Mary couldn't believe how early it still was. 'I will not move,' she laughed, imitating him.

He kissed her. '*Gut!* There is tea in the pot. I will make a cup to you. And I will telephone Gwyneth. I must tell her we will *both*,' he stressed the word, 'be coming home to Llamroth.'

Mary smiled. 'She will be pleased.'

'It is what she has been wishing for all these months. So, stay still. I will come back with the tea. And then I have something to tell you. I have news of my own.'

There was a burnished hard-edged radiance to the morning. The kind that makes you feel glad to be alive, Mary reflected. She sat, nursing the cup of tea between both palms, savouring the stillness around her. Six o'clock in the morning and the sun already warm on her face when she closed her eyes and tilted it upwards to the sky.

Thank you Tom, she said silently, for watching over Linda, for bringing her back to us. She squeezed her eyes tight and swallowed. And helping me to forgive Peter. It's what you would

298

have done – did. She believed that now. Tom had known it was Peter who'd killed Frank and kept quiet. 'Because that was the kind of man you were, Tom,' she murmured, 'our happiness meant more to you than anything else.' She felt a split second of shame and guilt. She held up her hands as though in supplication, the cup between them, and rested her forehead against the warm smooth surface.

Peter came out of the house and leant on the yard wall next to Mary. He was grinning. 'Gwyneth sends her love.'

'Go on then,' Mary said, smiling, 'tell me your news.' She waited, unable to read his expression.

'I have a job.' He took a long slurp of tea, savouring the moment. 'I have a job at the doctor's.'

'But…' Mary's stomach lurched. 'Will they let you…?'

'No, not as a doctor,' Peter said quickly. 'Not yet anyway. Doctor Grimstead has offered me the job as caretaker for the surgery. The last one has left.' He squatted down resting his clasped hands on her knees. 'We will not any more have to do the…' He tapped his fingers on her leg impatiently. 'The – what do you call it? The scrapping around for money.'

'Scratting.' Mary smiled. 'Scratching around for money.'

'That,' Peter agreed. He laughed in triumph. 'Now I can provide for you, for my family.' He sat back on his heels, watching her reaction.

The fact that they would have regular money coming in was like a great weight lifted from her shoulders, one that she didn't even know was there. But then something struck her. 'You said,' she spoke slowly, 'as a doctor "not yet"?'

'That is what is best.' He beamed at her. 'Doctor Grimstead has said he will make enquires to see if I will be able to practice again. I have all my certificates and papers. He says that sooner or later there will be new laws that will enable me to do that.'

In a voice filled with awe, he said, 'One day, Mary, one day I will become a doctor again.'

Chapter 88

'And, perhaps, one day you will become a nurse again.' He stroked the side of her face. 'I know you must miss that as much as I have missed being a doctor.'

His concerned remark gave her a spasm of regret. She'd fought her father to become a nurse. He'd wanted only that she brought money into the house. She'd loved her job, especially being Matron at Pont y Haven. And she wouldn't have met Peter if she hadn't worked in the hospital at the camp. But now she had a whole new life to look forward to.

'I think this baby will be more than enough for me for the time being. One day – who knows?' She leant forward and, pushing against his shoulder, stood up. 'I must go to the lavvy.'

'You must go slowly.' He steadied her but she pulled him with her, laughing.

All at once she felt a sudden pressure on her bladder. She couldn't move. 'Peter?' Water gushed from between her legs onto the flags. She stared down at her feet, unbelieving. 'Oh no!' She doubled over in pain. 'It's too early,' she cried, 'Peter, it's too soon.' She stayed still, trying to catch her breath. 'Peter, it's too soon.'

For a second he froze and then he lifted and carried her into the house, inwardly cursing himself. 'When I was a doctor at home in Germany, I have delivered many early babies. You must not worry.' He should have known, should have made plans for this. 'From what you have told me, it is only three or perhaps four weeks early.' He laid her on the rug and placed cushions around her, anxious to reassure her. 'Your waters have broken, Mary, so we must be prepared. We must take off your underclothes, *Liebling*. Try to lift yourself up.'

She groaned as she helped him. Her stomach rippled but there was no pain, only a dull ache.

'We must telephone the midwife.'

His composure stopped her panic. 'The number's on the sideboard.' She pointed upwards, towards it.

'There is pain now?'

'No. But—'

'It will be fine.'

'It's too soon. The baby will be too small.' It was almost a question. She searched his face.

'No, the baby is fine. I think perhaps he – or she,' he added, 'seems impatient to be with us. We should try to get you upstairs on the bed.' She would be more restful there, he thought.

'I'm not moving.'

He wouldn't argue with her. 'Then we must put the towels under you and make you comfortable here.' He moved around her as he spoke, tucking towels under her buttocks, arranging the cushions.

'Peter!' The ache increased, travelling down her legs and around her pelvis at the same time. 'Peter.' She clutched his hand, her eyes wide with terror.

'Stay calm,' he said, 'it will be fine.' He kissed her forehead. 'I will telephone.'

'Don't leave me.' Mary rose up on one elbow.

'I will only be in the hall. Try to relax.' His prised her fingers gently away from his and pressed on her shoulder until she was lying back on the cushions. 'Stay still for a moment.'

When he returned he was carrying a sheet and two pillows. 'The midwife,' he said, 'she will be here soon.'

'When?'

'Soon.'

As he covered her with the sheet she curled up again, unable to speak until the surge of pain subsided. 'That was worse.'

'You did well. It will be fine.' He bent over the fireguard, putting a match to the newspaper in the grate. 'It is good that it is always set.' The flames died down and then began to lick around the wood.

'I'm too hot already,' Mary complained. The sweat was beaded on her top lip and over the bridge of her nose.

'You will need the warmth later. And so will the baby.' He sat beside her. 'Stay on your side,' he said, 'it will make you feel better.'

'No, I need to walk around.' Mary flung the sheet away from her and pushed herself into a half crouching, half standing position. Peter didn't stop her. Supporting her weight he rubbed the small of her back.

Mary could hear herself grunting. 'Talk,' she said eventually, when the next pain receded. 'Talk to me … anything … say anything.' She held the weight of her belly in her hands. 'Where the hell is that midwife?'

Peter had no answer. He continued to massage Mary's back. 'When this baby is born … we will go home?'

'Yes, we'll go home.' Mary crouched down. 'I think it's coming.' Pushing Peter to one side, she collapsed onto the floor on her back, hearing herself scream, cutting off the noise by biting down on her lip and burrowing her face in the cushions. The contractions were almost continuous, she couldn't take much more; the pain was tearing her apart, all there was was agony.

And then she saw her mother's face, felt her cool hand on her sweating forehead. *Mam?* She was wearing the flowery wrap-around pinny she always wore.

Shush now, Mary. Winifred smiled at her. She smelt the blend of carbolic soap and lavender. You'll be fine. She was leaning over Mary.

But then she was gone and it was Peter parting her legs, looking at her. 'You should push now.' His voice was low but definite. 'Mary? Now push.'

'The midwife?' Mary gripped hold of one of the cushions and pulled it over her face and screamed into it. Soon it became a rhythm of pain and release. With each contraction she felt the increasing fullness between her legs. And then there was a sudden rush of pressure.

'It's a boy.' She heard the smile in his voice but the pains increased again.

Another voice. Not Mam's, not a voice in her head, another presence following a waft of air.

'Mary? Nurse Patterson. I'm here now.' The midwife tried to bustle Peter from Mary's side but he didn't move.

'The ambulance?' He questioned her, his old authority emerging.

'I'm afraid we're on our own. Two of them are already out on calls and the third has mechanical problems, I believe.' She smiled briskly at Mary. 'Now mother, let's see what's going on here.' She rifled through her case to find gauze, clamps and scissors. 'You can go now,' she said to Peter, preparing the cord.

'I will cut it,' he said.

'No, father, this is my job.' She looked askance at him.

'I know how to do this.' He didn't explain any more. 'And, as you say, I am the father.'

'Well!'

Smiling, carefully taking the scissors, he slowly cut through the umbilical cord between his wife and his child and lifted the baby onto Mary's chest. She cupped her son's head.

Nurse Patterson sniffed, resentful. She started to speak but then Mary panted, 'I need to push.'

'It's the placenta.' The midwife glared at Peter. 'You will allow me?'

'I will take our son.' He reached over to the fireguard and pulled down the towel that had been warming.

Mary only had time to hand the baby to him before the scream erupted from her.

Nurse Patterson quickly examined her. 'It's not the placenta, there's another baby.' She looked shocked for a moment and then glanced at Mary and smiled. 'Well, we didn't see that coming, did we mother? You're having twins, my dear. Next contraction, push.'

Mary threw her head back against the cushions and rode the wave of pain as the baby slid out with a tiny cry.

'It is a girl.' Peter gazed enthralled at the child in the midwife's hands.

Taking advantage of his bewilderment, she laid the baby on Mary and clamped the cord in two places. At the last moment he realized what she was doing and, holding out his hand, he said, 'Please?'

Reluctantly handing the scissors to him she shuffled back. 'Thank you,' he said, passing the little boy to her. 'I did this for my son. I need that I do this for my daughter as well. I would never forgive myself if it was otherwise.' Cutting the lifeline between his wife and children created a bond between himself and the babies.

Chapter 89

Mary was laughing and crying at the same time. She held the little girl next to her face before exchanging her daughter for her son so the nurse could wrap her up. Even the temporary separation felt unbearable. 'Two babies, Peter, we have two babies.' Both children were crying now, thin wails that made Peter's heart feel as though it would burst in his chest with happiness.

The midwife placed the baby girl next to her brother and went into the scullery, reappearing with a bowl and cloth. 'Have you thought of names?' She stood back, smiling at them.

'*Meine Geliebte?*' he said. He leaned towards her and stroked the wet strands of hair away from her face and kissed her. Her lips were slick and tasted salty.

'Do you want to choose?' Mary whispered, her mouth still close to his. 'Any of your family names?'

'No.' There was a small sadness in him but he knew what he wanted for his children. 'No, it would not be the right thing. I would like them to have English names. It will be easier for them.' He touched the top of their son's head with the back of his fingers. 'We know they will have much to deal with.'

'We can protect them from all that,' Mary said. 'We will protect them.' She emphasised her words. 'Heaven help anyone who crosses us, Peter. We're a family.'

He smiled, the words echoed in his mind. 'We are a family,' he agreed.

Mary hesitated. 'Before, when I did think about it, I thought about Victoria for a girl and Richard if it was a boy?'

'Victoria and Richard it will be.' And I will love them more than life itself, he thought. And I will always idolise you, *Liebling*.

'Peter.' She touched his cheek, her hand falling back on the sheet. She hurt, but right now it was nothing; the pain over the last few hours was pushed aside with a rush of the earlier guilt. 'You forgive me?'

'Forgive? What is there to forgive?'

'For everything: for leaving you, for not telling you about them.' She choked on her tears. 'For not forgiving you right away about … about …Tom.' She looked down at the babies, both firmly swaddled in towels, their skin mottled and bloody. Exhausted by the effort of being born, their eyes were swollen and closed and their heads flopped forward. 'And for not resting in bed this morning. What if they've been born too soon because of me?'

'There is nothing for me to forgive.' He dared to add, 'It was always for you to forgive me.' There was still that small stab of fear in him.

They held one another's gaze.

'Babies decide when they'll come.' The midwife spoke briskly as she carried the metal bowls holding the remnants of the birth into the scullery. 'Now father, you wash mother's face, while I deal with this.' She began to clean Mary's thighs before pausing for a second. 'They're good strong babies. Small, but healthy. Twins often come early, you know. You should know. You've been the nurse.' She smiled up at Mary between her knees. 'But I'd like to get you to hospital as soon as possible. We need to get the babies, and you, checked over, my dear.' Nurse Patterson addressed her next words to Peter. 'Father, will you telephone again for the ambulance, while I finish cleaning mother up?'

Mary and Peter exchanged amused glances. 'Mother?' Mary mouthed. 'Mother?' She pulled a comical face.

'Father!' He winked before turning to go into the hall.

When he returned, shaking his head, both women looked at him.

'The ambulance?' Nurse Patterson said sharply.

'Peter?'

'The two are still out on calls, the other is not repaired. They say one will come when it can.'

'Not good enough. We need them now.' The midwife stood, hands on hips.

'Why?' Fear caught in Mary's throat. She looked from one baby to the other and then at the woman. 'Why, what's wrong? Peter?'

'There is nothing wrong.' He glanced at the midwife.

'No need to be hysterical, mother.' But the woman moved closer to Peter, turning her head away from Mary. 'We need to get them to hospital. I am worried about the little boy's breathing and he's slightly jaundiced.'

Peter had already noticed. '*Ja,* it is best, I think.'

'Do you know of anyone with a car?'

'*Nein.* Mary's brother-in-law, but he is not here.' It was too complicated to explain. 'I will look outside.' He moved quickly.

He didn't realise he was in his stocking feet until he was standing on the road looking left and right. Nothing. Nobody.

And then he heard it, the whine of an engine. The milk float. He ran towards it waving both arms in the air. It stopped with a squeal of brakes.

The milkman jumped from his seat. 'What the heck, mate?' He was clearly shaken. 'You could have got yourself killed.'

306

'My ... er ... wife,' Peter said. 'My wife has had babies. Two of them. Twins. We need for them to go to hospital.' He looked behind the man. 'So?'

The driver gaped and then looked over his shoulder at the milk float. 'No,' he said, 'I can't. More than my job's worth. I'm on my way back to the depot with the empties.'

Peter began to take off the crates.

'Here, you can't do that.' The milkman tussled with the crate Peter was holding.

'It is happening.' Peter glared at him. 'With or without your help, it will happen.' He waited until the man let go of the crate and he stacked it with the others by the front door.

The milkman flung out his arms in despair. 'Okay, okay. I'll do it. You go and get your missus. The name's Joe, by the way.'

Peter ran into the kitchen. 'I stopped the milkman.'

Mary began to laugh.

The midwife looked horrified. 'Really, that's not necessary.' She hurried out to the hall. 'I'll try for the ambulance again.'

'Peter?' Mary whispered. 'I don't care how we get there. It's these two I'm worried about.'

The milkman appeared in the doorway. He tipped his peaked cap to the back of his head and ran a hand over his mouth, obviously embarrassed. He coughed loudly, his large Adam's apple moving rapidly up and down his throat. He looked at Peter. 'We can put your missus on the back now ... on a mattress or summat?'

The midwife returned. 'They say we have to wait. It really isn't good enough but that's all we can do, I'm afraid.' There was a worried furrow on her forehead. 'I'm sorry, there's nothing else for it.'

Peter and Joe spoke at the same time. 'There is the milk float.'

'My milk float,' Joe said. 'I cleaned it out this morning. You could eat your dinner off the back of it.'

'Slightly different than carrying two small vulnerable babies,' she said sarcastically.

'We are wasting time.' Peter ran up the stairs. 'Come, help with the mattress and blankets.'

The midwife shook her head in despair. 'If you're so determined—'

'We are,' Mary said. 'Now, please, help me with these two.'

'Well, I suppose there's nothing else I can say.' Nurse Patterson expertly took both babies in the crook of her arms. 'But I have my dignity. I will follow on my bicycle.'

'All okay back there?' The driver peered through his mirror at them and shouted for what seemed to Mary the hundredth time. Deciding his precious load was worth working overtime without being paid, Joe was driving slowly and steadily all the way to Bradlow Hospital.

'Yes.' The chorus was the same each time, although Mary, lying in on the back of the float and almost smothered by the number of pillows and blankets Nurse Patterson had put around her, winced with every bump and hole in the road. Peter, wedged beside her, a baby in each arm, sat with his back to the cab.

Once a woman tried to flag the float down. 'Any to spare?' she called.

'Sorry, missus, no milk on board and I have two half pints of my own to deliver,' he shouted.

They left the woman staring after them.

Despite her discomfort, Mary giggled quietly at the ludicrous situation they were in. She leaned against Peter and tipped her head back to receive his kiss. What a story to tell the twins when they were older.

*

The light from the parlour window falls across the two figures standing so close in the garden they could be one. The air is still, soft in the warmth left over from the day, barely rippling through the full-leaved branches of the trees on the opposite side of the road. The moon hangs between the stars, hoary against the blue-black of the night. On the beach the waves collapse in the familiar monotonous rattle on the pebbles. The cliffs jut out, darker than the sky.

Peter turns Mary's face towards him. They kiss. 'Welcome home, *Liebling*,' he says.

ABOUT HONNO

Honno Welsh Women's Press was set up in 1986 by a group of women who felt strongly that women in Wales needed wider opportunities to see their writing in print and to become involved in the publishing process. Our aim is to develop the writing talents of women in Wales, give them new and exciting opportunities to see their work published and often to give them their first 'break' as a writer. Honno is registered as a community co-operative. Any profit that Honno makes is invested in the publishing programme. Women from Wales and around the world have expressed their support for Honno. Each supporter has a vote at the Annual General Meeting. For more information and to buy our publications, please write to Honno at the address below, or visit our website: www.honno.co.uk

Honno, 14 Creative Units, Aberystwyth Arts Centre
Aberystwyth, Ceredigion SY23 3GL

Honno Friends
We are very grateful for the support of the Honno Friends:
Gwyneth Tyson Roberts, Jenny Sabine, Beryl Thomas.

For more information on how you can become a Honno
Friend, see: http://www.honno.co.uk/friends.php